Sudden Light

Donegal's Novel

Also by J.A. Greenleaf

Donegal Fairy Stories
By Seumas MacManus
Edited by J.A. Greenleaf

Real Irish Fairies of Donegal
By J.A. Greenleaf

Sudden Light

Donegal's Novel

J.A. Greenleaf

Cover Art by

John Quigley

Published by

Swordpoint Intercontinental, Ltd.

Cataloging in Publication Data is available from the Library of Congress

The author's moral rights are asserted.

ISBN: 978-0615447957

Typeset in Contenu Book Display, Phonetica, and Silvus
By Swordpoint Intercontinental, Ltd.

Swordpoint Intercontinental, Ltd.
7202 Giles Road, Suite 4212
La Vista, Nebraska 68128 USA
www.swordpoint.com

Table of Contents

DEDICATION

No one has stood by me and encouraged me more than my wife, Karlene, to whom this book is dedicated, with both love and gratitude.

My sons, Joseph and Jacob and to the memory of Benjamin (1979-1999), Daddy's Wee Beans.

Thanks, too, to my friends, Dudley Corner, John Quigley, Dan Pieri, Paul Reilly, Tim and Mary Porter, Ger and Síofra Moyne, Vern Taylor, Janet Smith, Marcia and Kristin Greger, Charles Sands and Mary Moore. There are many others—you know who you are.

SUDDEN LIGHT

You have been mine before,—

How long ago I may not know;

But just when at that swallow's soar

Your neck turned so,

Some veil did fall,—I knew it all of yore.

Dante Rossetti

1 DONEGAL CASTLE, IRELAND: 1589

In the cacophonous tumult of the battle, Máire was surprised to hear a bee or wasp fly mightily by her. She almost swatted it with her hand as it flew through the narrow arrow loop cut in the massive walls.

There were many young girls and boys taking refuge on the upper floor. Most were huddled in the corner as the stone shuddered with each impact of heavy cannonballs. Two, who could not contain their rapt curiosity, had been near-mesmerized by the English ranks arrayed around the castle, firing cannon, muskets, and arrows at the castle and its defenders. The girls were peeking through the arrow slit at the incredible spectacle below, their arms around one another's shoulders, when one of them suddenly, breathily, called out, "Oh!" in a soft voice.

Her arms flew out from her sides and she fell back, almost as if she had slipped on the woven rushes laid across the wooden floor. Máire instinctively moved to catch her but brought her hands to her mouth to try to stifle a scream. An iron-tipped arrow had flicked effortlessly through the girl's jugular vein and great steaming gouts of blood were drenching both her and the girl. Máire knelt at her side and tried to staunch the pulsating blood with her hands, but the light in the girl's eyes went out like a guttering candle. Máire thought how she'd never seen anyone die before. She had seen dead people, but not someone

1

who'd just been killed. Máire's arms and green woolen dress were awash with congealing blood. How could one person have so much blood, she wondered? As she laid her down on the rushes, two more arrows flitted through the window and skittered across the floor, burying themselves under the rushes. The one that had killed the girl stuck in the floor, dripping blood like the Devil's quill.

"Away from the windows and arrow loops!" Máire shouted. There was, in truth, no need to say anything, for they all moved as far from the walls as they could. The oldest of the boys hesitated and said they needed to be lookouts. Máire agreed, after a moment, and told them to stay at the arrow loops, for they made smaller targets. She felt brave enough to observe from a loop herself, although she was violating her own commands.

Some of the English were moving boldly forward. Several were stopped, brought to their knees, by the defending archers. Others moved ahead, their shields over their heads. A cheer rang out from the Irish as the castle door banged open, and then shut as quickly, condemning the three swordsmen who sallied forth to death or victory. Death would be seen to be the only course, for there seemed to be hundreds of the English. Máire could see that two of the swordsmen had fallen almost immediately. The third was surrounded. He hacked mightily with his sword held in both hands as he stood his ground. Máire craned her neck to see if it was her husband, Uilliam, whom she knew was on the ground floor with the other men. No, she thought, she believed it was not, but she agonized for all three. She loved them all. There were relatively few clansmen in the castle, and they were all family. The last one fell heavily, and she knew he was gone. One of the English horses screamed wretchedly as it was hit in the rump by an arrow that seemed to bury itself to the feathers. It must have been a crossbow's bolt. The horse stumbled sideways, almost dislodging the young man, who dropped the reins. As the smoke from the cannons cleared in the wind, she saw several pikemen yank the horseman from underneath the settling horse.

2

She could see soldiers holding their matchlock muskets, with long smoking wicks dangling from the weapons. The wicks moved toward the barrel as plumes of white smoke gushed from the barrel and touchhole, as well as wafting from the wicks. The musketeers immediately moved to recharge the matchlocks.

Máire wanted to go down to find Uilliam, but she knew she must not. Would he risk all to vaingloriously sally forth? To be sure, she reasoned. He would throw his life away almost casually if he thought it would delay the English by a tick of time. Several of the girls and a few of the young men went down the curving stone stairs set in the corner of the castle. Máire made no move to try to stop them. The dead girl on the rushes was mute testimony that it was not safe in the upper reaches either. Máire felt she could not leave herself, however. Uilliam had sternly told her to stay.

She gathered the remaining children around her at the side nearest the River Eske, for the bombardment seemed less there. She stole a quick look toward the river and saw massed Englishmen on the far bank. Some had fallen on the shore, and a few were splayed, awash in the river, while a number were standing amongst their fallen comrades, and were firing at the castle. Another fell with a great splash, and she turned around.

The heavy walls, amazingly enough, were shuddering with the tremendous forces of the cannon-fire. One cannonball penetrated the stone roof and caromed off the far wall, bowling over two children before smashing into the fireplace. Máire and two other women ran to try to help the children, but stopped suddenly when they saw the bright white, shattered bones of what was left. The two women went to their knees, vomited and commenced to wailing. Máire choked back the bile in her throat, and went to try to put out the fires started by the scattered flaming turf that had been burning in the fireplace. She trod on some of it, and doused the rest with a bucket of water that had been near the fire for cookery.

3

Although the fire was out, she could still smell the smoke. The cannonball was not the red-hot variety she'd heard about. She looked towards the stairs and was shocked to see smoke roiling upward towards the high, pitched roof. She knew, instinctively, that they would have to leave instantly if they were to survive.

She knelt and placed her flattened palms on the floor. It was hot! Where some of the matting had burned away from the turf fire, she could look down through the thin gap between the planks.

Máire saw what she'd both expected and hoped against—orange flames licking at the floor from below. The circular stone staircase was contained within the walls, and had doorways to each floor. If she could usher the others down, perhaps they could make it to the ground floor where the animals and supplies were housed. She knew there was no other way out. The windows were too small to escape through. Even if the fall didn't kill them—which it most assuredly would—the English archers would finish the task.

There was no choice. She shouted at the women and children in rapid Irish, and some of them obeyed her, but most ran excitedly around the great room, clearly panicked beyond all hope.

At that instant, the floor broke through where it had apparently been weakened by that rocketing cannonball, and the room was enveloped in smoke. Flames thrust their fiery tendrils upward, igniting all that was combustible.

Sunlight made faint beams through the smoke, and she could faintly see the outline of the others, moving, ghost-like, through the room. Both Máire and the others were soon coughing and gagging. Máire fell hard against the enormous oak wardrobe that loomed over the room from the riverside wall. She could feel herself slipping into unconsciousness as the room spun around her. She felt as if her lungs were being squeezed.

In that moment of twilight before dying, she thought of Uilliam. She felt a moment of peace, and could even feel his great arms around her and his quiet voice in her ear. She even turned to see her imagined husband. To her amazement, he was there. He was badly wounded, and was missing fingers on his sword hand. Apparently oblivious to the pain, he settled beside her and held her with his good arm.

She could not imagine how he had made it up the stairs. She was prepared to risk the flames to find him, how could she not believe he would do the same?

Uilliam was barely visible in the darkness of the smoke, but she could see his brilliant smile. He smiled! Máire knew that nothing else would matter now; they were together.

"Together forever, my wee one," he whispered, his voice hoarse from the smoke. "It shall always be 'Uilliam and Máire,' lovers for all time."

They held one another tightly as the flames found them and held them both.

2 DETROIT, MICHIGAN, USA: THE PRESENT

Somewhere behind the clapboard houses and graffiti-splashed stores, a tire was burning. Perhaps it was a car. This was, after all, the inner city of Detroit. Motown. The city had been punched hard—a body blow—in the race riots of 1968. It never completely recovered.

"God, I love this town!" Marisa thought, as she dodged a pothole in the street. The city reminded her of the 6 o'clock news film of Beirut. It was not Chicago—the "City of Big Shoulders" to quote Carl Sandburg— but the "City of Slumped Shoulders," to quote herself.

"Bomb crater?" she said, to no one. With a single finger on the steering wheel Marisa turned the car, grazing the edge of a pothole.

She was going too fast. At the last moment, she noticed a still-open gas station. She was almost past the entrance ramp. Without warning to the man next to her, she turned suddenly into the station. Her passenger clutched the door frame and his seat belt. The Mercedes two-seater convertible, riding springily on its Teutonic, computer-designed suspension, bounced over the driveway and curb. If the top had been on, her passenger would have hit his head on the overhead. September in Michigan was hardly time to put on the top, by her view.

The car was her one passion. Even though it was new, cost hundreds of thousands of dollars, and was still under warranty, she only trusted it to a small garage called, "Ben's Benz," where the owner and chief mechanic, Benjamin, treated it with such love that Marisa was convinced he dreamed of her car. She would buy her gas from Ben if she could, but this station would have to do.

"Dee-troit" in September was often cold, as it was today. It occasionally snowed, both in September and October, thus giving trick-or-treaters, in their ghost-sheets, the look of mountain troops reconnoitering a bombed-out city in winter camouflage. Perhaps that wasn't too far from the truth.

She remembered the Detroit of years ago, as a child. It wasn't Paris, but there were people, stores and shoppers, even after the riots. Now, you could fire a cannon down Woodward Avenue downtown and not hit anything. "Shouldn't think that," she smiled to herself, "someone will try it!"

Dull red and orange leaves pirouetted from trees near the gas station, falling on her car and into the car's interior. Although the temperature was only about ten degrees above freezing, Marisa declined to put up the top. There were some people who didn't believe her Mercedes even had a top, as they'd never seen it up. Marisa had the heat blasting in the winter, and the air conditioning set at "meat locker" temperature during the summer. Regardless, short of a tornado or blizzard, the top stayed down.

The moment the car stopped, she deftly flipped the driver's visor down, and began inspecting her makeup in the lighted mirror. Without looking at the gas station attendant as he walked slowly toward her, she raised her hand in the air, palm down. She made a half-wave of her fingers upwardly. With this, she both wordlessly dismissed the attendant and implied that she wanted the car filled.

The gas attendant, a dark-haired man in his thirties with the weathered skin of one who worked outside, reached for the most expensive pump. Although he did this, in his mind, to somehow punish this princess for treating him like he was invisible, in actuality, she wouldn't have cared if he'd pumped Chanel No. 5 into the car—as long as (a) it would run, and (b) they would take her black American Express card.

The man yanked a faded red wiping rag from his rear pocket and scrubbed imaginary grime from the fender of her car as the gas pumped.

He glanced over at her. "Nice," he thought. Late 30's, rich, obnoxious, and probably hates men. Stockbroker, lawyer, advertising...something like that—an overachiever. Not medicine, he considered. The car matches, but not the attitude. He wondered why they were on this side of Detroit, anyway. Must have gotten low on gas on the Lodge Expressway and pulled in. With the current rash of carjackings, you'd think they would call in a helicopter with emergency fuel, rather than risk coming close to the Great Middle Class.

As he leaned against the car with one hand propping himself, he held the gas nozzle with the other. He looked at the car, and its two passengers. He noted the top was down in cold weather. She was a fool to drive this car in this part of town, especially with the top down. Her diamond rings—there were several—flashed lightning bolts around the car and onto him. People would cut her just because she was white and in their 'hood. The jewelry and car would just be a bonus.

She's totally oblivious to her surroundings, he thought.

The boyfriend was on his telephone, speaking too-loudly and gesticulating wildly. The attendant had no cell phone and had no interest in having one. Who would he call?

The passenger punched the hang-up button an instant after he shouted, "Just do it, Sol!" He punctuated the end of the call with a single word, "Asshole."

The attendant laughed to himself at this. Everyone is someone else's "asshole," he guessed. There was a big chart somewhere, showing the pecking order of assholes. They probably had ranks. This buttercup would be "first class," without a doubt.

While the car was filling—they were low—the attendant asked the woman if she wanted the oil checked. She didn't answer, but merely pulled the handle to release the hood. Sweet, he thought. They obviously are genetically suited for each other.

She picked up her iPhone with her right hand, and plucked her earring off with the left. She tossed it like a broken Christmas tree ornament into the carpeted area behind the seats, and started punching a number into the phone. The attendant wondered how many thousands that trinket cost. The boyfriend began to tell her about his problems with "Sol," but it was apparent that she wasn't interested. Even this jerk could see that—couldn't he? No, the attendant guessed not. He continued to explain to her about how Sol was supposed to have done something or other. The attendant didn't much care, either. She was hearing some distracting noise from her boyfriend, so she looked at him with eyes that must have flashed more than the diamond earring, for the boyfriend shut up in mid-sentence.

He could hear her talking to someone as he bent under the hood. The oil was fine. Clean. In fact, from the looks of the engine, the car was new. He shut the hood and twisted the wiping rag around his fingers, wondering what to do to pass the time. It was cold. He was wearing only a blue cotton work shirt with a thermal underwear long-sleeved shirt underneath. His greasy Levis had holes in the legs from spilled battery acid.

He walked back to the pump. He had set the automatic pump shutoff at the first, and lowest, notch. It was a slow day, and he was happy to get out of the station. The station owner was banging on a car that should have been razor blades years ago. The owner had him changing mufflers, always a "treat."

The boyfriend looked like he went shopping with a copy of this month's GQ. The attendant imagined the boyfriend handing the magazine to the clothing store manager, telling him, "I want to look like that," as he pointed to the cover.

The boyfriend was in his late thirties, early forties. Tennis/golf tanned, $250 haircut, $30,000 teeth—which he flashed constantly—and expensive clothes. Gold Rolex, gold pinkie ring. He loved this guy, he thought, ruefully. He leaned over to see if boyfriend had a diamond earring. He didn't—a disappointment.

She finished what he presumed was her "power call," and flicked the phone onto the dashboard. The boyfriend renewed his banter.

"Ees," he said, "Ees, are you going to go to the Island or not? The whole gang is going."

The attendant thought he heard him call her "Ees." What the hell kind of name is that?

The attendant heard her for the first time when she answered the boyfriend. Her voice had a strange, magical kind of sound to it. "No-can-do Philip—I have a brief due on Monday, and I have to work on it all weekend."

A lawyer, the attendant surmised. I was in the ballpark.

The boyfriend whined, "Aw, come on Ees—you promised. Get some clerk to do it. You're a partner!"

She laughed a beautiful concerto of musical notes. "Yes, but partners bill out at $1,500 an hour. Clerks, regrettably, do not."

As she laughed, she tossed her hair back. It wasn't particularly long. As he walked to the driver's door to collect the money, the attendant was trying to judge what color her hair naturally was. At first he thought it to be a very dark brown, but he looked closely at it, and saw that it was an incredibly dark red, like black cherries. As she held her chin up, turning toward him, a cloud opened and bright sunlight illuminated her face.

The attendant's heart seemed to stop. He stood there, stupidly. Almost as a reflex, he looked down at his rough hands when she looked toward him.

Filled with bravado, the boyfriend lifted himself half out of the seat with his left hand and knee, and said, "What do you want, jerk-weed?"

The attendant ignored him, and the boyfriend said nothing more. This was mainly because he realized that, at around 200 pounds and obviously well muscled, the attendant could make short work of him. He recognized the obvious—the attendant simply wanted to be paid.

The woman pressed her head back against the headrest, and stared directly at him. She noticed he had his name, "Gene," embroidered on his blue work shirt. He had hazel eyes, with tiny particles of gold. They looked deep inside her and made her tremble with fright. As one who was supremely self-possessed and confident, it was a highly unusual feeling.

The attendant held out his hand toward her and she cringed. She was convinced, for some implausible reason, that he was deranged and was going to strike her.

The boyfriend saw her recoil from the attendant, and heard her quick intake of breath. It puzzled him, but he did nothing.

Inexplicably, she took her own hand and touched the edge of the attendant's thumb, as if testing it for heat. Instantaneously, an overwhelming, almost orgasmic, feeling of passion washed over her. Her finger burned without being hot. Both her hands clasped the man's heavily muscled forearm, to her boyfriend's utter disbelief.

"It's you!" she whispered in a throaty, almost disembodied voice. "It's *you!*"

She essentially shouted the words the second time. As she did, the attendant seemed to snap out of his fixation, and looked at her hands clutching his arm. He yanked his arm away and tried to say something. He couldn't understand her actions and he couldn't fathom why she was looking at him like that. Did she know him?

The boyfriend was almost out of the car. He didn't care if he was going to get a beating. He had to do something.

The attendant was alarmed. Was he being accused of some horrible crime? With the commotion, the station manager stopped work and was walking toward the car.

The attendant saw that this was going badly. He had a criminal record, and had lied on his application a few days earlier. Why should it matter, here in the "combat zone?" Now this nut case is going to ID him as some kind of rapist or something. He turned on his heel and ran away, leaving the station in a dead run, down the street.

"Did you get that butthead's name, Ees? I can't believe this shit. This city is out of control. Christ. Ees. Are you okay?"

She was staring at her hands.

"Hey, you've got grease on your fingers." He reached for his handkerchief, dabbed it on his tongue, and moved it toward her hands.

She slashed at him with the edge of her hand and shouted, in a too-loud voice, "Don't touch me!"

Philip was surprised by her vehemence—as was she. "Oh, I understand—'evidence.' Let's call the cops and sue this place for assault."

She laid her hand over his as he started to dial 9-1-1 on the cell phone. He looked up at her. She looked very different. She wasn't in "control" any longer. She had undergone some type of transformation, but he couldn't understand what or why.

"It's him," she said quietly.

"Of course it's 'him,' who the hell else would it be?"

"But his name was 'Gene.' It's always 'Bill' or 'William' or some variation. Never 'Gene.' But it's him. Oh, God!"

"What in sweet Jesus' name are you talking about, Marisa?"

"I'm in love," she said, with a little sob, bowing her head slightly.

"I know, sweetheart. I love you too."

"No. Not you. Him. I love him! It's him! It's always been him!" She held the steering wheel with both hands, rested her head against her forearms, and began to cry.

3 DETROIT: THE RENAISSANCE CENTER: THE PRESENT

They arrived at her office high in the Renaissance Center, a futuristic complex of four tall, round, glass-walled office towers, forming four corners around a larger, and much taller Center tower—also round. This was a hotel. The entire RenCen, as it is commonly known, is located on the shore of the Detroit River, overlooking both the river and Windsor, Ontario, Canada, on the opposite shore. Windsor is the largest Canadian city south of a major American city—owing to a bend in the river. She hadn't said anything on the fifteen-minute ride downtown, except, muttering several times, "It's him."

The only thing Philip could think was that this guy was a missing witness in some legal case Marisa had. This seemed unlikely, as the only people she seemed to encounter were rocket-propelled corporate board members and CEOs.

Philip looked at her as if for the first time. She seemed so different since this startling event. She even seemed to walk differently. Philip escorted her to the reception area. One of the secretaries came up to Marisa and said, "Miss Marisa, you have a little something on your hand," holding a Kleenex and making a wordless offer to remove it. Marisa made a half-turn away to avoid the help. Philip noted that she didn't break the secretary's arm, as she almost had done to his.

"Thanks, Heather, I know."

"Are you going to be all right, Ees?" Philip said, as he held her arm.

13

She waved him away. He offered an "air kiss," but she had already turned to go to her office. Heather, watching this, smiled. Not many liked the overbearing Philip.

Heather followed Marisa into her office, reciting phone messages that Marisa wasn't listening to.

"Ticklers: don't forget the brief is due Monday. Absolutely. Want me to come in tomorrow? I don't mind a Saturday. I could use the extra hours of overtime. Car payments."

"Brief?"

"Yes, *brief.* Court of Appeals. Remember? Deadline?"

"What case is that?" she asked.

"Are you with it? What case? We've been living and breathing this case for weeks! Rothman!"

"Rothman," she repeated, trailing off her voice, as if she'd heard the name for the first time.

"Yes, Rothman. Remember Patrick Ignatius Johnson, Asshole-at-Law, on the other side?"

"Johnson." She said it without seeming to comprehend. She continued to touch her burning ear.

"That's him. You know, Mr. Syphilis? Want me to come in?"

Marisa smiled at the syphilis reference. Amazingly, it was true. Equally amazing was that she knew about it. She ran into Johnson at O'Hare Airport in Chicago a number of years ago, and he'd been waiting for hours for a snow-delayed flight. As was his habit, he spent the time in the lounge, drinking Seven and Sevens. He was already at Seven to the 10th power when he spied her. They'd never been friends—she didn't believe he allowed himself friends—or perhaps it was the other way around. In any event, she was a familiar face in a strange city. He greeted her like she was a newly rediscovered pal, like being in Europe and seeing someone you know, however distantly. You act like you were

Brownies together. She cultivated people, even people she didn't like, so she accepted his invitation to go into the bar for a drink. He'd had too many already, but ordered another. In a boozy voice, he inexplicably began to tell her about himself. Personal, gut-wrenching secret things, as if he was exorcising himself by telling her. She was ill at ease, but the story was fascinating. He told how his father was now 87 years old, and had always been a small town doctor in a little upstate Ohio town. His father had married in the 1930's, but never had children. His wife wouldn't have anything to do with him, but his receptionist, who was getting all sorts of "raises" and "bonuses," would. In the process of playing "doctor" with his receptionist, whom he liked to describe as his "nurse," a real-life diagnosis of pregnancy soon followed. It was the 1940's, so the good doctor had her go to visit "relatives" out West, where Johnson was born. Old Doc, with the connivance of his old pal, the Probate Judge, legally adopted little baby boy Johnson. Marisa found it hard to imagine this lifeless husk of a man as a child, running and playing with trucks, eating raw apples. He probably spent the time cheating his schoolmates out of their toys.

Doc Johnson's wife knew what was going on, but she felt trapped by circumstances. She went along with the adoption, but never warmed to little Patrick.

The Doc was too busy with his practice and a string of new "nurses" to notice Patrick's taking up space on the planet either. Ultimately, little Patrick was packed off to a rich man's baby sitter: military school. He languished there, an uninspired student and a worse cadet, until he graduated from high school.

Marisa obviously knew none of this, and she listened intently. When he told her how he went to college, he took a gulp of his Seven and Seven and said, almost as an aside, "And that's where I got syphilis."

"What?!" she exclaimed, sitting up straight.

"Huh?" he answered, taken aback by her remark. He looked around and noticed that the suddenness of her outcry had attracted the attention of others in the bar.

He realized, too late, that he had plumbed the depths of his most frightful secrets. He had told her, another attorney, the most horrible of them all and didn't recognize he had.

He almost sobered up, and, wiping his lips with the back of his hand, said, "Nothing. Didn't mean it. Happened to another student. Not me. No. Not me."

With this, he jumped up, bumping the table and knocking his glass onto the floor. He stepped into the broken glass in his rush to the door, crushing it into the carpet, literally running away in his haste to distance himself from his secret.

She couldn't imagine what demons inside him caused him to tell her these things. Ever since, he treated her as his sworn, blood enemy. When she saw him, she imagined there were some vestigial remains of the syphilis, bandy legs, chancres, whatever, although she was sure he'd had millions of units of penicillin to knock it out. Was it still there? Did that explain his viciousness? She was hard, but not vicious. He was like a wolverine, killing for sport. She was a formidable opponent. As a precaution, with Johnson, she followed up every conversation with a fax, saying, "We talked today. You said 'hello,' I said 'hello.' You said you would grant me a two-day extension of time to answer. I will send you a written stipulation to that effect."

Another attorney had once called Johnson and asked for an extension of time to file an answer to a civil lawsuit complaint Johnson had filed against the other man's client. The lawyer explained to Johnson that that day was the last day to file an answer or motion in response to the complaint. Would Johnson grant him a two-week extension so he could prepare an answer, as the client had only retained him that day?

"Sure, sure," said Johnson. "No problem, Old Buddy."

The attorney thanked him, and hung up.

Johnson hadn't noticed that it was the last day for answers, so he had his law clerk check to be sure. It was true. The next morning, the moment the court opened, Johnson was there filing a default against the other man's client.

When the attorney found out, enraged, he called Johnson. Didn't Johnson agree to an extension? "Ah, yes," answered Johnson, "but when you didn't fax me over a stipulation, I thought you didn't want one any longer."

The trial judge, being the least common denominator, as is often the case, refused to set aside the default. At a hearing, Johnson admitted that he made an oral agreement to extend, but pointed out that such things must be in writing. "The Court speaks through its orders," repeated Johnson. The case was appealed to the Michigan Court of Appeals. To the dismay of almost all legal practitioners, the Appellate Court upheld the ruling. It stating its displeasure that Johnson had not followed his own oral agreement, but cautioning the Bar at large that such agreements must be in writing.

The other attorney ended up being sued by his client, and the lawyer had to pay the entire judgment himself. He had no legal malpractice insurance, and was a broken man. Johnson was a pariah in the legal community, but he was curiously popular with clients. Some thought he had "runners" to get him cases, and all lawyers dealt with him as if he were nuclear waste with an icing of Ebola virus. Unfortunately, like a 2,000-pound gorilla, they couldn't ignore him.

Marisa kept that nugget of information largely to herself. Heather, her friend and confidential secretary, knew, but she talked to Heather about many things, far beyond the office. Marisa didn't socialize with lawyers, and didn't enjoy their company. All they talked about were either their own cases, or someone else's. The discussions were either derogatorily or in admiration at a big settlement. Boring.

"Call Johnson and ask him to stipulate to an extension. Tell him I'll extend the time for him to file his answer."

"You know he won't agree. That's why he's an asshole. Assholes don't agree. He belongs to the Wild West. Southfield lawyers never agree."

"Call him anyway—and hold my calls."

Heather, still holding shorthand notes regarding telephone messages, turned and walked away, greatly puzzled.

Marisa sat on the edge of her desk, picturing Gene in her mind. The name, "Gene," was still a wonderment. "He was always 'Bill,' 'William,' or some other derivative," she thought.

Heather stuck her head back in the door. "Mr. Penicillin is on the line, personally. Wants to know the reason you want an extension."

"Tell him—tell him—I'm in *love!*"

"Oh, *great! That* will convince him for sure!"

4 DETROIT: MARISA'S OFFICE: THE PRESENT

Heather obeyed Marisa's request that she didn't want to be disturbed. She was even prepared to bar a rather dotty old senior partner who seemed to pass his days by disturbing the work of others. He was a pleasant old curmudgeon, but he brought in no new business. He wore ties from the 1950s, with large art deco style pictures on them. The ties were complete with soup stains and dried food that were probably older than many of the firm's associates. He had been a state senator in the 70's, and was still called, "The Senator" by many, always with affection. The managing partners considered asking him to leave, but they knew it would kill him. Besides, they still had clients who threatened adversaries with "The Senator," remembering the formidable swath he cut during his prime. Clients still telephoned and his secretary—on orders from the front office—deftly passed them on to his associates. He didn't seem to notice.

The afternoon seemed interminable. Her office was befitting that of one of the "rainmakers" of the firm. She had a commanding view of the wide Detroit River and Windsor beyond. Her office cost something like $300,000 to furnish, complete with an original Toulouse-Lautrec poster.

She couldn't think of anything but "Gene." This still troubled her. "Gene." No, it couldn't be his name, she considered. For four hundred years, it had been one version or another of 'William.' "Uilliam," she recalled. A single salty tear touched the corner of her mouth, and she tasted it with her tongue. "Uilliam, my lost love. Have you come back to me again?" she spoke out loud. Other tears joined the first, and soon she

19

had her arms crossed on her desk, her head cradled in them, as she sobbed.

Earlier, she'd found a gray legal pad in her desk, and tried to make notes about the appellate brief. She purposefully didn't use the ubiquitous yellow pads, simply because most other lawyers did. She couldn't write. She broke pencils and a $750 fountain pen. She tried to dictate but found she couldn't remember how to work the machine. She turned to her iPad, but her mind simply wasn't on her work.

Philip had called several times, but couldn't get past Heather. His office, in a brokerage firm, was in an adjacent tower in the Renaissance Center complex. Philip wasn't subtle in his sheepdog-like love for her, but, more often than not, she wasn't even aware that he was in the room.

Marisa was a meticulous person, in both her mannerisms and appearance. Today, however, she was a different woman. Her makeup was streaked from tears, and she had smudged her mascara and lipstick in trying to wipe her eyes. She had not washed the grease from "Gene's" hand from her own, treasuring it somehow.

Should she call this "Gene?" No, he never remembered her from the past. He clearly thought of her as some sort of "crazy lady" after she clutched his arm at the gas station. She must try to see him, though. To warn him. To be with him. To be anywhere, go anywhere, just to be with him. She—they—were cursed, to be sure, but such a sweet curse! To love a man like Uilliam for all the ages! If only he would remember some part of it! This was, undoubtedly, part of the curse. She could remember everything, while he recalled *nothing!*

Heather eased herself into Marisa's office, walking gingerly. She had a sheaf of papers in her hand.

"Marisa? Are you okay?"

"Fine. I'm fine."

"Honey, you don't look fine. You look like you've been dragged over twenty miles of railroad track."

"No, I'm fine. Really."

Marisa didn't believe her own words, but she didn't want to concern Heather in her personal problems, although Heather certainly had no hesitation about telling Marisa about the "Boyfriend-of-the-Month Club" she seemed to belong to. Heather was lovely as well as smart, but she seemed attracted to the lowlifes of the world.

"Ah, Marisa, Patrick 'The Chancre' Johnson, amazingly enough, agreed to an extension. I think he really wanted one for himself, but was afraid to ask. By agreeing to yours, he gets one too, and can lord it over you. You need to sign this. The messenger will bring it to Johnson for his signature, and the messenger will take it to the Court of Appeals."

Marisa stared at the stipulation, seeing but not reading.

"There. Sign there."

Marisa scrawled her name.

"Thanks," Heather said, walking briskly out the door.

The days were growing shorter, now that winter was approaching, and although it was only five o'clock, it was dark outside. Marisa didn't like fluorescent lights, and only used the table lamps in her office, as well as a halogen desk light. She had turned off the lamps earlier in the day, and only the desk light glowed in the otherwise dark office.

When Heather returned, Marisa was a tiny figure in a dark corner of the room. She was sitting in an overstuffed chair, her legs scissored under her. She held herself tightly in her own arms. Only her eyes looked up as Heather approached.

"The messenger called on his cell. Johnson grumbled about some of the wording in the stipulation, but, since it was a plain 'vanilla' stip, he signed it. Soon, the courier was on his way to the Court of Appeals. That was an hour and a half ago, so I'm presuming that it will be filed on time. It's only Friday. Your brief isn't due until Monday, so we could have filed it even then, but I hate to wait."

"'Kay, thanks," Marisa sniffed.

"Listen, Marisa, my boyfriend has to work tonight—or so he says. You want to have me stick around? Girl talk? Maybe grab a bite someplace?"

Marisa snuffed noisily, and wiped her nose with her sleeve. When she saw this, Heather believed this was a "DEFCON 5" emergency. The sleeve was on a six hundred-dollar silk blouse.

"Heather, can—*would*—you do me a personal favor? You don't have to if you don't want to."

"I don't mind. What?" Heather was surprised at the gentleness with which Marisa spoke. While Marisa was always cordial with Heather, she wasn't usually so soft-spoken. She didn't consider the staff to be serfs like many of the attorneys in the office. Marisa did have a commanding presence, however. When she asked Heather to do something for her, she simply said, "Here's what I need you to do . . . "

"Ah, I saw someone today. A man. I knew him from before. From school. At least I think I saw him. His name is 'Gene.' I think he's changed his name, though. I knew him as 'Bill,' or 'William.' I don't remember his last name, and if he's changed his name, I don't know what it is now. Anyway, he is working at the gas station on Woodward Avenue near the big Baptist church that says, 'It's ll pm. Do you know where your soul is?'"

Heather smiled and nodded. She knew the church. It was something of a legend, and she smiled as she recalled the sign.

"I don't know the name of the station, but maybe you can find it on the Internet. Can you...do you think you can call there and see if Gene can take a minute to talk to me? It's very important."

Heather couldn't imagine what school this Gene and Marisa could have gone to together. The University of Michigan Law School? Aquinas College? This sounded fishy, but she'd do anything for her, and this was nothing.

"No problemo. I'll get right on it. Can I get you anything? I have some rose hip tea?"

"Any Irish tea?"

Heather laughed. "No. Fresh out. Made the last pot of 'Darby O'Gill' earlier today," she joked.

She stopped laughing when she saw the look of puzzlement on Marisa's face. She really did want some Irish tea. There were many odd little shops in the RenCen, so she would send one of the mail boys down to the gourmet coffee store to see if there was any Irish tea.

After she did so, she checked online. While she was on the Internet, the mail boy came back with a red pasteboard box of "Ty-phoo" leaf tea. "No Irish, but here's some English tea," he said. Heather, one who tended more toward the "designer" teas like Celestial Seasonings, didn't know how to brew loose tea. She almost poured it into the teakettle as she began to boil water on the small stove in the coffee corner. Few people used it anymore, content to use the microwave, as she was usually. "A teaspoon for each cup, and one for the pot," she remembered her grandmother saying. "Teaspoon." She'd never made the connection before.

Before long, she had made a murky, almost viscous fluid that she presumed must be English tea. She found Marisa's coffee cup and filled it, adding sugar and milk. Marisa was one of those lucky women who only counted calories if she were in a marathon race and needed to *add* calories. Heather gained weight by watching food commercials on television. As she brought the cup in to Marisa, steam trailed from the hot tea like smoke from a mountain train.

Marisa took it with both hands. It was good to see her smile.

"Irish?" she asked.

"No. Ah, *English,*" answered Heather.

"English," repeated Marisa, pensively, with a slight furrowing of the bridge of her nose, as if in displeasure.

"They didn't have anything but English. It's the same thing, isn't it?"

23

"No, but that's all right. Fine. Tastes great. Did you have some, or are you still drinking bluebird wing tea or something made from an angel's halo?"

Heather smiled. It was good to see something of Marisa's wit, even if it was at Heather's expense.

"I'm going to have some tea made from Egyptian mummies' toes right after I get a call back on my inquiries on the station. Wait. There's the phone. Be right back."

Heather was gone for fifteen minutes or so. Marisa had finished her tea, and turned the tealeaves in the bottom of the cup with her fingers, wondering what the tealeaves said was her fortune. She'd gotten up from the easy chair and moved to the heavy plate glass window. She stood leaning against it. She stood with her arms extended above her and her palms against the glass.

She turned her head as Heather re-entered the room, a peculiar look on her face.

"Say, Marisa, ah, just how well did—do—you know this Gene person?"

"Did?" repeated Marisa, ever the lawyer, listening to precisely what people said, rather than just hearing concepts and sounds, as did most non-lawyers.

"Do, I mean, do. Was he, like, a boyfriend or anything?" The thought of this person being Marisa's boyfriend sounded highly unlikely.

To Heather's surprise, Marisa said, "Yes. You could say that. Years ago. What did you find out?"

Heather inhaled sharply and decided to just get the words out of her. "I called the station, and when the phone was answered, I asked for 'Gene.' The guy wanted to know if I was a relative, which I thought was odd. I told him I was calling for a friend, and he got real inquisitive. 'Who was the friend?' 'What, exactly, was the reason for my call,' and so forth. I don't know what kinds of lies I told him, but it must have been convincing. He told me."

"He told you *what?*" asked Marisa.

"He told me—that—Gene had been in an accident."

Marisa paled. The feeling of déjà vu swept across her. Had her heart stopped? She couldn't tell. Heather had noticed the instant reaction and paused, not knowing if she should continue. Marisa was looking at her so plaintively, Heather could not but relate what she'd heard.

"The man on the phone said he was a police detective. Detroit PD. He said that he was at the 'crime scene,' and that this Gene had been killed in a 'robbery armed.' Cops always said that backwards. You'd think he was speaking French. I'm sure it wasn't the same 'Gene,'" she lied. She'd tried to interject a molecule of hope, but the moment she had told Marisa Gene was dead, she saw that the news had shattered Marisa. Her shoulders slumped, and her knees began to bend. Heather jumped forward and put her arm around Marisa and guided her to the chair, into which Marisa fell heavily.

"Baby, were you that close?" Heather inquired, rubbing Marisa's forearm, for what reason, she didn't know.

"I've loved him for lifetimes, Heather."

"'Lifetimes,' what the hell did that mean?" thought Heather.

"Could I have some more tea, Heather?" Marisa asked, in a tiny voice that sounded like someone else.

"You gonna be all right if I go out to the coffee corner?" asked Heather.

"I'll be just fine. This isn't the first time."

The paleness of Marisa's skin and the lost soul quality of her voice didn't reassure Heather, but she went out of the room anyway, moving quickly. Within moments, she'd returned with two cups of tea and a bottle of brandy.

"This booze was in the cupboard, and has been there since a Christmas long ago. We will put it to good use," Heather announced, as she poured a generous portion into each teacup.

The brandy had a harsh edge to it, but it warmed each of them as they drank. Heather had pulled up a straight back wooden chair over to Marisa, and sat in front of her, her elbows resting on her knees, the teacup in both hands.

"Want to tell me about him? Were you close?" asked Heather, clearly wanting to know everything.

"You wouldn't believe it. I'm not sure I believe it," responded Marisa. "Maybe I've just dreamed it all…"

"Tell me," pronounced Heather, pleadingly.

5 DETROIT, MICHIGAN, USA: THE PRESENT

A vee of Canada geese could be seen from Marisa's office window as they flew southward over the river, toward Windsor. Their moving wings looked like oars on a fleet of Phoenician war galleys as they followed some primeval compulsion and their leader.

Marisa, glancing up at them, felt like she and "Gene"—no, she couldn't call him "Gene"—that she and Uilliam were following some greater obsession. The centuries were the "sky" they flew across, alighting briefly in one era or another.

"Sometimes we find each other, but sometimes I don't think we do. But that's later. Let me tell you from the beginning. Promise me—promise me—you won't think I'm absolutely insane, although, to tell you the truth, I think I am, or have been. Perhaps that would be a blessing. To remember! To remember and he *doesn't!* What a terrible, soul-searing burden! I have never told anyone, not in four hundred years. I could never tell Uilliam. I couldn't find him for years. Wasted years. He didn't understand; he never could. He doesn't know me. We are sometimes near each other in age, but in some lives, we have been decades apart. At rare times, are of different races. Always man and woman; me a woman, of course. We are always 'Uilliam' and 'Máire,' or some variation of the names, though—at least until now. Can't figure that out," she mused, half to herself.

Heather didn't say anything, but this metamorphosis of a tungsten, depleted uranium-tipped legal "killing machine" to this tiny bundle was almost more incredible than the fanciful story she was hearing. She listened, though. Marisa was her boss, but they'd been together for a number of years, and Heather considered her a friend, even though Marisa sometimes didn't notice she was on the earth. That wasn't Marisa's fault, though. Marisa often soared above lesser folks. Many people complained—as gently as possible—that they'd seen Marisa driving past them. They'd waved, honked their horns, and just about crashed into Marisa's car, but Marisa, in her sporting version of a German Panzer tank, didn't give them a sidelong glance.

After the other person had left, Marisa and Heather had joked about it. "Marisa was probably thinking of a cure for cancer, or an invention to get water from sand dunes," they said. It probably wasn't far from the truth.

Heather urged Marisa on, asking her to relate her story.

"Tell me everything, from the start. When did you meet Gene? In school?"

"Uilliam. His name is Uilliam."

"I'm sorry, okay, 'Uilliam.' In school? What kind of name is 'Uilliam'?" asked Heather, rapid-firing her questions.

"You haven't been listening, Heather. I met Uilliam—which is an Irish name for 'William,' in County Donegal, Ireland in the late 1500s. My own father, of the MacSweeney clan, was one of his father's men. Uilliam was one of the O'Donnells, who were the chieftains of that region. Uilliam was the Chieftain's eldest son, and I was his wife."

Heather jumped reflexively, spilling tea on the $1,200 a yard carpeting, thinking that Marisa was "around the bend." Marisa continued.

"I had known Uilliam since we were children, but I was sent to a convent school when I was a child. My father wanted me to be educated, although few girl children were. My mother didn't think it was necessary. 'What did a wife need of Latin?' my mother would ask. My father loved my mother. He swatted her on the rump and laughed, 'So she can pray for her father's salvation!'"

"Like most little girls, I thought young Uilliam was a pig. He made faces at me, and would belch my name whenever he said it. He did it to infuriate me, and it worked. I was happy to go to the convent, because I didn't have to endure him and his nasty little friends. All they did was play soldier, batter each other with wooden swords, and clamber up and down Uilliam's family castle."

"Castle?" Heather asked. She scolded herself for interrupting. She'd had told herself she wouldn't. Talking, even this fantasy, was Marisa's therapy. "Castles are *so* romantic," she thought.

"Yes. They had a castle. Uilliam's ancestors, the early Chieftains, built it many years before. Oh, it isn't like the storybook castles on the Rhine, or like Neuschwanstein, the Mad King's castle in Bavaria. It was every inch a castle, though. Massive, just massive walls. They must have been—be, that is, the castle still exists—fifteen, twenty feet thick. It was squarish, more like a rectangle, quite high, with the Chieftain's chambers on the highest floor. It was in Irish Tirconnell, 'O'Donnell's territory,' in what is now Donegal, in County Donegal, in the ancient Province of Ulster, in the northern part of the Republic of Ireland."

"The River Eske makes a bend right there, where the castle was situated in the curve of the river. It was not far from the bay and the sea. I loved it, even as child. We didn't live in the castle, my family and I. We had our own smallholdings, a half-day's ride from the castle. We would go to the castle often, though, as my father often had business with the Chieftain."

"I was thirteen when I returned from the convent, and Uilliam fifteen. I almost didn't recognize him when I saw Uilliam that day in the Great Hall. I had been home before, for visits, but the young men, and some boys, were constantly out hunting, warring, wenching or whatever it was they did."

"I felt so foolish. All the girls were trying to attract his attention, but I was too shy. I could hardly think of his nasty little-boyishness, all warts and elbows. Now he was beautiful."

"There were four or five girls around me, and minstrels were playing music in the Hall, as they often did in the evening. The young men were talking amongst themselves, and they stood stock-still as we girls strolled in. It wasn't as if we were raving beauties, it's just that it was as if 'new' girls were suddenly dropped from the sky. We weren't 'new,' of course. We all were from the village or the surrounding area, and had been born there. We had simply been away at the convent, becoming 'young ladies.' The boys immediately began to make hand gestures and talk animatedly, pointing out this girl or that. My ears burned, because I was afraid they were talking about me."

"Uilliam was the only one who didn't say anything to the other boys. He was tall, and had curly black hair. His eyes were coppery hazel. They were just like 'Gene's'." She sniffed at the recollection of her lover, whom she thought she'd seen only this morning.

Heather was fascinated, and she repressed her desire to ask a hundred questions. She didn't believe a particle of any of it, but it was so interesting. A castle!

"I remember what he was wearing—a short, green leine, or waistcoat, with a shawl collar, and pleated ruffles around his waist, like the pictures of Sir Walter Raleigh's collar you see. It had slashes at the shoulder, and there was red cloth underneath. It had a cape of pale yellow that matched his shirt, which went to mid-thigh. He had on white tights with stirrups. He had a little skein, or dagger, that hung thigh-low from a long leather thong that went around his neck, and he was holding a falcon on his right wrist, atop a heavy leather glove. The falcon had a little hood on his head, and jesses floated beneath his claws as Uilliam walked toward me."

"I wanted—but didn't want—him to be coming toward me. One of the girls said, 'Uilliam! What do you call your falcon?' He didn't turn toward her, but spoke to me. He answered the other girl's question as if I had asked it myself."

"The girl who had asked fumed when she saw that Uilliam was answering her question by telling me. I looked over at her helplessly, but she obviously hated me."

"Arrow," he said. "I call him 'Arrow,' because I loose him at a bird or rabbit and he flies, unerringly, to the target."

"'I didn't ask. *She* did,' I said, sarcastically, pointing at the other girl. By now she was glowering at me with unreserved disgust."

"Uilliam ignored this, and took my arm in his left hand. Both he and the bird were an overpowering presence, and I was frightened. My throat was tight and I found it difficult to speak. My breath came in shallow gulps. I said nothing as Uilliam guided me away from the other girls, to one of the tall, narrow windows in the Great Hall."

"There was a fragrant breeze that blew my long hair—the same color as it is now—and tendrils of hair covered my face. I bowed my head slightly, and moved my hair back with two of my fingers as I shook my head, freeing my hair. I noticed a sharp intake of breath from Uilliam at this, and I was amused. Did I have this effect on him just by combing my hair? Was I a woman, after all?"

"Sunlight from the window mined the copper from his eyes and it dazzled me. His teeth seemed so white, and his smile was freshly minted only for me—or so I felt."

"When I finally got the courage to speak, I said something stupid, 'Are you going to belch my name?'"

"He reddened instantly, and laughed. I wanted to die. What a foolish, little-girl thing to say!"

"No, Máire. From this day on, I will only sing your name. In my heart and on my lips!"

"It was a grandiloquent thing to say, but it was poetry to me. I was smitten."

"For reasons that I will never know, at that, I ran away like a startled doe. Faster, probably. I went out of the castle, and found myself at the very edge of the river. The water reflected the clouds, and it seemed like the world was upside down. Had I ruined my chances? Did I want 'chances?' What were they, anyway?"

"At that moment, a hand gently rested on my shoulder, and I whipped around, not having heard anyone approach. It was Uilliam. I almost fell into the water, I was so taken unawares."

"He continued to hold my shoulder as I faced him, as if to prevent me from bolting again. I would not."

"Do not be afraid, Little One. I am heartily sorry for the callowness of my youth. How is it that they say it in English? My "salad days"'?"

"He'd switched from Irish to English. The nuns had taught us Latin and English, and some French. Still, it was hard to change thoughts from one language to another."

"He went on, in Irish, 'I hardly recognized you when you came in with those little girls.'"

"'Little girls,' I thought, with some amusement. Most were older than I."

"'I knew who you were immediately,' I heard myself lying."

"'I must be famous!' he laughed."

"'No, you were the most awkward of the boys in the Great Hall,' I said, meaning none of it, but wanting to hurt, for some unexplainable reason. He was a magnificent ram among goats, but I couldn't tell him. He was conceited enough as it was."

"'Ah. That's probably true. I had to crab my way from the other boys before they raced ahead of me. Being awkward and clumsy, I needed the head start!' As he spoke, his eyes seemed to laugh, and tiny wrinkles formed at the outer edges of his eyes. I wanted to touch them. What was happening?"

"'I—I didn't mean it that way. What I meant to say, was, you were so mean to me when we were children.'"

"'I was an idiot. I will never be mean to you again. I will be your "Champion," and I will ride my charger into battle with your scarf at the tip of my lance. I will name my armor after you. You will be my armor and my amour.' This last sentence was spoken in French, bewildering me. He looked deep into my eyes as he said this, and I felt my face flush again, for I realized that he meant each word."

"From that day on, we rode horses into the countryside, walked in the rain, threw flowers at each other in verdant fields, and loved one another. He became the love of my life, in the grandest sense of the word. He became the love of all my lives. I have loved him for four hundred years! And I've lost him, Heather, I've lost him again!"

6 DETROIT, MICHIGAN, USA: THE PRESENT

Heather had been sitting, cross-legged, on the small Oriental rug that lay in front of Marisa's chair. She had been listening to Marisa, without really questioning what she'd heard. She felt as if she was a little girl and her mother was reading her a bedtime story. No matter how incredible "bedtime stories" were, you never questioned their veracity.

Marisa had paused for a moment and gently wept, breathing in short gasps. Heather reached forward and touched a small hankie to Marisa's tears. At that moment, Heather realized what Marisa had been telling her. She looked at Marisa intently, searching for a sudden smile that would signal a grand joke that Marisa was playing on her.

"Ah, 'Reese, are you sure you're okay? Do you need a doctor, I mean, in case you're hurt?"

"Heather, my friend, I'm not insane. I don't know why I'm not insane. As each year, decade, century goes by, and I endlessly find and lose my own life's love, I sometimes wish for the peace of losing my mind."

Heather glanced quickly around the room, not knowing what she was looking for. She couldn't find a clue to this completely bizarre transformation of a polished, urbane, beautiful corporate attorney to this bundle of rags.

"Let me get you some tea," Heather said, determined to master the situation. It certainly wasn't a resolution, but it would give her a chance to step outside and catch her breath. Perhaps she'd think of a solution. Should she call Marisa's mother? She had her number in her iPad's contact list. No, Marisa's mother didn't seem like the type that would treat this aberration with any humor or compassion. She'd probably have Marisa in a private mental hospital with a prefrontal lobotomy scheduled for the morning, like the young Kennedy girl in the 1930's. Did they still do those or was that just in "One Flew Over the Cuckoo's Nest?"

She looked back into the office, and Marisa was still in the chair, in as close to the fetal position as you could get in a chair. She could see her shoulders moving slightly; she must still be crying.

Was it the gas station guy's death? No, that couldn't be. She said she knew him, but she must be mistaken. What was all this "Uilliam" nonsense? It was a romantic tale, but it certainly existed only in her imagination.

Heather noticed that, while all the staff except she herself had left the offices, virtually every attorney was in his or her office or the halls, going to and from the library. "They may make the 'big bucks,'" she thought, "but they have no personal life. They get here at six or seven in the morning and don't leave until around 11 pm. If they don't, then they do not have the 'dedication' to be partners."

Heather went to her own desk and coded the telephone to block calls to Marisa's phone. Heather was going to wait this one out with her boss—her friend. It was odd, she considered. Marisa and she had always had something slightly more than the usual employer/secretary relationship. Heather couldn't exactly call it a friendship—they never talked after hours, or saw each other socially. This wasn't a conscious decision on either's part. It was a tacit acceptance of the difference in their social status. It meant, of course, that Heather was from Hamtramck and the daughter of Polish immigrants who left Warsaw after World War II. She wasn't from Grosse Pointe Shores. She didn't think that Marisa even knew that Heather was really "Wanda." She'd adopted the name "Heather" when she applied for her first legal secretary job. It sounded more "citified" than the provincial "Wanda." What she really meant was, it didn't sound as "Polish." She wasn't ashamed to be Polish; she exulted in it. She was "Wanda Kaminski" the moment her feet hit the sidewalk. She spoke nothing but Polish at home. She still lived with her parents in Hamtramck, a small city surrounded by Detroit. Hamtramck had Polish newspapers, radio stations, stores, and thousands of Poles, some of whom had only just arrived from the Old Country.

She just didn't want to seem too "ethnic" to get a job in a top law firm. In secretarial school, "Wanda" had that notion told her on an hourly basis. She wondered how many "Candys," "Debbies" and "Cindys" in offices throughout the city were really "Olgas," "Barbaras" and maybe "Wandas?"

She had the hot teacup in her hand, and she placed the cup on her desk, grimacing as she spilled some on papers. "Probably important," she thought. "To hell with them—that's why God invented laser printers!"

She had a "speed dial" number for a restaurant in the RenCen that both she and Marisa liked, and she punched the button, quickly ordering two meals, charging it to Marisa's account there. She added a bottle of Chateau Lafitte Mouton Cadet 1990. Rather daring of her. She'd had some on a date a few months earlier and loved it. "Was that her last date? No, couldn't be. Maybe . . ." she thought, pensively.

Marisa looked up slightly as she walked in, a heartbreaking, heartbroken cry for help. Heather rushed toward her, spilling more of the tea.

"I ordered some food from downstairs," she said, adding, guiltily, "and some wine."

Marisa only nodded.

"Marisa, I don't know what this is all about. It's hard to believe—it's amazingly hard to believe—but you believe it, don't you?" Heather looked at her for any signs that this was, after all, some colossal prank. It appeared not to be.

"I sometimes think it is all a hallucination, some kind of fairy tale, but it is devastatingly real. It isn't just a wisp of a thready, smoky dream-scape. It is boneshakingly, slap-in-the-face, historically real. Christ, I can remember the colors, sounds, and the smells! I can, O God!" Marisa's voice increased in pitch to a virtual wail. "I can smell Uilliam burning!"

They both were crying uncontrollably when the delivery boy from the restaurant arrived. He'd delivered to Marisa's office before—she was an after-hours devotee too—and the security officer at the front entrance to the office didn't escort him any longer.

He stood in the door with the food, the wine bottle dangling in a net bag from his little finger. Not much respect for an expensive bottle of wine, Heather thought, sniffing.

She rushed over to him.

"Grandma died."

"What?" he said.

"Her, ah, Grandma died, and she's, like, sad."

"Was it your Grandma too?"

"No, I'm just sad for her."

"Women," the delivery boy muttered. He gave his best, "Big Tip" smile and "Thank You!" and looked down at what had been scribbled in the tip space on the bill as he turned to leave. "$10! Great!" he thought. The door was shut behind him, and he heard the heavy "snick" of the lock being thrown.

"Lezzies," he said, aloud. "Gotta be lezzies. The ten bucks is 'conscience money.'"

"Picnic time!" Heather said, a little too brightly. "Hungry?"

"If I don't eat, maybe I'll just die. I won't see him until the next life, Heather."

"Oh boy," thought Heather. "This is going to be a long night."

"Wanda," Heather heard herself saying.

"What? Wanda who?" asked Marisa.

"Wanda *me*. Call me Wanda. I hate Heather. Sounds like that movie. I'm really Wanda. Heather is made up."

"I knew that."

"You *did?*" asked Wanda.

Marisa didn't notice that she had picked up a fork and started to eat. "We do background checks on everyone. Your social security number has to match the name. I like 'Wanda' better anyway. 'Wanda's' my friend; Heather's my employee."

Wanda melted at this. She truly liked Marisa, and saw through the Ultra Bitch she portrayed to everyone but her. For all Marisa's money and power, she saw that she was a sad character, who was lonely even when she was with her usual entourage. At that moment, Wanda was resolute—she would hear this through, and reserve judgment, no matter how mad it all seemed. She heard herself say, "Tell me about the next time you met!"

Wanda had the bottle of wine opened by then, and they both sipped from the wine glasses, as Marisa settled back into the chair.

Marisa took a long breath and began to tell the story of Uilliam and Máire.

"We were married the following Spring. I had garlands of flowers in my hair. The young girls all wanted to be my handmaidens—even the one whom I'd apparently offended when Uilliam answered her question as if I had asked it."

"The Bishop married us in the castle chapel. There had been some behind-the-scenes maneuvering by some of the Chieftain's right-hand men, saying that Uilliam ought to marry the daughter of another high Chieftain, perhaps an O'Neill, who were a powerful family to the East. My father was one of the Chieftain's clansmen, one of his kinsmen, and a powerful chieftain in his own rite. This was very persuasive to the

38

Chieftain, but no more so than Uilliam's fierce determination to marry ME."

"I was so happy, and my mother and sisters were radiant. My father's chest was so puffed out with pride, I thought he was going to explode! I only saw this all fleetingly, for I only had eyes for Uilliam once he came into view."

"We lived in the castle, of course. The castle had a large chamber on the first floor, a great room. Here the soldiers and others slept on rushes and straw. The top floor was mostly for the Chieftain and his wife. Others came there often, and it was time and again the scene of music and dancing. Lutenists, harpists, pipers and minstrels would often travel to our town, as did jugglers and others. It was a happy time. I especially liked to be in the upper floor on cold, snowy evenings. The fireplace glowed hotly with a turf fire."

"It was on such a wintry day as this that the Chieftain, my father, and a number of clansmen were away from the castle. They were involved in yet another of the endless border wars with nearby clans. Uilliam was left in charge of the castle, along with a small contingent of kinsmen. I was not unhappy that he didn't go with his father, as he had in times past. Uilliam still bore the deep scars on his thighs from sword cuts of foot-soldiers who attacked him as he fought on his horse. The wounds were cauterized with hot tar, and were ugly. I shivered each time I touched them. They were so horrible. Uilliam didn't seem to mind, although he confessed that they ached at times. He was alive, though. Others had left, never to return."

"We had heard reports for weeks that the English, who previously had confined themselves to the areas around Dublin—like the Norsemen before them—were moving through the countryside, pillaging as they went. We were far to the North, hard against the sea. We felt we would not be a target. If we were, we had heavy cavalry and a strong castle to defend ourselves."

"As fate would have it, while that very cavalry was away, runners came, breathless, to the castle. They cried out that English soldiers, 'a thousand or more,' were on the move, heading in our direction."

"This report was not taken too seriously. First, a thousand soldiers and knights would be highly unlikely. Who could have such an army? Secondly, what interest would they have with us? We had little gold. Our few cows, sheep, goats, pigs, horses and chickens wouldn't interest a band of Vikings, much less the English army!"

"Uilliam was ever cautious, though, and ordered the guard to be set. He commanded that weapons be prepared and measures taken for the defense of the castle, including filling the water kegs and bringing animals into the castle itself."

"I tried to help, and attempted to move a cask of wine by myself. It rolled away from me. Uilliam was nearby and I saw him, poised to shout at the idiot who moved the cask. He saw it was I, and closed his wide-open mouth, just as he was about to say something harsh. Without a word, he took me by the shoulder and told me to go to the upper floor. It was the highest point in the castle and had the greatest visibility. He said he wanted me to be one of the lookouts. I knew it was just a ploy to get me out of the way, and be safe. The year was 1589."

"He said, 'I'm sure it is a false alarm, or perhaps a small band of vagabonds, enlarged in the telling, but be awake, and send a boy with the news if you see anything.'"

"I don't know if he believed this, or if he was just saying it to comfort me. We'd been under attack before, usually in retaliation for a raid by our men, but a thousand soldiers? I trembled at the thought. Could it be real?"

"The walls of the castle are so thick that the stairs to the upper reaches are inside the walls. It was dark in the stairwell. The only light trickled in from arrow-loops cut into the walls. I was winded when I got to the top, holding up my skirts. I positioned myself at one of the windows, where I could see well beyond the town and the hills beyond."

"Several hours later, as I peered from the windows in the walls, another lookout pointed to several horsemen and foot soldiers who had appeared in the distance."

"'There, there!' we all shouted, in chorus, pointing excitedly at the small band. 'Not much, would you say, Mâire?' the boy of ten or so said, with obvious bravado."

"'No,' said I, 'not much, indeed, but run and tell Uilliam that our 'guests' have arrived.'"

"They all laughed at my calling them 'guests,' and it took some of the tension out of the air. Two or three raced off, each wanting to beat the other to the ground floor to tell Uilliam."

"Uilliam was schooled in the art of war, and his scars attested to his bravery and prowess. In truth, I knew him to be inexperienced. I silently wished the Chieftain had been there to direct our defense. Perhaps they would arrive in time? It was a fanciful thought and one I didn't really believe myself."

"It seemed like only a moment that Uilliam, with two of his cousins, were there at my side, gently moving us out of the way. I beamed when I saw my love. It was frightening to see him girded for war, with his heavy sword at his side as he studied the scene from the window."

"'A small band,' said one of the cousins, a young man admired by one of my close friends. 'Yes—for now—but perhaps an advance guard?'"

"The lieutenant was about to say something. Suddenly, as if on cue, the crest of the small hillock on which the enemy gathered blackened with what seemed to be hundreds of men. A thousand? I didn't know—perhaps there were more. There was a sharp intake of breath from Uilliam and he drew back quickly. I could tell he was surprised—even shocked."

"'Look at that!' called out one of the girls, almost crying. There were shrieks from two others, and the soldiers quickly went down the steps to the great room. I made to follow them, but Uilliam told me to stay where I was. If they were unfriendly—which seemed likely—he wanted me out of harm's way. I made to protest, but he said that the younger ones needed me, and he would be sending others up to where I was. I bowed my head slightly. He was my husband. He lifted my chin with the edge of his right forefinger, and softly kissed my lips. Tears coursed down my

41

cheeks, and I was deathly afraid for Uilliam, but, oddly enough, not at all for myself."

"There were weapons stored on each of the floors, and we made to prepare them. The castle was quite old, and some of the weapons were ancient and largely antiques, fit only for practice and display."

"We'd positioned longbows and quivers of arrows, crossbows, quarrels and pikes at what we thought were strategic positions around the room, mostly at the entrance to the stairway. After all, no one could scale the walls, and the castle was impenetrable. Built like most other castles, it had incredibly thick walls, stout oak floors, and a roof of thick stone shingles. There was no moat, but the main door was massive oak, studded and banded with iron. Rushes and hay covered the floors, and this room had a woven matting. The walls had many decorations and tapestries. I thought it was beautiful."

"The wind shifted slightly, and we could hear shouts and war cries coming from the enemy soldiers. They had various colored banners, which meant nothing to us; perhaps they did to Uilliam and the other soldiers. They looked fearsome though, beating their spears and swords against their shields. If their intention was to terrify us, they succeeded—at least with those of us on the highest floor."

"I directed the girls to stoke the fire. I didn't know if the chill was in the air or in the shouts of the barbarians outside. They seemed pleased to have something with which to keep themselves occupied."

"The English—if that is what they were—stayed beyond arrow-shot. Their belligerence and evil were proven as several ranging shots flew from the bows of the enemy yeomen. It was a very long distance, yet the arrows shattered against the stone of the castle. We were doubly frightened at this. Nothing we had could go three-quarters the distance. What did this mean?"

"One of our bowmen came up to where we were and positioned himself at an arrow loop. He drew his stout bow back until the arrowhead fairly nicked his fingers, and let fly with a 'woof!' of expelled air. We all looked to see the arrow's flight. It fell short. I knew him to be our best, and my body seemed frozen. I could neither move nor speak."

"After an embarrassingly long moment of silence, I said I thought he was hindered by the arrow loop, but did not suggest a second shot. The English were shouting derisively at us for this short shot, and peppered the castle walls with an answering volley of hundreds of arrows, almost all of which struck the walls. They broke harmlessly enough, but the effect was devastating."

"They did not seem interested in sending an emissary to talk to Uilliam, or to have anyone go to them. They had quickly surrounded us. I think the number mentioned of a thousand enemies was perhaps understated. I couldn't count them."

"They lit fires and pitched tents. They were moving into some of the evacuated houses, and I could see them carrying out their loot. They torched the houses as they left, which sent an angry boil of smoke rolling toward us on the wind. I could hear women crying from below, perhaps the occupants of the houses. The meager possessions of the townspeople would soon be on the backs of the English horses."

"'What do they have against us? We didn't do anything to them,' I asked aloud, to myself. I was surprised I'd spoken aloud, something I didn't realize until a woman nearby answered me, saying she knew not. I reached over and put my arm around her, to both comfort her as well as myself."

"It did not seem that the English had been there for very long, but suddenly we all were startled by what sounded like a tremendous clap of thunder. We didn't expect it—the clouds were white, and the sky blue. We ran to the windows, and saw a large cloud of white smoke from the English lines. I immediately hoped that God had sent a lightning bolt down to vanquish the English. Almost immediately, I saw a large clod of dirt fly up from the courtyard. What was it? Soon after, another thunderclap battered us, and this time, there was an answering crash as if something huge had struck the castle, as if we were next to a cliff and a huge stone fell down and hit the walls. This was terrible. These must be the 'cannon' that Uilliam and the other men had been discussing for some time. I'd never seen—or heard—one before. I remembered what Uilliam had told me about these new and fearsome weapons developed across the Irish Sea, in France and elsewhere. I didn't understand what he was talking about, and quite frankly, wasn't too interested. I wished then that I'd paid more attention. I recalled something about a mixture that exploded in a tube and propelled a ball or something out the unsealed end. It all seemed rather fanciful. How could this ball travel so far through the air? A catapult? I had seen drawings of them in the convent, but the noise? Surely the English had none of these 'cannons'!"

"I began to grow more fearful when the pace of the muskets and the large, booming, thunderous ones—the cannons—seemed to increase in frequency. The walls were thick, but could they withstand this? I didn't know. I didn't want to find out."

"The castle seemed to rock slightly as several projectiles hit the walls within the space of a split-second. I had never felt it move, even in the fiercest of gales whistling in off the slate-gray ocean seas a stone's throw to the west."

As Marisa told the end of the story, describing herself as Máire in her blood-soaked dress and Uilliam with his useless arm hanging from his side, she began to cry as she vividly remembered every detail

Her throat seemed to constrict once again from her remembrance of the killing smoke, and, as the crying Wanda put her arms consolingly around her shoulders, Marisa remembered that final instant with Uilliam's arm around her.

How it all ended—and how it all began.

7 LONDON: 1666

Wanda was gripping the wine bottle to her breast, tears coursing down her face and onto her blouse.

"Oh, Marisa! That sounds so real! It's like you were actually there!"

"But I was, Wanda. I don't know the reasons why things happened as they did, but Uilliam and I both died in the fire. We had no way out; there was only one entrance and no escape. Even if we'd gotten out, we would have been slain by the English. Their numbers were overwhelming."

"How come you never told me this—*er*—story before?" asked Wanda.

"I didn't remember it myself, until Uilliam had touched me. Some part of the 'curse,' if that's what it is, dictates that, if we touch in another life—and I'm presuming we don't, sometimes—I remember everything, but Uilliam, *the lout!*—oh, I'm *sorry* Uilliam!—remembers absolutely nothing. As I said, I tried to explain it to him once, in another life, and he thought me mad."

"There will be a day, I know, when he'll remember me. I just know it in my heart. I've loved him for four hundred years, and he's always loved me—I absolutely am positive of it. He just doesn't know it!"

45

"Isn't that just like a man? Doesn't know he loves a woman until the woman tells him so!" Wanda laughed, and Marisa smiled. It felt good to smile.

"Were you always a lawyer, Marisa?" The more Wanda spoke of it, and heard, the more she found herself believing.

"No, thank God. I was all sorts of things. Would you like to hear some of the things that happened to Uilliam and me? I warn you—there has never been a happy ending. Maybe there never will be. I'll be ten thousand years old, and Uilliam will never love me—or know he loves me." Marisa sniffed again, and grabbed a Kleenex from the box nearby.

"I was a scullery maid in London in the latter part of the 1600's," Marisa began.

"Charles Dickens?" Wanda interjected, a bit too brightly.

"No, Dickens wasn't until many years later. This was the old London that had built up from the ruins of Londinium, the Roman London. There were still many signs of the Romans—walls, statues, and even some buildings. I lived near the Thames River, and I can remember it well. Thinking back, it stank—the city reeked—even the people smelled. The streets were very narrow and people used to throw their 'night soil'— turds and piss—into the street. Some streets had a gutter in the middle, and some of this raw sewage washed away, but most didn't. People— sometimes—would shout out, 'Gardy loo' which was a corruption of the French, 'Gardez l'eau' when they were going to empty the pisspot onto your head. More often than not, they would just open the upstairs window and 'let fly.' I came close to getting hit more than once. You take to walking under the overhang—many of the houses crowded out over the street farther than the ground floor walls, to increase the size of the upstairs rooms."

"My Master was Thomas Faryner, a baker in Pudding Lane, near Fish Street Hill behind Eastcheap, and we lived above the bakehouse. Master Faryner was a great man, both in size and stature, and he was the King's Baker. He'd send me with the bakehouse boys to get flour and other things in the handcart. He didn't want to trust them with any silver or coppers because he knew he'd never see them again. I was pleased that he trusted me. There was another girl who worked there, but she was not too bright. Agnes was her name. I liked Agnes. We were friends."

"Did she die?" interrupted Wanda. Wanda realized as she spoke that Marisa was relating events that—to her—took place three hundred years before, and everyone was dead. She saw the irritation in Marisa's face at being intruded upon in this journey—of fantasy. She resolved to remain silent.

"The boys fetched water from the Thames, and we used it to make bread. There were public fountains and watering troughs, but the water was often foul, and rats were everywhere. Other ingredients were purchased in various parts of the city. London wasn't all that large—certainly by today's standards—but there were many, many people compressed into a small area. Throughout the night you could hear people shouting and fighting, babies bawling, horses neighing, all of that. Sometimes a house would burn, and there was the clamor of people trying to put it out. They usually just let it burn itself out. They always did."

"When we went with the cart to buy flour, the boys would kick aside the legs—or just a single leg—of war veterans who begged along the streets. I knew they were veterans because they wore the tatters of uniforms, and a few had medals they held onto, even in the face of starvation. I gave one a crust of old bread from the bakehouse once, and I still remember his eyes. They looked like they were dead, but he could see. His hands were festered and grimy, and you could see the white of bones through the sores. I thought he had the Plague. The year before was horrible. Thousands died from the Black Death. I was afraid to go out of the house. I looked out the windows and saw them haul hundreds of dead away on the carts. I heard they buried them across the Thames from the Isle of Dogs, where the King kept his hounds, but I certainly wouldn't go there to see. What a horrible sight that must have been. I saw many, many go down the river. I think they were just thrown in. Once, when I was fetching water, I had just drawn the bucket from the river, when I noticed that there was a decomposed body close by. I dumped the water out, and went back without any. My Mistress took a willow switch to my backside for this, saying that I should have brought the water anyway; he was dead, and couldn't hurt me. Little fish were feeding on him, Heather—Wanda—and I couldn't do it."

"The air was always heavy with the smell of wood fires, and the sulfurous stink of coal burning and the church steeples were often enshrouded with smoke. Listening to the bells ringing from a haze of smoke was a strange sensation. Each church had different sounding bells. You could pick them out, especially St. Paul's."

"My family bound me to the baker when I was 14. They didn't need another mouth to feed. We'd lived in Whitechapel then. It was bad when I was a child, but I heard later that it had gotten worse. I never went back. I saw one of my brothers once, and he said he was apprenticed for seven years with Stokes the goldsmith at the Goldsmith's Guild. This was quite an achievement, and I told him so. He said that my parents were well, but that one of my brothers and two of my sisters died in the Plague. I asked them which ones, and felt badly. They were my family, but we seemed so far apart, even though I could have walked there in a day from Pudding Lane. I knew I'd probably never see my brother again, and I hugged him when he left. One of his friends was with him, and my brother was obviously embarrassed. It didn't matter."

"I remember the day well. It was the second of September 1666. Agnes was to have pulled the fire out of the hearths below the bread ovens each night, and doused the coals with water. For reasons I'll never know, she didn't rake and douse the coals. The water cask was probably empty and she didn't want to walk to the river in the dark—I don't blame her. In any event, she must have pulled the coals from the fire and left them on the floor, which was hard-packed earth by the ovens. Some bavins for the fire—some sticks of wood—were stored nearby, and they must have ignited in the night. It had been a hot summer, and buildings were very dry."

"I think I was the first to raise the alarm. I woke up choking, coughing and hacking. My room was filled with smoke. It was about two in the morning. I was only wearing my nightgown, and I ran out of the garret, screaming 'Fire!' I'd forgotten about Agnes, who slept with me. My screaming woke her up, and she followed me out. The Master and Mistress slept in the rooms below the garret, and they were soon out of their bed. They were unclothed, but didn't seem to notice. The Mistress ran for their children, who were young. There were five in the family, including the baby."

"The Master started to go down the stairs to the bakehouse, which was on the ground floor. Below the Master's sleeping quarters were the dining room and kitchen. He made it part way down, but at this point there were already flames around the edge of the doorway to the dining room, and smoke was filling the room. We could hear the sounds of the wood crackling in the flames, and we were terrified, especially Agnes. She did not seem to be able to move."

"The Master looked out the window, and I followed. There were already people trying to put out the fire, including our two bakehouse boys, who slept in an outbuilding at the base of the rear garden. 'At least they were safe,' I thought."

"'Come along everyone. We must go over the roofs to the other houses and safety!' he shouted."

"My Mistress went first, carrying the little one. I followed, calling to Agnes. Agnes reminded me of a horse I'd seen in a burning stable. Although the path was clear, it wouldn't leave. Its eyes were wide and white. 'Agnes! You must leave or you'll die!' She wouldn't move."

"The Master handed me the children, and I passed them behind me. He turned to Agnes and reached for her. I don't know what she was more afraid of—the fire or the clutches of this naked bull of a man, black with soot, his eyes the only whiteness. She shrank back, covering her breasts with her arms."

"'Come, little one! The house is afire! Come to me!'"

"I saw that she was no more going to leave the house than that horse did in the burning stable."

"My Mistress and I called out in one voice, 'Agnes!'"

"She heard us and looked at us, but I don't think she saw us."

"The flames were racing across the ceiling, and out the window. My Master's hair was aflame as he leaped out the window onto the roof where we stood. I covered his head with my nightgown, and put out the flames. He was burned. I glanced back, and saw Agnes framed in the window, like some Madonna of the Embers. It was a vision of hell, as I saw her consumed by flames and fall back inside the house. The heat of the fire and what had just happened—in what seemed like only moments—caused me to swoon. My Master, even in his pain, caught me, or else I would have fallen from the roof."

"I coughed and wiped the back of my hand across my face. I, too, was black with soot."

"The bakehouse was old and made of wood, pitched, as were most of the houses and buildings in London. It burned like a bonfire. There was a very strong wind from the east, and it fed the flames, blowing them to other houses and buildings nearby. When I walked to the quayside, I could see the large quantities of goods stored in the warehouses, and I could smell the pitch stored in barrels. There was also any manner of combustibles: oil, hemp, flax, tar, cordage, hops, wines, brandies and cloth. These all, I am sure, fueled the fires."

"Fires were an everyday occurrence in London. While the people living nearby—who had the most to lose—fought hard to put them out, the Trained Band didn't seem to take too much interest in them. Two of the Band could be seen lounging from a safe distance, watching the spectacle. Leather buckets, axes, ropes, ladders and big iron fire-hooks were stored in St. Botolph's Church. I didn't see anyone doing much, and no one was using any of the tools to pull down buildings to make a firebreak. I recognized one of the constables and a beadle, and they were shouting officiously and pointing with their staves, but no one seemed to be listening. I could hear people shouting, 'Fire! Fire! Fire!' from the darkness, but it hardly seemed necessary, given the clamor and tumult in the streets. Within a few minutes, I could hear the familiar cry of the Trained Band, as they ran to fight a fire, crying, 'Hi! Hi! Hi!'"

"Even my Master, who had lost everything, said it would burn itself out."

"We made our way across the roofs until we found someone in a window. We must have looked like Lucifer and his minions just arrived from hell. This wasn't far from the truth."

"I knew the old woman who stood in the window as we approached, as did my Master. She didn't recognize us, and made the sign of the cross, urging us back to the Nether World. She must have thought we were from Hades."

"Once the Master called out to her and identified us, she must have recognized his voice, and reluctantly bade us to come in."

"Almost as if she had been carrying it around, she instantly produced a dress for my Mistress. The Master was large, and nothing would fit him. She found a blanket and put it over his shoulders in a motherly way."

"'I cannot pay you for any of this, Good Lady.'"

"The old woman raised her hand and bent her wrist in his direction. 'You will be back in business in a week, and I shall eat bread for a year!'"

"He cheered. 'Two years!' he replied."

"She went before us and unbarred the oak front door. As we stepped into the street, we all looked toward the fire."

"They, like I, were astounded at the speed and intensity of the blaze. 'Could this really go out by itself?' I thought. I'm sure the others felt that too."

"The Master turned to the old woman and thanked her profusely. 'Come with us. I fear your house will soon follow ours.'"

"She looked at his shining white eyes and glanced at the approaching fire. She quickly bent down and grabbed a calico cat that had been rubbing up against her legs, and held it to her."

"'Let us spare no time,' she said, resolutely."

"Without bothering to close the door, she left her life behind her and walked hurriedly away with us. The moment she left her doorstep, street people rushed in and began ransacking her home. She seemed not to care, but I knew she did. She had simply lived long enough to accept the inevitable."

"We made our way through the streets, but not without difficulty. Footpads and cut-purses abounded in London, and the Trained Band merely pushed them aside. They knocked a few heads and arrested a few, but Tyburn wasn't a large enough gallows to hang them all."

"The Master took a staff and dagger from one of them who came at us from the shadows, and we went forward armed. I wished the bakehouse boys would have found us, but I was confident they would be all right. The fire would burn itself out."

"Although it was night, by the time we got to London Bridge, the sky had a reddish hue from the fire."

"The Master spoke prophetically: 'This one will be the death of London. It will not burn out until London is no more.'"

"'Could this be?' I wondered. 'Surely he is just overwrought from having lost his bakehouse, home, and serving girl, Agnes.' Agnes. I hadn't thought of her since we left her afire. Oh, Agnes! Why couldn't you have gone with us?"

"My Master had a brother who lived on London Bridge, above his apothecary shop. I had once gone with one of the bakehouse boys down Fish Street Hill to deliver a parcel of bread to him, and to get some potion in return. The Master announced that we would go there."

"We were a pitiful-looking load of baggage as we made our way through the streets. Several times we were confronted by ruffians, and my Master's staff on their heads and shoulders kept us from harm. With each sally, he would roar like a bear, and many ran from this alone. It was fortunate for them that he did not have a pike or halberd."

"Many were carrying furniture, chests and valuables. From the looks of many of their rags, they did not come by them rightfully. The Star Inn on Fish Hill Street was quickly being consumed in the flames. Hay and straw were stored there for the animals, and this provided ready fuel to the fire. We could feel the heat of the fire as we ran past. It was like the sun on a hot summer day."

"The wind was still blowing fiercely from the East, and as we ran into a wall of smoke I wondered if we would come out again. I held my arm against my mouth and tried to keep from breathing the smoke, but it was impossible. Several of the little ones appeared to be close to fainting, and I was greatly concerned for them. Suddenly, we were out of the main smoke. When I looked up, we were under a canopy of flames that roared from the rooftops to the east. It leaped across the street to the houses on our right. These, too, quickly ignited."

"My Master, like most Londoners, was used to going about in the dark, for there were few street lights. His guidance brought us to London Bridge."

"There were many houses and shops built on top of London Bridge. Walkers, horses, and carts passed under them to go across the Thames. It was a truly dangerous place at any time, but particularly so at night."

"Fortunately, my Master's brother's home wasn't far from the north bank, where we were. Surprisingly enough, he was out of his house, with a torch and a sword, when we approached. He didn't even realize who was hailing him from beneath the blanket. He only saw the staff and dagger and raised his sword in defense"

"My Master called out to him by name, and said his own. The brother must have recognized the children, for he almost dropped his torch as he ran toward us."

"'The fire, brother! I saw the flames from my window, and worried that it might be near your bakehouse.'"

"'It was my bakehouse, Cedric. Burned to a cinder. Gone.'"

"'Come inside, quickly. It is not safe here. You will be at home with me. The fire will be out soon.'"

"Although I had heard this from everyone, I believed it less as I saw the flames steal the sky. Would we be safe even here?"

"Cedric's wife found me an old dress belonging to one of their daughters, and I put it on quickly. Some water was splashed on my face from a bowl, and I soon found myself being toweled by Cedric's wife, Anne."

"'Thank you, Mistress Anne,' I sputtered, through the water.

"I was offered food, but I only wanted a drink of water, which I soon received. It was dark and murky river water, but it tasted wonderful."

"I found a place on the floor and a blanket was placed over me. I quickly went to a dreamless sleep."

"The sun was up when I awoke, but I could not see it. I think it was Tuesday. I looked out the window, and all I could see was the fog. At that moment I understood that it was not fog, for I could smell the heavy smoke. London was covered with smoke. I looked toward where the bakehouse had been, and I could see flames though the smoke. The smoke was black, gray and white, apparently from the different buildings and their contents. There were warehouses near the river, and they held any manner of things from across the world. These, too, were blazing."

"I went to the highest window of the house, and I could see down into London, or as well as the smoke permitted me. I could see a large party, and could tell from the colors, ribbons and flags that it was the Lord Mayor, Sir Thomas Bludworth, and his council. There was much pointing and hand waving, but no one seemed to be paying attention to any of them, including the Lord Mayor. He had a scarf around his neck, which he unwound and used to mop his forehead. Shortly, they went away."

"It was nearing six of the clock in the morning, and I was shocked to see the fire burning so far down Fish Hill Street toward London Bridge. I thought we had escaped, but the fire was coming to us!"

"I ran to tell the others, but they were already assembled."

"'Where were you, Mary?' asked my Mistress. 'We looked for you and called out.'"

"'I was in the garret, Mistress, watching the fire. I saw the Lord Mayor! Perhaps he will put out the fire!'"

"'I doubt he could put out his pipe,' chuffed my Master's brother."

"'We have to leave, Mary. It is thought that the fire will not spare the bridge. We will go across the bridge together and find safety on the south side of the Thames,' pronounced my Master."

"I had nothing of my own; even my dress was borrowed, but I helped carry bundles of what I do not know. I heard them clink, and presumed them to be silver or some metal. I know they were heavy enough to make my legs quaver. Each was in a tablecloth or bedclothes, and I dared not suggest that the three I was given were too much for me, for the others had even greater burdens. Even the children were carrying all they could. I remained silent."

"The smoke, a foul witches' brew of yellow and white, which I could taste, was enveloping the north end of the bridge, where we were."

"I stopped for a moment in the walkway to try to adjust the bundles that were already seeking to trisect my body."

"'Hasten, Mary! Come quickly!' my Master called from over his shoulder, apparently not seeing me at his elbow.

"I started to answer, when suddenly I was hit hard from behind and I went sprawling, my arms flying out. I hit the walkway hard, and felt my nose begin to bleed profusely. I grabbed at one of the tablecloths to stanch the flow, and in yanking it, caused one of the corners to become untied. Silver plate cascaded out onto the stones. I was amazed at the beauty of it all."

"I wasn't the only one who was surprised. Two cutthroats hurrying by with their own packages quickly dropped what they had and made a lunge for mine."

"Although I was in pain, and bleeding, I cried out to them to stop, and my Master heard me. How he did so in that bedlam, I cannot imagine."

"The Master said something to his brother, and held back a hand when it was plain that Cedric was going to join in the affray. Cedric was perhaps fifty years old, and obviously elderly."

"My Master handed his packages to his brother, and, wielding his staff, rushed to my side. I like to think that he was saving me, but he could just as easily have been saving the silver."

"One of the thieves had a broken draw-shaft of a wagon, and he swung it at my Master. The heavy end of it missed him, but in completing its arc, struck me on the right shoulder. It was if a giant had me in his clutches and flung me like a rag doll. In an instant I was somersaulting in the air, off the bridge and into the swirling waters of the Thames, far below the walkway of the bridge."

8 DETROIT, MICHIGAN, USA: THE PRESENT

Oh, Marisa!" cried Wanda, on the edge of her chair with excitement. "I hope you weren't *drowned!*"

Wanda was flustered at having made an outburst in the middle of Marisa's story.

"I mean, I guess I mean, I know you didn't live for three hundred and fifty years, but I don't want to think you *died!*"

"Not-to-worry, Wanda. I know what you mean," said Marisa. "Time for more tea, anyway!"

Wanda jumped up and made her way to the teapot, ignoring all the angry flashing lights on the telephone.

They would have to wait—she was going to *London!*

9 LONDON: 1666

I hit the water hard, and went deep," continued Marisa. Although I never considered myself a swimmer, but I had splashed along the shores of the Thames with other girls, and somehow managed to stay afloat."

"My eyes were open wide, and I could see the light of the sun. Somehow, my thrashing around got me to the surface and I filled my lungs with air mingled with smoke. Nothing tasted better!"

"I was already some distance from the bridge, for the water flowed swiftly under the pillars of the bridge. I could see small figures on the bridge, and saw that the northernmost houses had ignited."

"I must have looked like a drowning dog, for I was paddling like one. There was a large quantity of furniture, boxes and other debris in the river. A small child, face down, floated by me, and I screamed. I reached for a wooden box just as my strength and resolve were about to fail me."

"I was closer to the north bank of the river, near the Billingsgate docks, as near as I could tell, but there was no salvation there—all was an inferno. The south bank was well beyond my meager swimming abilities, so I just drifted, kicking my feet to escape the dead child who was haunting me."

"The box was too small to climb upon, and almost too large to hold onto. The corners and edges cut into my skin. I was still bleeding from my nose, and I could taste the iron blood."

"There were many boats and lighters upon the river, and, although I waved my hand at them, and tried to shout, I was not very loud, and no one noticed me."

"Just as I was about to sink away into a quiet oblivion, hoping for the salvation of the Lord, I felt something touch my shoulder. I whipped my head around, thinking, in fear, that it was the dead child seeking to embrace me and take me to Eternity. It was a rowing boat, and there were two gentlemen, finely dressed, along with an oarsman. One of the gentlemen, a portly old man of perhaps fifty-five years, with a powdered wig and brocade waistcoat, held one of the oarsman's oars, and was probing me with it."

"'She's alive, Pepys!' he called to the other gentleman."

"'Right you are, M'lord!' he answered."

"'M'lord?' I found myself wondering to myself. 'Was a member of the aristocracy actually rescuing me?"

"I let go of the box and lunged for the oar, holding it for dear life, for that is precisely was what it was."

"He pulled me toward the boat with the oar. The oarsman grabbed me unceremoniously by the back of my dress, and hauled me aboard like a fish. I'm sure I must have looked like some sort of sea monster, bleeding from the nose. My auburn hair hid my face as I flopped in the water at the bottom of the boat."

"'Are you going to live, little one?' asked the one named Pepys.

"In answer, I coughed and sneezed, spraying droplets of blood over the other gentleman's white stockings and silver-buckled shoes."

Pepys laughed at his companion's discomfort, and said, "'She'll cook up nicely, this fish! She'll survive 'til we get her in the frying pan!'"

"I know now that it was his odd sense of humor, but at the moment, I almost cast myself back into the water, thinking that I had been captured by cannibals!"

"'You are scaring her, Samuel!' said the older man. To me he said, gently, 'We will not hurt you. Are you injured?'"

"I wiped the back of my hand across my nose, and saw that there was blood on my hand."

"'Nose,' was all I could say. It must have sounded idiotic."

"'Yes, that is your nose! It must be a lovely one when it is not doubling as a fountain!' laughed the portly gentleman."

"I was fuming, and felt like a half-drowned rat. I rolled over and got to my knees. My dress clung to me and I could feel the men's eyes on me. I was mortified."

"'Th-thank you, sirs,' I sputtered."

"'She will survive, Pepys!' said the older man.

"'Young Miss, I am Samuel Pepys, Esquire, and this good gentleman is Sir Batten. You are?'"

"'Mary Goode, serving Master Faryner, baker to the King,' I managed to say, in a cracked voice."

"'How very "good," my dear. I hope Baker Faryner is not now down in the depths from which you sprang—I have eaten his bread, and would miss him most terribly,' said the man named Pepys."

"He continued, 'We humble boatmen are out upon this pest-strewn river to survey the damage and the ongoing fire for His Majesty. Shortly I will go to Whitehall to report to him.'"

"'The King?' I asked, incredulously.

"'Certainly the King. Who else can order the seas of fire to part?' said Pepys, still making sport of me, I am sure."

"'Oarsman, make for the Watergate at the Tower.' said Sir Batten."

"My heart stopped. The Tower! People went to the Tower and never were seen again, except on the gallows on Tower Hill, near the Roman wall. I had been near it, but the moat and the soldiers were most forbidding. She often wondered what was inside. She had heard of the Watergate—the Traitor's Gate—through which the doomed, the condemned, would pass on the way to the chopping block. I shivered unintentionally."

"As we approached the Tower, I could see the pennants snapping in the wind as they flew from the heights of the White Tower. The oarsman paused slightly. We quickly began to drift in the current, although the wind was still blowing from the east. We were downriver at that point."

"The gentlemen could sense the boatman's apprehension; the Tower was the stuff of nightmares and horror stories to scare children—of all ages—with. To many, it was a one-way trip."

"Both the oarsman and I looked up at the same time, and saw soldiers armed with muskets at the battlements near the Watergate, and they were pointing them in our general direction. They gave me gooseflesh."

"'You in the boat!'" hailed one of the sentries, "'come no closer. What is the password?'"

"Sir Batten looked over at the oarsman, wondering if he should give the password out loud. I noticed he did not look at me; I must not have seemed like a threat to the Crown Jewels! Apparently thinking the boatman was not either, Sir Batten called out, in a deep voice, edged with authority, 'Crown of Roses! Sir Batten and Mr. Samuel Pepys.'"

"'Advance!' called the soldier, but I noticed that he still trained his gun at us.

"The large wooden gate with rectangular openings began to creak and slowly open. Murky Thames water eddied around it as it moved. The tide was high, and it took a few minutes for the gate to open enough so we could move through. Clearly, this was the oarsman's first trip through Traitor's Gate—as it was mine—for his head was almost like it was on a swivel, it turned so. His eyes were wide. I doubted he would be returning later with the password on his lips."

"The bow of the boat nudged the stone of the quay, and an officer strode confidently toward us. He took in the gentlemen's clothes, swords and finery in an instant, and judged them to be Quality. He saluted in their direction."

"Sir Batten identified both himself and Mr. Pepys to the officer, who I think was a captain, but I could not identify the ranks very well."

"'Sir!' was all that the captain said, but he said it in such a loud, authoritative voice, that it startled me. Two other soldiers were behind the captain, and they stiffened."

"Mr. Pepys had already alighted from the boat, and Sir Batten turned to the oarsman. Without a word, he flipped him a silver shilling, which the boatman caught with obviously practiced ease. I knew it was a shilling for he held it to the light and smiled a gap-toothed grin."

"He peeled off his grimy wool cap and bowed from the neck, saying, 'Thank ye, Your Worship! Thank ye!'"

"Sir Batten then turned to his next problem—me. I could see that he was debating whether to leave me with the boatman. The boatman appeared to have the same idea. He was now discovering, as he rested on his oars, that I was only wearing a thin dress that was clinging wetly to my body. I could feel my cheeks burning as I sought to cover myself with my arms. I looked at Sir Batten with what must have been a baleful gaze. A strand of his powdered wig had fallen down over his left eye, and he brushed it back unconsciously. He was a heavy man—no, a fat man—and he had a large mole on his nose. His right eye seemed to droop slightly, for some reason, and he had a nervous tic on the other side of his face. As he brushed back his hair, I could see that he had a number of gold and jeweled rings on his fingers. Both they and his fingers were oversized. He could see I was assessing him, and he cleared his throat, 'Harrumph!' I was startled by this outburst."

"He spoke, 'And you, my young woman. What would we do with you? We cannot have you go with this boat master, can we? He might feed you to the fishes again if you cannot pay his fare.' I was sure what 'coin' would pay my passage. M'lord knew as well."

"'I–I can walk back to London Bridge, M'lord. I am indentured to Master Faryner, the King's Baker, and they are awaiting me, I am sure, at the bridge,' I stammered.

"'London Bridge! So that is where you went swimming from! We did not ask you in the boat. However, my dear, from what we could see from our vantage point on the river, the bridge itself is in flames. There is no going across the river, short of being rowed across by our boatman here,' waving a fat finger at the oarsman."

"The boatman, seeing his chances for a 'fare' renewed, opened his toothless maw in a grin. Seeing this, Sir Batten seemed resigned to be encumbered with me, at least for the moment."

"'Oh, come along then!' he said, a little too impatiently for my sensibilities, but he was my benefactor and savior, after all."

"He held out his chubby hand to help me from the boat. I gathered up my skirts around me with one hand, and reached for him with my free hand, all the while trying to keep my balance in the rocking boat. His hand gripped mine to help me out, and it felt as if I had thrust my arm into the furnace that was London! Everything went white and then colors swam dazzlingly before my eyes! In an instant, I was back in Uilliam's castle, and I 'remembered' everything that had transpired in my life—and death—as Máire! I could not breathe, I was so overcome. Yet, I did not understand—I was still in London, in the Tower, and I could not escape the fact that London was burning at that moment! These thoughts flashed before me instantly, and just as suddenly, I shouted out, 'Uilliam! You have come back to me!'"

"I said this very loudly, and it obviously startled Sir Batten for he moved back suddenly at the sound of my voice. I had his hand in a death grip, however, and he plucked me from the boat like an apple from a tree. Amazingly enough, although I saw that it was Sir Batten, I knew it was my Uilliam, although it was plain that he did not know me."

"I knew not how I suddenly remembered all of my life in Ireland, but it was all as real as the stones of the Tower to me. I released a broadside of furious Irish at Sir Batten, and he twisted his hand to be away from me. Surely I was possessed."

"Pepys was standing nearby, and he was clearly amused by all of this. 'She appears to know you, Sir William. At least you are on a Christian name basis with her. I don't recall anyone mentioning your Christian name to her. That gibberish is, I believe, Irish. Is there something you wish to tell me about your trips to Ireland, Sir William?'"

"As I heard Pepys say Sir Batten's name was William, my heart began to pound even harder. I flung my arms around him and embraced him. I saw in his eyes that it was my love, my Uilliam. While his present appearance in the form before me made no sense, the tide of love was as high in me as the water was in the River Thames."

"The captain and the other soldiers, as well as the boatman, were each bemused by all of this. Their obvious smirks and 'knowing' looks—which were not lost on Sir William—only served to infuriate him further. Angrily, he thrust me back at the end of his arms.

"'Enough of that!' he commanded. 'I never saw you before, and I do not know you. You seem to know my name, but I am not an insubstantial figure in the City of London.'"

"This was my first reincarnation, and I was confused. It had been nearly a hundred years since Uilliam and I had died in the castle, but it all seemed like present memory to me. I couldn't differentiate between the two eras."

"I knew he was Uilliam, but he didn't look like him. It was Uilliam, of that I was absolutely positive. I didn't make any more advances to him, but I wanted to crush him in my arms. I couldn't understand how we had escaped the fire, so I asked."

"Excuse me, Sir William, but how did we escape the fire?" I asked.

"'"Did" escape? Past-tense? My good woman, if you haven't noticed, all of London appears to be a flaming hell, all about us. We have not escaped anything!'"

"I mean the castle," I said, plaintively.

"'We are in the Tower itself, madam. The White Tower is just there. We have not, but shall, escape the fire. First there is work to be done.'"

"I decided to keep my tongue, as I didn't want to lose Uilliam—or 'William'—whom I'd only just found after almost a hundred years of oblivion."

"'Pepys,' said, Sir William, "we've work to do. Do you think this young woman can make her way safely?'"

"Pepys inclined his head sideways to the leering boatmen and Sir William understood immediately. No woman, highborn or lowborn, should be left to the likes of these."

"'Oh, very well, come along then Miss,' said William."

"'Mary,'" I said, "'I'm your Mary.'"

"Pepys chuckled at this and chided Sir William: 'Sir William, if you'll take 'your Mary' with you, I'll take along some men and follow right behind.'"

"Sir William glowered at this reference to 'his Mary,' but I beamed."

"Shortly, there was a small band of us moving, inexplicably, toward the raging inferno that I had just escaped!"

"I remembered the fire in our castle—it seemed like earlier today—and I felt a great clutching pressure on my chest and was gasping for breath."

"'Are you quite all right, Madam?' William asked of me."

"Yes, Sir William." I made myself smile. "I am quite all right—*now.*"

"He smiled back at me, and I saw the old Uilliam! Nothing really had changed!"

"I knew, for sure, that he would recall all that had gone before, just as I did, but it would take a little longer. He was, after all, a man."

"As we walked, Sir William explained to me that both his and Pepys' houses were near the Tower. We had to salvage certain of their possessions."

"As several of the men had spades, I presumed that we were going to bury them, whatever they were."

"We'd not walked far when a swath of black, stinking, smoke washed over us, making us all cough. The men carrying the shovels looked around, dropped their tools and ran off. This left only Sir William, Mr. Pepys, Sir William's man, and me."

"'Cowards,' muttered Sir William, clutching the hilt of his jeweled sword, as if he'd go after them and cut them down."

"'Why didn't you run off, little one? You're braver than those curs.'"

"I glowed in the attention he was giving me, and I reached down and picked up a spade. 'I'll dig for you, William. Anything. I won't leave. I'll never leave you!'"

"He seemed concerned by what he must have taken as a mad woman's ramblings. Regardless, he picked up a spade and began to dig a deep hole at the base of the old Roman wall. I knew that the wall had once surrounded Londinium, the ancient Roman city of London."

"'Just as well—they'd come back and steal it all, anyway,' said, William, speaking to no one in particular."

"I joined in—I was a strong girl—and began to dig quickly, next to William. Before long, we had a very deep hole. Pepys did not dig, as he had gone to his house, which was farther away. Soon he returned with some bags and bottles of wine and other things. He deposited them in one of the holes."

"William moved off and went to a house near us. It was made of wood, like most of the others. I noticed the thatched roof was already beginning to smolder as I went with him. It was a splendid house. I hoped it wouldn't burn, because I dearly wanted to live there with William. Was he married? My heart stopped at the thought."

"I ventured a question: 'William, has your wife escaped?'"

"'She died in the plague last year,' he said, gruffly."

"The plague had struck down thousands in the year of our Lord 1665, and London was visited with this terrible fire only the next year!"

"I told William that I was sorry, but, secretly, I was not."

"He opened a wooden chest and took out an obviously very heavy iron-bound strongbox. It had a heavy lock, and leather handles. I made to take one, but he stopped me."

"'It is far too heavy for you. I will take it. Carry those candlesticks and wrap the paintings in the oilcloth, if you please, and we shall go. This house is going up in smoke!'"

"We scrambled out of the house, and if by a self-fulfilling prophecy, the house ignited like tinder behind us. In moments it was as if we were in the castle once again. We weren't though—we were safe."

"William's back was bent like a bow under the weight of the box. What must be in it? I glanced at the painting under the oilcloth. It was of a rather severe looking woman. His mother? Lady William? I hoped not. I couldn't bear to be saving her. I caught myself at this—jealous of a dead woman. Didn't I have him now? Well, not quite, but close!"

"Pepys saw us and scampered over, with William's man, to help us. They lowered the strongbox into one of the holes, which was a good four feet deep. This surprised me, but then I realized that Sir William's man must have continued digging while we were gone."

"The strongbox went in the hole along with a gold chalice and the candlesticks, which seemed to be silver, went next to it. William carefully placed the painting to the side of the box, and threw his cloak over it. He took much care for an old man, I thought, grimly."

"They placed a flat stone over the treasure and carefully shoveled earth onto all the buried goods and glanced around, apparently to take their bearings. I, too, looked about, but didn't really know what I was seeing, other than the Tower and the old wall."

"They flung the spades away from them, perhaps to not guide others to the burial site. William said, 'Pepys, I have to go to the King. Are you coming with me?'"

"'No, Sir William, I mean to write down my recollections of this day. Who knows? Perhaps some day someone may be interested in reading of this fire? Be careful. Shall I take the young woman with me?'"

"Before William could respond, I said, adamantly and resoundingly, 'No!' I startled both myself and them, that is certain."

"Bemused, William said, 'Very well, come along. I shall leave you at St. Paul's. Surely the clergy can make some use of you.'"

"I had no intention of being left at St. Paul's or anywhere else. I knew I was inseparable from William."

"We walked at a quick pace, with the intention of skirting the fire. People were rushing here and there, and soldiers with pike poles were debating on whether to pull down buildings to stop the fire. They did not agree, and were arguing as we hurried by."

"We had to go by a circuitous route to get to St. Paul's. I knew the way better than William, so I treaded us through the crooked, nameless streets, cluttered with debris and packed with people, going in all directions. I almost got separated from William. He saw that I was going to be lost, and grabbed my hand and held it tightly in his large, strong—but soft—hand. My heart leaped! I knew he loved me! Did he? I gripped him as tightly as I could."

"Several footpads crashed into us, and looked William up and down, gauging his mettle, I presume. William sensed this and drew his sword rapidly with his free, right hand. I clutched his arm. He swung his sword in a circle around him, causing it to make a fearsome whistle. The bandits backed off quickly. Although armed with clubs and knives, they saw they were no match for what appeared to be a trained swordsman."

"I was coughing from the smoke, and Sir William reached into his laced cuff and pulled out a beautiful nosegay. He handed it to me, and I stared at it. 'For your nose,' he said."

"'Not likely,' I thought, as I tucked it into my bosom. It smelled mightily of cologne—*his* cologne.*"

"We fairly ran, hand in hand, through the clogged streets of London, vaguely headed for St. Paul's, and the King beyond. None of the landmarks seemed to be familiar any longer, and several houses we ran by were aflame. I pointed excitedly to St. Paul's cathedral in the distance. Its huge gray mass of stones was recognizable to anyone."

"As we got closer, we realized that the unthinkable had happened: St. Paul's was ablaze! We stopped suddenly when we saw that the streets were awash with some sort of liquid that was glistening in the gutters. 'What is it?' I asked William."

"William considered my question for a moment and answered, 'Lead. It is lead from the joints between the stones. It is a deadly heat that must be causing that. It is like leaden lava.'"

"I didn't know what 'lava' was, but I was certain I didn't like it."

"As we ran along the street to the side that didn't seem to have any rivers of lead-lava, I heard the booming of cannon once again! Had history come full circle? Were these English cannons, bombarding our castle once more?"

"William pointed to the lead-lava side and said, 'They are exploding from the heat! The stones are erupting! Quickly, move very quickly!'"

"Almost immediately, the stones nearest us began to leak the lead-lava. It spattered on me, burning instantly through my clothes and my skin. I screamed in abject pain."

"William stopped and ripped his beautiful shirt from his body. He wrapped me with it. He had powerful muscles, I could see, even though he was much older than he was in Éire."

"We moved off. Just as we seemed to be away from the worst of it, a stone burst just to the side of us, deafening me for a moment."

"In my confusion, I'd let go of William's hand. *William!* Where was he? The smoke was thick, but I could see him, on the cobblestones, a great shard of granite protruding from his chest. I wailed, and rushed to him, kneeling by his side. He made a weak smile at me, but I could see he was close to the end. I bent down and kissed his chest, his neck, his chin and his soft lips. As I put my head against him, covering his terrible wounds with my long, dark-red hair, I knew he was gone. I couldn't leave him even if I wanted to, for the river of lead-lava was closing in on us from all sides."

10 BORNEO: 1699

I looked up from the fire when I heard the men shouting. My youngest child was suckling on my breast and I stood up and he opened his mouth in surprise as he continued to stand there, his arms upraised to me."

"I paid him little attention and he soon ran off to join the other children. I walked across the dusty clearing at the end of the village and to see what the noise was all about. The warriors of the village were expected back at any moment, and I wanted to see if they brought food from their hunt."

"I was immensely fat; my mahogany-hued skin could scarcely seem to contain my girth. My huge, pendulous breasts rested on my big belly. I was proud to be so fat—it was a sign of great prosperity."

"My mouth began to water at the thought of fresh meat. It had been days since the village had fresh food, for the men were on the hunt far afield."

"We women held back, and chattered between ourselves about the hunt and how it appeared, from the men's shouting and outcries, that it was immensely successful. My mouth watered in anticipation."

"Our men lined up, facing one another, making loud cries of triumph for a successful hunt. They raised their weapons in excitement, and boasted of their bravery and prowess in battle. Their naked bodies glistened with sweat and with the blood of their quarries. I was sexually aroused and felt my heart beat faster. I peered through the line of men to see what they had captured."

"Soon I could see some movement. It was long pig! How I loved long pig!"

"The first long pig moved between the men, who were blocking its escape. It was bound with vines, but it could still walk. I could almost taste the long pig, cooking slowly over a fire! I would cook one myself! I felt I could almost eat a whole long pig by myself, I was so hungry."

"The other women pointed at the seven or eight long pigs that had been captured, and talked incessantly between themselves, how this one was fat, or that one was lean and probably tough. You could see how hungry they were!"

"The Chief had positioned himself at the head of the gauntlet, and the first long pig came up to him. This long pig did not seem to be as frightened as the others, who were cowering under the blows from the warriors' clubs and other weapons. The long pig had long, black hair and was very pale. I had never seen a long pig so pale. The Chief was saying something in a loud voice, but I couldn't understand him over the commotion from the long pigs, the warriors and the women and children near me."

"Suddenly, the Chief reached out to the first long pig—the brave one—and ripped an ear from the long pig's head and began to eat it. The long pig screamed in pain, and it excited us women even more!"

"Blood was coursing from the long pig's head and it was cuffed by the Chief on the shoulder. The long pig wavered for a moment, and then stumbled forward."

"Within a few moments, all the long pigs were encircled by the warriors, and, with an almost imperceptible nod from the Chief, the warriors fell on the long pigs with their weapons and in what seemed like seconds, they were all killed."

"We women soon added wood to the present fires, and started more cook-fires. The long pigs were beheaded and thrown on the fires to roast. We all could breathe in the scent of the roasting long pig, but the men would eat first. Large portions were cut away and eaten ravenously. The men's naked bodies were coursing with blood, fat, and sweat, and several were moving towards the women and roughly taking them sexually. No one paid any attention; it was a rite of the hunt."

"The sun was hot and the raging cook-fires made it even hotter, but we were hungry and could hardly wait until the men were finished eating. We brushed back the children who were trying to tear off pieces of the long pigs. It sometimes happened that a man would club a child to death who was trying to eat before he finished. Sometimes it was the man's own child, but no one protested, for it was his right."

"The Chief soon lifted himself from his haunches before the cooking fire and stood to survey his warriors either eating busily or rutting with the women. He smiled and I could see his white teeth, filed to sharp points, daubed with blood from the long pig he had just eaten."

"He noticed me as he looked around, and wiped the gore from his chin with the back of his hand."

"The Chief had fastened the head of the first long pig by its hair to a vine around the Chief's waist, and it swung like a pendulum as he walked towards me, his great spiked war-club in his hand. The club had bits of hair and flesh on it, and it was dripping blood as he stood over me."

"The Chief was obviously aroused, and his great, black penis stood out from him in solid erection. He untied the head from his waist and let it drop heavily to the ground."

"In his hand, he held the penis of the long pig, a great delicacy to our people, as were the ears and lips. He held out the severed penis to me and I reached out for it, only to have it pulled back. He laughed and his great saw-tooth teeth glistened."

"He dropped the penis next to the head and moved toward me. I knew what he wanted. He was so beautiful! I twisted about and went on my knees and showed my great rump to him. He swiftly entered me, and gloriously mounted me for what seemed forever."

"Spent, he pulled out and I turned around, a smile on my face of pure satisfaction. My husband! I was so proud to be the wife of the Chief!"

"I knew he had saved the long pig's penis for me, and I was pleased. He reached into the dust and picked up the penis and made to hand it to me, obviously saving the best part for last. I didn't mind; I was famished!"

"I was still on my knees when he handed me the bloody penis. I felt like I had been hit between the eyes by the Chief's war-club as I clenched the penis in my fist. I fell backwards onto my rump in the dirt and screamed in Irish at the top of my lungs, causing all the birds in the trees nearby to take flight:"

"'Uilliam! *Go madh dó féin bhus céad mairg!*'"

ll DETROIT, MICHIGAN, USA: THE PRESENT

Oh, my God! Marisa, I'm not sure I've remembered to *breathe!* I am so upset about this! I can't *bear* it. What happens next? Are you still in London when you find William again? You *do* find him, don't you?"

"Yes, I do. I find him many times over the centuries. How can one heart be broken so many times? Will it be broken again, in *this* life?"

"Tell me more! It is after-hours and the damned phone should stop soon. I'm surprised they haven't sent the building security up her to make sure we weren't murdered!"

"The next time I found Uilliam was, as fate would have it, back in Ireland. Not in Donegal Town, but in the County of Donegal, in Raphoe, which was, and is, the seat of the diocese, both Catholic and Protestant. I was a Protestant woman..."

12 RAPHOE, COUNTY DONEGAL, IRELAND: 1741

As I saw the gaunt figure dressed all in black at my doorway, I made a small cry, thinking it was the Angel of Death. As he pushed back the hood of his black cape, I saw, with relief, that it was our church's minister, Reverend Liam Doherty."

"With some difficulty, I pulled at the heavy oak door and it moved slowly inward on noisily protesting, frozen hinges."

"'Reverend! Come in! Come in! It is so amazingly cold outside. Come in and get warm!'"

"The preacher, never other than a wisp of man, weighed no more than his shadow, as he moved into our house. He recognized, I'm sure, that it was surely no warmer in the house, for there was no heat."

"'God Bless All Here,'" he intoned, nodding his head to the wooden crucifix in the entryway."

"I made a small curtsy, and took him by the elbow, feeling nothing but bone through the woolen cloth."

"'Reverend, have you eaten? I must have something here? Let me find you dinner!'"

"I meant it, but, God's truth, I did not know what I could find him. I'd eaten some molding turnips yesterday, perhaps, or was it a week ago? I was no longer hungry; I didn't know why."

"'Have you supped today, Máirín Caít?'"

"'Ah, sure, Reverend. Didn't I have a fine, young swan with dumplings and wine sauce, just this afternoon?' I said, with a faint smile."

"Pastor Doherty nodded solemnly, a line of gray hair falling, bisecting his wrinkled forehead."

"'Máirín Caít, I cannot stay long. Since last year's terrible winter, and this summer's awful famine, my flock is anguishing. I must be on my way. Máirín Caít, let me say, straightaway, what I am about. You love Jesus, don't you? Of course you do. What a question. This is most difficult. I, ah, I am here to take your wee babies, the twins, to Jesus. Sure, and they are baptized in the water of the Lord. They are in Heaven, my dear. You and I know they are. Sweet innocents. The cold, the devil's frozen finger, has touched each home in the county.' "

"I started at his words, and my hands flew to my mouth to stifle my cry, but I could not."

"The Pastor touched my shoulder as lightly as a butterfly's wingtip, and pursed his lips almost imperceptibly."

"I had long ago stopped wondering how the minister knew so much about what went on with his flock. But, didn't my sweet babies fall into everlasting sleep just this morning? Or could it have been yesterday? The day before? My breasts knew; the babies no longer gently kneaded them to express the thin, blue milk I had left."

"I cried softly as I thought of my little girls. Identical twins, born just this past Spring. 11 May 1741; I will remember it always. 'Oh, God!' I murmured."

"'Yes, my child. God. Our God, great plowman, the grand farmer, has called your tiny babies to His majestic harvest. We all are harvested; some wheat, some chaff. Your wee babies were in the highest state of Grace. Did not I baptize them myself? Hold fast, my dear. Your husband will be home soon. I know it has been weeks that he has gone to Dublin to petition the government for help. County Donegal might as well be in Siberia. It is Siberia, it is so cold. No one, even the Old Ones, can remember such cold! I have heard that you can walk across Lough Swilly, and Swilly is salty!' the minister's voice trailed off."

"I nodded, not knowing what I was agreeing to. I had not been to Lough Swilly since the summer of 1740, when it was warm, with normal weather. It was now so truly cold. So crazily cold. The winter's fuel for last year did not last anyone through the winter. We were burning our house, literally. Several of the inner walls were built from bricks of turf. Caomh, my husband, broke the walls down. I don't know how he knew of the peat, but he did. He was so wise! He was a solicitor, an important man in the community. It was decided—by him, mostly—that he would take our scrawny horse and cart to Dublin. Dublin was days away in the best of conditions, but in this deadly cold, it wasn't strange that he would be gone so long. He'd be home soon. He'll die when he learns of the babies!"

"'Máirín Caít, let me take them. I shall put them in consecrated ground, beneath the flagstones of the church. They are with the Baby Jesus. These are their mortal remains.'"

"He glanced around, hawk-like, looking for them. He spotted the basket and glided quietly to it. I started to move to stop him, but I hesitated."

"He stooped to pick up the two little bundles, and tucked them under his cape."

"'Burn the basket as fuel, Máirín Caít. Stay in the smallest room in the house, and keep it warm. Your man will be home soon, perhaps tomorrow.'"

"'Let me go with you!' I called, holding out my hand, palm outward."

"He shook his head, and said, 'No, my daughter, I am God's shepherd, gathering the lambs. You cannot come. God bless you, and keep you safe.'"

"With a swirl of black as the cape billowed in the flint-hard wind, he was gone. I was alone. So very alone."

"The days had been short, and what passed for light was gray, like dirty water after a wash. I walked back into the house, leaving the door open. What did it matter? The house was as cold as the outside. I would have sat down in a chair, but I had burned them long ago. I had no fire. I would not burn the girls' basket. Never."

"I leaned against the paneled wall of what had been a fine house. Only the Bishop of Raphoe had a finer house. His house was a castle, a palace, by any other description. I had heard that it had cost £3,500 to build! What would that treasure have bought in food this day! I had been in it often, in better days. Bright lights, cheery fires, and warm laughter. All gone. Did the Bishop burn his furniture? Probably."

"I looked to the door, and considered the pastor's words. I needed to be there when my babies were laid to rest! Why couldn't I die? I only lived for the little ones. I only ate so my breasts would give them milk. Their tiny coughs echoed in my ears. They had food; I still had milk. I held them close to me at all times, but I was so thin, I don't think I had much warmth to share. I wrapped us in every blanket we had, but they just slipped way in the night. I carried them, I held them, I put them to my breast, but finally, I realized they had gone on a journey from which they would never return."

"I cried and cried, and then decided, suddenly, that I should have made a mistake. I should have gone with the minister!"

"I stumbled toward the door, and pulled my scarf around my face, so only my eyes were visible. I was lashed by the wind, and tiny needles of ice sought to force their way through my dresses. I looked down Sheep Lane, toward William Street, but there was no one in sight. Snow and ice covered everything like some Arctic tundra. This was not the Ireland of my youth. Something had gone terribly wrong with the weather last year, and this year as well."

"I slipped and fell on the ice, and I thought I'd broken my wrist as I struck the road, breaking my fall with my hand. I struggled up. My lungs were burning from the cold."

"I walked past a pile of something, and saw it was a dead horse. Though there wasn't much to eat, ravenous dogs looked up from it to me, perhaps judging which meal was better. I really didn't care if I was next. I had to find the minister first of all."

"As I walked toward the church, I bent into the wind. It seemed to be so dark, but wasn't it midday? Perhaps not. I really didn't know—or care."

"Two black and white collies, the essence of gentleness in kinder times, bared their teeth at me. They were moving towards another bundle in the road, circling it widely as they judged their prey."

"I was startled to see some slight movement in the bundle. Was this horse still alive? As I got closer I realized my foolishness. It was far too small to be a horse. It was a person. The dead both walked and lay in the streets of Ireland this winter. I moved towards the body, dusted with snow. The dogs growled ferociously at me, but I ignored them. What did I care of dogs?"

"I started when I saw the body of a neighbor woman. Her name was Fidelma. She lay on her back, and one of her breasts was bare to the wind. It was frosted with the cold. She had to be dead. I moved back her scarf to look for signs of life, and as I touched her I recognized the terrible coldness."

"What was the movement?"

"I moved her cloak aside and saw a tiny baby. A baby! At first I thought it was one of mine, in my sorrow, but then I remembered she had given birth a week ago. The wee child moved!"

"His little mouth was on her cold, dead nipple, and he made soft murmuring sounds."

"In an instant, I swooped up the bundle of cloth he had been wrapped in, and covered his head. He made a little cry, and I could feel my breasts begin to leak my watery milk."

"'Let down,' I though, 'the same as when my own sweethearts would cry out.'"

"I smiled to myself for the first time in forever. I was a mother again!"

"I looked frantically for a place to take the little baby, and escape the ice."

"The door of the bakery banged open and closed in the wind and I moved quickly toward it. The shop was abandoned, like everything else, it seemed. The ovens were dark and cold. The bakery would shelter 'my' baby and me from the night."

"I kicked the door shut with my foot behind me as I moved inside, but it sprung back, half open. It was bitterly cold inside, but not windy."

"I called the baby by boy's names, as if he would answer. In truth, I didn't know if he was a boy or girl, but I unconsciously willed him to be a boy, for another little girl would wound me too deeply."

"'Michaél? Is that it? Fine, Michaél it will be.'"

"I could feel my milk again, and I looked for a place to nurse Michaél. I spied the baker's little wooden creepie stool, and pushed aside the detritus of bread-making, some gnawed by rats, or whatever was still moving in this town."

"I plunked myself down on the worn stool and gently brushed back the blankets from Michaél's face. He was so thin! There was no baby fat, and it was frightening. My babies, 'til the end, were not so thin. But still, they died, I sorrowed. But still they died."

"I could do something wonderful here. I could suckle this little one, and save him."

"I could save him!"

"His little blue eyes fluttered open and he looked up at me!"

"Michaél! I'm your mammy now. I'm here for you, my wee one."

"I bared my own breast for him, ignoring the temperature. Little droplets of milk trickling from my erect nipple. I smiled the smile of a mother as he ravenously began to nurse."

"I was immediately struck with a thunderbolt's revelation!"

"'Uilliam! Uilliam! Oh, *Uilliam!*' I called out, as the snow began to fall."

13 DETROIT, MICHIGAN, USA: THE PRESENT

Marisa! I could not *stand* it! I don't know how you live—*have lived*—with this heartbreak! Knowing that you have lost your sweet Uilliam so many times. It is, simply, too much to bear!"

"Oh, Wanda, he was always my 'Uilliam,' but I can assure you, he wasn't always *sweet* Uilliam.' He was always mine, but I was not always 'his.'"

14 PARIS, FRANCE: 1788

wasn't always low-born, as I was in London. I was once a Duchess, a real lady. The newly formed United States of America had recently defeated the English. In 1788, I was forty-seven. I know this doesn't seem too old now, but then, especially with the diseases and accidents that befell so many people, to live to sixty was an accomplishment."

"I was very rich, but it did neither my husband nor me much good. We had wanted to leave France, to travel to England or elsewhere, but we had waited too long."

"We were living in our chateau about an hour from Paris, by carriage. My husband was a kindly man, somewhat older than I was. We felt that we had been gentle with our peasants, and treated them fairly. However, the harvest in the year 1788 failed, and it was an uncommonly harsh winter. There was unrest throughout the countryside, though, and our peasants joined hundreds of others and burned not only the chateaux of our friends and neighbors, but also our own beautiful chateau. Some say it was to destroy the records of the manorial dues they did not pay. This was doubly tragic, for my husband, the Duke, did not hound them for their dues, but he knew that others—his friends—did. We had to flee with a few loyal servants to our townhouse in Paris, on the Champs-Elysées. Everyone called that time 'Le Grande Peur,' which means, 'the Great Fear.'"

"On the 17th of June 1789, while we were still in Paris—unable to leave—a mob attacked the Bastille, and destroyed it. We lost several of our retainers during that time, as they ran off, and we were careful not to make a show of wealth at any time. We kept the house dark at night, with only a few candles in rooms away from the street. We did not wish to invite undue attention."

"The second week in October, we were surprised to see a young man appear in our garden. Although he wore threadbare old clothes, I knew him to be a cousin of my husband. He was brought to us by one of our servants."

"He expressed his regrets that he could not get us out of Paris. He could not leave himself, even with his disguise. He told us that, for appearances sake, he had been part of the mob that marched to Versailles on the 5th of October and brought back King Louis and his Queen, Marie Antoinette, to Paris. They were being held as virtual prisoners. They were to be protected by the Revolutionary National Guard who were commanded by the Marquis de Lafayette, who had distinguished himself in the American Revolution."

"'If the King himself is captive,' mused my husband, 'then we have no hope.'"

"I tried to comfort him as best I could, but in the end, it was he who needed to console me."

"The young man left, after we pressed some silver coins and a single gold coin on him. We wished him Godspeed."

"We lived like hermits. Months passed and became years. We grew vegetables in the garden, and our clothes—and bodies—became thin. We'd let all of our servants go, except for old Pierre, who was older than us, and had nowhere else to go. Our house was in great disrepair, but we could do nothing about it. My husband's health was failing, and he died of pleurisy in January of 1791. I was totally alone, except for Pierre, who did what he could to comfort me. Now I could not leave. I had no where to go, and no one to protect me."

"Later in June, the King fled Paris to Varennes, and was taken into custody. This news quickly came back to Paris, and the population was in a great fervor over it."

"I don't know how I survived those days, but I did. I became so gaunt that I could see blue blood in my veins through my parchment-like skin. After all, wasn't it my 'blue blood' that had made me a prisoner in my own home, in my own once-beautiful Paris?"

"I felt so lost without Guy. I wanted to die, to be with him in heaven. Strangely, though, I couldn't leave Pierre. He had a family somewhere—a son who was a priest at the lovely Mont-Ste.-Michel—but he had not seen him in many years, and didn't even know if he lived. There was nothing a priest could do except pray—and God's ears must have ached from listening to me."

"I thought that the situation could not get worse when the Reign of Terror began in 1793."

"Members of the Committee of Public Safety—their safety—I might add—were rounding up all aristocrats. Gunfire could be heard through our barricaded doors. Screams and shouts cut through the night."

"I looked out the windows at night, and saw the peaceful stars twinkling in the night sky. I wondered why God had abandoned me—why Guy had abandoned me. Pierre heard me crying, and gently tapped on the door-frame of my room."

"'Yes, Pierre, what is it, old friend?'"

"'Madam, I do not know what I can do to be of help, but perhaps you wish to merely talk?'"

"'I would very much like to talk with you Pierre, but I fear I would only depress you.'"

"He smiled a gap-toothed smile, and sat down beside me. The years fluttered by like wind blowing the pages of a diary as we spoke of old times, of lost youth and missed opportunity. I felt so good. I was at peace for the first time since Guy had died."

"Pierre was brushing my long, white hair with his hand when I sailed gently onto the sea of sleep, still in my armchair."

"The next morning, I was stiff from having slept in the chair. I got up, creaking, or so it seemed to me. I went downstairs and found Pierre in the kitchen, holding two wrinkled potatoes. He was apparently wondering just what he could do with them."

"He coughed quietly into his sleeve, and looked at me with rheumy, tired eyes."

"'Good morning, Madam,' he said."

"'Pierre,' I said, gently, 'we have known each other for more than thirty years. Surely with all that has transpired, you can bring yourself to call me by my Christian name. It is "Marie," you know.'"

"'I know, Madam, but, no, I cannot bring myself to call you anything than that which I have for so many years. But thank you.'"

"I sighed, but realized he wouldn't change. I said to him, 'Pierre, I have not been out of the house in weeks. You are not well. I will go to the market and find us something fine to eat—perhaps a chicken! Would you like a fine capon?'"

"'Madam is hallucinating, I fear. There isn't a gnarled rooster anywhere to be found. The only "crowing" is by the damned—excuse me, Madam—rabble that shouts "Liberty! Equality! Fraternity!" all the night and day! I'd like to give them "equality" and cut them into equal parts!'"

"This was fiery talk for old Pierre. I patted him on the shoulder and told him I would return before long. I had several copper coins in one pocket, a few silver in another, and a single gold coin in my shoe. I kept the gold for the most dire of emergencies."

"As I ventured out onto the street, I was taken aback at the smells. The street was awash with night soil and the foulest of garbage. Even so, urchins were routing through it. They gave me a sideways glance. I undoubtedly looked like poor pickings, and they returned to their trash."

"I made my way to the small market area, and was almost run down by several horse drawn carts, carrying a heavy load of human cargo. Some were dressed in finery I hadn't seen in a long time. I brushed back a tear as I recognized two of them, a man and wife, as old friends and companions. They saw me, but I'm sure without recognition. I heard one of the Committee members say something about 'Madam La Guillotine,' and I froze. Executions, by whatever means at hand, were an hourly occurrence. I was not aware that they brought them there by the cart load!"

"As I stopped to stare, a woman came up to me. She seemed vaguely familiar. She was wearing the red, white and blue cockade of the Revolution, and looked directly into my face from a distance of only a few inches. I was almost overcome by her fetid breath. I mouthed something, but I don't know what. It seemed my voice, even as thin as it was, apparently was what caused her to be convinced she knew me. It was then that I realized I did know her: she was one of my old maids, Joan."

"I started to say something to her in greeting, but she grabbed me roughly by both arms and shouted out, in a voice that nearly blew me off my feet, 'Here is one! An aristocrat! An *aristocrat!* A Duchess!'"

"The second cart came to a clumsy halt. Two Committeemen came over, apparently bemused by the ravings of this woman, especially as they saw what I looked like."

"'What have you been putting in your wine, woman? This bag a Duchess? Perhaps Marie Antoinette in disguise?'"

"'Ha!' she cried, '"Marie" it is, but not the Queen! A duchess! I once worked for her. Cruel she was to all of us.'"

"I struggled to keep from crying. I had held Joan in my arms when one of her babies died, and sobbed with her. Cruel? This was cruel. My arms ached so from her death grip. I recognized it for what it was."

"'What does one more aristocrat, more or less, mean to us?' slurred one of the Citizens, obviously drunk. 'She is old. Look at her. Sixty, seventy.'"

"They started to turn to leave, but Joan was persistent. 'She has money. Millions. Check and see!'"

"'Millions indeed,' I thought. This stopped them. They went through my pockets and found my few coins, which together, wouldn't probably buy the mythical rooster."

"They still weren't going to take me, but they did capture my few sou. As they prepared to leave again, they were berated by Joan."

"'Are you Citizens of the Republic, or aristocrats yourselves? Surely the headsman doesn't notice the difference between brocade and cockade, what?'"

"One of them cuffed Joan with the back of his hand, while the other lifted me off my feet—I didn't weigh much—and plopped me into the center of the cart."

"'Farewell, Duchess,' called Joan, merry with her conquest. What had caused her to be so venomous?"

"I was disconsolate. I was beyond tears. I could only think of Pierre, waiting for his rooster. 'He would wait an eternity,' I mused."

"I wondered if there would be a trial, but then imagined not."

"One of the women in the cart asked me if I had any money. I thought this was odd—what would she do with money on her way to the guillotine or the noose? I asked her why? I added quickly that I didn't have any, that my few centimes had been stolen by the Citizens."

92

"She said that the guillotine was fast and sure, but executions were so common that they were using axes and even long, executioner's swords, in the classic French style. She told me that one of the wives of the English King Henry VIII specifically asked to be beheaded with a French sword rather than an ax—which could sometimes take several blows. If the prisoner gave money to the headsman, he might make a swift, hard blow, and get it over with instantly."

"I shuddered at this thought, and remembered the gold coin in my shoe. I thanked her in a barely audible voice. The last thing I would buy on this earth, after a life of ease and privilege, would be a headsman's stroke. How plaintive."

"Before long, we reached a square. I could tell from the large, rowdy crowd that there was to be no trial today. I would need my gold. I thought of Guy, our chateau, Pierre, and my formerly happy life."

"There was no guillotine, or even a headsman's ax. Instead, it was the French sword so 'loved' by Henry's Queen! I was grateful for my coin."

"I could not watch what went before me. Each time I heard the sword whistle through the air, I died a little. If so, perhaps I would simply expire before I climbed those bloody stairs."

"Before long, it was my turn. I was not bound like the others. I presented neither escape risk nor danger to anyone. I squinted my eyes so I could not see the mound of decapitated corpses and the baskets of heads. I did, regardless."

"I looked up as I got to the scaffold to see the headsman, dressed in black with a black, leather hood over the upper half of his head. He was sweating and breathing heavily from the exertion and was leaning on the hilt of his long sword. The great sword was covered with gore, as it rested, point-down, between his feet, with blood coursing from it, pooling unnoticed at his feet."

"I saw that the purse hanging from his belt was bulging, and thought of my gold coin. I wanted to see the likeness of the King one last time."

"Strong arms pushed me to my knees. I saw from the first execution—before I turned away—that the victim dies while kneeling, head high. I knew now why Henry's Queen wanted it that way. To bow down to this human trash would be to dishonor all that I believed."

"I didn't begrudge the executioner—he was merely trying to earn a living. He probably had a family, children—perhaps even a rooster! I smiled at this, gaining a stare from the citizens."

"The headsman walked toward me, moving gingerly since the boards were awash with wet blood, glistening red in the bright sunlight."

"I held up one hand to stop him, while I reached for my shoe. He hesitated."

"'Something for you, Sir.' I quietly said, as I retrieved my gold. 'To strike a hard blow.'"

"He nodded, and waited."

"I found the coin and looked intently at it. I could see the executioner smile a yellow-toothed smile beneath his hood. Few of his victims had gold, apparently!"

"As he moved closer to me, I said to him, in my firmest voice, 'Kind Sir, I give you all that I have. You must, in turn, give me all that you have. Strike hard! Strike hard!'"

"On my knees, ignoring the raucous crowd, I reached to his outstretched hand to press the coin into the hollow of his palm. As my bony, white fingers touched his palm my world disintegrated and reformed. I could barely speak, I could not move. All I could do was whisper, my voice cracking: 'Strike hard, Uilliam!'"

15 EDINBURGH, SCOTLAND: 1828

When I was younger, I had no problem climbing the hill to the Castle. I loved to see the Black Watch soldiers in their kilts, parading about the castle gate, their muskets glinting in the low Scottish light. One of the officers would lead the replacements, to the skirling of bagpipes. He held a long sword against his shoulder, and saluted with it."

"I would bring my lunch, a piece of bread, sometimes with a dot of jam, and a jar of tea, to sit across from the soldiers to watch them."

"I was fresh from Galway, Ireland, and my ears burned hot when I saw the soldiers looking at me sideways. They dared not turn their heads, but their eyes were their own—when the officer wasn't watching! I confessed to Father when he came to our house, but my penances were never very much. We were all breaking the law by going to confession, and taking Holy Communion. It was against the English laws to be Catholic. I didn't know why, and didn't ask. Father came to our houses and said Mass to a few who gathered there."

"I knew why the young men's eyes followed me. Wasn't I a looker? I had ugly freckles, but the lads seemed to like them. I found the Scottish boys to be very strange. It wasn't just the way they spoke: Irish and Scottish Gaelic are near enough to follow, but it is just all their 'lassies,' 'laddies,' 'wee bairns,' and all of their strange ways. The food! Who can get used to haggis! Sheep's stomach, stuffed with something horrible—I don't know what. Barely a decent potato in the place!"

"I had little choice for being there, though. One of twelve children, and nine girls at that, I was a burden on my family at home. My Da was a farmer, and my three brothers were in a fistfight all the time, it seemed, about inheritance. You'd think Da was on his deathbed. I don't know why it should be so, for wouldn't it all go to Liam, the eldest? To be sure, to be sure."

"We didn't have much of a place. Rocks seemed to come out of the ground. We'd pick them, pile them, and more would appear."

"It was potatoes for us, although we did raise a few other crops for sale to the gentry. We never had meat, but had a little milk with our potatoes on Sunday. Once in a while we would have a fish to share between us all. It wasn't much."

"When I came to Scotland, it was to work for a fine family. I had a room in the garret, directly beneath the slate of the roof. It was the worst place, the butler thought, but I liked it. I liked to hear the rain on the roof, for it reminded me of Galway."

"As the years went by, I sent whatever shillings I could to my Da. I never heard back from him, but that didn't surprise me. Neither my Mammy nor Da could write, and I, myself, had to have the butler address the letters. After about ten years, I had a visitor. I thought it was a wraith: myself come back to me in ghostly form, somehow, for I was seeing myself as a young girl!"

"After the shock wore off, I heard her say she was my little sister. I held her tight; I fear I cut off her breathing! She had to push me away for a moment to gasp in some air! I felt terrible; I thought I'd injured her!"

"She was only a little one of seven when I left, and now, he she was, this freckles peppered across her nose, bright blue eyes, and dark red hair that glistened in the afternoon sun!"

"Her name was Anne, and she was the one I felt the worst about leaving, as she was my pet."

"Anne told me she was going to work for a family in England, in London, and that she had dreamed about seeing me before she left, perhaps for good."

"I cried so hard when I heard how she'd saved what little money she could to travel all the way to Scotland."

"I didn't want her to see the little cell I had in the garret, so I told her to wait there, in the garden, while I rushed upstairs. I must have looked a sight, holding up my skirts as I flew up the stairs! I had five pounds that I had been saving for four years. I had a thought that it might be my dowry, but as each year went by, and the heavy toil took its toll on my hands, skin, and beauty, fewer soldiers each year turned their eyes toward me. I was becoming an old woman, and I was only in my late twenties!"

"Despite Anne's protestations, I pressed the five pounds on her. She could not even stay the night! They were expecting her at a place called Grosvenor Square, in Westminster, which is part of London, and she had a coach to catch. The butler grumbled when I asked if I could walk with her to the coach-house, but after I begged him, telling him it was my own baby sister, whom I hadn't seen in ten years, he relented."

"The coach-house was not far from my master's house, and I knew it well. I, myself, had arrived there so many years ago."

"As we walked, my sister told me of the family news. My second and third-eldest brothers had emigrated, one to America, and the other to Australia. Three of my sisters were married, and I was an aunt! Da was not doing well, physically, having broken his leg the winter before. My mother was fine, she said."

"I don't know if it was more torture to have seen Anne, than to simply live with my memories of her and the others. It pained me to learn of my brothers, gone off to the other side of the world, and that

Da was badly-off. Liam had taken over the daily work on the farm, and had married a girl from a nearby farm. Anne said her name, and I'm sure I wrinkled my nose: I didn't like her. Perhaps she'd changed. They had no children, and this bothered Liam."

"The tears ran in the street gutters when we two were finally separated. Anne promised to write, but I didn't hold out much hope. She clutched the five-pound note in her hand, and I told her to hide it. It was terrifying to think of her alone on that coach, all the way to London."

"It was cruel of Fate to allow us such a short time together. She had great difficulties finding my master's house. She had never been in such a great city before, and was overcome with vertigo just looking at the tall buildings. She was speechless at the sight of Edinburgh Castle, dominating the craggy mountain on which it stood."

"I, myself, never married. I never did hear from Anne again. I did get a letter from Liam, asking for money to help bury Da. He'd died a year after Anne came. I sent all the money I had, but it was only one pound, six pence. I didn't hear back from him."

"I had toiled many years for my master and mistress, when one day, as a bent and work-worn scullery maid, I was on my hands and knees scouring the kitchen floor with a scrub brush and a rough bar of lye soap. The soap was of the type that had long ago burned my hands so they cracked and bled from time-to-time. I brushed back the wisps of white hair out of my face, as I heard the butler—not the same one, but one of his successors—there'd been three after the first one—call my name."

"Holding my hand against my back, I painfully brought myself up, so I was on my knees, looking up at him. I couldn't see too well, unless something was up close. I blinked and tried to focus, but couldn't."

"Speaking to me in his very direct way, he asked me to come into his tiny office, where he bade me to sit in a straight back chair next to his desk chair."

"Never one to mince words, he said, 'Mary, we are going to let you go.'"

"I said, rather stupidly, 'Sir, I have not asked to go anywhere.'"

"He paused for a moment, apparently absorbing this, and then recognized that I thought he was talking about running an errand, or going on a trip or visit."

"'Ya dinna understand, Mary. We have no further need of your services. You are too old. What are you, fifty eight?'"

"I couldn't take this in. No further need for my services? What would I do? Where would I go?"

"I couldn't speak, and only moved my lips. Nothing came out."

"He continued, 'You will be compensated handsomely, and I have made inquiries. The vicarage needs a charwoman, and they have a small flat that goes with it. It is hard work, but you are strong, are you not?'"

"I finally found my voice, and protested that I had lived there for most of my life, begging him, throwing myself to my knees, to let me stay on."

"He was resolute. I asked if our Master and his Mistress knew about this? It hurt deeply when he said they did, and agreed."

"That was that. The 'handsome' compensation was a five-pound note. It reminded me of the one I'd given Anne so many years before. Five pounds for forty years toil."

"The other servants bade goodbye, thinking, 'there but for fortune, go I,' I'm sure, and I was out of the house within the hour."

"The butler had given me the address of the vicarage, but by the time I'd hobbled down the hill, the note had disintegrated from perspiration. I knew the vicarage, which was Anglican, of course. The minister was a thin, hawk-faced man, who never smiled, for religious reasons, I supposed. He asked me if I was a member of the Church. I was, of course, a member of the Catholic Church, but he didn't specify which church, so I honestly said, 'Yes.' He nodded, and introduced me to his wife, who was a heavy-set woman of forty or so. She had very bad teeth, and a terrible odor about her. I didn't know what it was, but it burned my nose. I wondered how the vicar could live with this cesspool of a woman. I had bigger problems than this."

"The 'flat' the butler promised me was a cold, bare room, smaller yet than my garret, positioned above the stables. The smell of the animals below was an improvement over my Mistress. I would go to sit with the animals late at night, after I completed my work. I spoke with them, and imagined they answered me. Perhaps they were Irish, for they seemed to respond best to the lilting sound of Irish songs I sang them. The words sounded strange in my own ears, as I had not heard Irish spoken in so long!"

"Days turned into months, and then years. I had a small charcoal brazier in my room, and the winters were cold. My joints ached, and I could hardly move. My fingers knotted and knuckles bulged, the effects of years of heavy work, I presumed."

"I dared not complain, for I was afraid that even this would be taken from me."

"One day, as I was washing the pews in the church, I overheard people talking about the funeral that was scheduled for later that afternoon. I was surprised to hear them say that they had made arrangements for a guard over the body. I thought this strange; who needed to guard a body?"

"My questions were answered by one of them, as he explained to the second man of how there had been many grave robberies of late, so many so that people were hiring guards to watch over the bodies of their loved ones, at least until they corrupted and became worthless. Bodies were being used for medical experiments at the universities, and were in great demand with both the universities and private doctors."

"He said they were entitled to the bodies of executed prisoners, but there was a shortage all around. Perhaps the answer was more hangings, they said, laughing."

"I was aghast at the thought of it all, but I eavesdropped all the more, fascinated as I was by the tale."

"The one doing all the talking said that there were a number of missing persons in the city, and talk was that the grave robbers, having been stymied by the guards and other precautions taken at the graveyards, had taken to killing people to sell their bodies to the medical schools! This was perhaps the best way, because they would have a 'fresh one.' I thought this all to be quite horrible. They spoke of human beings as if they were a leg of lamb! Fresh, indeed!"

"The thoughts of all of this stayed with me throughout the day, and into the days after. It was dark when I walked the short distance to begin work, and dark again when I was done. Everyone was a grave-robber, in my mind. This was compounded by the fact that the stable was only a short distance from the churchyard. They buried that person that first day, and, sure enough, there were two rough looking characters sitting on gravestones throughout the night and for three days thereafter. It was consecrated ground, and they were drinking and smoking. I didn't say anything to the vicar. After all, it was Protestant ground."

"I could see the churchyard from my tiny window, and imagined shapes gliding through it each night. I wasn't afraid of the dead; they couldn't hurt me; but I did sleep fitfully thinking of the ghouls I imagined out there, spading piles of damp, musty grave-soil in heavy piles around the freshly re-opened grave! A terrible thought."

"One night, after spending what seemed to be hours peering out my little window, I finally went to bed. It was cold, and frost was on my breath. I had only a thin nightgown, and a worn comforter. I wished I had a little dog or cat, but I'd little enough food for myself. I was too thin, but it was the work more than the poor food, although the odd potato and yam I ate, with an occasional carrot if I were lucky, wasn't enough to feed anyone."

"I was startled from the beginnings of my fitful sleep to hear voices at the bottom of the stairs. The only door was one at the ground level. There was no lock, but there was a heavy iron hasp. I heard the hasp grate and my heart leapt into my throat."

"I held the comforter to my chin, and listened intently to see if someone were coming up the stairs."

"I heard a woman's voice—this was reassuring, for no grave-robber would be a woman, to be sure. Who could it be, at this hour?"

"The visitor called out, 'Mary? Are you there, Mary?'"

"I didn't know if I should answer. I didn't recognize the voice, but she did know my name."

"She called to me again, but still I didn't answer. I then heard the light thread of a woman's footsteps coming up the stairs. A moment later, I heard second, heavier, footsteps!"

"The sounds echoed off the stone the stable was constructed of."

"In terror, I finally called out, 'Who is it? What do you want? I'm not alone!'"

"'Calm down, Mary, it is friends. From Ireland,' called the woman, obviously closer."

"Sure, and there was a bit of Éire in her voice. I said to her in Irish, 'If you are a friend, state your name!'"

"I got no answer but heard the second person, a man, saying, 'What is that she is saying?'"

"He said it in such a gruff voice that I could hear my heart. I had nowhere to run to, and I couldn't escape if I wanted to, I was so crippled up."

"He got an answer from his companion, 'It is Irish, you idiot? What kind of Irishman are you, William Burke!'"

"He laughed a deep, humorless laugh. Who were they?"

"In a moment, they came into my room. The woman was carrying a hooded lantern, and I tried to focus on them. My eyes were too bad. All I could see was the small shape of the woman, and the very, very large hulking body of the man. Both were dressed in dark, perhaps black, clothing."

"'Just here to say hello, Mary, just to say hello,' said the woman."

"I regained my voice. 'God save me! Go away! I have a knife!'"

"I had no such thing, and I'm sure they knew it. The woman waved the lantern, and it played over me. In an instant, the big man was on top of me, crushing me with his immense weight. The suddenness of it forced the breath from my lungs and I heard the cracking of my ribs. I felt no pain, strangely enough."

"I was still clutching the comforter in my rough-red hands, as he turned his massive head toward me. His breath was overpowering, smelling of whiskey. My head was reeling, and I felt myself on the very edge of passing out. I opened my mouth to scream, but I had no wind for it."

"He saw me begin to cry out, and clamped a horny, callused hand over my mouth."

"Tiny stars and red and other-colored visions that had been swimming across my eyes suddenly gave way to the face of my Uilliam, as the room went black."

16 CAPE HORN, SOUTH AMERICA: 1848

In 1848, I had long wanted to travel to California to visit my sister, Fiona, who now lived in San Francisco with her husband and children. I had not seen her for over five years."

"Fiona and I lived in Boston, on Beacon Hill, as children. We were very close, and I had a very difficult time when her husband, who was an Army Officer, was transferred to the captured Spanish fort called the "Presidio" in San Francisco. Fiona wrote me and told me about San Francisco."

"We both wrote one another expansive letters, but it took so frightfully long for letters to reach their destinations the news was ancient when it arrived. I was a maiden lady, still living with my parents. Oh yes, I had my little dog, Gypsy. She was the product of a back-fence romance between a neighbor's flirtatious terrier and a carousing mongrel."

"I cherished the letters I received from Fiona, with stories of adventures in the West, the Spaniards, sailors, cutthroats, soldiers, dance-hall girls, and all the rest. She sent me a silhouette cut from black paper, showing profiles of her and her two daughters, Agnes and Anne-Marie."

"I was especially fond of my niece, Anne-Marie, since Anne-Marie was named after me! I hadn't met either of the girls, of course."

"I sent small packages of ribbons and treats to the children, even though the shipping cost was terribly expensive. I confess that I kissed the ribbons I sent to little Anne-Marie! I wondered if she favored my looks? I hoped not!"

"Mother and Father were indulgent in my whimsy, as I was their only remaining child at home. I had two brothers who were off on their own, and, while they came to our house from time-to-time, I was nowhere as close to them as I was to Fi."

"I was only 17 when she, a woman of 20, married her dashing young West Point graduate. His name was Eamon O'Flynn. I wanted to go with her, but that was, of course, impossible."

"I had studied music at the Conservatory since I was a child, and was an accomplished violinist. My father—ever indulgent—bought me a violin made by the famous violin and music instrument-making family of Amati of Cremona, Italy. It had a label in it, in Latin, which said Nicolo Amati made it in 1680. It played so sweetly! I can hear it in my head, even today! I know that he paid two hundred dollars for it—which was a shameful amount—but the first time I laid eyes on it I was smitten! It even came with a letter that said my violin had a name, 'Lady Constance.' I don't know anything else about the history of my fiddle, but I loved her still."

"I often would remove Lady Constance from her case and stroke her back and sides. There were two black dots on the back, at each end, which, I was told, was a trademark of the Amatis."

"I taught violin in the parlor of our home. We lived in a large, brick house that was built in the classical style. My father was a Judge, and I adored him. I loved Mama, too, of course, but Father was so great and good!"

"Although I was in my early twenties, I had largely despaired of ever finding love. Except for my musical abilities—they were hardly that consummate—I had no real social skills that I could perceive. On top of that, I was what people generously called 'plain.' This meant, of course, that I was not pretty. I didn't even consider myself to be good looking. My nose could provide a perch for robins, and I always wore my hair so as to hide my hideous, elephantine ears. My hands and feet were huge. I was tall for a woman, and too thin."

"My mother and her lady friends were constantly discussing suitable husbands they thought I would be 'right for,' or even just 'get along with.' I had read too many Shakespearean sonnets and the English poetess, Elizabeth Barrett Browning. I had a well-worn copy of her book of poems, 'Poems of E. Barrett,' that was published in 1844. When she married Robert Browning two years ago, I felt I was at the wedding! What a couple! Of course, many people believe, as I do, that she was the better poet of the two!"

"Father and Mother were born in Ireland, and spoke of their time there as if it was yesterday, even though they were in their teens when they left."

"Father was very active in the 'Liberators,' an Irish secret society in the United States that I was not supposed to know of. It was an offshoot of the National Repeal Association, started by Daniel O'Connell, 'the Liberator,' who died tragically last year while on a pilgrimage to Rome."

"My father was in Ireland in '43—1843—when O'Connell called his 'monster meeting' at the Hill of Tara, and Father was one of a half-million people who attended the meeting. He met Daniel O'Connell and they became fast friends. Father was thunderstruck when O'Connell died, and was convinced he had been murdered by the English."

"My parents spoke Irish when they didn't want me to know what they were talking about. I knew a few words—you couldn't help but pick up scraps when you heard it all the day long—but I just wasn't interested."

"Boston was undergoing a great influx of Irish immigrants, what with the potato famine that had begun in Ireland four years earlier. Most of the new arrivals possessed barely more than the clothes they wore as passengers on the 'coffin ships' that left Ireland and England with so many and arrived with so few. Many of them spoke only Irish, which wouldn't do them in particularly good stead in America!"

"Sadly enough, it was usually Irishmen—speaking Irish—who fleeced these tired, sick arrivals of the few meager belongings they managed to bring with them—in the guise of 'helping them.' In point of fact, they were helping themselves."

"Those thieves who were prosecuted—and there were precious few— were dealt with leniently by most judges, who had the opinion that it was riffraff stealing from rabble. They rued the day that they appeared before my father, however! I was in court visiting him on one of those occasions, and, after my father gave the Defendant a tongue-lashing, he sentenced him to the rock pile, on the spot! In that case, the victim spoke only Irish. With Boston being an Irish town, both the policeman and city attorney were Irish-speakers. Although it was likely against the law, they conducted the trial in Irish! I'm sure it was a first for the United States!"

"No one said anything against my father. He was, after all, the Chief Judge. In point of fact, the real reason they gave my father ample leeway was because of the Liberators. It was widely rumored that Father was a principal in the Liberators, an organization that was known to deal harshly with those who chose—rather foolishly—to tangle with it."

"I once asked my mother an oblique question about the Liberators, and she professed to not know anything about it. It was like the little people. She once said of leprechauns, 'I don't believe in the "wee folk," but that doesn't mean they don't exist!'"

"One of Father's many friends, and a frequent visitor to our home, was a man named Donald McKay. Donald was thirty-seven, and was born in Nova Scotia. Father loved boats, and Mr. McKay was a naval architect. Donald was all-afire about a new type of ship called a 'clipper ship.' Ever since the Rainbow was launched in New York three years earlier, it was all he and my father talked about. The Rainbow was what Mr. McKay called the first true clipper ship. He discounted the Baltimore clippers that were blockade-runners during the War of 1812—and were currently being used in the West African slave trade. Slaving was something I found despicable."

"I enjoyed listening to them talk animatedly about the glories of clipper ships. The ships were over two hundred feet long, they said, and they carried more sail than any other ship their size."

"The Western United States was opening, and there was money to be made in shipping. Fiona and her husband traveled by ship, of course, but it was a very long journey. It was safer than traveling overland—what with the Indians and all—but when she told of the storms at the bottom tip of South America, where the Atlantic and Pacific oceans came together, I could hardly contain myself. I tried to put myself in Fiona's position, and didn't think I could survive such a voyage! The thought of it excited me, though!"

"Donald McKay had big plans to build his own clipper ships in a shipyard he'd established in East Boston in 1845. He carried around a leather case that held large drawings of all aspects of his planned ships."

"I don't know who was more excited about the idea, Mr. McKay or my father! Father would talk to Mother at a rapid pace in Irish about them. I knew he was talking about 'his' clipper ships, because Father apparently didn't know the Irish word for 'clipper,' if there was one. The English word 'clipper' was liberally interspersed in the Irish, along with 'McKay'—that came out as 'Mick-eye'—the way Donald pronounced it."

"Mr. McKay was putting together a syndicate of investors to back his first clipper, the Stag Hound, which he thought could be built in two or three years."

"Mother told me she was dubious. To invest tens of thousands of dollars in a risky venture—and have no return for years, if at all! 'This was the way of madness,' she said."

"All of their talk about the speed of the clipper ships, and how they could cut weeks off the passage from New York to California soon got me thinking about being very, very adventurous. When I thought Father was in the best possible mood, after dinner and a cigar, I gently tapped on the door to his study. When he answered the knock, I quietly opened the door a crack and peeked my head inside, saying, 'Father, do you have a moment?'"

"He, of course, did, as he rarely, if ever, denied me time, and I came in and sat down in a leather chair near his easy chair."

"The lamp was lit, and he was reading 'Typee,' by Herman Melville."

"'Is that a good book, Father?' I asked him."

"'I have not quite decided about this chap Melville, Anne-Marie. The man deserted his ship, became a virtual South Sea Islander, and, I think, is an atheist. It is interesting enough, but I am not sure I shall read another. What can I do for you, my dear?'"

"'Father, I, ah, have something special to ask you,' I stammered."

"He smiled, and put down his cigar. 'Yes, love, what would that be? Don't tell me you need a new violin because yours is "too old"?' He knew he could 'play' me just as well as I could play 'Lady Constance.'"

"'Oh no! Father! You are just joking. I *love* my violin. No, what I, what I would like to do, is sail to California to stay with Fiona for a time, and help her with her children.'"

"'California!' he exclaimed, 'California is on the other side of the globe! Does your mother know about this?'"

"'Well, yes, she does—and she thinks it will be a good idea! She thinks I might find a husband!' I blushed at this. I didn't want to be an old maid, but mercy only knew what sort of ruffians were in California!"

"He started to say something, but I needed to make the bargain—I was my father's daughter. I cut him off: 'I could sail on the new clipper ship, and send you a full report!'"

"This was a merciless ploy on my part. Father, usually very vociferous, was quiet. I knew he was thinking of McKay's clipper ship that they were both planning."

"'A clipper ship,' he mused, tapping his teeth with a pencil. 'That would be advantageous to the syndicate. But what of your safety? Thousands of miles with only men? That would not do!'"

"I had a ready reply to that one. 'There is a group of nuns traveling to the missions in California. I can travel with them. The ship leaves next month. Can I go? Can I?'"

"He wanted endless details on the sailing, the schedule, which order the sisters belonged to, when I was to return, and many other things, most of which I was prepared for. In the end, he agreed. I was going to write my sister, but then realized that a clipper ship would probably beat my letter to San Francisco!"

"Within a fortnight, I was packed and ready to go. Father and Mother rode the train with me to New York, and saw me off. Mr. McKay asked Father to go on-board the ship and to take copious notes, which Father was more than happy to do."

"I admit to being more than a little afraid as the ship made its way out to the open sea. While I had been on boats before, it was never out of Boston Bay, and always on a calm day. I introduced myself to each of the sisters. They seemed very young, even younger than I was. I then began to explore the ship."

"The ship was the very one, Rainbow, that had caused such excitement in my father's study—the first true clipper ship. We had gotten what must have passed as a 'welcoming speech' from her captain, Capt. William E. Devereaux, who was a tremendously large and powerful man, with graying hair and long sideburns. He wore a dark blue ship's officer's cap that was stained with salt, worn low over his eyes, and looked very threatening."

"Captain Devereaux told us that this was a working ship, a cargo ship, and passengers—there were about fifteen of us—would not, *shall not,* get in the way of the sailors."

"I brought some food with me from home, but my cabin was small and I had to share the cabin with three of the sisters. I was afraid the food would spoil, so I shared it with them. They didn't seem to have much."

"Once we got away from land, the ship heeled sharply as the sailors went aloft to set the sails. The rigging began to creak and strain as more and more sail was set. I was convinced that the masts would be pulled right out of the ship, with the strain of all the sail."

"The Captain didn't seem to mind that one of the young officers, Jimmy, was showing the passengers what the different parts of the boat were, and telling us the proper names for things. I soon began to call the floor the 'deck,' the stairs the 'ladder,' and the kitchen the 'galley.' I did inspect the galley, where there apparently was a single cook, a German fellow, and two or three Chinese helpers. I didn't bother them."

"Food was reasonably good, but in no great quantity. As each day went on, and we sailed farther south, it got worse, as did the water. Stored in casks below, the water soon took on a very brackish taste, as if it were contaminated by the seawater. Perhaps it was; I didn't know."

"The crew eyed us women on every occasion, even the sisters. The sailors were a rough lot. Their hair was tarred, and they had little square flaps for collars that kept the tar from their shirts in the back. Their pants had bell-shaped bottoms, which they rolled up as they scoured the deck with 'holy stones.' These were, I found, rectangular stones held in a wooden holder. They are moved back and forth by a stick, scouring the deck. It looked very difficult. I noticed that a number of the sailors had tattoos on the tops of their feet: a pig on one and a chicken on the other. I asked Jimmy about this and he said that sailors are a superstitious lot, and few learned to swim, because it would invite a shipwreck. Pigs and chickens hate the water, and they felt that if they had them tattooed on their feet, they would always stay 'dry,' and never drown!"

"The common sailors lived in the forward part of the ship that Jimmy said was called the 'forecastle,' but he pronounced it 'fo'c'sle.'"

"Days evolved into weeks, and the boredom was palpable. When they weren't working—which wasn't often—the sailors contented themselves with knot tying, scrimshaw, and carving."

"I had a few books with me, but had read them each more than once. I began to wander around the ship in hopes of borrowing, or trading a book. I did get to look at a copy of Nathaniel Bowditch's 'Practical Navigator,' but I couldn't make much sense of it."

"As we neared the Equator, it became unbearably hot. Our cabin was like a crucible, and we all slept on deck, under the watchful eye of the mate. The sailors had stripped off their shirts, and their tattoos and scars were plainly seen. It was frightening, but also interesting, in a macabre sort of way."

"We put into Rio de Janeiro and anchored in Guanabara Bay. The ship's sailors were anxious for shore leave, which the Captain seemed reluctant to grant. In the end, he did, allowing a few at a time. He knew that they would get into trouble there, he told us, but if he refused them, some would 'jump ship,' and desert."

"I asked about going ashore to look around, but the Captain said it was a dangerous place. It looked beautiful, though. He pointed out Sugarloaf Mountain towering above the bay, and said he had once climbed it as a young man. It was hard to imagine him as young, but he was so strong, I'm sure it wasn't difficult for him to climb Sugarloaf, or any other mountain. Jimmy said the Captain's wife used to sail with them, but she died of consumption last year. Ever since, the Captain hardly ever went ashore."

"I'd thought his sullen attitude was due to his manner, but this information put him in a different light. I felt sorry for him."

"After two days, we had reprovisioned, and gathered up all of the crew except one. He'd simply vanished. He was a 'topman,' who worked the highest sails, and would be missed, said Jimmy."

"The crew seemed happier, although a few were nursing knife cuts, blackened eyes and missing teeth. All had hangovers from strong drink."

"I tried a banana! There were large bunches of them. The Captain said to eat up, as they wouldn't last long. I rather liked it, and wrote about it in my diary."

"I didn't miss the heat as we went farther south. I looked at the charts in the navigator's room, and saw how the tip of South America, called 'Tierra del Fuego,' was very close to the South Pole."

"Jimmy showed me on the chart where we planned to sail, through the Straits of Magellan. He said that ships used to go through Drake Passage, but that Magellan was a better, safer passage, adding that any passage was a nightmare: rounding 'the Horn' was the worst part of any voyage. Many ships simply broke up, and a few went on the rocks at the false Horn, to the North of the real Cape Horn."

"Captain Devereaux cautioned the passengers to stay in their cabins as much as possible during the passage. He constantly eyed the sky and took many sightings with his sextant. He seemed possessed."

"I was somewhat surprised that we didn't take in sail as we got closer to the Horn. The sky was slate-gray, with tendrils of clouds flitting by overhead. An occasional rain-squall would douse the deck, and make it slick. The crew-members wore oilskins to try to stay dry. I had a set, but they smelled so badly, I couldn't bear to wear them."

"Jimmy told how a ship such as ours, a 'square rigger,' couldn't easily turn around. If anyone went overboard, they would be lost, for we couldn't go back for them. For this reason, it was very important to stay below, in our cabin, or the small saloon. The sailors tied ropes, or 'lines' down the length of the ship, to act as safety lines. I couldn't see how it could make any difference. Many times, as we went farther south, the sea broke over the ship and the ship shuddered as it sought to shake off the weight of water. I got a soaking myself, being nosy one day, and the water must have been direct from the South Pole—it was near freezing!"

"Jimmy came for me one day, and showed me the wreckage of a ship on nearby rocks. I asked him if anyone survived, and he said he thought not. I felt colder at this than I did from the drenching I'd received. What if that were us?"

"The Captain did order the sails to be taken in, or 'shortened,' as Jimmy called it. This was a sign to all of us that it was going to get worse, as it shortly did."

"The wind was so fierce that a sail split down the middle with a tremendous thunderclap sound. I pitied the poor sailors who had to climb aloft to take it down. They did not put up a new sail just then for it would be futile."

"The conjunction of the two oceans and the pole's effect on the weather created such great forces that it seemed as if we were mocking God to attempt a passage. I think the nuns agreed, for they hadn't stopped praying from the time we hit the bad weather."

"One of the longboats broke loose in the middle of the night and broke open the door to the passageway leading to my cabin. Instantly, a great wave followed, and what seemed to me to be millions of gallons of water flooded our compartment. We all woke from our fitful sleep to believe we were drowning!"

"There was no light, and we collided with one another in the India-ink blackness. We screamed and shouted for help. We knew the ship was going to sink; that we would be another lost ship. Jimmy told me before how Lloyd's of London, the insurance syndicate, recently acquired a bell from a wreck. The bell was called the Lutine Bell. They rang it once for good news and twice for bad. They rang it twice for each ship that was lost. Would we be the next double ring?"

"We could hear the boatswain's whistle sounding over the noise, as he called the sailors aft. Shortly, several came in with lamps. They took a long look at us four women, wet in our nightdress, and asked, brusquely, if we were all right. We were, but we were very afraid."

"We could hear them manning the pumps, and the sounds of wood being nailed up to close the gap where the door had been, apparently."

"The sailors left us a lamp, and we huddled together in the near darkness, still wet and wrapped in a damp blanket. We looked like drowned kittens."

"Jimmy came to our door the next morning, very early, to ask us if we wanted to eat! Eat! What a thought!"

"As the faint sunlight came in through the small porthole, we found whatever dry clothing we could find, and dressed. The sisters were giggling when they had to put on my clothes. I never considered myself to be much of a fashion queen, but they thought it was high fashion!"

"Even the Captain came to check on us, and grunted what must have been approval when he saw that we'd all survived. He said that the ship had taken on a great deal of water. Planking was opening up, but that the pumps were handling it for the time being."

"Later that day, as I was on deck trying to clear my head, I watched one of the Chinese cook's helpers go to the rail to heave some slop over the side. The ship took a lurch and the Chinaman hit the rail hard. In an instant, both he and his copper kettle were over the side!"

"I shouted out, 'Man overboard!' in my loudest voice, pointing to where Ling, I think his name was, went over."

"The Captain, who was on the quarter-deck, as usual, had his head craned aloft. He was looking at the sails or sky; I don't know which. He instantly looked over and saw Ling hit the crest of a large wave. In less time than it took to think about it, the Captain reached for a rope that was on the deck, saw that one end was secured, and dove over the side with the loose end of the rope!"

"I rushed to the rail, taking care to hold onto a safety line myself, so I wouldn't join Ling at the bottom of the sea. The Captain was swimming very strongly toward Ling, who by then was almost out of sight. I could see the two of them join, and before long, the Captain and

Ling were pulling, hand over hand, along the rope back to the ship. I laughed with delight, not the least of which was to see that Ling still had a grip on the copper kettle!"

"A Jacob's ladder was hung from the rail on the lee side, and the Captain and Ling, neither looking any worse for wear, came aboard."

"I hurried to my cabin to get blankets, and went on deck with them. I gave one to each of them. Their lips were turning blue, and they were shivering. The Captain ordered rum, and the cabin boy rushed off to get the Captain's bottle."

"The captain took a deep swig from the bottle, and was about to hand it to Ling, when he ordered a cup be brought. I thought this was rather strange, but remembered how Jimmy told me that the Captain was very race-conscious. He was raised in South Carolina, and, had Ling drunk from the same bottle, the Captain wouldn't drink from it again."

"The Captain made to go below to change clothes. He still looked formidable, standing there with water running from him. It was by far the bravest act I had ever seen. He handed me the wet blanket and reached out for my hand."

"I didn't know what to make of it, and I hesitatingly presented my small, white hand. I was astounded when he bowed down and kissed my hand. Suddenly, it seemed as if a fever overtook me. No man had ever kissed my hand! I felt faint."

"In a moment, I recovered. He thanked me for crying out when Ling went overboard. 'He is a good Chinee,' said the Captain."

"By the next day, we had gotten clear of the worst part of the storms, and the wind, while strong, seemed to blow in only one direction. This was unlike the Straits of Magellan, where it appeared to blow from 360 degrees simultaneously!"

"I, too, was feeling better, so I was on deck, the only one from my cabin to be able to move and not be seasick."

"The salt air agreed with me. I was happy to be sailing, but even happier that I wasn't a sailor! I couldn't imagine diving overboard to save someone! Thinking this reminded me of Ling. I walked to the galley and stuck my head in through the Dutch door, which was open at the top."

"It was dark inside, and it was a moment before my eyes grew accustomed to the dim light."

"I saw the cook and asked him how Ling was doing after his swim. He didn't answer, but rather, made a jerking gesture with his head to dark figures in the background."

"Ling came toward me, and I could see that he had injured himself, as there was a dirty bandage swathing his forehead. It was bloodstained on the front. He obviously suffered an injury at some point, probably when he hit the rail, but the astringent nature of the seawater must have acted to close it when I first saw him. I gasped a bit at the wound, as I hadn't expected it."

"I asked him if he wanted me to look at it, and after a moment, he smiled and nodded his head up and down, as he understood."

"The cook watched with amusement as Ling went out on the deck, for Ling was still carrying the same copper pot! 'Did he go everywhere with it?' I wondered."

"I fished around in my sleeve for a handkerchief, and found one. It was man-sized, one my father had given me. It was clean and white."

"I didn't want to get blood on my fingers, so I carefully reached behind Ling and pulled the rag off by the 'bunny ears' made when the knot was tied."

"This wasn't very good nursing, it appeared, for the wound had clotted and I had only served to tear off the scab and cause the cut to bleed profusely. I handed him my handkerchief, and he pressed it against his forehead, all the while holding that foolish pot!"

"Over Ling's shoulder, I could see the Captain watching us intently. Nothing seemed to be missed by our Captain, that was sure."

"After Ling stanched the blood flow, I reached for both ends to tie them behind his head. He turned to accommodate me. I was interested to see his long, black pigtail, something Jimmy said was very important to a Chinaman. Ling was shorter than me, and had prominent cheekbones and large front teeth. I'm not sure he was very smart."

"I wanted to feel what his pigtail felt like and, emboldened by my 'nursing,' I made to move it aside."

"As I touched it, it was like touching an electric eel! I let out a scream, and dropped it! What had I done?! What was it?!"

"Ling whipped around and stared at me, open-mouthed. His narrow eyes widened, and I stared into the Oriental face—the face of Uilliam! All before me flashed by, and I knew it was he, this foreign face! Uilliam! I began to cry, and Ling moved backward. I didn't care who saw me. I rushed to him and kissed him hard upon the lips. He tried to get away, but I held him in a crushing grip."

"In seconds, the Captain was upon us. 'Willy!' He shouted, wrenching us apart. 'I give you heathens Christian names, take you aboard ship, and what do you do? Attack white women! Right before my bloody eyes!'"

"At this, the Captain swung the short length of rope he had in his hand across Uilliam's face, dislodging the bandage and causing a fresh gout of blood to flow. Uilliam—Ling—began speaking in rapid Chinese, which only seemed to enrage the Captain even further. The Captain's neck muscles knotted and his veins stood out on his forehead, under his cap. I tried to speak, but couldn't, I was crying so hard."

"The next few moments seemed to go in a slow motion. The Captain cursed Ling for being a rapist and an idolater. Before anyone could intervene, the Captain, his powerful back arched, lifted Ling over his head and threw him like a dart into the angry sea."

Sudden Light

"'I plucked you from the sea, Chinaman, and I can put you back where I found you,'" he said, though clenched teeth.

"I rushed to the rail to see Uilliam, clutching the copper kettle like a buoy, disappear into the wake of the Rainbow."

119

17 TOMBSTONE, ARIZONA TERRITORY: 1883

The sun was firing glinting sunbeams at the unpainted shacks and bawdy houses of Tombstone as I stumbled out of my room to use the privy out back. I had a chamberpot in my room, but I hated to use it, ever since I spilled it once on the way to empty it. I was a little drunk."

"I wrapped myself in an Indian blanket and walked, barefoot, down the dusty path to the outhouse. Somewhere a horse was whinnying, answered by a barking dog. Didn't dogs ever sleep?"

"The smell from the privy was overpowering, but it was unavoidable. I looked at the torn mail-order catalog, and admired the ladies' dresses. I couldn't read, so I didn't know what they wrote about them. The prices were too high for me. Who could afford $1.25 for a dress? I glanced at a torn copy of the Tombstone 'Epitaph,' the town's newspaper, but there weren't as many pictures."

"By the time I'd finished, nearly every dog in town had joined in, echoed by shouts from men in the boarding houses. A heavy-caliber pistol blasted into the air, causing a brief pause in the barking. It lasted only a moment. It certainly woke up any remaining dogs and sleeping drunks."

"I sighed and gritted my teeth. Another day in Tombstone."

"I'd been up most of the night. I worked as a 'dancer' at the Bird Cage Theater. Sure, I danced, but I spent most of my time under the stage. We were all whores, but the cowboys liked to call us, 'soiled doves.' Wasn't a dove white? This was funny, for I was as brown as a beetle."

"My name was Marianna, and I was, I guess, about twenty-six. I was what the whites called an 'Apache,' but we called ourselves Nde, 'the people.' I was Chiracahua, and had lived most of my life in Sonora, Mexico."

"I had been married, and had two sons. For reasons I'll never know, I allowed myself to be seduced by another man in the tribe, and we were caught by my husband. The council tried me, and it was ordered that my nose be cut off, to show the world that I had committed adultery. I could not believe the pain and blood. My little sons, who were about ten and eight, cried as loudly as I did, but my husband stood by, his face like rimrock, his arms folded across his chest."

"I was given a dirty rag to stop the blood—without much effect. I was given a knife and a small—very small—bag of food, a gourd of water, and banished from the camp."

"My last memories were of my sons being held back by their father, and of the man who caused all of this. Nothing happened to him; his nose wasn't cut off; and he wasn't banned from the tribe and his children!"

"I wanted to die, and came very close to it. I walked for hours, weak from loss of blood. I lay in a hollow under an outcropping of rock throughout the day, and ate most of the food and consumed almost all of the water."

"I didn't care."

"I was going to just stay there and be eaten by animals, but I thought of my sons. They hadn't condemned me. If I could only live, someday I could go back to them, or find them!"

"The sun cast long shadows as it silhouetted the giant Sonora cacti, then disappeared."

"I heard the sounds of night, and imagined animals in the darkness about to eat me."

"The moon was bright, and I walked in the relative coolness of the evening. I decided to walk only at night, as the old ones always advised."

"My water soon ran out, and I cut open a cactus to suck on the meat. The pain in my nose had subsided to an aching throb. The wound had scabbed over, and I tried to remove the rag. It stuck to the scabs and caused the bleeding to start again as I tried to remove it. I left it."

"I was a strong woman, used to hard work and long walks. Although the men rode horses, we women never did."

"Days blended into nights. I don't know how long I walked. Finally, I came to a mission, and knocked feebly on the great door. The friar who came to the door took a quick look at me, covered with dried blood with my nose wrapped in a bloody rag, and knew instantly that I was what he called a 'fallen woman.'"

"The people at the mission were kind enough, and I understood some of their Spanish. They wanted to save my soul, but I wanted nothing to do with their Jesus."

"After I'd healed, they said it was time for me to leave. I didn't mind. I still could not get used to the stares and whispers of the people who came to the mission and who wanted to see the 'squaw.' Little children, unafraid, would come up to me and want to touch the stub of my nose. I couldn't bear it."

"I was a woman of the fearsome Apaches, which had ruled these hills for hundreds of years."

"Two wagons carrying traders were heading North to Arizona Territory, and the friars arranged that I would go with them. They said that I could work for a farm family, or perhaps, a couple with small children in a town. I understood most of this, and appreciated the kindness."

"It was obvious that the traders had different notions on my talents, and they weren't in the child-rearing area. It was common knowledge that an Indian woman without a nose was an adulteress, and for some reason this seemed to entice them, regardless of the fact that I was so ugly."

"I had long, black hair that went below my waist, and my breasts were still firm. My waist was thicker than that of the Mexican women, but I was led to believe that some of them used devices under their clothing to make their waist smaller, for some reason."

"In any event, we'd only gone over the first hill, when the wagons stopped. The men, most of whom were Americans, numbered about seven in all. They started talking among themselves, and pointing at me."

"One took a drink from a bottle and handed it to the others, who took swigs. The one who'd drunk first swaggered over to me and started talking to me in English. I had no idea what he was saying."

"He began to unbutton his trousers, and I knew what he wanted. I had been untrue to my husband, but I wasn't a wanton woman. I'd known only my husband before my fall. I let out a small cry and held my hand to my mouth."

"The others laughed and the man grinned at them. He had only a few teeth, and tobacco juice was rolling down the corner of his mouth. He spat on the ground and lunged to me, grabbing me by the ankle."

"As he pulled me across the wagon floor, my dress went up around my waist, exposing me to him. He said something in a loud voice to the others, and they all came over, cheering him on, and shouting. I was terrified."

"He grabbed at my clothes and ripped my blouse, exposing one of my breasts. The shouting grew louder."

"I was yanked bodily out of the wagon and fell heavily on the hard ground. I hurt my arm in the fall, and cried out."

"My wailing and tears had no effect on them, and the man stood over me, holding himself in his hand, laughing. I looked at him and was amazed to see that it appeared as if the end of his manhood had been cut off in some way. I found out much later than he had been circumcised, but I had never seen a man done so before."

"I knew he would take me, regardless of what I did to resist, and I didn't want to be torn and hurt by his forcing himself into me."

"I rolled over and went on my knees, my elbows resting in the dust."

"He pushed me over roughly, and flung my legs apart with his hands. What was happening, I thought? I held my hands against his chest, in protest, and, to my amazement, he entered me from the front!"

"I scrunched my eyes tightly shut as he rammed at me, sweating and grunting like a hog. It was over in a moment, and I could feel his stickiness on me and in me. It was horrible."

"I started to crawl away, when, to my horror, another one took his place, and then another, until they all had me—each from the front."

"They stood around, laughing and, I guess, congratulating each other. I went under the wagon, and curled up in a ball, whimpering softly. This was part of my punishment, I presumed."

"Several of them went a short distance away and urinated into the ground. They were so like animals."

"Before long, two of them reached under the wagon, and with some unintelligible statement, pulled me out and threw me into the back of the wagon, onto some blankets and things they'd traded for along the way."

"The sun was hot, and I went under the blankets. I didn't want to see them, nor have them see me."

"That night, they camped, and the nightmare began again. It wasn't all of them, but it was the first man, whose name was Bobby, and several of the others. Bobby had removed all of my clothes, but a little more gently this time. They still had me from the front, which I found was the white way. It was odd. I felt no pleasure, only shame."

"In the morning, I found a few coins atop my clothes when I awoke. I had heard that white women were given money for sex, but I couldn't believe it."

"The money and the sex continued each day, and I grew resigned to both. When we came to a small town just over the border, I bought a few beads. There was a looking glass there, but I could not go near it. Many had thought me pretty before my fall, and I was proud of their admiration. I knew I was no longer pretty."

"I kept my few coins in a small leather bag that I hung from my belt. I was learning a few words of English, and understood the meaning of 'whore.' I knew I was now a 'whore.' I didn't care."

"Several weeks had passed since we'd left the mission, and the wagons pulled into Tombstone."

"A man with a shiny metal star on his shirt, carrying a shotgun and wearing a large pistol on his belt, with many cartridges in loops, came up to the wagons and stopped them."

"'No guns in Tombstone, gents!' he shouted."

"There was much protesting from the men, but the look of the man with the star, glaring at them though little slits for eyes, with his huge red face and giant pair of mustaches, was enough to stop the objections."

"Wordlessly, they handed over their gunbelts and rifles to the little man who stood next to the star-man."

"I found out later that the star-man was the Marshall. He had replaced Wyatt Earp who'd left town a few years earlier after a gunfight at the O.K. Corral."

"The O.K. Corral didn't look like much then, and even less later after I'd heard the story of the gunfight."

"I was told to wait in the wagon, and did so for what seemed ages. Before long, Bobby came back with a woman who was, I guessed, in her forties. She was white, and wore a black dress with a lot of lace. It was the most beautiful dress I'd ever seen. It looked, though, that her breasts, large white globes, would fall from the top of her open dress!"

"The woman said something to me in a high voice. I didn't understand her. She motioned me to get down from the wagon."

"She began speaking Spanish that was worse than mine, but I understood most of what she said."

"'I hear the "boys" had a good time with you on the way here, and tell me you are a real professional,' she said, as she looked me up and down. 'I have seen "button noses" before, but yours is more of a "dress hook."'"

"I didn't understand her meaning, and asked her what she meant. She laughed and walked away, thanking Bobby as she went. She stopped a few feet away, and turned over her shoulder to see I hadn't moved. She bade me follow her with a wave of her hand. I moved toward her, and Bobby slapped me on the rump as I went past him."

"Thus began my life as a 'dancer.' As before, the many men who came to the Bird Cage Theater seemed oblivious to the fact that I was missing my nose. I had dresses that the woman—her name was Alice— gave me to wear, but they were costumes, really."

"We would dance, and then go under the stage to the beds there to 'entertain' the men. Some of us would go to one of the fourteen 'bird cages' that hung from the ceiling. They appeared to be opera boxes, but they were for prostitution. Alice collected the money, and gave us a little of it now and then."

"Although there was a 'no gun' ordinance in Tombstone, it wasn't particularly effective. Guns were a part of Tombstone, and I even had a little .41 caliber Remington derringer that I kept in my dress."

"Once, during a show at the Bird Cage, there was a conjurer—I don't remember his name—who had a trick where he was pretending to catch a bullet in his teeth. During his act, a whiskey-soaked cowboy drew a Colt .44 from under his coat and took aim at the magician."

"Luckily for the conjurer, the shootist couldn't aim straight, and the bullet went low, through the wood at the front of the stage. Several of the girls and I were under the stage with customers, however, and the wood shattered as the heavy bullet thudded into the wall only a few feet from us!"

"Two of the men pulled on their pants and stormed out. They beat the cowboy with his own gun, and threw him into the street. We were cheated out of our money, on top of all of that."

"There was much gaiety and music in Tombstone, as the cowboys and silver miners came into town, throwing their pay onto the gaming tables, saloon bars and into the purses of Alice and the other madams."

"The miners worked the mines outside of town, and celebrated the coming of each Saturday night, after working hard for six days. The cowboys came and went—we saw a few regulars, but most were strangers."

"Even the law officers were customers at the Bird Cage, as well as the other dancehalls and saloons."

"I never went to any of the other saloons or dancehalls myself, although the Silver Dollar was nearby. I knew some of the other girls, though, and two others were Apaches, although one was a Mescalero and the other a Jicarilla. They were friendly enough, but my missing nose meant more to them than it did the white women."

"I had picked up a smattering of bar-room English, and this, with my little Spanish, got me by. A few men even knew a few words in Nde, and this surprised me. Some spoke of how many they had killed, and then wanted me. I no longer felt any emotions; it didn't matter whether they lied or told the truth."

"I was curious why the first 'bird cage,' the one closest to the stage, was always occupied by what seemed to be the same men. One of the girls explained that the same man, who was supposed to be a member of 'Russian royalty', had rented it for the past two years. They said that a brother of the Russian Tsar, who was like their King, was on a grand tour of America, and he found himself in Tombstone. He liked it so well, he decided to stay."

"This wasn't too surprising, as I had heard that many writers told stories—and lies—about the West and included Tombstone. The Earp brothers and the O.K. Corral only added to the 'allure' of Tombstone. He'd probably read about Tombstone and wanted to see for himself just what it was all about."

"I didn't know if the Prince, or whatever he was, was genuine, and didn't really care. I was curious to see him, though."

"The girls said he paid $25 a night for his 'bird cage,' which I was sure was untrue. $25! If he did, he must be a prince. I meant to ask Alice if it were true."

"That night, I made an effort to look past the lights and see who might be in the first 'bird cage.' I could see a tall, shadowy figure, dressed in cowboy clothes, all in black. I saw he had dark, wavy hair, and a great mustache. He looked intriguing and I imagined him as a Prince."

"There were a few books that people had left at the theater, and one had pictures of Kings and Queens. They were of Queen Victoria of England, someone said. I imagined 'England' must be near 'Russia,' if they both had Kings and Queens. I didn't think the United States had a King."

"Did this 'prince' dress in royal finery like those around Queen Victoria? I imagined so."

"I began to wonder if he would come below the stage. Several of the other men would come and go, as did a parade of the girls. I was an 'under the stage' girl, and no one ever asked me to go to one of the birdcages. The Prince—I soon found myself calling him that—never left. Sometimes he would clap his hands and cheer during the show, obviously enjoying himself. When I wasn't onstage, or 'under,' I would peek out from behind the curtain to watch him."

"I suppose it was because I felt so lost and abandoned that I began to fantasize about the Prince. I imagined he was watching only me, and that he had a strange attraction to me. It had to be 'strange,' I thought—considering how ugly I was!"

"This didn't matter. I thought of myself in Queen Victoria's beautiful dresses, and appearing in a large room full of wonderful people, officers in golden uniforms, the Prince at my side."

"In my dreams, I had a beautiful nose, and my skin was fair. I would have his children, I thought. This, too, was pure illusion, for the town doctor told me—and several other girls—we had caught the 'clap'—some disease gotten during sex—and that we could never have children. Most of the girls were pleased with this development, as it uncomplicated matters, but I felt sad, as I thought of my little boys."

"Dreams have no restrictions, and I bore the Prince many sons, each a Prince. By then, I made one of the girls who could read recite the entire Queen Victoria book to me, and I soon felt I was an expert when it came to royalty. Surely Russia couldn't be much different. The book even said how the Queen was related to the Tsar and someone called the Kaiser. There was a picture of a Russian aristocrat, a soldier with his coat over one shoulder. He was beautiful, but he wasn't the Prince."

"I stole glances at the Prince at every opportunity. He had dark, tanned skin, and a deep, rumbling laugh that made me giddy."

"He had the biggest hands! I so much wanted him to go under the stage with me. I almost asked him, but he hurried upstairs to his box. $25 a night, I thought!"

"One night, there were several girls in the Prince's bird cage. They hung all over the men, and one was trying to sit in the Prince's lap. I could hear his thunderous laugh as he picked her up and placed her down next to the man beside him. He must be very strong, I thought. I was glad he didn't fancy her, but I had no illusions about what went on in the bird cages."

"I imagined I must love him, a very strange sensation. I hadn't loved my husband. I liked him; I loved my sons in a motherly way, but this feeling I had for the Prince—it was hard to explain, but it was a nervous, warm, bubbly feeling that seemed only to increase. I felt jealous for the first time in my life when the 'soiled dove' tried to sit in his lap!"

"I danced my best for him alone, and was as flamboyant and risqué as I could be without simply stripping off my clothes!"

"I smiled when the Prince cheered, along with the rest of the room. I quickly covered my mouth, because I didn't want the Prince to see my missing front tooth."

"After two years of coming to the Bird Cage every night, suddenly, neither the Prince nor any of his usual three friends appeared."

"I was alarmed. I went to Alice to see if she knew anything."

"'Alice, Alice!' I said, breathlessly, running to her when the show started without the Prince. 'Have you seen the Prince? Why isn't he here?'"

"Alice seemed amused at my interest. She looked up from her ledger and said, 'Marianna, I do believe you actually *care* about someone—and a "Prince," no less!'"

"I blushed and swept the hair back from my face."

"'I—I have seen him here, and was, I was just wondering if he was all right—that is all.' My ears burned with the lie."

"She laughed and said she didn't know, but she would find out, since I had such 'great concern' for one of the customers."

"He neither appeared that night, nor the next. Alice, true to her word, made inquiries around town, but didn't find out much. She did learn that the Prince had only left to 'experience' the 'real West,' and would be back.'

"It was all a great costume ball to the Prince and his group, she said. They dressed up like gunslingers, and threw gold coins around like they were pennies. They went into one of the silver mines one day, dressed as miners. They worked a few hours so they could 'experience' what it was like."

"On the third day, there was a great commotion in the street, and I heard the flat sound of a shotgun blast. I ran out into the sun, to see the black-powder gunsmoke drift lazily away in the light breeze. There was a great crowd of people, both on foot and on horseback. The other girls and I ran down the board sidewalks to see if we could see what was going on."

"There were lawmen in the lead, and they were holding the reins of several horses. On those horses were men tied up like trussed pigs, rope wrapped all around them. One was the Prince!"

"I couldn't believe it! My heart stopped!"

"I asked one of the men who was walking with the crowd what happened. He looked at me for a moment, taking in my missing nose and horrendous accent."

"'Rustlers, Squaw-woman. Horse stealers. Low-down, rustlers.'"

"'Rustlers!' I said, 'how could that be? He's rich! He could buy a thousand horses! He pays $25 a night for a bird cage!'"

"The man took a twisting bite from a plug of chewing tobacco, and said, 'I do not know 'bout that, but if he rustled them cayuses, he will have a new "necktie," that's fer sure! 'Course he'll only be able to show it off in Boot Hill!'"

"I couldn't believe it! Hang the Prince? How could they?"

"I pushed through the crowd and tried to get close enough to talk to the Prince. I knew he didn't know me, but perhaps he'd remember me from the Cage."

"I couldn't get close enough to talk to him, but I called out, 'Prince, Prince!' There was a great deal of turmoil, and I went unheard."

"I moved along with the crowd, looking all the while at the Prince. He had lost his hat, and, of course, his gun. He had longish hair, and it went down over one eye. He couldn't brush it aside, and he tossed his head to move the hair. I wanted to comb it for him."

"We got to the Sheriff's Office and before long, both the Sheriff and the Judge came out. They talked between themselves, and then the Sheriff began to speak. The crowd quieted a little."

"'All right! Who accuses these men of horse stealing? Anyone here say they did it!'"

"A short, bald man with bad skin came forward. He took a blue bandanna out of his pocket, removed his hat, and wiped both his forehead and the sweatband of his felt hat before placing it back on his head."

""'Lo, Sheriff. Clyde Timkins. You know me. You arrested my Pa last year. Let him go. I remember that, and I am obliged. These four jaspers came onto my spread, bold as brass, and cut out four of my best stock from the herd and made to take off with them. Me and my men not being a hundred yards away, eatin' our beans!'"

"'Huh,' said the Sheriff, absently. 'Right there in front of you?'"

"'Ayep, right bold of them. If they's gonna be rustlers, they best be better thieves than that!'"

"Everyone laughed, except the Russians and me. I began to cry."

"The Judge, a dour man who looked like an undertaker, spoke up, 'They will not have a long career, so I would not worry about how good they are at it.'"

"This caused more laughter. It was all a joke to the crowd."

"'Anybody else see it?' inquired the Sheriff."

"Two other of Timkins' men came forward and said the same thing. They pointed at the Prince and his friends, who, by now, realized the gravity of the situation."

"'Anything you want to say, gentlemen? Did ya do it?' asked the Judge."

"The Russians looked at one another, and one began to speak. The Prince said something to him in a rapid language that I presumed was Russian. It sounded odd. The man went quiet."

"The Judge spoke again."

"'"Russian Bill" I think they call you? Wanna say something? Guilty or not?'"

"'Your Excellency,' said the Prince, evoking more laughter. I knew the men jokingly called him 'Russian Bill,' but I didn't think that was his name, and I never thought of his as that."

"'Your Excellency,' he repeated, 'I am afraid that my friends and I are, well, have been caught in an embarrassing moment.'"

"His voice was full and deep, and he had a heavy accent. I could hardly understand him as he continued."

"'You see, Sir. We have been experiencing your wonderful country, and thought it would be a grand lark if we "rustled" a few horses. We were going to take them away, and then return to pay—pay handsomely—for them. I have gold, silver. I have "greenbacks." We can pay.'"

"'Is that "Guilty" then, Russian Bill? Are you guilty?'"

"'Guilty of being foolish, perhaps, but we meant no harm, Your Excellency.'"

"The way the Judge spoke through clenched teeth and spat in the dust after he talked to the Prince, I knew he was doomed. The Prince didn't realize it though, and continued to try to talk his way out of this dangerous situation."

"'Your Eminence. Your Worship. I assure you we did not intend to keep the horses. We can pay!'"

"'And so you shall, Mr. Prince. So you shall,' said the Judge, his mouth a thin line."

"The other men looked around, and saw someone in the crowd swinging a knotted noose-end of a heavy rope. He paled."

"The Judge spoke a few words in private to the Sheriff, and took out a huge pistol. He rapped the butt onto the wooden hitching rail, and the crowd quieted. The Judge spoke in a loud voice."

"'What we have here is one of the most dastardly crimes in the West. A man who has his horse stolen is a dead man. Left alone in the desert, he will croak. Without a horse, a man is not a man. Sure, I know these fellers are foreigners, but that does not count. They gotta have laws in whatever hellhole they sprung from, too. Cannot believe horse thieving is not against the law in Baghdad or wherever in God's name they's from. I heard the evidence, I heard the confession. They's guilty as hell. I fine them—I *fine* them—all the money they have, and their guns and horses. Oh yeah, and they's to be hung. Right now. Guilty. Guilty, *Guilty!*'"

"With each pronouncement of 'guilty' he slammed the butt of his pistol onto the hitching rail, splintering both the wood of the rail and the gun butt."

"I could not believe what I heard. The Prince was talking in Russian to the others, and they began to speak loudly in Russian."

"As if done by the conjurer, nooses for each of them appeared at the front of the crowd, and were slung over the balcony railing of a nearby building."

"I tried to move forward as the crowd led the Russians to the side of the street, near the nooses. I couldn't move at first, but I could see them lowering the ropes over their necks. The others were shouting in Russian, but the Prince was silent."

"I pushed and elbowed my way to the front, and made my way to the Prince's horse's head. I was a few feet from the Prince, when he looked down at me! My heart beat strongly within my breast as I looked up at him, looking so royal there on the horse. I could imagine him with Queen Victoria! I was crying, and called out, 'Prince. *Prince.* Don't leave me!'"

"He heard me, and said something I couldn't hear. I had to get closer. The crowd was clearing from in front of the horses, and I knew in a minute the horses they were riding would be stampeded and they'd be killed."

"The horse's eyes were wild and white, and his nostrils flared. He stamped his feet, barely missing my own. I didn't care."

"I moved to the side of the horse, and reach up to clutch the Prince's leg in my arms. He looked down at me the instant I held him, and it seemed as if lightning flashed! I felt as if I had been punched in the stomach; I couldn't breathe!"

"I heard myself speaking in a language I didn't know I could speak. I called out, 'Uilliam! Uilliam! Is it you, my darling?'"

135

"He looked down at me, and I could see my own, sweet Uilliam, his hair again over his eye like a blackbird's wing. He smiled gently at me and his lips parted a little and I could see the white of his teeth."

"I felt, rather than heard, the gunshot from the Sheriff's pistol and I could feel the heavy muscles of the horse tighten and spring him forward. Uilliam, wanting a quick end, spurred the horse ahead and his leg was wrenched from my embrace."

"The riderless horses ran down the street to the shouts and cheers of the bloodthirsty crowd as Uilliam and the others hung unnaturally from the railing of the boarding-house, swinging widely at the ends of ropes."

"I was on all fours, my head craning to see Uilliam, as my tears wet the dusty street of Tombstone."

18 YPRES, BELGIUM—THE WESTERN FRONT: APRIL 22, 1915

The machine-guns sounded like woodpeckers to me, calling and answering each other. Canadian and German woodpeckers, very near me, in the trenches."

"I was a nursing sister, and my ambulance was irretrievably lost in the quagmire of ponderously heavy mud some yards from where I leaned against the shattered stump of a tree."

"My driver—now lying, arms and legs splayed, near the front fender of the ambulance—had slid off the corduroy log road and into a swamp of ooze. Both he and I were trying to push it out—an impossible task— when I heard a 'whack' sound, like something hitting a board, hard. I looked over and saw what could only be surprise on Johnny's face. He sank to his knees and the light went out of his eyes. I stripped off his uniform shirt and saw the small puckered puncture wound in the middle of his back. It hardly bled at all. I had seen so much death since I'd arrived from 'Old Blighty'—England—at Calais, some weeks before, but never so close, so personally."

"Johnny was seventeen years old, he'd told me. He lived on a farm in Michigan, Port 'Something' or other, and had joined the Canadian Army in Sarnia, Ontario, after the Christmas of '14. It was so sad. It wasn't his war, to be certain, but I certainly didn't feel very 'possessive' of it myself."

"I covered him with his greatcoat, and softly touched his eyes closed with the tips of my fingers."

"I tried to cry, but had no tears left in me."

"There were no wounded in the ambulance, but I couldn't lift Johnny. There was another stretcher-bearer, but he had cut his arm badly as we were transporting injured soldiers through the damned barbed wire. It wasn't like farm barbed wire, this military 'war wire.' It had fangs: rusty, omnivorous red fangs."

"The doctor was worried about tetanus—lockjaw—as was the stretcher-bearer. I hoped he would be all right."

"My skirt was sodden and heavy with mud. I contemplated cutting off most of it with the bayonet Johnny had given me a few days before. He said the Huns would have their 'way with me' if they captured me, nurse or not. He left unsaid whether I should use it on the Boche or myself, but I understood. He didn't know that I had a Mills bomb hand grenade in one of the large pockets of my dress. A soldier told me how to detonate one, not knowing I had one—or my intentions with it."

"Women were not supposed to be this close to the front lines, but fatigue, dysentery, wounds and death had left fewer men to go forward. I went willingly, but with a deep fear of the unknown. I had seen so many limbless, sightless and horribly wounded young men coming to the rear from the 'Quiet' Western Front, I knew it was Death."

"I could hear the whistle and scream of the German artillery shells, and looked for cover as the tremendous detonations began to 'walk' toward me."

"I scrambled to a deep shell hole and rolled in, trying to slow my descent by digging my fingers into the slimy sides."

"The muddy countryside seemed to absorb the shells' blasts more effectively than dry earth, but the shock could be felt through the mud with each impact."

"I heard a sharp 'cranggg!' sound and saw shards of metal whipping through the air over my head and figured the ambulance had been blown up. I thought of Johnny. It couldn't hurt him, of course, but was he gone?"

"There was a large pond of water at the bottom of the shell hole, and it was rippling with each explosion. To my stunned horror, a severed human head rolled lazily to the surface and grinned at the sky. Rats swam across the water and one scrambled onto the head, submerging it. I vomited dryly onto the front of my dress, hacking away the memory of the head. White bones were exposed in the banks of the hole where I had slid down. The Front was an immense graveyard."

"The Canadian soldiers said the Frenchies buried their dead in the walls of the trenches and the dead became exposed with rain and shellfire."

"I now knew how grim that would be."

"The shooting stopped abruptly, and, after waiting a minute to be sure that it wasn't just a momentary reprieve, I began to slowly climb from the hole, dislodging more bones in my climb. I gritted my teeth and continued upward."

"As I neared the lip of the shell hole, I could hear voices. I couldn't recognize the language. Was it the Germans? I'd heard about how they cut off Belgian babies' hands. I clutched my Mills bomb in my pocket. I'd lost the bayonet in the death-pit."

"Just over a small hillock of mud I could see helmeted heads bobbing. Were they the flat, low helmets of English and Canadian troops or the dreaded 'coal scuttle' helmets of the Hun?"

"They were ours! Two soldiers, walking in a straight line, appeared above the hill, their helmets at a jaunty angle."

"'Hallo! Hallo!' I called out, in my loudest voice."

"They stopped stock-still, feet still poised to step. I could now see that they were carrying a man on a stretcher between them."

"'Christ! Are we hearing goddamn angels now, Gord?' said the front one."

"They unceremoniously dropped the stretcher and the wounded man cried out loudly in pain."

"'Sorry, Cap,' said the second one, addressing the man on the stretcher, as he unslung a rifle he had over his shoulder. Stretcher-bearers weren't supposed to be armed, as non-combatants, but perhaps these were front-line soldiers, pressed into stretcher-bear service. I thought of my Mills bomb."

"'Here! Over here! I'm an English nurse!' I called out."

"The one with the rifle moved forward slowly, in a low crouch. 'Front-line troops' I thought. I'd seen that 'look' before. The other one had extracted a pistol from somewhere under his greatcoat and was moving toward me. Woman or not, they were cautious."

"'I'm standing up!' I said, as I tried to get to my feet. My dress was heavier than ever."

"I'm sure that I didn't look very feminine standing there, covered in dun-brown mud, but I was dressed the 'part' and I was only five feet tall, and not particularly threatening to anyone."

"'Be careful, Gord! It might be a Hun trick!' said the soldier with the pistol."

"'Right, Billy, I think I recognize her! It's the Kaiser's girlfriend!' he chuckled as he lowered his rifle."

"'Howdy, Missy. Not a very nice neighborhood to be strolling in. Nurse you say?' asked the one named 'Gord' in a young-sounding, pleasant voice that sounded Canadian—or American."

"'Yes, yes,' I stammered. 'I was with that ambulance over there,' glancing over my shoulder. There was no sign of either the ambulance or the men, only a smoking hole!"

"'Yeah, those ambulances have a way of sinking out of sight,' laughed Gord. 'No, I see the engine and a wheel. Big shell. How'd you make it?'"

"'I-I was in that ghastly hole over there. I think I'd stay with the ambulance rather than face it again!' I said."

"I was gushing out a torrent of chatter as we moved through the mud to where 'Billy' was with the wounded soldier."

"I knelt down in the ooze next to the stretcher and tried to assess the wound. There was a large field dressing over his forehead, covering his left eye."

"Answering the unasked, Billy said, 'Head wound. Shrapnel. Blinded him. He's our Captain.'"

"'A man of economical speech,' I thought."

"I spoke to the wounded man. 'Who are you?' I said, softly."

"'Patricia,' came the startling reply. 'Patricia' I thought, what kind of name is that for a man?"

"'What? How...' I began, haltingly."

"'Patricias, Missy. We'll all 'Patricias,' said Gord, sensing my utter confusion. 'Ain't our name—we're part of Princess Patricia's Canadian Light Infantry. 'Patricias.'"

"'Oh, I see,' I responded, rather unconvincingly."

"Gord was obviously amused by it all, as he stood over me, leaning on the muzzle of his rifle, the butt of which rested on the soft ground."

"Speaking again to the wounded soldier, I asked, 'I mean, what's your name?'"

"'Thomas, W.L., Captain. Is that you, Mother? Mother?'"

"'He's out of his head, Ma'am,' said Billy, stuffing his pistol into a cavernous pocket. In the same motion, he pulled out a piece of moldy cheese, and took a large bite. With filthy fingers, he thrust it toward me, and, through a mouthful of cheese, said, 'Wa' some?'"

"I hadn't eaten all day. In fact, I hadn't eaten since midday the day before, so I took it eagerly, green mold and all. I took a large bite and ate it slowly. I handed the piece back, and said my thanks. In truth, the bite of cheese brought back my raging hunger."

"I made to look at the man's wound, but was stopped by Gord, who told me he had just changed the dressing. From the looks of it, I couldn't imagine with what he'd changed it *to*, but I left it alone. 'Thomas, W.L.,' didn't seem to be in any particular distress."

"I stood up, and suddenly became dizzy. I didn't know if it was from lack of food, terror or the shellfire. Billy reached over and grabbed me around the shoulders to keep me from falling."

"'You wounded?' he asked, in a concerned voice."

"'No, no I haven't been wounded. Just been through a lot. Not like you boys at the Front, but a lot.'"

"'Lady, you *are* at the Front. Right over there. Hundred yards. Can't you hear the woodpeckers?' said Billy."

"I smiled that Billy called them 'woodpeckers,' just as I did."

"He continued: 'We was taking the Captain over to the aid station, but the aid station is blowed to Mars about now. So, we was moving him to the rear, when the big guns opened up. There's dead everywhere. Goddamn Austrians!'"

"'Austrians?' I asked, surprised? 'Not Germans?'"

"'They's all the same: Germans, Huns, Boche, Austrians. Krauts. They all like kraut. Got one of the Austrian pistols.' He patted his trench-coat pocket, where the pistol was."

"I nodded, silently."

"'This ain't healthy, standin' around here,' said Gord, authoritatively. 'We better move on. You come with us,'"

"'The "Corp" is right, Ma'am. You'll be all right with us. Going to be dark before long, and the Austrians send out patrols that sometimes get behind our trenches.'"

"I shivered at the thought, and nodded my agreement. I could see that Gord wore mud-splattered corporal stripes, and this was, somehow, reassuring."

"The two lifted the captain with a grunt and stumbled toward the direction of the shattered ambulance. The mud made a sucking noise as it tried to hold them in place."

"I followed closely behind. Once I stumbled, and fell forward, reaching out to Billy's back to keep from falling. He wavered, and I was afraid I'd cause all of them to fall, injuring the captain more. He kept his feet, but said, over his shoulder, 'Hold onto my rucksack. It'll keep you from falling, Ma'am.'"

"I held the rucksack strap, and could feel the cartridges in the cotton bandoliers he had slung over both shoulders. The accoutrements of war were frightening."

"We had traveled only about a hundred and fifty yards, when I heard renewed gunfire, coming from behind. It was distant enough—the Germans—or 'Austrians'?"

"Gord said, 'Take cover! Them's German shells!'"

"We didn't need much coaxing, and the four of us soon found shelter in another, much more shallow, shell crater. I looked for more signs of carnage, but saw none, thank God!"

"Gord slithered up the side of the crater to peer over the edge, just his eyes over the lip, in an obviously practiced manner."

"'Nothing there. Odd shellfire. Stuck in the mud, maybe. Duds, maybe. Can't trust the Boche. Troops come after an artillery barrage. Almost always. Don't hear our counter-fire.'"

"He was speaking in a quiet voice, as if to himself. Suddenly, he called out loudly, 'Look! Lookit that!'"

"He'd raised himself up and was pointing in the direction of the trenches. He was plainly alarmed."

"Billy and I bracketed him on each side, and peered out to where he was pointing."

"There was a ghostlike cloud of greenish-white smoke moving ominously toward us. We all stood, stock-still, in awe and wonderment at this new and strange development."

"'What the hell are the Austrians doin' now?' asked Billy."

"'Dunno. Dunno,' said Gord, in a quiet voice."

"As the cloud came closer to us, I could smell the definite odor of chlorine. In nursing school, the chemistry professor had us identify various chemicals by their smell. He told us how chlorine gas could be deadly, and how a janitor had died at his university while working around chlorine."

"'It's chlorine! It's a gas! Poison! Cover your mouths!' I shouted."

"Gord and Billy thought me insane, I'm sure, but an instant later, as the cloud reached us, and they began to cough, Gord reached in a pocket and yanked out a mud-soaked handkerchief and began to breath through it, and Billy put the cotton webbing of his bandolier over his mouth. I used the bottom of my skirt, and in an instant I could feel a burning in my throat and lungs. Billy pitched forward onto his face."

"Gord had a wild look of panic on his face and pointed to the Captain, who was clutching his throat with both hands."

"I moved quickly toward him, seeing the abject fear on his uncomprehending face."

"I reached for him, and touched the dried mud on his cheek. Recognition of the ages flashed from my fingertips to the very cortex of my brain."

"'Uilliam!' I cried out. Oblivious to the passage of time and circumstances, I removed the hem of my skirt from my own mouth and placed it over his. I smiled the sweet smile of recognition as Death rolled over the lip of the shell-hole and swirled around us, a will-o'-the-wisp of eternity."

J.A. Greenleaf

19 MALIN HEAD, COUNTY DONEGAL, IRELAND: ST. PATRICK'S DAY, 1927

My name was Mary. I walked along the coast road, my bare feet kicking up puffs of dust as I continued. My silver-colored Kerry Blue Terrier, Murphy, watched me, protectively. His dark eyes looked first to me, and then at nearby sheep grazing next to the road. Murph liked sheep and most other farm animals, and, oddly enough, cats. He had no use for other dogs and could be counted on to run off any who might be bold enough to come near him, no matter how large and fierce they may be. Murphy feared no dog."

"The Vikings had been here eons ago, I thought, and sailed their long boats to these very shores. Malin Head, being the northernmost point on the island of Ireland, would have been a promontory that the Vikings would have had to sail past in order to travel to the western shores of Ireland. I knew that two huge rocks, small islands in themselves, near Hell's Hole, just over the rise, still were known by their Viking names, which means, 'Shield'."

"As I walked, I carried a long switch of wood that I had picked up along the way, and swatted at rushes as I strolled. Murphy stopped along the road and appeared to have found something that was unusual to him, and looked back at me, as if to ask me to wait a moment while he determined if it was safe to proceed."

"I shielded my eyes from the unaccustomed sunlight to try to see what Murphy was interested in. There was a little motorcar, an unusual thing here in itself, and, nearby, I could see the figure of a man, looking out over the water. Murphy came to me, both for permission to run ahead as well as to collect a gentle scratching behind his ears, which he craved on a constant basis. I marveled, as usual, at his soft, curly fur. Softer, somehow, than a lamb's wool. If Murphy only shed his fur, I would spin it on me wheel and make meself a silver Kerry Blue scarf!"

"I sang softly as I walked, and the man, whom I could see now was a painter, was sitting at his easel. He could hear me, even over the sounds of the waves coming ashore. He looked up and saw me and held up his brush in the air in greeting. I lifted my switch, and whirled it in the air in reply."

"Murphy couldn't contain himself with this new and interesting development, which was decidedly different from his usual walks. He ran ahead, first sniffing the automobile and, lifting his leg against one of the tires, he baptized it with his mark and then trotted over to the artist who promptly set his brush down on the easel. He paused to talk to Murphy in the way that all dog lovers did, asking him what his name was, where he was from and was he enjoying himself?"

"I said good-day to the man in Irish and he replied, but in English."

"Murphy had clearly found a new friend, and was begging for attention, in between investigating the painter's box of paints and wetting down one of the three legs of the easel."

"'I'm so sorry, sir, but that dog is like a canine watering can. He seems to have an endless supply of his water. I will get some water from the sea and wash off your wee stand for ye'.'"

"'Ah, don't give it a thought. As long as I can keep him from giving my shoes a shower bath, I don't mind, for he is only marking his territory. I'm proud to be part of his territory. What do you call him?'"

"'Murphy. His name is Murphy'.'"

"'Like the stout?'"

"'You mean Guinness porter?'"

"'Well, in a manner of speaking. In the southern part of Ireland, in Cork, there is a type of porter, or stout, sold by the name of Murphy'.'"

"'A drink by the name of Murphy! Sure that would be something to see. If my boy Murphy could be something other than a dog, he would like to be strong drink. I don't know if you believe in past-lives, but I believe that Murphy must have been a human man in another life and would have been a pub brawler for certain'.'"

"'Reincarnation. That's what scholars call living past-lives. I believe in it, for how can you not? Surely, God would not waste a perfectly good soul and could not resist fitting him into a new body for another chance to make the world a better place. I'm sure that young Mr. Murphy here was someone in another life or two. By the way, my name is Jack. And you are?'"

"I sized him up before answering. He was well-dressed, in a dark suit, and had a colored stone stickpin at the top of his tie. I took him to be around 60 years old—near the age of my father, had he not drowned while fishing off Inishtrahull Island north of Malin Head, some three years ago, when I was 15."

"'I am Mary Doherty, sir,' giving a little curtsy."

"The artist stood up at this, and smiled at my formality, making a show of bowing in return."

"My eyes flashed and I replied, hotly, 'You make fun of me, sir!'"

"'Not at all! Not at all! Please forgive me, but you are so sweet, curtsying like that, I couldn't resist returning a formal greeting!' He reached for his folding stool and thrust it toward me, saying, 'Sit! Please sit! I have to say, I never let anyone watch me paint, not even my good lady wife, Cottie, but it is the least I can do for having offended you in some way'.'"

"I hesitated for a moment, but he did speak of his wife, and that meant that he probably wasn't a lecherous old man out to lure young girls into his motorcar, and Murphy, a fine judge of character, had obviously approved of him for he was showing him more attention than he did to me at the moment. I walked over and gingerly sat down in the canvas and wood contraption, something I had never seen before."

"Jack removed the small canvas that he had been working on, and set it aside. Walking over to the boot of his car, he rummaged around for a moment and returned with a fresh canvas in a wooden stretcher. It was about 20 inches by 30 inches, and white."

"'A new canvas for a new beginning,' he said, placing it onto the easel. 'I have contented myself to paint with brushes in the past, but I'm going to try something new that I have been experimenting with in my studio, using a palette knife,' holding up a small, flexible blade with a rounded tip."

"'I'm going to make an oil painting of this small bay yonder. I like the way the single headland on the left and the two headlands on the right frame the waves and brilliant blue sea between them.'"

"'The warhorses,' I stated, matter-of-factly."

"'I beg your pardon, Miss?'" he asked.

"'The breaking seas, sir, we call them 'warhorses' for they look like great white horses carrying armored knights coming ashore'."

"He looked past his canvas at the seas and remarked, 'Why, yes they do at that. They do at that.' He smiled to himself and continued to make preparations to begin painting."

"Murphy was sniffing at Jack's wicker basket and Jack remembered that he had not eaten. 'Would you care for a sandwich? I have, I think, two or three different kinds.' Sensing my reluctance, he continued, 'Please do, I often get so involved in my painting that I forget to eat and they end up going to the birds—or for some ravenous creature like Murphy here'."

"'Well, if it isn't too much trouble...' I answered, remembering that the bowl of porridge I had was before sunrise that morning."

"Jack handed the basket over to me and Murphy, sensing a lunch of his own, scampered over to me, who daintily picked what I took to be the smallest of the sandwiches, Murphy and I eying him carefully."

"'Thanking you, sir,' I said, demurely."

"Soon Jack was lost in his work, applying great squirts of different oil paint from what seemed like a vast supply of different tubes, some new, some rolled up and a few crumpled. He left the caps off of them, some of which fell to the ground at his feet. He did not notice. I was excited about seeing the bay, which I had seen almost every day of my life, magically appear on the canvas before me, the sea-foam a creamy yellow and the deep blue of the sea accented by warhorses. Jack worked furiously, the palette knife spreading the paint in strokes that seemed both bold and abandoned. He also captured the reddish color of the rocks and the shore. I lost track of time, as I leaned forward to watch this curious man create a painting that was part of my life."

"Having worked without taking a break, Jack finally finished the painting, and stood up, pulling his shoulders back and stretching his arms behind him."

"'Well, what do you think?' he asked, expectantly."

"'Oh, sir! It is truly the most amazing thing I ever saw! It is like a photograph, but only, somehow, better! I mean, in a photograph, I would see the bay, but in your painting I see and *feel* the bay. Does that sound mad?' I pulled my eyes away from the painting and looked at him, my red hair across my face, blown by the sea breeze. I pulled it back with two fingers."

"'Mad? It is the type of reaction that all artists yearn for, but rarely get! I can have a thousand people look at one of my paintings and say how very nice it is, but 'nice' isn't what an artist slaves away for. A true artist lives and breathes for the kind of honest remark that you just made, and I thank you for it.'"

"Jack removed the painting from the easel, turning it to look at it in different light. He was careful not to smudge the wet oil paint."

"'Mr. Jack, it is a masterpiece. I never knew that a painting could be made so quickly and with a knife! It will look grand hung in some great house. Are your paintings very dear?'"

"'Dear? I think that they are a bargain, myself, although some will argue with me on that point,' he said, smilingly. 'This one? Considering it is a top-quality canvas stretched over some of the finest timber that money can buy, painted by myself, I would imagine this one would fetch, oh, 30 pounds in a Dublin gallery.'"

"I quickly crossed myself with the sign of the cross, exclaiming, '30 pounds! Jesus, Mary and Joseph! No one has 30 pounds! No one has 30 shillings!'"

"'Oh, they do, Mary, and some, bless their souls, are even willing to send it my way in exchange for one of my humble paintings. This shiny motorcar you see before you was paid for with money earned from my meager skills.'"

"I looked over at the black automobile, in awe, not quite sure if he was, once again, making sport at my expense."

"'This one, however, will never see the Dublin sales gallery'."

"'Sir! You must not destroy it! It is a thing of wondrous beauty, an amazement, a joy to see!'"

"'Destroy it? No, it is the very first palette knife painting I have ever made. I will do another one today, of what I remember Derrynane in Kerry to be like. No, I think our friend, Murphy, would bite me if I destroyed the painting belonging to his mistress.' He smiled as he handed the painting to me. 'Mind the wet paint, Mary, for it will never come out of your dress'."

"It took me a moment of stunned silence to realize that Jack was giving me the painting. I stammered, 'Me? You're giving this to me?

Surely, you can't be serious! I don't have 30 pounds—I don't have 30 pennies!'"

"'Payment is paid in full: the company of a beautiful, ginger-haired girl with green eyes on St. Paddy's Day. Who could ask for more? Take it, with my thanks for the company. Give Murphy a sandwich. Hasn't he earned it, protecting us from bears and wolves as we work away, painting God's wonderment?'"

"Unable to believe what had taken place, I could only stammer my heartfelt thanks, as I walked towards home, holding the painting before me. I looked over me shoulder, seeing that Jack was back on his chair, starting another painting, lost in his work already."

"My house was at the foot of the hill known as Banba's Crown, after one of the three legendary Queens of Ireland, on top of which was an ancient tower and Marconi's wireless station. I went to the house and put the painting on the mantelpiece above the fireplace. I stepped back to enjoy it when my mother came into the room, drying her hands on her apron."

"My mother asked me, in Irish, where in the world that picture came from, and I told her, briefly, how a man named Jack had just painted it down the road, and made me a present of it."

"Like all mothers, mine told me that I shouldn't be accepting presents from gentleman, and didn't even need be talking to them. She looked at the painting and asked what the words scratched in the paint on the right side meant. I said I didn't know, but he said his name was Jack."

"At that moment, we both turned suddenly at the sound of a gunshot from the direction of Banba's Crown. Murphy, who had been sleeping on the floor, suddenly leaped to his feet and started barking."

"'What could that be?' cried my mother."

"'Surely, I cannot know,' I answered, but I mean to find out, as I rushed out the door, Murphy close behind, at a run."

"My mother called out to me to stop, to come back, that it was too dangerous and none of our concern, but I paid her no heed. This was something happening in my own back garden, as it were, and I would get to the heart of it as quickly as possible. I scrambled up the steep hill towards the tower and saw a number of men with what looked like rifles and a few pistols, shouting angrily at one another. Some men were on the ramparts, shaking their fists at the armed men on the rocks below the tower."

"The men looked over to me, swinging their weapons towards me and just as quickly, swung them back, recognizing that I was just a girl, and no threat to them. I recognized some of them, just as I knew most of them in the tower. Civil war had not left the Inishowen Peninsula and Malin Head, although it was largely resolved in the rest of the country, with the Free Staters triumphant."

"One of the men, whom I knew as James from Malin town, held an antiquated pistol at his side and walked towards me, an angry scowl on his face, shooing me off with his free hand, telling me, excitedly, 'Be off with you, girl! This is men's work!'"

"'This is the work of mischief, James, and you know it! I will leave when you leave!'"

"Murphy stood solidly in front of me, growling, with his teeth bared."

"'Call off your damn dog, Mary, or it will be a bullet that he's getting!'"

"'Bullets indeed! Would not your own blessed mother like to be hearing what's coming out of your gob, James?'"

"The other men on the ground laughed at James' distress and did not notice the movements above them on the parapet of the great stone tower or see the huge block of stone that scraped for a moment at the edge and rocketed to the ground below. None of the men on the rocks had time to shout a warning although one did point upwards as he saw the stone come over the edge."

"Seeing the movement of the pointing man out the corner of my eye, I stopped in mid-sentence and looked up to see the massive stone plummeting towards me. I raised both hands in vain defense, but the block struck me full on with a sickening sound as it slammed me to the rock on which I stood. Murphy cried plaintively and scratched at the stone to try to free his mistress."

"White faces, with Os for mouths, appeared over the edge of the tower."

"One wailed aloud, 'Bill, you daft prick! You have kilt our own sweet Mary!'"

20 SAN FRANCISCO, USA: NOVEMBER 1941

My nurse poked her gray head around the partially-opened door and told me that my last appointment for the day was here. I always knew what the 'last appointments' were. They were unspoken 'consultations,' but they were set for the end of the day—or weekends—or nights—or holidays—any time but the normal appointment hours for my 'regular' patients."

"The reason was obvious. What I was doing was something I truly believed in, but which was terrifyingly illegal in the United States in 1941."

"'Abortion' is such a horrid word, I thought, as I considered the patient about to see me. Medically, it was simply a 'procedure,' like lancing a boil. I kept no records of these patients. This was contrary to my medical training. I had been a physician in Germany and, for the past year, in the United States. I was incensed that narrow-minded politicians could make a medical procedure illegal. Who were they to impose their will on women? The damn Nazis? Was it not a woman's own body? The politicos were obviously male, as were the Christian church leaders who palmed their beliefs into the many handshakes with the politicians."

"I knew, as a Jewess, that my Faith also forbade termination of pregnancy, but I preferred to blame it on the Gentiles."

"I smoothed my white cotton coat and glanced in the mirror. Gravity had not been my friend, and I looked stern. I seemed to always have looked stern, but now, at only twenty-nine years of age, I had gray hair! I refused to do anything about it, for I felt a doctor should look older; it instilled confidence. My earrings seemed to strain my earlobes, as if my skin had lost its elasticity. I looked at the back of my hands, and saw my mother's hands. I could not allow myself long, feminine fingernails, as my mother had. This was a concession to the practice of medicine. I thought of my mother's soft hands and quiet beauty with a smile, and quickly glanced at the mirror to, once again, see Doctor Marion Weiss, scowling back at me in her usual style."

"I ushered the patient in. She was accompanied by a darkly handsome man wearing the uniform of a United States Navy officer—I had no idea of his rank—who fell in behind her."

"I gave this man a longish look of disapproval, and he stopped, seeing my flinty eyes."

"'I, ah, was going in with her,'" he stammered, self-consciously."

"The woman, heavily pregnant, put her hand on her belly, defensively, in the manner of all pregnant women."

"'There's no need, Captain,' I said. This is a 'woman's world.' Men are neither needed nor necessary. You've obviously done your work elsewhere!'"

"I don't know why I was so harsh. There certainly was no need. It was, as I had noticed in myself before, perhaps envy, or even a certain anxiety at being in the presence of such a Greek god, and a naval captain to boot, that caused me to overreact with the voice I usually reserved for the most troublesome of patients and tradesmen."

"I gripped the navy blue wool of his uniform with my left hand as I held the door with my other, barring the way. I felt a small thrill as I could feel his knotted muscles. He hesitated."

"The woman began to wail and pleaded with me to let him in, and my nurse gave me one of her long-suffering, conspiratorial looks reserved for a partner in crime—for that was, technically, what we were."

"I turned back to the woman and said, '"boyfriends" stay in the waiting room or the bar down the street, not in my examination room!'"

"She commenced to blubbering, and said, through the tears, that the sailor-boy was her husband, of all things, not her boyfriend."

"This was highly irregular and unlikely—if they were married, wouldn't they want a child, at their age—which was, perhaps, their early twenties?"

"I had never been married, and never had even come close. Certainly my family in Germany tried the matchmakers and every friend and relative to find me a 'suitable young man,' but I found none of them acceptable, and now there were only unsuitable old men. This one would have been 'suitable'—especially 'without his suit'—I thought, licentiously, surprising myself."

"The woman could see that I was relenting, and rushed over to gently open the door against my softening grip. I relented, not knowing why, but perhaps it was the sheer masculine presence of the young officer. He troubled me in a way I could neither understand nor recall ever having felt before."

"He moved in past me, and I could smell pipe tobacco on his uniform, and I thought of how I would love to have him by my fire, smoking his pipe! I was aghast at my thoughts! He walked athletically across the room and deposited himself next to his now-seated 'wife'—if that is what she was—in the wooden armchairs facing my desk."

"I quietly shut the door, passing an irritated glance at the now-smirking nurse."

"'Lock the door for the day, Agnes,' I said, unnecessarily. Agnes was not altruistic about this 'business,' but she was paid better than other office nurses because of her complicity."

"'Right, then,' I said, without much reason for doing so, as I sat in my worn, black leather chair, to a chorus of creaks and squeaks from the ancient seat, much to my annoyance."

157

"'You say you're married? I don't doubt you, really I don't. It is chust—it is just—that I don't see married, ah, couples.'"

"I was unhappy that my Germanic accent could not be suppressed in moments of stress. It wasn't that I was agonizing over the 'procedure,' for it was just that, although this woman was huge—obviously in the last trimester. It was just that—this Man—for I could only think of him in capital letters—was so *unsettling!*"

"'I,' he began, correcting himself, *'we* decided that, what with the war in Europe, and the likelihood that America will be in the thick of it before too long, that this just wasn't the best time to have a baby. I've been at sea—and my rank is "ensign," by the way. I'm a long way from "Captain"—and I, er, *we* think it would be best to wait until after the war's over. It should be quick, once the United States Navy is on the job!'"

"He smiled with a mouth full of teeth and it almost rocked me backward. I barely noticed the woman in the room with us. *I* would have this one's baby, I considered. I could not believe what I was thinking! Not only was it unprofessional, it was so unlikely! My brothers used to say their old boots were prettier than I was. I think it was true. As the years went by, I threw myself into my studies, getting my degree years ahead of my peers. I seemed to seek out 'old lady' clothes and shoes, and did what I could to diminish what few good physical features I had by refusing to wear makeup, and wearing the most severe hairdos I could. Today my hair—with its white strands—was pulled back in a tight bun, almost stretching my facial skin."

"The woman cleared her throat, as if she'd heard my scandalous, innermost thoughts, and said, 'Doctor, we think that my career—I'm an actress—would suffer by having a baby right now. We will have another—a dozen—when Willy gets back from the Navy.'"

"I glanced over at Willy, and he nodded agreement."

"'We can have a house full of children when I get back' he said. 'I'm off to Pearl Harbor, Hawaii, from here; I'm on leave. Beth can't go to Hawaii, and I'm stationed on a ship, the battleship *Arizona.*'"

"'This is highly irregular. Have you thought about adoption?'"

"They were ready for this one, it would appear, for they both harmonized together, 'We couldn't give her up if she were born!'"

"'Her?' I inquired, looking over the tops of my spectacles."

"'Oh, we don't know what she is for sure, Doctor, but there are girls on both sides of our family. Willy has four sisters, and he's the only boy.'"

"Hardly a 'boy,' I thought, lustily."

"'Look, folks, if you feel so strongly about it, why not just have it?'"

"'We can't—right now,' Willy pronounced, with finality."

"I had done my part, and I wasn't about to let a $100 fee walk out the door. I had few patients, and I felt word of my 'activities' was making the rounds. Pregnant women came in and 'un-pregnant' women walked out. San Francisco was more of a village than Munich."

"'Have you ever been given a due date? I presume you have had some prenatal care?' I inquired.

"'Yes,' she answered. 'And I know what you're thinking. It is late. The baby is due in a month.'"

"I heard myself repeating, *'a month?'* I unintentionally looked up at the Texaco calendar on the wall, doing quick mathematics."

"They both shifted uneasily in their seats. Willy responded, 'I've been at sea, like I said. Beth didn't want to make a decision without me. She didn't want to have the—*ah*—what do you call it—without me being present."

"'Firstly, it is a procedure. Nothing more. It isn't a "baby" at this point. It is a fetus, the product of pregnancy. Nothing more, perhaps less. It isn't alive, and is never alive until it is born. It is neither a "she" nor a "he," it is an "it." Just that—"it." It is like removing a growth, a tumor. A tumor isn't a "she," even if removed from a woman. It, too, is an "it."'"

"Having completed pronouncing my dogma, they seemed stunned by my abruptness."

"You couldn't be present during a natural birth, and you cannot be present during this procedure. Nothing personal, you understand, but it isn't for men."

"He shifted in his chair, and leaned forward, resting his huge forearms on my scarred, second-hand desk. I moved backwards unconsciously, as if afraid he might strike me."

"Look, Doc. I understand rules and all. I'm in the Navy. I also understand this is all illegal. I accept that. I don't like it, but I accept it. Beth is fragile. She needs me to be here with her, for moral support."

"I could feel myself weakening in the presence of this man. I knew I could not resist his persuasion."

"I muttered something incomprehensible, and stupidly nodded my head like some disjointed manikin."

"'There needs to be an examination. You understand that there are many—physicians—who would not perform a—procedure—on a woman who was this far along, unless it was to save the life of the mother. This we need to determine.'"

"'Is there an additional fee for the exam? I'm only an ensign, Doc.'"

"I hated talking about money matters, preferring to leave that to Agnes. I had to reply, though, saying that there was nothing more."

"'Please wait outside, Ensign. This won't take long.'"

"Willy looked at Beth, who nodded almost imperceptibly, and went through the door."

"As Beth climbed onto the examination table and put her feet in the stirrups, I pulled on a pair of gloves. To my aggravation, the glove split down the middle. I'd had Agnes buy the cheapest gloves on the market, and I think she bought 'seconds' of those, and pocketed the difference."

"I snapped the torn gloves into the trash and, more gently, pulled on a fresh pair."

"My examination was cursory. The pregnancy was normal; Beth was normal. I had to rationalize my actions, however, so I told her what she wanted to hear: 'Beth, the procedure will be necessary to save your life.'"

"Beth commenced to wailing, and Willy rushed in, expecting the worse. He saw Beth exposed in the stirrups and his mouth gaped open. Agnes was right behind him."

"'All is in order,' I exclaimed, rather Teutonically. 'You both might as well come in. I have just advised my patient that the procedure is necessary to save her life.'"

"Willy nodded his head absently, while Agnes simply smirked. I fired an angry look at Agnes."

"'Have the other matters been taken care of, Agnes?' I asked"

"'Yep,' said, crudely, 'paid-in-full!'"

"I hated talking about money matters. Back home, there were no money worries—at least until Hitler took power. Now our grand home was probably full of Hitler Youth, I thought, wryly."

"Both came in and Agnes set about readying the room for the procedure."

"I took Willy by the hand, rather unnecessarily, and plunked him down on a stool at his wife's head. He gave me a quizzical look, staring at my hand on his, and then I realized that I was still wearing the rubber gloves. I quickly moved to the end of the examination table."

"I readied the saline solution and other preparations I needed, and Agnes set out the tray of instruments, then adjusted the lights."

"I filled a large steel syringe with a sedative and squirted an arc through the air."

"'What's that,' said Willy, alarmed."

"'Pain reliever. It will make her drowsy. She won't feel anything. Standard procedure.'"

"I tied off her arm and found the vein in her forearm very quickly. Rather roughly for me, probably wanting to punish her for having this man, I gave her the injection."

"I put a cotton ball on the entry point, and had Willy hold it, mainly to give him something to occupy himself."

"I quickly went about the procedure, with Agnes peering, owlishly, over my shoulder. I gave her quick commands, and she did as I asked."

"The matter was taking much longer than ever before, and Willy was obviously agitated. Beth was coming out from the effects of the sedative, and her head was lolling back and forth, as she began to moan."

"I tried to move the fetus more quickly, and finally delivered it."

"To my utter disbelief, the fetus appeared as if it were full-term! It was a male—a fact echoed by Willy as he shouted out that it was 'a boy!' as if he were the proud father."

"Willy was on his feet, having abandoned his wife, who was babbling deliriously."

"'Oh God! He's perfect. Look at his blond hair! Beth's hair! Blue eyes!' Is he alive?'"

"'"It," I corrected. 'It is not alive. It is a fetus. It is not a child. It is not born, it is aborted.'"

"Willy began to cry inconsolably, and I was as moved by that as I was by the image of this fetus before me. Agnes, too, was crying. Had the world gone mad?"

"To add horror to tragedy, the fetus began to breathe and cough, as it lay in the metal pan on the rolling cart."

"I held Willy back with my hand, and the gloves smeared bloody gore over his beautiful blue uniform and white shirt. He ignored it all as he strained to see 'his son.'"

"I turned my back on him, and Agnes stepped between us. I took a cloth and placed it over its mouth to stop the crying and the breathing. It was only a procedure, I reminded myself."

"As the little chest movements began to subside, I reached for a bottle of ether, and my damn flimsy rubber glove ripped on a metal corner, tearing the rubber from my fingertips. I cursed the glove and myself. I had become the *verdammt* Nazi I had fled!"

"Willy moved around Agnes and came forward, his look murderous. I held up my comically half-gloved hand for him to stop, and, surprisingly, he did."

"'It is gone,' I pronounced, with medical finality.' Willy's head seemed to rest on his chest, in abject sorrow."

"I removed the cloth from the still face of the fetus, and, absentmindedly, brushed the hair away from the tiny nose with my bare fingertips."

"To the everlasting wonder of those in the room, I immediately tried, in vain, to resuscitate the tiny boy, attempting, in rapid succession, every lifesaving technique that I could imagine."

"I clutched the lifeless body to my breast and held the little head against my lips."

"No one could understand why I stood there holding him, seemingly forever, saying nothing but, 'It is he! *It is he!*'"

21 DETROIT: MARISA'S OFFICE: THE PRESENT

W anda blew her nose loudly into a wad of Kleenex and began to wail in anguish.

"Oh, Marisa! It is so sad! So *sad!* You found him, you found him after all those years, and each time either you or he died! It all seems so real!"

"It *is* real. It may sound like a lunatic's raving, but I swear to you, I swear to God, it is all true. My mind knows it, my reason tells me it can't be so, but I remember each and ever second of all of my lives, over four centuries!"

"I recall lives when I never found him. There were other times we found each other that I didn't tell you about, but each time it ended in tragedy, just like now. I just can't get over the fact that his name is 'Gene' now. That's the first time his name wasn't some form of William."

Wanda got up from the floor where she'd sat, cross-legged, at Marisa's feet as she listened, enthralled, to Marisa's stories of her lost love.

"Oh! I am so stiff! I'm starved. Can we go get something to eat, Marisa?"

"I guess I'm hungry too. Yes, let's go."

They had talked all night, and dawn was breaking over the Canadian skyline. They walked a short distance to an all-night diner.

"Do you, I mean, should you go to the, ah, funeral?" asked Wanda.

"Funeral. Hadn't thought of that. I suppose, but does it really matter? He's gone. I'll meet him again. It will all happen again—it always does!" Marisa spoke softly, crying quietly.

"Sorry I brought it up. Here. We're here. Eat. You'll feel better."

"Wanda, are you my 'missing' Polish grandma?" Marisa said, chuckling.

Wanda gave Marisa a little hug before they went in. "I like to see you laughing again."

They threaded their way around an old black man who was panhandling an obviously agitated couple sitting in a booth.

"Back here. Let's get far away from the 'ex-Mayor'" whispered Wanda, pointing surreptitiously at the bum.

A much-folded copy of the Detroit Free Press was on the counter, and Wanda grabbed it as they walked by. "Maybe there's a story about the, um, robbery."

The bored waitress took their orders for two "number 3s," and they each took a section of the paper, searching for the story. It didn't rate the front page, but that didn't surprise either of them. This was Detroit, and the murder of a gas station attendant hardly made the paper at all, much less the front page.

"Here! Here!" exclaimed Wanda, excitedly pointing at a small photo-piece as she pushed the coffee cups on the table aside.

They both bent over the paper and read it intently. In her hurry, Wanda had folded the paper so the picture was hidden. She folded it back, and there was a picture of 'Gene'—a black man, in his late forties!

"It isn't him! There's two 'Genes' or something, but it isn't him!" Marisa said, stating the obvious.

Wanda was finishing the article as Marisa stared out the window, thinking of possibilities.

"Uh-oh. Bad news," said Wanda.

"What is it?" Marisa quickly asked, a hint of trepidation in her voice.

"Says that the suspect worked there. 'Police sources stated that an attendant, one Bill O'Donnell'...*Bill O'Donnell*, Marisa!" Wanda interjected, the excitement in her voice was apparent. "Wasn't that his name in Ireland? 'William O'Donnell'?"

"'Uilliam Ó Domhnaill' was his name. Translated, it is William O'Donnell," Marisa responded, thoughtfully.

"Is that an omen or what?" said Wanda.

"An omen, perhaps. It was never thus before."

"Let me finish the story. '...Bill O'Donnell who was seen running from the scene shortly before Gene Washington was found by customers, shot in the head.' 'Money missing,' blah, blah, 'no weapon,' Listen: 'O'Donnell had recently been released from the State Prison of Southern Michigan where he had served a nine year sentence for armed robbery!' Your Bill is an ex-con!"

"I don't care, Wanda. It doesn't matter what he's done. It isn't the same Uilliam. It is 'Uilliam' in another body. We have to find him now!"

Marisa started to get up to go, but Wanda gently pressed her down into the booth. "Eat your swill. You—we—need our strength. We'll find him, I promise. He'll be safe. There's nothing we can do at this hour, anyway. C'mon. Eat."

Resignedly, Marisa sat back down and began to pick at her food.

"Uilliam, Uilliam, Come back to me!" she said softly.

167

22 DETROIT, WOODWARD AVENUE: THE PRESENT

hat bitch was fuckin' nuts," thought Bill as he slapped his biceps with his hands, trying to stimulate a degree or two of warmth.

After running from the station, he realized that he'd overreacted. "Fuckin' bitch," he muttered, remembering his mad race from the woman's Mercedes after she started freaking out.

After he rounded the corner, he realized that "bloodhounds" weren't after him and he felt a bit foolish for "legging" it out of there. After just getting out of the Joint, he was more than a little gun-shy. He'd done some short flops in a couple of county jails for a misdemeanor or two, including one unarmed that was pled out to assault, but this was his first hard time. 4000 Cooper Street, Jackson, Michigan, was not an address he wanted for the rest of his life. He did a flop of nine years and did it all at Jackson. No camps for him. He had a high-risk classification, and was considered an escape risk just because he was out-of-place a couple of times. The other cons thought it was amusing that Bill, with an "A" prison number prefix, meaning he was on his first sentence, had a security classification. Most of the inmates were "B's" or "C's," and a few even higher. The "C's" were usually lifers, having been "habitualized" as career criminals.

He grew accustomed to prison life, but it was hard. As a white male, he was in the minority. The "brothers" hung together, as did the Chicanos. Many of the whites were in their own gangs, such as the

Aryan Brotherhood, but he didn't join. Most were bikers, devil's disciples, or some other loonies. Then there were the assorted "freaks": those who were so intent on one thing, it overshadowed everything else. There were the "Jesus freaks" who talked your ear off about being "saved" all the time—worse than being caught in a stuck elevator with an insurance salesman, the TV freaks who watched the tube every waking moment, the appeal freaks, who did nothing but appeal their fuckin' hopeless cases, write letters to the judge, governor, whoever, and then there were the exercise freaks. These guys did nothing but work out with barbells and other exercise equipment. Some states did away with the exercise equipment, saying they were just "bulking up" the convicts so they could be stronger criminals. Bill thought this was bullshit.

Bill started out doing hard time by not conforming. He'd gotten into a number of fights with other inmates, and on one occasion, he looked sideways at one of the guards, and later that day the guard, a huge mother, showed up with his twin brother. They beat him unconscious.

Other cons said he should file a grievance against them, or at least send a "kite," a prison letter, to the warden. He did neither. Bill had always been in reasonably good shape, but the drinking and occasional drugs that came his way took the edge off of any "condition" he might have been in.

After the beating, he became an "exercise freak." The remaining nine years of his sentence were spent in working out. If he wasn't in the Yard, using the barbells and other equipment, he did pushups, sit-ups, jumping jacks, and squat-thrusts in his cell. There wasn't much room, but his cellmate was a TV freak so he had the floor to himself. After awhile, he was able to not even hear the endless game-shows and soaps that his cellmate had on.

Bill had dropped out of high school midway through the ninth grade. He had never been much of a student, and didn't see much future in it. He'd gotten a job as a flunky in a local gas station, and before long, he was doing oil changes and tune-ups. He was paid less than the minimum wage, but he couldn't complain, as he was underage.

His father had been a drunk, and used to work out his frustrations of not having a job by slapping his mother around. He tried to stop him once, and had one of his front teeth knocked out for his trouble.

No one shed a tear when his father left town with some bimbo he met at a bar.

He had two sisters and a younger brother. Each stayed in school, which made his mother happy.

They lived on food stamps and Bill gave almost all of his money to his mother, except for a few bucks he kept out for booze. He'd acquired his father's taste for the malt. He had to buy a quart of beer for his "buyer"—a local bum who would buy for any kid—but he got a quart himself. He would sit out in the shed behind the house after work and just drink. He felt good, but never had enough money to get roaring drunk.

As time went on, he realized he could "boost" a few things from local stores and either sell them for pennies on the dollar, or keep them himself. He was caught for the first time when he was fifteen. Nothing happened to him except for a "stern lecture" from the local Probate Judge. Unfazed, he did a couple of B&E's—breaking and entering—of some houses, but didn't get much. His was a poor town. A load of bird-shot whistled by his head on his last B&E when he'd stumbled over a footstool and awakened the homeowner. Being shot at was "uncool," and he gave up being a B&E artist.

By the time he was seventeen, he was a "keeper" and was charged as an adult. His first time in jail was for probation violation, and he did 45 days. He hardly ever slept, as the perverts were after him all the time. "Sweetmeat" they called him.

After he got out, he got a second job unloading trucks, and it wasn't long before he went back to jail again, this time it was for simple assault. He spent 30 days in jail. He broke the nose of the first pervert that went for him, and that ended anyone coming after him in jail.

He thought about joining the Army, but he couldn't pass the entrance test. He blew it off, figuring he couldn't pass the background check anyway. He briefly thought about getting his GED high school equivalency, but it cost money, and he was still handing over most of his pay to his mother. More and more went to booze, and by now he was nineteen and had ID showing his age as 22, so he bought his own.

He was hitting the bottle pretty hard by the time he robbed the local convenience store, what he called the "Stop 'n' Rob." He had no gun, but stuck his hand in his jacket pocket as if he had one. The Armenian who ran the store didn't point a finger at him in response—he pulled an absolutely huge black automatic pistol that looked like a bazooka as he gaped at the muzzle aiming right between his eyes.

The cops came and roughed him up a little. This was to be expected. "Resisting arrest." He didn't, but that didn't matter.

He was charged with armed robbery, even though he didn't have a gun. He asked his bored court-appointed lawyer how they could do that, and he said, "alleged weapon." That didn't make much sense, but he got no further explanation.

In the end, the lawyer told him that he got the prosecutor to drop the felony-firearm count, which would have given him a two-year flop at the beginning of his regular sentence, in exchange for a plea "straight up" to the robbery, armed. He bought it, and was surprised to get a 10 to 15 year sentence, a sentence that the judge based on his "previous record."

The court-appointed lawyer said that he was "real surprised" to hear the sentence, and that he should think about appealing.

Bill didn't appeal, even though he found out from one of the jailhouse lawyers in the joint that the felony-firearm count and plea-bargain were "illusory" since he didn't actually have a weapon, but it was all the same to Bill. He knew if he went through all of the appeal process, they'd just try him again and find him guilty. He was guilty. Drunk, but guilty.

There was applejack, raisin wine, and other booze in the joint, not to mention a cornucopia of enough drugs to open a pharmacy, but he didn't use any. It wasn't that he didn't want any—he was an alcoholic—it was just that he didn't have any "green money." Currency, although illegal, bought and sold everything—including life—in the joint. Some people used tokens, the prison coins, but green money was preferred.

He got a postcard or two from his mother. He could hardly read her childlike scrawl. He never replied.

Other inmates had money in their prison accounts, and they used it to buy any number of things, including TVs. His account had nothing, and he bought nothing.

His civilian clothes, which could be worn inside the walls, wore out and he wore nothing but prison blues and prison made boondocker boots.

He kept to himself, and as he worked out more and more, was left to himself.

He was convicted on a Proposition B offense, and did his statutory minimum of ten years.

The world had changed dramatically during the time he was in prison. Since he never watched TV, listened to the radio, or read newspapers, it was as if he had been in a spaceship for ten years, and returned to earth after a long space voyage.

They gave him a cheap suit and $200, took him to the bus station in Jackson and handed him a bus ticket to Detroit.

Since he had done his minimum sentence, he wasn't on parole, and didn't have to stay in a halfway house.

He thought about cashing in the ticket and spending the money in Jackson, but he needed to get out of Jackson County. When the bus came, he got on and found a seat near the front. He spent the entire trip looking out the windows at the new cars that flashed by. They were really something, he thought. He had never gotten a real driver's license. He drove on his fake ID, but had never gotten stopped. He would like to drive one of those new ones.

Detroit had suffered in the past ten years, and he was surprised to see so many of the stores closed, especially J.L. Hudson's, which took up an entire city block.

He wandered around for several hours, carrying his little prison-issued gym bag with his meager possessions. He felt foolish wearing a suit, and finally sold it for $25 at a used clothing store he came across. He spent the $25 and a few dollars more on a pair of Levis and a flannel shirt. The store owner said, "Just get out?"

"What'd you say?" Bill said, surprised. He'd heard him, but didn't think he was that obvious.

"Your clothes. Prison junk. Your boots. Prison made. Chrome rivets. Spot 'em a mile away. Wanna sell 'em?"

"Only shoes I got," said Bill.

"Trade you for some sneakers?" asked the owner.

"Naw. These are broke in. I'll keep 'em," replied Bill.

It had only been a few weeks that he'd been out that Bill found the job at the filling station. Gene, the owner, was an ex-con, who had done hard time for some kind of gang warfare. He didn't talk much about it. He tried to help out another ex-con if he could do it without getting robbed. Bill was ten years out of date and didn't know one new car from another, but he could still help out around the garage, pump gas, and do a couple of oil changes now and then.

Gene even gave him a couple of his old blue work shirts to wear, complete with "Gene" patches above the breast pocket. He used to kid Bill about being "twin brothers." He was always joking around, and made Bill laugh. It was a strange sensation—he hadn't laughed much in prison.

Bill lived in a boarding house a short bus ride down Woodward Avenue from the station. He didn't drink. Booze had destroyed his father's life, and most of his to date, and he knew he couldn't handle it.

After he ran from the station and the "crazy bitch," Bill went around the corner to a dirty little coffee shop and had a cup of gritty coffee and a stale doughnut. He dunked the doughnut to try to soften it a little. As he sat there, thinking of how paranoid he was for running away, he looked at his oil-stained, rough hands, and wondered how things could have been different back when he was a kid.

Here he was, 33 years old, and the only thing he had to show for it were biceps that could rip open the sleeves of his "twin brother" Gene's shirt if he flexed them and about two bucks in change. He could take the bus home tonight, but he'd have to walk in tomorrow. Payday was Friday, three days away. Supper and breakfast were included in the boarding house rent, so he'd survive; he was paid through the end of next week.

He finished his soggy doughnut and washed it down with the last black gulps of coffee left in his cup. Bill wiped his mouth on the sleeve of Gene's shirt and left a dime tip.

"Sure you can afford it, Chief?" sneered the overweight black waitress.

Bill leaned over and picked up the dime, shaking it in his hand. "Nope, you're right. I can't!"

He walked away, pocketing the ten cents, and headed back toward the station. He hoped that bitch had left and didn't cause any more trouble. Gene didn't need it, and Bill, himself, sure as hell didn't.

When he ran out of there, he wasn't wearing a jacket, and the thin cotton shirt didn't keep him very warm. It was dark, and the buildings he walked by were abandoned. The neighborhood smelled like stale urine and garbage.

Just around the corner from the gas station, he could see red lights flashing against the sides and windows of buildings. He stopped suddenly. "Cops," he thought, "don't need no fuckin' cops."

He thought of what could have happened? The bitch called the cops? They wouldn't send all these cars. He could see an ambulance reflected on a window as he peeked around the corner. Was somebody sick? Did Gene have a heart attack or something?

He hadn't heard any sirens at the coffee shop, but that didn't mean anything. Sirens and even gunshots were "background noise" in this part of town, and didn't "register."

He'd been gone about an hour, and had no idea what could have happened in the meantime. He wasn't anxious to find out, so he walked slowly away in the opposite direction.

A blue and white Detroit cop car went flying by, paying him no attention. "Those assholes always speed, no matter what," he thought.

His instinct of self-preservation told him not to go back to the boarding house, so he began to look for a place to hole up. A wooden clapboard house that looked as if it had never been painted had a fire in the upstairs, burning most of the roof off. "Must have been Devil's Night," he mused, thinking of the day before Halloween each year, when, for some inexplicable reason, Detroiters burn down buildings. A wooden door hung crazily from rusted hinges at the back of the house, and he made his way carefully up the shattered wooden steps. A kick of his boondockers finished off the door and he made his way in.

The house stunk of fire, urine, feces, vomit and cheap wine, but it appeared to be empty. He propped the door up and leaned a broken table against it. It wouldn't keep anyone out, but it would be an early-warning alarm for him.

The sodium vapor lights of the streetlight outside cast an eerie yellow light through the dirty window glass. He could hear tiny claws running on linoleum somewhere. "Squirrels or rats," he speculated, hoping it was squirrels.

He found an old, musty blanket and a full sized mattress that was half-propped against the remains of the kitchen cabinet. The house felt like it would come down around his shoulders at any minute. He didn't much care, though.

He wrapped himself in the rank blanket and lay down on the mattress, which itself smelled of urine.

He dreamed of green fields, mountains and the most amazingly blue water. He also dreamed of the bitch in the Mercedes. She was smiling at him and holding out her hand. He had an erection when he awoke in the early morning hours.

The sun was just rising, filtering red through the windows. "Red sky at morning, sailors take warning." He didn't know where he'd heard that, but it was true enough. Probably be a shitty day today, he thought.

He urinated through a hole in the floor, adding to the "bouquet" of this shattered house. Somebody had probably gotten a beating for dropping ice cream on the floor of the house when it was new, and lovers swept into each other's arms in delight at finding such a wonderful place.

He saw now that there were needles and burned spoons on the floor, and realized this was, or had been, a "shooting gallery" for drug addicts. He didn't use drugs, and didn't want any of them to show up. They were "shooters" in more ways than one. They'd kill for no reason, even after they got their money.

"Had Gene been robbed?" he wondered, aloud. "Hope he wasn't hurt."

He was stiff from sleeping at an awkward angle, and he did a few quick arm exercises. He'd do a jumping jack or two, but was afraid he'd end up in the basement.

176

Bill moved the table from against the door and went outside into the dawn. There was dew everywhere, and it sparkled in the reddish sunlight.

He rubbed his hand on the stubble of his beard and imagined he looked—and smelled—pretty rough. He'd head back to the boarding house and take a long "hotel" shower.

Bill counted his change and decided to walk back home. Ever-cautious, he took a parallel side street, rather than walk down Woodward.

Woodward Avenue used to be the street to be seen on, back when he was a little kid. All the fancy cars and even fancier women drove up and down Woodward. As urban blight moved out from downtown Detroit, the cars and white people disappeared. After the '68 riots, everyone seemed to disappear.

He had seen a documentary film about the riot: the screams, sirens, and the fifty caliber machine guns of the Michigan National Guard hammering away at real and imagined enemies. His own neighborhood was decimated, but his family stayed. It was before he was born. They had nowhere else to go.

As he got to the side street that led to his rooming house, he slowed somewhat. Down the side street, about a half block from his place, a car was parked on the wrong side of the street. This wasn't too unusual; people around there parked everyone, including on the sidewalk.

This was a stripped-down Chevrolet sedan. The engine was running and clouds of exhaust vapor floated upward in the chilly morning. There were two men in the car, drinking coffee. He moved a little closer and could see the telltale antennas on the trunk of the car. "Po-lice," he said softly to himself.

They could be there for any number of reasons—this was a high-crime area—but he sensed that they were there because they waited for him.

177

He backed up slowly, and vaulted over a low chain-link fence, moving quickly amidst the broken toys and old tires in the yard.

He got to the alley behind the house, and dogs began to bark.

He cursed them quietly, under his breath, and moved away from the sound.

Within ten minutes, he was several blocks away from the area of the boarding house, and went back onto Woodward Avenue. There was a McDonald's restaurant nearby, and he would buy a breakfast burrito and a cup of coffee.

He got to the restaurant and went first to the men's room. He looked at himself in the mirror and grimaced. He splashed some tepid water on his face, and attempted to straighten his hair with his fingers, without much effect.

The morning crowd wouldn't notice one more stinking bum, but he tore off the "Gene" oval name-tag from his shirt, leaving a dark blue spot where it had been. He tossed it in the plastic trash bin and went out into the restaurant.

There were the maple syrup-splattered remains of today's Free Press so he picked it up, discarding different sections until he found the small article about the robbery and *murder* at the station. He was not much of a reader, but he felt his face grow hot when he read that the police were looking for "a white male, 6 foot tall, black hair, blue eyes, age 33, who goes by the name of William O'Donnell." Why wouldn't he "go by" that name—it was his name.

He threw the paper down angrily on a nearby table and was startled to see a large man in an ill-fitting tweed sport coat standing in front of him, a thin smirk on his face.

Bill gave the man a quick once-over look and gauged his strength. He saw the glint of a badge at his waist. "Police," he thought. "A detective."

Bill looked behind him and saw another one, leaning, too casually, against a table.

"Got some ID, asshole?" said the man in front of him, moving his coat back to show a large automatic pistol in a belt holster.

"What for? I didn't do nothin'!"

"ID, shithead, or I'll frog-walk you out of here without it! Am I bugging you?" growled the detective.

Bill patted his pockets, and said, "I don't have any with me. Musta left it home."

The big detective leaned around Bill and laughingly said to his partner, "Eddy, he 'left it home.' Isn't that special?"

Bill looked at Eddy, who wasn't smiling. This was bad, thought Bill.

"No, really, my name is Bobby Winters," giving the name of his old cellmate, whose date of birth and background he could rattle off in a pinch.

"Okay, 'Bobby,' when did you get outta the joint?"

"I ain't been in prison," Bill started, catching himself knowing what the "joint" was."

Both of the detectives laughed. They moved quickly for such big men, flipping Bill around and pinning his arms behind him as they crunched the handcuffs together, cutting off circulation in his hands.

"You just gotta lose those prison boondockers, you asshole," smirked the second detective as they hustled Bill to the still-running plain Chevrolet parked outside.

J.A. Greenleaf

23 DETROIT, MICHIGAN, USA: THE PRESENT

Bill was swiftly charged with Felony Murder and Armed Robbery. Marisa seriously considered defending him herself, but realized that this would be the height of folly: she had never tried a single criminal case, not even a misdemeanor—and this was a capital offense!

The District Judge appointed a defense attorney, electing, as he could, to not appoint the Public Defender's office. Court appointments were a bit of largesse that judges could mete out to lawyers they liked, took pity on because they maybe didn't have much of a practice—and thus, income—or, in rare cases, considered the defense attorney to be the best lawyer for the case. Marisa, who was following the case closely, sized the lawyer up when he appeared for the scheduled Preliminary Examination, or "Prelim," when the Prosecutor was tasked with proving to the Judge's satisfaction that (a) a crime had been committed and (b) that there was probable cause to believe that the defendant had committed it. It wasn't much. Even Marisa knew this with her limited experience—nothing more than Crim Law in law school.

She'd had him checked out: James Fennimore Wilson (Marisa considered that one for a moment when she heard it), a native of Indiana, a retired detective from Indianapolis, and a very experienced criminal defense attorney. He seemed to do little more than court-appointed cases, which troubled Marisa? Was it that black defendants—the majority of Detroit's defendants—wanted a "Jewish lawyer from Southfield" and not one of their own, and a retired cop to boot?

180

She was sorely tempted to take him aside and grill him, but that would be highly unusual and Marisa decided to stay in the shadows and watch.

Wilson had a quick talk with Bill at the counsel table and then rose to tell the Judge that his client was waiving the Prelim and a reading of the charges. The judge looked at Wilson over his half-lens glasses and said nothing more other than setting the case for arraignment in Recorders Court, two weeks hence.

Marisa was a little taken by surprise at the swiftness of the procedure, but presumed it was due to her lack of criminal experience. Civil cases were like another country.

Later that day, she spotted a lawyer she knew who did some criminal work and asked him about what happened.

"Looking to steal some criminal cases from me, Marisa? Didn't think they had deep enough pockets."

"No thank you very much. One of the secretary's sons has a joyriding charge and was assigned James Fennimore...."

"Wilson?" The man continued her sentence. "Ol' 'Plea and Flee?" he said, grinning broadly at his own wit.

"What?" she replied, stunned at what she thought she'd heard.

The criminals have a saying about him, "The only thing that beats his clients to Jackson Prison are the headlights on the bus!"

"Oh, my God! Should this defendant dump him?"

"Not necessarily. He can do very good work. He is just 'inconsistent.'"

"We, the firm, could pay for a better lawyer...." Marisa added.

"Quite the fringe benefit. Are you hiring?" he asked, only half-jokingly. "You could hire, say, *me!*"

"I appreciate the offer. I'm sure you'd do well. Come on by. I'll take you to lunch," she said softly, handing him her engraved business card.

He took it gently and was still staring at it as she slipped out of her chair, seeing a fee slip away but a 'power lunch' in the future and, maybe a new job!.

Although mightily tempted to hire a Dream Team to defend Bill—and not the crazy ones led by Michael Keaton's character in the movie of the same name—she didn't, ignoring her deep-seated misgivings.

The case was set for trial some weeks into the future when Heather came in with the daily paper, a story deep inside circled in red ink.

Marisa set down the interrogatories she'd been poring over to read the article.

Throwing the paper hard against the opposite wall, she let out a decidedly unladylike blast of profanity that would redden a muleskinner's ears.

"That miserable *fuck!* I knew it! 'Plea-and-flee!' That little shit pled him out to a capital offense! Natural life! My God in heaven!"

Her shoulders heaved with sobs as she collapsed into her chair as Heather rushed to console the inconsolable.

24 DETROIT, MICHIGAN, USA: THE PRESENT

After Bill was sentenced to "natural life" in prison—to Marisa's utter dismay—Marisa began a campaign to represent him on appeal. First, she met with the managing partner and the management committee of her firm, giving them a pitch that they needed to do more pro-bono work in general and criminal appeals in particular. They could hardly believe their ears, for Marisa had never suggested anything even approximating this. Her firm was very active in doing pro-bono work and, when they didn't feel they had done enough themselves, they made substantial donations to the appropriate State Bar of Michigan department, earning a mention in the State Bar Journal and a nice tax deduction.

She smiled sweetly and pretended to rummage through a file—a file that contained only one case—Bill's—and said she had her law clerk do some research and he had found a case "at random," none other than Bill's. She pointed out that he had been convicted after a guilty plea and had been sentenced to "natural life" in prison.

One of the partners said, "Marisa, I don't claim to be a great criminal defense attorney"—earning guffaws and agreement from the others—"but aren't guilty pleas nigh unto impossible to win on appeal?"

She'd anticipated the question and quickly pointed out that this was the "beauty" of such a case: the Firm would do pro-bono work, but not have a great outlay in either time or expense. She said she felt the exposure would do her good and keep her "sword" sharp.

Several of the partners pointed out that she had the sharpest "sword" in the Firm, but all agreed that, if "Marisa wants, Marisa gets." She earned the Firm millions each year. How could they deny her this otherwise bizarre request?

She enticed the Senator to contact the Judge in Bill's case, one of the Senator's golfing buddies, and pass on that one of the premier firms in the State of Michigan and one of its leading lights wanted to represent a criminal appellant and had picked William O'Donnell "at random."

The Judge saw that this was an easy way to save the taxpayers a few thousand dollars and quickly agreed.

Marisa took one of the firm's pool cars—a Cadillac—and drove to Marquette, in Michigan's Upper Peninsula. Bill had completed his 45 days of in-processing at the State Prison of Southern Michigan at Jackson—his old "alma mater," and was quickly transferred to "maximum" at Marquette. Marquette is the permanent home of the hardest cons.

Marquette State Prison was located across the state highway from Lake Superior. Built a hundred years or so ago, it looked like a castle and was closer to a dungeon than most prisons in America. It was a cold, depressing place, in a very cold part of the United States.

Marisa's office had called ahead and ensured that she had an appointment to visit Bill.

She drove north along Interstate-75 and crossed the Mackinac Bridge, the suspension bridge nicknamed, "Big Mac," to arrive at the Upper Peninsula and then traveled across the UP to Marquette.

It was a pleasant trip, but her mind was preoccupied with what she was going to say to Bill. What if he rejected her representation? He had a right to ask for someone else. Would she be able to even *talk* to him, knowing, as she did, that he was the reincarnation of her long-lost husband of four hundred years ago? It even sounded insane to Marisa, herself, as she thought about it. What am I doing? This whole half-baked plan is destined to fail.

She parked her car and walked in through the large entryway. There were a number of visitors queuing up to visit prisoners and they looked as lost as she, herself, felt.

This was all a new experience for her. She had never represented a single client in a criminal case, not even a parking ticket. She strode purposefully to the reception counter, wearing a trim tailored suit and carrying an expensive, pigskin briefcase. Her high heel shoes clicked loudly on the terrazzo floor and several of the Corrections Officers looked up at the sound, quickly paying close attention to her as she walked across the large room towards them. Each of them hoped that this vision would stop at their location that they could be the ones to help her.

Marisa sized them up quickly and walked up to a small, round, balding man of about forty-five. He sat up straighter and cleared his throat, spreading his hands out, palm-down, on the Formica counter-top.

"How can I help?" he asked, sincerely.

Marisa gave her name and State Bar number, indicating that she had an appointment to see a convict for an attorney visit. The CO, or Corrections Officer, made a show of looking up her Bar number on a computer.

Satisfied with his search, he made a phone call and muttered something unintelligible into the telephone.

"Fine, Miss. There are some lockers over there. You can't bring anything in except legal papers, note paper and writing instruments. Do you have any weapons? No, I guess not. Lock the locker, take the key and your name will be called. Okay? Super."

Marisa found the lockers and locked both her purse and briefcase in the locker and took the plastic-headed key, noting the location of the locker, and then seated herself amongst the visitors.

A small black child came up to her and asked, "Are you going to visit my Daddy too, Lady?"

"Maybe next time. This time I'm going to see my nephew."

The child didn't appear to know what a "nephew" was and quickly went away, distracted by other children playing with some well-worn toys in the corner of the waiting room.

After what seemed like a very long time, but was actually only about fifteen minutes, her name was called and she walked to the heavy steel door that led into the inner reaches of the prison. She was more than a little anxious about going into "the unknown," filled with murderers, rapists, thieves—and probably a few judges and lawyers, she thought, wryly. She hoped she wouldn't be locked away in a women's prison herself soon, but there was a very real possibility.

A mannish-looking female guard gave her a quick once-over and she passed through a metal detector. A large swab on a wooden stick was dipped into a jar and a figure was painted on the back of her hand. She couldn't see anything and looked up, puzzled.

"UV—ultra-violet ink. Put your hand under here," said the guard, pointing to a boxed light. Marisa complied and the figure, a "9," appeared.

"I see. Thanks. If a woman comes out, wearing a beard and my suit, if 'she' doesn't have an invisible '9,' you'll know it isn't me, right?"

The guard didn't seem to think that was particularly funny and just waved her through to the next door, with heavy bars. She looked through what was probably bullet-proof glass to a control officer and saw the humorless guard indicate that Marisa should be let through. She went a short distance, only to see another barred door. This was the "man trap" that she'd heard about. This was a very, very scary place.

She was further directed to a barren room with several Army-surplus chairs and a similar, steel table, also with the ubiquitous Formica top. Who decorated this place? The National Guard?

After a time, another CO came to the room, leading a handcuffed Bill, looking more than a little forlorn in his prison blue uniform. He had a sheaf of papers rolled up in his hands.

As the officer pulled out a chair for Bill to sit in, Bill looked up for the first time, a look of absolute shock and disbelief on his face.

"You!" he cried out. "What the fuck are *you* doing here? If it wasn't for you, I wouldn't even *be* here! Guard! Get me outta here! This woman's poison! Take me back."

The officer was perplexed. This had never happened before—most inmates were anxious to see visitors of any kind, much less a stunner like this one, who was obviously unhappy that this inmate didn't want to see her.

She stood up quickly, holding out her arms, urging him to stay, saying how important it was—to his "case." Finally, Bill acquiesced and sat down. What else did he have to do? He had a lifetime of imprisonment and sadness ahead of him; he might as well talk to this nutcase and see what she had to say for herself. Perhaps she could explain why he was in prison doing natural life!

The guard left and they both sat down, Bill slumping in his chair, his manacled hands in his lap, still clutching his rolled-up legal documents.

She paused a moment to let the "dust" settle, then spoke.

"Hello, Bill. Can I call you Bill? Anyway, my name is Marisa O'Brien and I'm a lawyer."

"I know you're a lawyer. I heard you talkin' at the gas station. What are you doing here? Suing me?"

"No, I'm not suing you. I'm here to represent you on your appeal."

"What appeal? I ain't filed no appeal."

"Your court-appointed lawyer filed an appeal on your behalf. Kind of surprising, since he was, in effect, filing an appeal against his own representation."

"Old 'Plea-and-flee.' That's great. Sold me down the river."

"I know. That's why my firm and I want to represent you. No charge."

"Better be 'no charge.' I have about $4 in my account."

"Regarding that, I will put some cash in your account before I leave. Would that be all right?"

"Court-appointed lawyer putting money in an inmate's account? *That* will be a first! Ain't never heard of that happening before."

Bill looked at her intently, in a new light. Who was this person and what interest did she have in him?

"I will put money in your account today, I promise. And, if you need more money, or anything, I—ah—my firm will be happy to provide it. First, though, I want to tell you that I had absolutely *nothing* to do with your arrest, charges or anything else. I was just buying gasoline. I'm sorry I—overreacted—when you were helping me at the station. It was something else. A great misunderstanding."

"I'd say. Landed me here. However, I didn't do it. I liked ol' Gene and he gave me a break, giving me a job. I wouldn't hurt him. I know, if I'd have stayed, I probably would have gotten drilled by the same gang-banger who killed Gene."

"That could well be. Before we begin, can I ask you, is it all right with you if I represent you? You can ask for someone else."

"Do you do a lot of criminal appeals? We got people here—jailhouse lawyers—who can do a pretty decent appeal. They aren't *real* lawyers, but that's what they do all day, all night."

Marisa hesitated. "I, um, have been a lawyer for many years. I—I don't want to give you the wrong impression. This is my first criminal case—of any kind!"

"Christ on a Harley! Your first case! Hey, keep your pity money. I'd be better off with one of the guys here, writing it out, longhand!"

"Listen, please. I'm very experienced in legal research, trials, appeals and all kinds of legal matters, with the exception of criminal cases. My firm has platoons of lawyers and we can do the job. What we don't know, we can hire out. We—I—want to represent you. If, that is, you want us too," she added, very quietly.

"Here we go again. Plea-and-flee and now this. What the hell. Might as well. At least you will put a couple bucks in my account."

"I have $500 in my purse out in the locker room and I'm going to put it in your account today."

"$500! Man, you must *really* feel guilty! More guilty than me!"

"It would be my pleasure. Now, since we have a lawyer-client relationship... We do, don't we? I have to ask you some—background—questions."

"Shoot," said Bill.

"All right. I know you remember me from the gas station, but I want you to take a moment—don't say anything right away—look at me long and hard and tell me, do you remember ever seeing me before, even *years* ago? In the dark recesses of your mind? Do you?"

Marisa was near-breathless as Bill, puzzled, looked her up-and-down, staring intently at her.

The suspense was excruciating. She reached across the table, unconsciously, and touched the back of his hand. To her relief, he didn't pull his handcuffed hands away. She felt electricity coursing through her hand, energizing her entire body. Bill seemed to have no reaction and she withdrew her hand.

After a very long time, Bill said, quietly, "Well, maybe..."

"Maybe?" Marisa replied, excitedly. "Like, maybe in a dream, almost, like you can't completely remember when and where?"

"A dream. Could have been a dream. I've had strange, unexplainable dreams. I can't really remember the dream in the morning, just sort of a *shell* of a dream, like when you know the answer to a question, you just can't remember what it is, even if someone has a bet on it."

"Did you feel anything when I touched your hand, Bill?"

"Is this lawyer stuff? I've had lawyers before, but they never asked me if I dreamed about them."

"No, it isn't. I just have the *feeling* that I knew you before. A long time ago. A very, very long time ago. I was wondering if you did. Can you remember anything at all about those dreams?"

"Not much. A little, though. I wasn't me. I don't know who I was. I don't remember you. Many people I didn't know. That's about it."

"Nothing else? No someone who, maybe, reminded you of me?" Marisa said, hoping a smile would bridge the ages.

"No. Sorry. That's all I remember. Oh, yeah. One more thing."

"What's that, Bill?" asked Marisa.

"Fire."

25 MARQUETTE, MICHIGAN: THE PRESENT

Marisa held her face in her hands, stifling a scream that was welling up inside her, unbidden. She could not contain herself. Bill was stunned by her response. After a long moment, Marisa began to speak, very slowly.

"That's remarkable, Bill. Really remarkable. This fire, was it like a campfire, a forest fire or some kind of building or house fire? Can you remember?"

"You aren't going to go all crazy on me, are you? I don't need all the drama."

"No. I'm sorry. I have a 'thing' about fire. I can't explain it. I was frightened by a fire a long time ago and I react, well, rather precipitously."

"You react *what?*"

"Suddenly. The drama you mentioned."

"I see. Kind of scary."

"Yes. Scary for me, too. But, back to the fire. What do you remember?"

"Not much. It was a big fire. Lots of screaming, shouting and, I think, people died. Maybe everyone died. I feel sad when I think about it. I don't know why. Maybe someone I knew, someone I loved died in a fire. I don't know why it is so depressing. It isn't like *I* died in a fire myself, right?"

Marisa was leaning forward, savoring every word. "Right. Of course not. Maybe someone, a relative?"

"Not that I can remember. Maybe I was a fireman in another life!"

"Do you believe that?"

"What, that I used to be a fireman?"

"Sort of. In another life? Do you believe that people live again, maybe many times?"

"I'd like to think, someday, I'd have a chance on redoing this life. I sure fucked up *this* one! But, no, I don't really think there's anything to that. I got a mean, drunk, uncle. I'd hate to think that he will come back to life, again and again. Holy shit!"

Marisa said, "If you ever remember anything, I'd be very interested in hearing it. You can phone me, collect. Here's my card and I've written my cellphone number on the back. Any time. Night or day. We never close!" she added, rather lamely.

He studied the card and turned it over, thumbing the edge of it, making it snap.

"OK. Good enough. You gonna get me out of this mess?"

"I can pretty much assure you that things are going to happen. It won't be right away, but I will be filing a motion for a hearing in the trial court. There will be a motion for a Writ of Habeas Corpus to have you attend the hearing, and we'll subpoena your trial attorney, too."

"Plea-and-flee?" he said, with a disarming half-smile.

"None other," she said.

At that, they went over some housekeeping matters and she gave him copies of various papers for his own use.

"That's it for today. You'll be hearing from me. I'll put the money in your account. Can you buy a TV?"

"I'm not a TV freak, but I do like watching sports, so I might just do that. Thanks, by the way."

"No, thank you for letting me—us—represent you." She flashed him a billion-dollar smile and he waved goodbye with his manacled hands.

26 DETROIT, MICHIGAN, USA: THE PRESENT

Marisa sat at her computer and booked a non-refundable, round-trip ticket from Detroit Metropolitan Airport, first-class, to New Orleans, and then a cruise on a Carnival cruise ship to Mexico, with the best possible room, all-expenses paid. It cost her thousands of dollars but, frankly, she didn't care if it cost sixty thousand dollars. She knew that she would be beyond her bank account soon anyway.

Next, she logged onto the Detroit FreeCycle website where people gave away things and knew that, once she posted the prepaid trip to Cozumel, her mailbox would be flooded with requests for it. She'd created a Yahoo email account just for this.

She tapped the "enter" key on her computer and went back to her work on William's motion.

She had put few details in the posting, figuring that she could work it out with some of the prospective recipients. She didn't want to sound like too much of a nut case and certainly didn't want to be the subject of an article in the local daily, "Crazy Lady Gives Away Trip!"

After an hour and a half, Marisa logged onto her new Yahoo email account. She'd already gotten fifty-seven messages! Good news travels fast!

She scrolled through them, deleting the ones from men. She had to find someone who could be her—so the messages from women were the only ones she kept. She hated to be discriminatory, but she deleted the

195

ones with ethnic-sounding names. She needed to find someone who could approximate Marisa herself. She answered the ones that were left, saying, succinctly, that she'd booked this non-refundable trip and, as luck would have it, had something come up that prevented her from traveling. She didn't have travel insurance, so she could either give it away or lose it altogether. She'd rather give it to someone who really wanted it. She asked the senders to tell her why they wanted the cruise.

As expected, within minutes she received replies from everyone. They were uniformly long and varied. Some were of Mexican heritage and wanting to go home for a few weeks, second honeymoons, chance-of-a-lifetime and everything in between. One caught her eye, one of several that included photographs as attachments. She was about her own age, with similar coloring and dark hair. Her name was, amusingly enough, Madonna Jankowski, and she was a school teacher in Port Sanilac, Michigan, up in the "thumb" of Michigan, north of Port Huron. She said she was divorced, without children, and had recently moved to the "thumb" from Lansing after her divorce. Because of the move, she hadn't had a vacation in several years. She had the time and wanted to go.

Since she'd supplied her telephone number, Marisa phoned her.

"Hi. This is the lady who posted the giveaway for the trip. Is this Madonna?"

"Yes! How exciting! Am I a 'finalist?' or whatever it is called?"

"It isn't a contest—just a 'random act of kindness.' But, yes, you're one of the few I've narrowed it down to. I can't promise anything—don't get your hopes up!"

"Oh, my, God!" she said, pacing her words. "I am over the moon!"

"I was impressed with your email. Have you ever been to Mexico?"

"No! I've never been anywhere. Cedar Point, Ohio, is about it. Not quite the same. Are you sure I can't pay you something for the trip? I mean, I don't have a lot of money, but I could make payments or something."

"Wouldn't hear of it. I'm a doctor, and successful at that. One of those hated 'rich doctors,' I'm afraid. My accountants will probably find some way to write it off of my taxes, but it is a gift, plain and simple."

"I just don't have any breath left!"

"I'm glad you're pleased. I'd like to give it to you. I'm going to be in Port Huron tomorrow for a little business and I could drive to Port Sanilac to meet with you, if that's all right with you."

"All right? Of course, it is all right. There isn't a 'catch' to this?"

"None that I can think of," Marisa lied. "See you tomorrow at one? Where would you like to meet?"

"We could meet at the harbor, down by the old lighthouse. Would that be all right?"

"Fine. I'll be driving a silver Mercedes."

"Wow! I'll be 'driving' black shoes with Levis above them, green sweater."

Marisa smiled. She liked her. "See you then."

27 PORT HURON, MICHIGAN: THE PRESENT

Marisa had reported her driver's license as lost and had a new one issued some time ago by the State of Michigan. She put it in a side pocket of her purse, along with her own "Passport Card," a high-security card issued by the U.S. Department of State for travel between the U.S., Canada, Mexico and the Caribbean, but only by foot, car, train, or boat.

The connection with the woman from Port Sanilac went well. She didn't look like a dead-ringer for Marisa, but she was of the same general coloration, height, weight, and age. She would have to do.

Offering the woman, a stranger, Marisa's ID would seem very suspicious, so Marisa spun a web, saying, innocently, "I hope you don't have any trouble using a ticket in *my* name."

She took the bait: "Oh! I hadn't thought of that! Do you think there will be a problem?"

"Hmm," said Marisa, with fake thoughtfulness. "I really don't know. I guess the worse that could happen would be that they'd send you back. I'm sure nothing worse could result."

"Really? I wouldn't be thrown in jail or anything?"

"I hardly think so. It isn't like you're a criminal or something, and no one's asking you to bring back a mysterious box, leaking a strange fluid!"

"Now you're scaring me! Maybe this isn't such a good idea, after all. I wish I had an ID with your name on it and my picture!"

"Sorry," said Marisa. I'm fresh out of fake ID's. Haven't had one since I was 19 and used my sister's!"

"Could I be your sister?" the woman said, pensively.

"My sister. Oh, I see what you mean. You want to 'borrow' me. Right?"

"It would be just for the trip. I'll send it back! I promise! I want to go so badly, I can taste it."

Marisa let a very long time go by and then she reached into the outside pocket of her purse and pulled out her original driver's license and Passport Card, handing them to her, saying, "Here, Sis. Have a great time."

The woman crushed her in a great bear-hug and started to cry. Marisa gave her the ticket and told her to enjoy herself. She truly hoped she would have a good time and that Marisa wasn't ruining an innocent life. God knows she'd ruined many in the past.

28 DETROIT, MICHIGAN, USA: THE PRESENT

Marisa had made preparations for some time, obtaining a Writ of Habeas Corpus, as she had told Bill in Marquette, to have him brought to Detroit for a hearing on a motion she'd filed for a new trial, contending there was newly-discovered evidence, which Bill would be required to testify about.

As the hearing was set for the following Tuesday, she knew that the Michigan Department of Corrections would transport Bill to Detroit in advance of the hearing date. While it was always possible that he could have been brought from Marquette well in advance of Tuesday, that seemed unlikely, since Bill was to be in Detroit only for the single day.

The State of Michigan, being broke as usual, wasn't about to pay perdiem and expenses for the transporting corrections officers to stay for a "mini vacation" in Detroit. It was all a calculated risk, but Marisa surmised that the DOC would bring Bill down the Monday before the hearing, a scant few days from now. She had much to do.

She'd purchased a mini-motorhome in nearby Toledo, Ohio, paying cash. She'd asked the seller if she could use the plates to get her home to Dayton, Ohio, and she'd mail them back to him. Hesitant at first, her luminous smile broke down his objections.

"Aw, hell, it ain't like I got a need for them. Send 'em back when you get a chance. You got my address. Make sure you got insurance on the bus, though. I don't want nothin' to happen, like an accident, and have it come back on me."

She assured him it would be covered from the moment she bought it.

That was all wishful thinking on his part, as she had no intention of either insuring the motor-home or anything that would link her to it. She already had a set of license plates—unexpired—that she'd gotten from a junk car. She kept a battery-powered screwdriver with her in anticipation of finding a suitable "donor" car.

The VIN data plate, which held the Vehicle Identification Number, was attached to the dashboard at the bottom of the windshield on the left side of the van, attached with special rivets that had notches out of the edges. On an automobile, with a steeply slanted windshield, she knew it was wildly difficult to get the plate off, short of removing the windshield. On the van, however, the windshield didn't have much of a slant to it, and it was relatively easy to get to the data plate, pry it off, and super-glue a new one—from a similar van at a "remove it yourself" junkyard, called "Larry's U-Pull It."

She'd removed the entire dashboard, something she found quite difficult, but she had an instruction sheet from online research, figuring that if someone at the factory had installed it, she could take it out. She knew if she'd only removed the VIN, it would be obvious to anyone coming by and she'd be found out.

After she'd gotten back to her rented garage, she removed the VIN plate, using a battery-powered Dremel tool and a small grinding wheel. The VIN plate and the stubs of the rivets came loose and she worked on the rivets themselves, grinding them until only the heads were left. More super-glue and the heads were glued onto the data plate. After removing the one from the van she'd purchased, mangling it in the process, she glued down the "new" plate, complete with rivet heads in place. It would take a very, very close inspection to see that it wasn't the original.

She looked around the van and found VINs on the driver's door, under the hood and in the glove compartment. They were on plastic, self-adhesive labels, showing the build date, tire pressure and any number of arcane information. The careful application of a heat gun let her remove them readily and some "Glue-Gone" liquid removed any trace of residual adhesive.

She "puddled" the VIN stamped into the engine with a very hot pencil torch, burning Mapp gas. Grinding the VIN off didn't do much, as the impression of the number went deeply into the metal, but puddling it—essentially melting the metal—in this case, aluminum—removed all traces of the numbers

Marisa knew, from her career as an attorney, that all modern vehicles had a Confidential Vehicle Identification Number, or CVIN, stamped in some out-of-the-way place on the vehicle's frame. This information wasn't even shared with most local police departments. A "Fed" would be contacted, and he would come to the vehicle, look up the location of the CVIN, and then crawl under with a flashlight, calling out the numbers as he read them.

Most car thieves weren't aware of the CVIN and few knew the location, and the location varied on different vehicles. She had no access to the CVIN list either, but she'd had a case a few years earlier, involving a large car dealer, represented by her, that was charged with fiddling with vehicle VINs and selling cars that had been stolen in other states, all with doctored titles and new VIN plates—although these "supposedly" came from the factory, compliments of a supervisor who had access to the blank plates and special rivets.

During the course of the trial, it was disclosed—reluctantly—on cross-examine, where the CVIN was located on this year and model of vans. Marisa, for some reason, had filed that information away in her mind and was able to draw it out now. She specifically bought a van of the same year and model for this plan.

Tying her long hair back and pulling her Detroit Tigers baseball cap down onto her head, she rolled under the van with a mirror in the end of a telescoping handle, compliments of Harbor Freight tools. Her brother called Harbor Freight "Mecca," as he regularly made "pilgrimages" to Harbor Freight, just to wander around and buy things he didn't really need. He dragged her along on more than one occasion.

With her small LED flashlight, she angled the mirror up onto the top of the frame, just forward of the right-rear tire. She was frustrated that she could not see the number, and reached for a small wire brush she'd brought with her under the van. Finally, holding the flashlight at a shallow angle, she was able to see the CVIN.

Marisa was aware that she couldn't "puddle" the heat-treated steel of the frame, but she did have the Dremel tool. She ground steadily onto the numbers and caused sparks to fly from the whirling grinding stone. She kept at it until the battery exhausted itself. Peering up at the place where the number had been with the mirror, she was satisfied to see that almost all of it was gone. Some remained, but she knew that simply contained the manufacturer's name, which was obvious anyway.

Two weeks earlier, she'd bought a very old Ford Taurus station wagon from an old woman in Mackinaw City, at the Straits of Mackinac. She wanted to have a "local" car, since each county had identifying license plates and a "down state" car, with Wayne County—"Detroit"— license plates would stand out like a beacon on a dark night. The old lady was very obliging and never even mentioned the license plates, which still had two months to run. The station wagon, she said, had belonged to her late husband, and she hoped that it could be "put to use" instead of just going to pieces from Michigan rust.

She parked the Taurus at a small, regional airport. Cars were never suspicious if they were parked at airports for up to a few weeks, as people went off to sunnier climes than Michigan—which was just about everywhere on the planet. She walked to the nearest town and took the bus to Detroit, which was a culture shock in no small degree. She was amazed at the strange people who took the bus—and "hung out" at the Detroit bus station. She'd put her backpack, containing just a few things, other than her "K-Mart" purse—part of her new "look"—and strategically placed it next to her on the adjacent bus seat. She purposefully sat on the aisle and had the backpack in the window seat. Several creepies asked if the seat was taken—one simply attempting to maneuver into it before being blocked by Marisa. The bus was nearly empty—she knew he was "looking for love in all the wrong places" and wasn't having any of it.

Her plan, such as it was, was to drive to a south-bound rest area, not far from Mackinaw City, and park the camper there and then make her way to the airport to pick up the Taurus, so she'd have both vehicles at the rest area where she would patiently wait for the transport car from Marquette Prison. She knew from the past that the Corrections Officers who where on prison transport always stopped at the rest area for a smoke, a toilet break and a chance to stretch their legs, as the "jump" from Marquette was the last place they'd been before driving eastward and crossing the Mackinac Bridge. They'd be looking forward to stopping at the rest area.

She anticipated parking the camper in the large, drive-through lanes reserved for trucks and RVs.

She'd filled up the gas tank on the camper before she drove it into the garage. She uncoiled the power cable from a small battery charger, connected it to the camper's battery and plugged it in. She didn't want the camper to have a dead battery when she came to use it.

Marisa gave a heavy sigh as she contemplated everything that she was going through. Was it all some kind of insanity? Did she dream all of this? What she totally and utterly mad? She knew, in the depths of her eternal soul, that she had lived all these lives, for four hundred God-damned years! "God-damned" was the only way she could describe it, in the most literal use of the expression, for it seemed to her, as it had in each of her lives, that she was suffering some incredible purgatory, punishing her for some, unknown, mortal sin that she could not, for the life—or "lives" of her—remember having committed. Surely, if she had been God-damned to what may well be fitful, soul-heartrendingly painful reincarnations for the infinity of time, then she must remember it! Perhaps it was something that occurred during a previous life, or "lives." Perhaps she was a vicious Egyptian princess who took fiendish delight in roasting her subjects over a blazing fire while she laughed and danced around the fire? God knows. God. Only God knows. She has prayed to Him for centuries. Has she had a "nod" from the Almighty or the lifting of a heavenly pinkie to acknowledge her, his lowly subject? Or, did he find pleasure in roasting her over the fires of a life without ending, being tantalizingly close to her beloved, and then to have him be pulled away—

or, worse—to cause her own death! Did God have a perverse and cruel sense of humor? Surely some reason exists for everything that happens—or has happened—in the world. Where was God? Did all the millions of people who worshiped, lived, died, killed, reveled, anguished, prospered, were tormented and dedicated themselves to God, Allah or whatever he was called commit a tremendous blunder of epic proportions? She could only believe that what had happened—and was happening—to her for four centuries was not normal, wasn't something that happened to everyone—to anyone—so there had to be a "higher power" who had his celestial hand on the tiller, if only casually.

Marisa remembered a story she'd read about the 2005 mega-hurricane, Katrina, and how a New Orleans neighborhood had flooded and people were being rescued from the rising waters, as it rose around their homes.

One old, black woman turned away rescuers in their boats, saying, each time, "God will take care of me." They left, but came back hours later, as the water continued to rise. Each time she said the same thing, "God will take care of me!" Finally, the water had gotten so high, the rescuers knew that, if she didn't leave then-and-there, she was going to drown. So, when she told them, "God will take care of me!" they replied, "God sent us for you." She looked at them for a moment, grabbed her cat, and stepped into the boat.

In a way, she was doing the same thing, for she'd planned that they leave North America by sailing away on a cargo ship from Toronto, Ontario, Canada.

On the other hand, she was planning—perhaps with a bit more madness—to attack a car with armed guards and free a prisoner, to spirit him away across the ocean. They may well react as most armed guards would—ripping their coats open and drawing large caliber handguns which would deal death to Marisa, Bill and everyone within pistol range. She had a sense of predisposition, sensing that, if she died in the attempt, it will have been a "worthwhile death," for, after all, if she didn't rescue Bill, he would molder away in a granite cell until he died, a bent, old man with rheumy eyes and phlegm in his throat.

If she was imagining or dreaming all of this, including the past lives, then she would suffer the ultimate ignominy: dying under the influence of an insane delusion.

Another great, heaving sigh, as she made preparations.

Her plan was undoubtedly flawed, but she couldn't see it. It wasn't as if she could Google the Internet for the "perfect" get-out-of-jail plan or have it reviewed by a committee at her law firm. She must draw on her own experience, intuition and basic understanding of human nature.

The die was cast: Bill, in the absence of some intervening higher power, would be transported from Upper Michigan to Detroit, located near the bottom of the Lower Peninsula. There was only one bridge, the Mackinac Bridge, between the two peninsulas. The only road of any consequence that led south from the bridge was I-75, where she would lie in wait.

If the transporting officers had kidneys made of cast iron and drove by the rest area she had dialed into her plans, then that was that. She would drive back to Detroit and go through the charade of having a Habeas Corpus hearing, asking for something she didn't want and suffer the anguish of seeing Bill, in chains, before the judge.

Perhaps he had committed murder. She didn't know for sure. He had pleaded guilty, but that wasn't much of a standard.

If this "dream" is true, and she fails in this attempt—or even is killed—then it will all begin again in some future life. She will be herself, although in some form she can't imagine, and Bill will be Uilliam once again. Perhaps they will be together at some time in the future or, failing that, throughout hundreds of more years. She knew in the essence of her soul that, somehow, they would be united. She thought of what Franz Kafka once said, "The heart is a seismographic instrument: it can record earthquakes, but it cannot predict them."

29 CENTRAL MICHIGAN: THE PRESENT

Marisa watched for southbound traffic traveling on Interstate 75. As she suspected, there were cars, SUV's and pickup trucks with one or two deer carcasses roped to the front fenders. One pickup truck, with a slide-in camper, had the deer mounted on the roof of the camper, its legs pointing forward and its head, a trophy buck, appeared to be flying like Superman. Cars going northbound, towards the Straits of Mackinac and the Upper Peninsula of Michigan, saw the spectacle and were flashing their headlights and honking their horns. One driver had both of his arms out his window and was waving wildly. He was driving wildly too, for his car almost went into the center median of the highway, such was his excitement.

Marisa was doing hunting of her own, but for two-legged prey—the kind that would shoot back. Under a newspaper on the seat next to her was a Charter Arms .44 caliber Bulldog revolver, loaded with blanks with realistic-looking wax bullets. She was more than willing to risk her own life to rescue William, but having lived various lives for 400 years, if she had learned anything it was that the Eternal Law of Karma was one law that she could never break. As a lawyer, she had more than a little disdain for the law, but she would not challenge Karma: she would not take someone else's life to save either Bill or herself—if they died, she knew, with certainty, that they would return to this world. It may be in 20 years or 100 years, but they would return, and, God willing, they would find one another.

It was for this reason she carried nothing with her that was actually lethal. Her equipment appeared to be lethal—that was the intent—in fact it appeared to be wildly deadly, but it was all Hollywood.

On the floor of the mini-motor-home she was driving were dummy Claymore mines along with arming wire and four large lever-operated suction cups, the type used by glass installers to carry large and heavy panes of glass to an installation site.

In the past weeks, Marisa had followed two Michigan Department of Corrections transportation vehicles as they left the Marquette State Prison for a prisoner transportation run to the Metropolitan Detroit area. It obviously had something to do with the number of hours that the transporting officers worked and the amount of time that it took to drive from Marquette to Detroit, but each of the vehicles left at five o'clock in the morning and traveled the same route southward, going across the Mackinac Bridge at about the same time and stopping at the same rest area on I-75. She, herself, drove a different rental car each time and she looked different on each occasion.

This time, she drove her dirty mini-motorhome. She looked like any other hunter, or, perhaps to the more cynical observer, one of the many prostitutes who traveled to Northern and Upper Michigan to provide services to hunters that the local Cabela's did not. That was fine with her, unless she attracted the attention of either the State Police or Sheriff's Department, or even a Conservation Officer, who drove police cars and had arrest powers.

She knew that the transportation car would have stopped for lunch west of St. Ignace, which was the small town anchoring the northern approaches to the Mackinac Bridge and that this routine stop at the rest area where she was waiting would be just far enough down the road from the usual lunch stop in the UP so that the guards were more than ready to stop, take a toilet break and smoke a cigarette. The inmates who were being transported ate box lunches and were not offered the niceties of a toilet break. Guantanamo Bay had taught state prisons a number of valuable lessons, one of which was the advantage of having inmates who were being transported wearing disposable diapers.

Naturally, the inmates absolutely hated wearing Depends, and several had filed fruitless lawsuits against the prison, claiming their constitutional rights were violated, the diapers were demeaning, and so forth, but the post 9/11 judiciary wasn't having any of it. One judge saying, in his ruling, that the inmate was lucky he wasn't wearing blackout goggles and earmuffs. Marisa was sure the inmate felt anything but "lucky."

There were no other cars or trucks at the rest area. She had first arrived there over an hour before and had installed a small battery powered gate motor on the gate at the entrance to the rest area. The gate, which swung down from the vertical, much like a railroad crossing gate, proclaimed that the rest area was closed. As soon as she installed it, a simple procedure, she toggled the matching remote control and the gate swung down. Considering Michigan's economy was always teetering on the edge of the abyss, drivers were not surprised to see the rest area closed. In fact, they would not have been surprised to have seen the Mackinac Bridge closed because of budget restrictions. When they saw the rest area closed, they gritted their teeth, crossed their legs or put their knees together and pressed onward. Even a police car passed by and didn't think anything of it.

Marisa could finally see the prison vehicle in the distance. She elevated the gate at the entrance to the rest area, hoping that the car nearest the prison vehicle would not need to make a "pit stop" as well. It didn't.

At a push of the button on her controller, the gate closed silently after the prison car was some 40 or 50 feet beyond it. She had to run the risk that a car may suddenly pull in from the expressway. She did not want to alert the prison officers that something was out of the ordinary. They appeared to be intent upon taking care of business at the rest area and did not seem to notice the gate closing.

Marisa was parked close to the rest area building but she left a parking space closer to the building, anticipating that the prison officer would park there. She knew that they would not get out immediately but rather would radio where they were and their intentions, take out their thermos jugs of coffee and have a cup or two before they went in, use the toilet, and smoke a cigarette or two.

She was higher than they were in their sedan, and she could see that there were two inmates in the back, each wearing orange jumpsuits and two uniformed officers in the front seat. The passenger was speaking into a hand-held microphone for the radio and then clipped it back onto the bracket on the dashboard.

At that, she stepped out of the truck, wearing an oversized snowmobile suit, a full-face Arctic weather mask and carrying a pair of wire cutters and large bolt cutters in her gloved hands. In a green canvas bag slung over her shoulder she had two dummy Claymore mines, the brown detonating wire and M142 Multipurpose Firing Device, the "clacker," an M5 Pressure Release Device, or "mousetrap" and the suction cups.

In one quick, practiced motion, she walked to the back of the prison car and snipped the radio antenna off at the base with the wire cutters she carried.

Seeing her motion, the guard in the passenger seat opened his door to look out to see what was going on. Marisa drew her revolver and pointed it at his face, bringing her left index finger to her lips, ordering silence.

The guard could see the round noses of the wax bullets in Marisa's revolver, and surmised that the pistol was loaded and she would kill him if he didn't comply.

She placed the dummy Claymore mine on the windshield of the car, turning them so the large, block letters, reading: "FORWARD TOWARD ENEMY" faced the men inside. She strung the arming wire around the other windows in an easy loop. She had a number of sheets of typewriter paper on which messages were laser printed in large letters. The papers were bound together in the upper left-hand corner, so she could thumb through them and find the message that she wanted. The first one said, "Claymore mine. Set to explode. Do not disturb detonating wire." She placed it, face down, on the windshield next to the Claymore. She could see the two guards' eyes become saucers as they read the message.

She turned to the next message and showed it to the guards: "Take out all weapons and cell phones by two fingers and put them out the driver's window."

The guards turned to one another as if to ask whether either of them were willing to forfeit their own lives to prevent an escape. Obviously, neither of them was, for they reluctantly complied with her order.

She took their equipment and placed it gingerly into her canvas bag. She signaled with a rotating moment of her index finger to roll the window back up, which the driver did. She placed the detonating wire against the window and secured it with a large piece of duct tape.

The next message she placed on the windshield was one the guards fully expected: "We want your prisoner." The two inmates, sitting in the backseat, behind the cage, were each reading the messages along with the guards, perhaps even more intently. Neither of them had any inkling of what was going down and they each presumed that this was a breakout planned by the other prisoner. In actuality, neither of them had any advance warning that the break was going to take place. This was to prevent any possibility of information leaking.

The two prisoners were each handcuffed with special prison-issued handcuffs that did not open with ordinary handcuff keys. Marisa had several of the keys. They each were locked to a chain which went to in eyebolt in the floor that was locked with an ordinary Master padlock. She heard a clunk as the driver unlocked the electric door locks.

She handed the special handcuff keys to the black prisoner who was sitting behind the driver. As she did that, she reached in and, using the long-handled bolt cutters, cut the chain. This allowed the black prisoner to unlock William's handcuffs since the black inmate could not reach the keyhole of his own cuffs. He passed the keys to William who then unlocked the first inmate's handcuffs. They both had leg irons on, which unlocked with standard handcuff keys, that were also on the ring Marisa had passed them.

In a moment, both inmates were out of the car, stretching their arms and laughing. Marisa slammed the door shut and strung the rest of the Claymore initiating wire around all the windows and, stretching it taut, secured it with tape.

Marisa terminated the wire at a small black box with three rubber antennas, commonly known as "rubber duckies," and stuck it to the windshield, next to the Claymore.

She showed the guards another message sheet which read, "Any cell phone or radio will detonate. Any vibration, glass breakage or a loud noise will detonate."

The guards turned pale and sat stock-still in their seats. Marisa removed a lightweight nylon car cover from her bag and, catching it in the light breeze, quickly enveloped the prison automobile.

Marisa motioned to the two prisoners to follow her. She tapped the black inmate on the shoulder and pointed to him to go into the camper. She took William by the elbow and pointed him to go into the cab of the pickup truck, which he did. He asked several questions, and she put her index finger to her lips, indicating silence. Reluctantly, he complied.

She started the engine, which, fortunately, fired instantly, slammed the transmission in reverse and backed out of the parking space. She drove quickly out of the rest area. She drove about two miles south to the next exit, which was a country road that passed over the Expressway. She drove across the country road and onto the beginning of the on-ramp and then stopped. She told William to get out and don't say anything, just to follow her.

She went to the camper and opened the door. She handed the keys to the black inmate, pointed to civilian clothes on the seat and handed him $500 in cash. He quickly put on civilian clothes and ran to the cab of the truck, jumped in and drove off, shouting his thanks and waving an arm out the window.

Marisa took off at a dead run across the overpass. Parked off the road, in a clump of trees, was the small, nondescript, 10-year-old sedan. Marisa opened the trunk with the remote and quickly started to undress, removing her wig and makeup. She put on a dress and flat shoes. William stood there in stunned silence and Marisa, seeing that he wasn't removing his *own* clothes, shouted, "Change-change-*change!*"

Soon William had changed his clothes and stood there, feeling wildly exposed in his hunter-orange pants and shirt.

"The best way to blend in as to look like everyone else. Everything, including the cows in the fields, are wearing blaze-orange during deer hunting season. Even if someone isn't hunting, no one wants to get shot accidentally and you don't want to get shot on purpose!"

They drove northward for twenty minutes, then pulled off down a farm lane. There were cars down every cow-path in Michigan during deer hunting season and aroused no undue attention.

"One last touch," announced Marisa, "your hair color needs to match your identification. Lean over the trunk."

Marisa snapped on a pair of latex gloves, pulled out a plastic pan and a bottle of red hair dye, which she quickly applied to William's head. In a moment, his hair and eyebrow color had been transformed. She took a clean towel and dried his hair the best she could, wrapped the dark-colored towel into itself and stuffed it into the roots of a nearby tree, kicking dirt after it, covering it.

"Am I supposed to have hair that matches the shirt?" William said, with a hint of a smile.

Marisa was shocked at the attempt at humor and laughed louder and longer than the joke deserved, but it made her feel good. William was secretly pleased that his lame joke had elicited such a positive response.

Together, they got into the car and continued northward.

Staying below the speed limit, they drove on secondary roads through the pinewood forests towards the Straits of Mackinac.

"William, I know you have 100,000 questions for me and I don't have 100,000 answers. Yes, it is I, your attorney and I have violated laws, oaths, principles and promises to help you escape. You were facing natural life in prison and I could not let it happen, for I made you a promise far longer ago than any promise I broke today. Hopefully, everything will make sense to you soon. Maybe it won't, but I fervently believe that I'm doing the right thing and hopefully we can pull this off."

Marisa looked over at William to see him nod gently, obviously hearing everything but understanding nothing. It wasn't but a moment before his head leaned over to the passenger side window and he quietly fell asleep from complete and utter exhaustion. Marisa smiled and gently touched his shoulder. It felt good.

30 NORTHERN MICHIGAN: THE PRESENT

Marisa was brimming with conversation, orders, directions and chatter. Bill raised his hand and she stopped talking.

"Excuse me just a God-damned minute," said Bill. "I've gone along with this. I don't think I was asked if I wanted to make a choice. We've added 'escape,' 'armed this-and-that' to my rap sheet. And, I might add, I wasn't guilty of murder, so this just adds icing to the cake. So, if you would, *please*, tell me what-the-fuck-is-going-*on!*"

He punctuated each of his last words by stabbing his right index finger downward in the air.

Marisa had anticipated both his frustration and anger. She took a moment to collect herself before she began. They were off the road on a two-track trail leading into a small copse of trees and the lights were off.

"I—I can explain. I think I can explain. I know you have no reason to trust me, to believe me, or even stay one minute longer. But, the die is cast and we must proceed. If you got out of this car, you'd be arrested within minutes and be back in the darkest hole in the Michigan prison system by noon tomorrow. I know."

Bill said nothing, which was good. Marisa took a breath and continued.

"I know you're not guilty of murder. Fact is, I don't really care if you did it or not. I was determined to get you out, no matter what. I will explain more later. I know some people who are, shall we say, very close to you. We go back a long way. A very long way. And, well, the time came and I stood up and went the distance. Do you like baseball?"

Bill nodded.

"Great. Me too. Let's just say that I'm the 'designated hitter.' I have special 'hitting skills' so I am 'at bat.' I don't know if that make sense." Marisa was on the verge of tears from pent-up emotions. She spoke again.

"You're going to pretend to be my brother. My real brother is in Australia but he left his Irish passport at home, figuring he didn't need it. Both of us were born in Ireland and came here as babies, but we have Irish citizenship. American, too, but still Irish. You don't look much like him, but no one sees beyond the red hair. You're Irish too. Do you feel Irish?" It was a rhetorical question—she didn't wait for an answer.

"We're driving to Cheboygan—staying off the expressway—then driving to Mackinaw City. We'll take a boat to Mackinac Island. Ever been there? No cars—horses only—and billions of bicycles. From there, we'll fly. I fly. I'm a pilot. We'll fly to Canada, then take a ship to England and go to Ireland. We'll be safe in Ireland. I always knew it would be Ireland."

"Ire-fucking-land! Christ on crutches!"

Although there undoubtedly would be a broad manhunt for Bill, they wouldn't be looking for this car, or a woman—although that was always a possibility, from simple deduction—and most of the searching would be to the south. Who would escape to the north-woods? Well, some would, but most would be going south, to the many big cities, or even out of the state. All of that was to the south. To the north was only the Upper Peninsula and, from Sault Ste. Marie, Michigan to Sault Ste. Marie, Ontario, Canada, a much bigger, far more industrialized city.

The car was running well. Marisa said, "Sleep if you can, Bill."

"Sleep!" he grunted. "Who can sleep?"

They arrived early in the morning at Mackinaw City. The car they were driving was a "local car," and, even beyond that, raised no interest. There were a few early "coffee shop" patrons around, some fishermen and no others. Although there were many tourists in town, they were all snug in their beds and saw no reason to get up so early.

"Bill. Grab these two duffel bags. I'll get the fishing poles."

"Fishing?" he inquired.

"Window dressing. You can fish if you want. Do you like to fish?"

He didn't answer, grabbing the army duffel bags. Marisa collected two tackle boxes and two fishing rods. She slammed the trunk, glanced through the car and locked the doors, pocketing the keys. Left in the parking lot with the many other cars at the ferry docks, it would attract no undue attention. People continually left cars there to go to Mackinaw Island, Boise Blanc Island or any number of other places, or just out into the lake for fishing, sightseeing or photography.

She led the way to the boat docks and stepped onto a finger dock, making her way directly to several small fishing boats, pointing a fishing rod at the last one on the left. Bill tossed the bags in and gingerly climbed aboard. He took the fishing rods and tackle boxes from Marisa and helped her aboard, then undid the two mooring lines from the dock.

"Do you know how to drive this thing?" he questioned.

"Of course! I was 'Daddy's Girl'!" Marisa answered, with more resolution than the facts deserved. It had been many years. She'd taken the boat out when she bought it a month or so ago, but not for very long.

She patted the pockets of her fishing life jacket for the keys, finding them, attached to a float in case they fell overboard. She had also found the car keys and deftly tossed them into the dark water.

Bill had noticed. "Guess there's no driving away. Shouldn't you have made sure the fucking boat would start first?"

Marisa flushed with the realization that he was completely right and was even more overwrought when the boat would not, in fact, start. It was a self-fulfilling prophecy. The electric starter spun the motor all right and the key was "on," she noticed. She was close to tears as Bill stared at her, wondering just what he'd gotten himself into. He expected the Coast Guard to descend on them at any moment, with boats and helicopters.

She thought about the starting sequence and then had a flash of inspiration.

"Prime the bulb!" she said, a little too loudly. "Over there. The fuel line. Squeeze that rubber bulb a few times!"

He saw what she was pointing at in the pre-dawn light and pumped the priming bulb in the rubber fuel line. In a moment, she tried the starter again and the motor popped and sputtered, then settled down to a steady sound. She was greatly relieved.

The motor clunked into reverse and she backed slowly out of the slip. Once she cleared the dock, she put the gearshift into forward and moved steadily away, causing no wake, in keeping with the large signs so ordering.

"We going to die?" Bill asked, sarcastically.

"Everyone dies. Some live forever, though," she added, cryptically.

31 MACKINAC ISLAND, MICHIGAN: THE PRESENT

It didn't take too long to motor across the Straits of Mackinac. Great, long, freighters—"ore boats"—plied the Straits, going west to Lake Michigan, south to Lake Huron and beyond, or north to Lake Superior, going through the locks at Sault Ste. Marie. They couldn't—or wouldn't—turn, so small boats had to be on their guard. The helmsman on the ore carriers wouldn't even feel a bump if they ran over almost anything but a very large vessel.

Tourists were on the move at the landing at Mackinac Island. Long a fortress and still there, preserved for hundreds of years, it was now a prime tourist destination. The movie, *Somewhere in Time,* was filmed there, starring Christopher Reeves and Jane Seymour. The Grand Hotel—with the "world's longest front porch" was the set for the movie, where Christopher traveled back in time to 1912 to meet Jane—'Elise'—only to lose her, rocketing back to the present day when he saw a modern penny he had with him when he journeyed to 1912. Marisa had always thought of *Somewhere in Time* as her favorite movie, but she never had a conscious reason for so thinking. Now, since the explosion of recollections had taken place, upon meeting Bill for the first time, she poignantly knew why she felt such kinship with the movie. She shared none of this with Bill, for he acted as if he were shell-shocked and she wouldn't add to it.

The boat was tied to a public dock and they disembarked, taking their duffel bags with them but leaving the fishing gear. The boat's key was pocketed for it wouldn't look right to see it in the ignition. She wondered about the fishing gear, but she saw gear in other boats. She presumed that the Mackinac Islanders weren't a larcenous lot.

Bill carried the duffel bags and she, her purse. She wore dungarees herself and a light jacket, as befitted the coolish morning.

Within a moment, they looked up and down the street of the town and soon spotted a horse drawn carriage near a sign that said, "Livery." An old word, to be sure.

They made their way to the carriage and saw the driver, pouring steaming coffee from a shiny thermos bottle.

He looked up, saying, "Mornin' Need a lift?"

Marisa nodded, and said, "Airfield."

This wasn't unusual, so the man finished his coffee as Bill and Marisa climbed aboard into the back seat, their bags at their feet.

The driver clucked to the horse and they pulled away, moving towards the Grand Hotel, going up a small hill. The horse strained in his harness as he moved forward.

"Live near here?" asked the driver.

"Windsor," responded Marisa.

"Ah. 'Canucks.' Get a lot of 'em here. 'Loonies' are doin' better all the time. Staying in town?"

Marisa closed the conversation by adding, "Mackinaw City," then saying, with false excitement, "Oh, look, Gord!" to Bill, "the fort looks so nice in the morning!"

Every other Canadian male seemed to be called "Gord," so the driver was content that all was right with the world and continued on, slapping the reins on the horse's rump, encouraging her to go a bit faster as Marisa pointed out things to the silent, red-headed, "Gord."

Within a short time, they arrived at the small airstrip serving the island. There were three aircraft parked on the tarmac.

The "cabbie" didn't go too closely to the airplanes as he didn't want to damage them in some way or spook the horse.

"That's $25."

"$25!" cried Marisa. "We didn't want to buy the damned horse!" She would have paid anything, but knew if she didn't protest, she'd draw undue attention to herself.

The driver was taken aback for a moment. "Ah, $20 Canadian, I meant."

Marisa grumbled but pulled out a Canadian $20 bill and handed it to him along with a gold-colored $1 coin—a "loony"—as it had the image of a loon, thus creating, forever, the nickname for Canadian dollars: "loonies." He looked at it too long then stuffed it in his pocket, happy enough for an early-morning fare, even Canadian cheapskates. The running joke on the island was that Canadians came to Mackinac Island with a Canadian $100 bill and one pair of underwear—and never changed either!

"Giddy-up, Emmy!" he called to his horse and moved down the blacktop road, away from the airfield.

There was no one at the field at that hour and dew covered the airplanes.

"Tell me we're going to fly in the big one," said Bill, not believing it himself.

"No, we're going to fly in that little white one down there, with the blue stripes and T-tail. These are American planes—their numbers start with 'N.' We're Canadians, so we're going in the one that starts with 'C.' Got it?" she said, more lightheartedly than she felt.

She unlocked the plane and motioned for Bill to put the bags in the open, carpeted area behind the two front seats.

"Don't you need to tie them down or something?" wondered Bill.

"No. No need. They aren't going anywhere that we aren't."

Since there were only two seats, she directed Bill to the right seat and told him to buckle up as she went around the plane, performing a preflight check, drawing fuel from each of the wing tanks to see if there was any contaminating water and checked the engine oil and other parts under the cowl, going around the wings, propeller, and tail. The plane had three wheels—"tricycle landing gear"—so it sat level on the tarmac.

Soon Marisa was inside, buckling up herself and fitting her headphones. She pointed to a set of headphones on the floor between them and Bill put them on, moving the boom microphone in front of his mouth. It almost looked as if he knew what he was doing.

Marisa turned on the key and checked the two magnetos and other gauges. Everything was in the right position. She went through the preflight: flaps, control wheel free, and so forth, then turned the key to "start." The propeller started to turn slowly, then more quickly as the oil warmed up. The motor started immediately. She waited until the temperature gauge was in the right place and then advanced the throttle after she checked the windsock for the direction of the wind.

Satisfied that she was taking off in the right direction, she moved to the top of the only runway. She could hear Bill's voice in a muffled manner, and then clicked the headsets over to "intercom."

"What?" she asked, curtly. Too curtly, she considered, but she was preoccupied.

"Are you sure you can fly this fucker? Aren't you the girl who couldn't start the goddamned boat?" he asked, clearly not a flier.

"How hard can it be? I played the video game!" she added, cruelly.

She glanced over to see Bill gulp as she pulled the throttle all the way, her feet still on the toe brakes, as she wiggled the controls one more time, then held them in the neutral position.

"See you on the other side!" she shouted, over the roar of the engine, as the plane accelerated down the runway, picking up speed and becoming lighter as it began to get airborne.

She turned to the left after she released the flaps, as she wanted one last look at "Big Mac," the Mackinac Bridge, glistening in the early morning light.

"Goodbye, Old Friend," she said to the bridge, "I'll see you on the other side, too."

32 DETROIT, MICHIGAN, USA: THE PRESENT

Ben's wife, Kristin, was in the office of Ben's Benz when she heard a racking sound of abject anguish coming from outside the office, towards the entryway. She hurried to the sound. The mechanics were busy with their jobs and hadn't heard the noises. Kristin quickly looked around, and, to her horror, saw Ben sitting on a case of oil, bent over, his chest heaving with deep sobs. She ran to him.

"Ben!" she cried. "What's wrong? Is it the kids? Tell me!"

Ben looked up, wiping his nose with the back of his arm, staining his blue coveralls.

All he could manage was, "Not kids. Car. Cash." He handed her a Federal Express box, ripped open at the end.

Kristin couldn't imagine what was going on. She shook the contents out of the box and the contents cascaded out of her hands. She was stunned to see huge amounts of hundred dollar bills, bound together with bank straps, a set of keys and what appeared to be a Michigan automobile title. A notarized Bill of Sale fluttered down. On one of the packs of money she saw a note, written with a fountain pen in a feminine hand.

"She's all yours, Benjamin. Take good care of her. She'll be delivered today. Here's some gas money. I can't thank you enough for being there for me. Love to Kristin. See you on the other side. Marisa."

"I don't understand. What is all of this? Is Marisa giving you her Mercedes? Money? There must be thousands!"

"Try $250,000. God only knows what the car's worth. Doesn't matter. I don't want any of it. I want my friend back. Fuck the money. 'Other side.' That can only mean one thing—she's gone." Ben sobbed again.

Kristin was thunderstruck. Ben had many friends but Marisa was very special to both of them. She rubbed her hand on his broad shoulders, trying to gather her toughest.

Quietly, she said, "Ben. Oh, Ben. I can't bear to see you cry. She'll be fine. You'll see. Call her. See what's going on. We can give it all back to her and have a big laugh over it. We were rich for ten minutes!"

Ben looked up at her, hoping she was right.

☙

Downtown at the law firm offices at the Renaissance Center, another FedEx messenger had just left. He wouldn't leave the delivery with the receptionist, although the receptionist very nearly insisted. Instead, Wanda was called and signed for it, after having to produce her driver's license.

Wanda rarely got personal deliveries at work and was curious. She took it back to her office, although the receptionist was clearly disappointed that Wanda didn't open it in front of her, sharing in the discovery of what it might be.

Wanda tore the end off the box and allowed a hesitant peek inside, as if there was a prank somehow attached. She looked up quickly, startled. She jumped from her desk chair and went to the floor-to-ceiling windows looking out onto the office itself and pressed the button that electrically closed the blinds.

Returning to her desk, she looked inside once more, disbelieving what she'd seen.

She reached inside and removed a pack of hundred dollar bills. She soon removed the rest, glancing furtively around. Irrationally, she thought there was a hidden camera, recording her taking illegal drug money. She envisioned a squad of black-clad cops with machine-guns rushing in and throwing her to the floor. Being cautious, she tucked the money into a desk drawer, quickly calculating that there was a quarter of a million dollars in hundreds. She felt like she wasn't breathing.

Looking expectantly inside again, she saw an envelope, which she poured out. Inside was a notarized and witnessed deed. Her own name was shown as the grantee and the grantor was—Marisa! Oh my God! She thought. Marisa! What has she gone and done?

The warranty deed was for Marisa's million dollar condo. The purchase price was $1.00, love and affection. She was overwhelmed with conflicting thoughts. Wanda lived with her mother in Hamtramck, an arrangement her mother loved, but which Wanda found chaffing. She looked for a note and found one, recognizing Marisa's handwriting.

"My dear Wanda. This isn't one of those 'If you read this, I must be dead' letters. I promise you, I'm starting a fresh life. I can't tell you more. In fact, shred this letter. I know you're a pack rat, and will want to keep it, but please, please don't. That which you don't know you don't have to lie about. My condo's yours, plus the 'milk money.' Nothing—money, houses—can repay you for your kindness and friendship over the years. Please call Benjamin at Ben's Benz and tell him not to worry; that I'm fine. I gave him my car and some gas money. I'll never forget you as a very special friend. Love, Marisa."

Wanda made a large explosion of breath and laid the palms of her hands on the desk, as if to hold it down. She folded the letter and made to tuck it into her purse and remembered Marisa's words. She leaned to the shredder near her desk and slipped the letter into the slot, hearing the whirring of the teeth as it ground the letter into tiny flecks of paper.

She reached for the phone and checked the number. In a moment, a man answered.

"Ben? This is Wanda. Yes, Marisa's assist....Marisa's friend. Did you get a package? Marisa's fine. Don't think terrible thoughts. No, she wants you to have it all. She's going to be just fine."

33 ONTARIO, CANADA: THE PRESENT

Marisa busied herself by turning knobs on the instrument panel and occasionally tapping gauges, while she looked both left and right for any other aircraft, for they were flying by Visual Flight Rules or "VFR." Bill, sitting uncomfortably in the right front seat, had no clue what any of the instruments or controls were, although he knew, instinctively, that if he touched anything, the light plane would immediately crash and scatter him for miles around.

The air was heavy with their silence. Since they flew out of the small airstrip on Mackinac Island, Marisa was busy getting, and keeping the aircraft flying, and Bill was not about to do anything that would jeopardize her ability to do so. He was deeply conflicted and more worried than he had been in a very long time. While he knew he was not guilty of the murder for which he was sentenced to life in prison, he surely was now guilty of prison escape, complicity in armed assault, escape and any number of charges that they could, and would, throw at him. When he was captured—and he knew he would be before long—they would chain him to the dank walls of the darkest dungeon in the Michigan prison system.

It sounded like a line from a television comedienne, but he asked, "Can we talk?"

Marisa almost seemed surprised that there was someone in the airplane besides herself, or that, perhaps, she was shocked to hear another person's voice. Startled a bit, she looked over at Bill. She tapped the large plastic earpiece of her right headset and tapped the extended microphone in front of her mouth, pointing at his headset's boom mike, which was askew, motioning for him to put it in front of his mouth.

Once he did, she fiddled with the intercom controls and he was startled to hear her voice loudly over the headphones. Sensing his difficulty, she turned down the volume slightly.

"I couldn't hear you over the aircraft noise. Did you want something?" she asked.

Now hesitant, perhaps because of the apparent personal nature of the intercom set up, Bill didn't say anything.

"All right, if you need something, let me know," she added, going back to her flying duties.

"No, wait! I, I, you have something to say. I mean, I guess I appreciate your breaking me out..." He stumbled.

"You guess? You *guess?!* Jesus H. Christ! You *guess?"* She sputtered.

"No, I mean, of course, of course I'm grateful. If you hadn't sprung me, I would rot in that shithole for the next 50 years if I didn't get stuck or clubbed over the head with an iron bar before them. What I'm trying to say is, you don't really know me from Adam, and maybe you think you feel something for me—many women are attracted to cons, especially lifers—but why would you risk everything for the likes of me?"

Marisa made an audible intake of breath and hesitated before she answered Bill. She was concentrating so hard on saying the right thing that she didn't realize that her right wing was getting lower with each passing moment. Bill looked out the windshield and saw that the horizon was at an angle and said, "Excuse me, but aren't we supposed to be flying level?"

"Jesus!" She exclaimed. "I'm sorry. I'm really sorry. I was just trying to concentrate on answering you. I have been expecting your question – – why wouldn't I?"

"Say listen, I don't really want you to crash the plane just to answer my question. We can talk about this later."

"I'm a very good pilot," said Marisa, softly.

Bill laughed suddenly and loudly, which elicited dark clouds and an instantaneous frown from Marisa.

"What's so funny? I am an excellent pilot!"

Still laughing, Bill replied, "No. Don't misunderstand. I wasn't talking about your flying skills. My flying skills would give us a quick dirt blanket. When you said that, it sounded like Rainman when he said, 'I'm an excellent driver'."

The smile returned to Marisa's face and she said, "But never on Monday. Definitely not Monday."

They both laughed together and realized that they had come closer, courtesy of the lame joke.

Marisa began slowly, "Do you, ah, believe in reincarnation?"

"You mean like coming back to life as a dog or a Shetland pony? That kind of thing?"

"Yes, that's reincarnation in a general sense. It is sort of like the Indians believe that each life is a different test or experience, and, when you die, you will come back to life, and what you return as depends on what kind of person you were in the previous life. I'm not talking about that kind of karmic experience, but I am trying to tell you that I believe that when we die we don't just turn to dust and become one with the earth."

Marisa looked intently at Bill's face and could tell that she was already losing him. He either didn't understand anything she was saying or patently disbelieved her.

"Bill, did you ever have the experience that so many people have, called déjà vu, where you feel like something you are experiencing in the present was something you had already done before or had seen in the past?"

"Of course, I think everybody has experienced that. I never heard a word attached to it. What was that word?"

"Déjà vu. It is the French expression meaning 'already seen'."

Bill was watching the emptiness of the sky as they flew, occasionally looking over at Marisa with a great deal of puzzlement. She was certainly a stunner, he thought, but also a likely head case.

Marisa forged ahead, saying, "Did you ever meet a stranger that you knew there was no chance of ever having met him or her before, but you were convinced in your mind that you knew this person?"

"Yeah, sure—sometimes. I just figure that they reminded me of someone."

"Tell me, Bill. When you first saw me at the gas station, or any time after that—did you feel that you had known me before? Remember I asked you something like this at Marquette. Think very carefully, if you would."

Bill paused for a long moment before answering. "I have to say, no. I don't want to hurt your feelings, but no. Do you think that I am the reincarnation of someone you knew before, maybe who died when you were younger or something? An old boyfriend or ex-husband?"

"No!" She blurted. "I've never been married, and there were damned few boyfriends."

"Sorry to hear that. Too much of the career woman for them?"

Marisa's face clouded over for an instant, but then she realized that he wasn't trying to be cruel. She answered quietly, "No. Certainly I have always been career-oriented, probably too much so, but there just never seemed to be Mr. Right. I know it sounds trite. There weren't even a great many Mr. Wrongs. I think I always had a deep set feeling that there was someone out there for me, but only one man, whom I never found."

"Since you committed a courthouse full of felonies to spring me out of prison, were you thinking that I was that guy? I mean, I'm honored that you might think so, but that is a damn poor reason to end up in prison or dead. I mean, you don't know me from the man in the moon."

"What I'm going to tell you will sound insane. I assure you I am not nuts. Please just listen to me, hear my story, and decide for yourself. I wouldn't blame you if you jumped from this airplane without a parachute after you hear this crazy lady tell her tale. Give me just one fighting chance to try to explain the unexplainable. Can you do that?"

Bill nodded quietly, giving her a strange look and readjusted his position in his seat, but his uncomfortableness had nothing to do with the seating.

"You and I knew each other in the past. The very, very distant past, about 400 years ago, in Donegal, Ireland. You are an O'Donnell now. You were an O'Donnell then. Your family were the clansmen of Donegal."

She looked over at him and saw his mouth partly open in abject astonishment. She soldiered on.

"In fact, you and I were married to each other. We lived in the castle of the Clan O'Donnell. Around the year 1600, the castle was attacked by the English and set alight. We could not escape the castle and we burned to death in the fire."

Bill said, "Come on, lady. I didn't just fall off the turnip truck. This is the biggest bunch of owl shit I have ever heard in my life. If I had parachute I would hit the silk. Did you just escape from the looney bin? I mean, give me a fucking break! Irish castles? 400 years ago? I must have looked like a prize turkey when you dreamed up this little number. If we weren't flying across Ontario, I would be looking for hidden cameras and figure I was on some kind of TV show. Do I look that stupid?"

"No, Bill, you don't look stupid at all. I told you this was going to sound bizarre. It sounds bizarre to me and I'm the one telling you. Will you just listen for a few more moments to hear me out? Please?"

"Well, it's not like I have anything better to do or any place else to go so spin your story," he replied.

"Thank you for that, anyway. As I was saying, we both were killed in the fire. According to Christian beliefs, we would go to heaven, hell, or purgatory. I think we went to purgatory and I will tell you what purgatory is. Purgatory is going to a place that you don't remember and suddenly find yourself as a new person, in a new body, perhaps even of a different race but always the same gender, and you don't remember anything that happened before. No, that's not precisely true. I went many years before I came back to life as someone else, and I never remembered anything that had happened before in Ireland, and I didn't remember you. During that new life I did finally meet you, and you were a completely different person as well. I did not recognize you but, when we chanced to accidentally touch, I instantly remembered my past life with you in Donegal and recognize you, even as your new self, as my sweet Uilliam. You, on the other hand plainly did not know me, either as the person I am now or as I was, many years earlier, in Donegal."

"That is an amazing crock of—that's an amazing story. So, did we get married in this new life and live happily-ever-after in a storybook castle?"

"No, Bill. There were no happily-ever-afters for us. You killed me."

J.A. Greenleaf

34 ONTARIO, CANADA: THE PRESENT

After what Marisa considered to be a horrific attempt at explaining the unexplainable as she told Bill about several of the past life events, he grew more doubtful with each revelation.

At one point he asked, "So, if I get this right, over the past four centuries I have pretty much ended each of these lives by killing you or somehow letting you die. End result is, each time you die and I live. Is that right? Is that what's going to happen this time—I'm going to kill you?"

"I hope to God that isn't to be. If the past is any prediction of the future, there is every chance." Marisa could see Bill's discomfiture and quickly added, "Do I think so? No, honestly, I *don't* think so. I want to only believe in good things and I want to think that, someday, you and I will be, well, we will be together." The last was said quite sadly.

They were driving across the Ontario countryside in an old car with Ontario license plates that Marisa had prepositioned at the small airfield where they had landed a short while ago. Marisa was pleased, at least, that Bill hadn't taken off on a dead run as soon as the plane landed. That was something. Perhaps it was just that he really had nowhere to go and he was a stranger in a strange country, and he might as well ride this out.

"I have absolutely no idea what you're talking about. Are you saying that we are really married and we are just celebrating our 400th

234

anniversary? What's the present for the 400th anniversary? Granite? Maybe a little granite pyramid?"

Marisa laughed. "I'm glad you can make jokes about it, even at my expense, but no, we aren't married. We may not even like one another, but I obviously have sacrificed everything I have and all that I ever will be because I truly believe what I just told you. I'm sure you don't believe a word of it, but I'm hoping that there will be some kind of revelation or magical moment or something that will bring you to the realization that it is all completely and absolutely true. And, thank you for not running, screaming, from the plane and making 'cross' signs at me with your index fingers."

He smiled at the idea, for he thought of doing something like that but sensing her absolute seriousness, he decided against it.

"Here's the plan. It isn't the best plan, but it is the only plan I have. We are going to Donegal, Ireland. I have never been there in my life—at least this life—but I am drawn to it like a lodestone. I believe in the core of my being that, if we can make it to Donegal Castle—which has been restored, by the way, according to my Google search back home—everything will come to light, the skies will open, the earth will move and the seas will part. Or something like that, anyway. We're going by ship because every flight from the North American continent is scrutinized for international terrorists and they will see us in a New York Minute. I'm traveling under my own name. My brother and I both have Irish citizenship and passports because we were born in Ireland. Not Donegal, as luck would have it, but Ireland nonetheless. I relieved my brother, Tim, of the burden of carrying an Irish passport with him and you are now he. He has red hair and freckles—inherited, no doubt, from both Granny and our Viking ancestors."

"Did I forget to tell you that you were my *idiot* brother Tim? You can understand, more or less, what people are saying, but please, for the love of God, don't say anything, to anyone. If they ask you a question, just give a monstrously big smile and pretend that you are a certified halfwit."

"That I can do. I'm very good at acting stupid. It must be my eighth-grade education."

"Eighth-grade? I would have guessed seventh-grade." She said this with a light punch to his left arm and they both laughed as they drove on.

She made a little square frame with her fingers and tried to imagine Bill passing for Tim and the photograph in Tim's Irish passport. She wasn't particularly pleased with the results and the likeness, but there wasn't anything she could do about it. She didn't have the capability to change the photograph—it was sealed under plastic that had security printing on it—so she just hoped for the best. She didn't think that the Canadians would much care who *left* Canada, as long as they left plenty of money behind. She imagined that most infamous Arab terrorist could probably doff his turban to the authorities on his way out and they wouldn't care.

They went through a drive-in at a McDonald's restaurant and she said, "Bill, in the glove compartment are some loonies. Give me some, please."

"Loonies in the glove box? I thought you were the only loony in this car," smiling as he said it.

"Absolutely hilarious. Loonies are Canadian dollars. We have to pay for this delicious lunch. Hand over some. What do you want?"

He quickly said that he would "kill for a Big Mac" then just as quickly realized what he said was likely to be taken the wrong way, in light of the conversation they had been having.

Marisa realized this, and assured him that she didn't take anything that he said to heart.

She ordered Bill not one, but two Big Macs, a large fry and a large Coke, all of which he consumed greedily. She enjoyed watching a hungry man eat ravenously. She tried not to think that the reason probably was because he had been in prison.

A month before, both she and Tim had driven from Detroit to Windsor, Ontario, and had shown their American passports when they arrived in Canada. The Canadians stamped their passports and she and Tim both asked if they could get their Irish passports stamped, since they didn't have any visa stamps in their passports. The Canada Customs woman hesitated at first, and then said, "Why not?" By this serendipitous action, Marisa had both her and Tim's passports, valid Irish ones, with genuine Canada immigration stamps within the time that Canada would allow Irish visitors to stay. She doubted that Canada Customs would be present at the departing freighter they were going to travel on, but it was likely that the ship's purser would scrutinize the passports and make sure that they had not entered Canada illegally. She imagined that there was some kind of fine for violation of these unknown rules and regulations; every government had a plethora of minutia to wade through.

As they neared the city center of Toronto, they realized how huge Toronto was, punctuated by the exclamation point of the CN Tower at the lakefront. She had been to Toronto a number of times before, but Bill had never been out of the United States and he gawked like a farm boy in New York City.

She consulted her newly-acquired portable Garmin GPS for the shipping company's dockside address and followed the precise statements of the GPS's computer voice, a woman. She had heard about people blindly following GPS instructions and driving down hills, off the road and along railroad tracks. She promised herself that she wouldn't turn into Lake Erie, even if ordered to by the robot voice.

35 TORONTO, ONTARIO, CANADA, ABOARD SHIP: THE PRESENT

They soon reached the dock and stared up at the huge ship which seemed like an aircraft carrier to them both. She found the parking lot that was described in the information packet sent her, and quickly made it past the bored security guard reading a girlie magazine in the guard shack. Some things never change, she thought.

They each had two suitcases—*apropos* for people heading for a European vacation.

"Let me guess," asked Bill, "all of the clothes will fit me perfectly."

"That only happens in spy movies. I took a wild guess after seeing you a couple of times in court. I can pretty much guess that they will be either too big or too small. If they fit, it would be a miracle."

"Well, that's something to look forward to. It is going to be a very long ocean voyage. At least I'll have romance with my ex-wife."

"You don't have an ex-wife that I know of, and I doubt very much there will be any romance. It would look pretty funny for a brother and sister, wouldn't it? We have separate staterooms. We will spend time together—the boat is big, but not that big—but we have to remember to act like we're brother and sister. You know, we pretty much dislike one another but don't choke each other so as to not upset the family."

They walked down the dock, each lost in separate thoughts. She wondered if she had made the most colossal blunder of her life because of some mad delusion that she had dreamed up. She thought not, but the entire premise was so fantastical that, were it true, it would be worthy of a Greek epic. She looked over at Bill, and he was obviously troubled. She wanted to hold him, but she realized that it was her lost love that she wanted to hold, not this stranger who may or may not be her Uilliam.

There was a long, precarious looking gangway leading to the ship and they trundled across it and into the bowels of the ship, where they were met by a smiling man in a trim Merchant Marine officer's uniform. He greeted them warmly with what sounded like a Scandinavian accent. He confirmed that by pointing to his name tag that identified him as Lars Swenson, the ship's purser.

Examining the sheaf of papers on his clipboard, he said, "Brother and sister? We get a lot of sisters—usually maiden sisters—but haven't had too many brother and sister passengers. Welcome aboard the Gulf Flyer. Your cabins are next to one another. I will give you time to get unpacked. Since we are still loading cargo, please don't go on the deck. You'll see signs that say no admittance, crew only and that sort of thing. Please obey them and there won't be any problem with anyone getting injured. This is a working ship. We take passengers, but it will work safely only if you remember our primary mission is as a freighter. People like to classify ships like ours as 'tramp steamers,' but tramp steamers are largely a thing of the past. I'm sure there are some in the Far East, Africa and in Latin America. We operate on a schedule and that schedule says we will depart at 1800 hours. We will have our evening meal a little later tonight because of our late departure. If you get hungry before that, there is always food available in the galley. You have only to ask."

"Irish, I see. We Scandinavians have a great kinship with the Irish, and, judging by your hair color, perhaps a little more kinship then we can admit to!"

With a smile and a wave, he handed them over to a smiling Filipino steward who beckoned them forward, grabbing the suitcases from

Marisa's hands. With Pidgin English and a gap-toothed smile, he marshaled them through the ship to their compartments. He took Marisa's suitcases and put them on the protective pad on the bed and showed her where the bathroom was, how to work the television and the location of the closet. Finally, he left and she breathed a heavy sigh of relief when the door shut behind him. She sat in the chair and softly began to cry, more from relief than anything else.

She desperately wanted to break down the door to Bill's stateroom and crush him in her arms—or, better yet, be crushed by him in a supernova of lust. She truly believed that she wasn't the cruel victim of some bizarre psychosis, as yet unnamed and undiagnosed. She felt like she was living the words of the American Revolutionaries who said they pledged their "lives, their fortunes and their sacred honor." She, like them, pledged her life, lost her fortune and destroyed her honor, and violated her oaths as a lawyer—for what? What jury wouldn't scream out, "Guilty! Guilty! Guilty!" thirty seconds after her trial began? Not even the most jaded forensic psychiatrist would believe anything she said—not even her name. Her name? What was her name? The name she was born with? When? Thirty-something years ago? Four hundred years ago? She felt like she was having an episode of vertigo. The stateroom rotated slowly around her as if she were on a carousel. It was a disturbing experience and she wondered if she was losing—or had lost—her sanity. What had she done? Was putting Bill—poor, simple Bill—in mortal danger the way she showed her—what?—four-hundred-year old "love?" By what definition was this madness anything approximating love?

Her quiet sobbing soon cascaded into a howling bawl that caused her chest to heave and the chair to quake with her cries.

She didn't realize the cacophony she was making until she heard a soft, metallic tapping on her stateroom door. She didn't hear the rapping at first, and then did, as it got louder. Quickly wiping and blowing her nose with a quick handful of Kleenex, she coughed and cleared her throat.

"Yes?" she asked, hesitatingly, her voice cracking.

"Señorita. You are OK, sí?" said the Filipino steward, whose voice she recognized.

"Yes. Sí. I'm fine. Bueno."

"I get your *hermano?*"

"Hermano?" she thought. Brother.

"No, it is fine. I am fine. Homesick. I'm homesick for my mother. Mi madre."

"I collect your *hermano, sí?*"

She cracked the door so he could see her.

"I'm fine. Really. Thank you. Just sad for home."

He smiled, displaying his gold teeth—clearly where a large portion of his steward's paycheck went—and seemed satisfied with her words and the fact that she wasn't injured in any way.

She saw him turn away and she shut the door, leaning against it, choking back yet more sobs.

The steward apparently was trying yet one more time, for she heard soft tapping on the door again. Still leaning with her back braced against the door, she called out, a bit too loudly, "I'm all right! Please leave me alone!"

She heard Bill's voice answer quietly, "Sorry. Didn't mean to intrude."

Fortunately, she hadn't relocked the door and spun around to wrench it open to see Bill turning away. "Wait!" she called. "I thought it was the damned steward. I mean, he meant well, but wouldn't take no for an answer."

Bill turned back towards her, taking in her disheveled hair and red eyes and puffy face.

"The damned steward," Bill said, smiling at the tiny joke, "called me 'Herman' and said you were sad and wanted your mother."

"Herman? No, *'hermano'*–brother. Remember?" Marisa smiled at the thought of Bill being called "Herman."

"All right. I'm off to check out this tub. You sure you're OK?" asked Bill.

"Yes. No. I don't know. Would you like to come in for a bit? I'm sure the steward won't mind." Marisa smiled sweetly and Bill entered the stateroom.

"Sit in my one-and-only chair. I'll take the bunk," said Marisa.

Bill walked over to her and gently moved her stray lock of hair back and over her left ear and stroked her left cheek with the back of his hand. Marisa felt her heart quicken. "Oh my God in heaven," she thought. "What demons cometh forth?"

She was shocked into silence when Bill kissed her tenderly on her lips, still with twinges of salty tears. She saw a kaleidoscope of images from hundreds of years of life, death, hope, misery, solitude and grinding hopelessness. She cried out at the experience of the unexpected kiss and the burst logjam of freed emotions. She put her hands up defensively and pushed Bill back.

Bill moved back a step and seemed confused.

"Listen, I'm sorry. It isn't you. I'm, I'm in a sorry state. The gravity of all of this is catching up with me. The kiss kind of surprised me. I appreciate it, I really do. But I need to explain what is going on—or what I think is happening."

"I get the picture, I'm your long-lost dead husband's ghost or something."

"You are the most solid ghost I've ever seen!"

"You've seen lots of ghosts?" he asked, smiling.

"I've seen ghosts for four centuries," she replied, feeling crazier than ever.

"Ghosts like hobgoblin ghosts—'Ghostbusters' ghosts?"

"Hardly. My ghosts were alive and sometimes well. You were one of my 'ghosts'—I was too. OK. Here comes more of the nutty stuff. If you want to write me off as a raving lunatic, go right ahead."

Pensively, Bill said, quietly, "No. Go ahead. I can pretty much guarantee, from what you've told me already, that I won't believe a damn word of it, but I certainly wouldn't object to hearing your story. You obviously believe it."

Touching him on the top of his forearm, Marisa said, "It is your story, too, Bill. Believe it or don't—at this point I'm past caring. I've jettisoned my entire life; money, friends, career and probably my liberty for what you think are delusions of a madwoman. I can tell you, if someone I didn't even know came up to me and told me all of this, I'd run for the nearest exit. Maybe it is lucky for me we are on a ship in the middle of the Atlantic Ocean—you can't get away, unless you're a very strong swimmer!"

She looked at him, pleadingly, studying his eyes and face for any signs of derision or ridicule. Seeing none, she forged ahead.

"OK, Bill. Here's the Reader's Digest condensed version. Can I prove a goddamned word of it? Not at the moment, but that's why we're going to London. I'll explain that in a moment."

"We knew one another from childhood as we lived in a very small community in what became County Donegal, Ireland. You were an O'Donnell, just as you are now, a member of the Clan O'Donnell and your father was the Chieftain. My name was 'Máire' and yours was

'Uilliam.' It was over four hundred years ago, towards the end of the 1500s."

Marisa paused for a moment, looking directly at Bill. He rubbed the whisker stubble on his chin, seemingly contemplatively, or at least she hoped. Hearing nothing, she continued.

"We were married and, by my estimation, could not have been more in love. When you were home, we were inseparable. You often went off with the men, hunting and warring or whatever it was that men did. This all came to a horrible, horrible end when, for no reason that I know of, the goddamned English attacked O'Donnell Castle. You and I were on the highest floor and there was no way out; the castle had been set afire by the Sasenach—the English. Why they did, I will never know. I have tried to determine what happened by researching the events in the past weeks, but, beyond the bare facts, the dates, the numbers of the Sasenach, estimates of the Irish dead: the stuff of history books. There was nothing as to why, in God's name, they would have done it. Regardless of the reasons, it happened."

"The stairs were engulfed in flames. Some young girls, together with you and me, were in the highest floor of the castle, on the side by the river. There were slit windows on the river side, but they were too small to allow anyone to get out, although several of the girls, screaming and shouting tried to get out. Even if they could have gotten through the opening, we were at such a height that jumping to the rocks or shallow river below would have been fatal. I'm sure anyone who could have gotten through would have preferred that to burning alive—at least there would be a chance, however slim. What little air came through the window was mostly blocked by the crying girls and only served to fuel the approaching flames. The heavy wooden floor was soon burning, along with the furniture and anything else combustible."

"We all crowded into an alcove at the windows and the fire reached us and took us all. I can remember it as if it were this morning—I hear every scream, I feel the burning, I smell the smoke and the young girls being consumed by that horrible dragon. Most of all, I remember you, Uilliam—Bill—standing before me, protecting me with your own body, until you fell, looking up at me with terrible sadness in your eyes as you touched me for the last time. I was there. It was real. It happened."

Bill was quiet—too quiet—and there was a very long pause in the conversation.

Finally, he spoke. "I, ah, I don't know what to say. I certainly don't remember any of that—not even in a dream—or nightmare. Wouldn't I remember it too? I mean, I don't rule out reincarnation. I think there really are genuine ghosts, although I haven't seen any. I have never been to Japan, but I don't doubt there is such a place. I'll keep an open mind. Hell, I'm here, aren't I? I'm wondering why I wouldn't have a glimmer of recollection about any of this. What happened during the next 400 years? Anything until now? I have to say, I can't remember much past my eighth birthday party. I'd have thought I would have remembered being an Irishman and roasting in a burning castle!"

"Please, Bill. It is real to me. I'd rather not have it treated cavalierly?"

"Treated what?"

"Cavalierly. Light-heartedly, jokingly."

"Hey, you're talking to Mr. Eighth Grade Education here. Keep it at comic book level!" he said with a smile that melted her heart.

He probably thought her to be ready for the Rubber Room, but at least he didn't express his doubts too strongly. She carried on with her story.

"I know you don't remember any of it. That is one of the stupefying things about it. I presume, although I can't say for sure, obviously, that we each lived many, many lives in the past 400 years. I do, in fact, remember many of those lives. I also think that there were likely other lives, but we never met—or, at least, if we met, we never touched. Touching seems to be the trigger that brings it all to the forefront. That's what happened when I first met you at the filling station. Before that day, I was happily unaware of any of these past lives and the implications of any or all of it."

"Of the lives that I know of—and there were many, many—there were certain similarities. I was always female—thank God!—and you were always male. We were sometimes old, other times young, we were often Caucasian, but sometimes we were of different races and ethic backgrounds. The key point always has been that, before we actually touched one another, I would never recognize you as my Uilliam. At the instant our flesh met, for whatever reason—hand-to-hand, a brushing contact, or whatever may have caused us to collide—I remembered all past lives. And you, my sweet Uilliam, you remembered absolutely, heart-wrenchingly, maddeningly, nothing! You were blissfully ignorant of anything beyond your own existence at that particular time and place. Maybe you were the lucky one—you never knew. You never had the ache of recollection and the broken-hearted knowledge of what had gone before."

"You say you can prove all of this. How? Old-timey pictures of you and me taken a hundred years ago, looking like we do today?" asked Bill.

"No. No pictures, paintings, records. Nothing. I have set a team of researchers out to find such things. They each were given a 'life' and asked to take it apart. Oh, it wasn't a complete waste of $250,000—that's what it cost me—for each of them were, for the most part, able to confirm that many, if not most, of the 'lives' took place, as near as can be confirmed from this point in time."

"Some things can be confirmed: historical events, dates, people—that sort of thing. Others cannot. For instance, I remember we were on a clipper ship that went around Cape Horn in the 19th century. I remembered the name of the ship and the captain's name, as well as the time of year—the month, but not the date. My researchers found that there was a clipper ship by that name. The captain's name was also uncovered. For a very large fee, the ship's log was found at Greenwich, England, at the Maritime Museum, and the log revealed that the ship had transited west-bound around the Horn—in the month I had indicated. There was an annotation of several passengers aboard and, buried in the log were their names, including my own—or at least the name I had recalled. There was no mention of a Chinese cook who went overboard off Cape Horn, but that isn't too surprising."

"Chinese cook? What does a Chinese cook have to do with the price of tea in China?" Bill barked an abrupt laugh at his inadvertent quip. Marisa laughed too, grateful for the "comic relief."

"The Chinese cook was flung overboard by the captain after being hugged vigorously by a certain female passenger. The last I saw of the cook was his shaved head and pigtail, bobbing in the gray seas, clinging to his copper cooking pot. That Chinese cook was...was you, Bill."

Bill was obviously stunned at the audacity of the notion that he had been a Chinese cook in the 1800s.

"I certainly think I would have remembered that, ah, wouldn't I?" Bill seemed subdued. "These researchers. They verified everything?"

"No, and I wouldn't have expected them to. They verified an amazing amount of material, which I consider to be a superhuman feat. Of course, the 'lash' of a quarter of a million dollars at their backs spurred them on to 'greatness,' it would appear." Marisa smiled, not at the expenditure of a fortune, but at the recollection of the demeanor of the up-to-then bored Deputy Head Researcher of an international firm of historical archivists. The woman had interlaced her fingers in what could only be a dismissive display of body language—particularly directed at another—prettier—woman. When I said it was important, time-sensitive, and worth $250,000 to my client, I got her attention. When I then wrote out a $100,000 deposit check, the archivist sat bolt-upright in her chair. The deal was done and, in what seemed like an amazingly short time, the ponderously heavy report was delivered to me.

"In each and every instance where I could provide names, dates, descriptions, places and events, the firm provided detailed verification— validation—what I said was true. Being the devil's advocate, I would say that the law of average would dictate that at least one, or even two, events 'might' be things that I had read about, forgotten, suppressed, and inadvertently recalled and served up as my 'remembrances.' There were far too many, over too long a period of time, to have been sheer luck. The old statistician's story about hundreds of monkeys banging away on typewriters will eventually result in their writing War and Peace just doesn't stand up to analysis. In fact, I'm my own worst critic. I took the results to a professor of statistics—now there's a spark plug, at the University of Michigan and asked him to form an opinion about the odds that a person reciting these events, with facts and figures, names and places, would have made them up or recounted them after seeing them 'someplace' but not remembering them otherwise. His conclusion, which cost me five grand, was that it was "statistically impossible" to have been happenstance. I'm not sure he used the word 'happenstance,' but you get the idea."

"That's a great deal of money, Marisa."

"Oh, I was going to walk away from the money anyway. It would only end up in a court somewhere, or the prison guards would sue me in absentia for all of their agony and anguish."

"If I live to be a gray-haired old lady and die in my jammies in a home for the silly, I figure I'll just come back—again and again—and have a chance at making another million or two."

"'*Another*' million?" asked Bill, his mouth agape.

"More than a few. I was—am—a very good lawyer. If I get caught, I will need those millions. *We* will need those millions."

"So, what you're saying is, this expensive report 'proves' that this amazing story isn't something out of The Twilight Zone and we shouldn't go 'do do do dah,' or whatever the 'Zone' theme song was."

"No. It certainly was persuasive. Very persuasive. It was what convinced me to break you out of prison. The real proof will be a certain treasure trove buried in the ground in one of the busiest parts of London."

"Buried treasure? London? Are you sure you didn't miss that spot by a few thousand miles, thinking of a desert island in the Caribbean instead?"

"I wouldn't mind being in the Caribbean and it will probably be easier to find than London, but London it is," said Marisa, firmly, slapping her palm on to the bed to emphasize her point.

Marisa continued, "Did you ever hear of the Great Fire of London? It happened in the 1600s. London was built largely of wooden structures, except for the fortifications, bridges, churches and other grand buildings. A fire started in a bakery—a bakery I remember working at—and the city was consumed in an inferno."

"A rich man, with whom I came into contact with, knew that he had to bury a large quantity of gold, silver and jewels or else it would be lost in the flames. I was there when he paced out a location directly out from an ancient—even then—Roman wall and buried it deeply. I obviously didn't tell my researchers about the treasure, but they confirmed that the wall was still there and nothing has been constructed in the area in question. They tell me their research concluded that nothing had been built there in recorded history—which goes back long before the Great Fire. No, that doesn't rule out the possibility that someone accidentally discovered it centuries ago, that a Nazi bomb in the Second World War didn't blow it to atoms or that a professor of medieval studies didn't find it while digging with his undergrads. I remember a gold chalice that had a golden horse, rearing, with a gold 'G' on his back. I had the archivists look for such a chalice—I provided a drawing, as best I could—and there is no such chalice known to the art world. Again, it could be in a private collection, or destroyed, but there it is."

"Tell me we're not going to go search for the God-blessed horse, are we?"

"That, precisely, is what we are going to do. If we find it, or even a gold sovereign, in that exact spot, then everything, no matter how seemingly insane, is true. I, myself, know it's true, but this will convince *you*."

"Does it really matter if I'm convinced? Hell, I'm an escaped convict. I'm a murderer on the run—or at least that's what the 'Wanted: Dead or Alive' posters probably say." Bill hung his head, obviously saddened at the realization of what the implications of all of this meant.

Marisa, touched by his emotions, leaned over and stroked his shoulder.

"Don't be sad, Bill. We're in this together. We will recover the baubles and go to Ireland. Have you ever wanted to go to Ireland? My brother and I went, years ago. 'Forty shades of green,' at least that's what Johnny Cash said."

"The Man in Black? What did he have to do with Ireland?"

"A great deal. He was flying there for something and, looking out the window, got the inspiration for his famous song."

"Can't be too famous—I never heard of it. 'Folsom Prison Blues,' now, there's a song after my own heart." Realizing the implications of that—especially the lyrics, "I shot a man in Reno—just to watch him die," seemed too close to home.

Rising, Marisa ushered Bill out the door.

"I'll see you for supper, Herman. I need to freshen up. I feel like I washed up on a beach."

○ঽ

The two had a number of different conversations during the voyage and Marisa told Bill about each of their past lives. He was surprised about most and shocked about some. There were instances when he tried to be amorous and Marisa fended him off, usually saying something about "brothers and sisters." That didn't always work. Finally, she said, "We were lovers and we were married, but those were different people in different bodies. I'm attracted to you, of that, there's no doubt, but I am on a quest for what is, for me, nothing less than the Holy Grail. Once that's found, or until I'm convinced it no longer exists, I cannot get emotionally involved. Please understand and believe me."

Bill finally seemed to accept that, however reluctantly. He spent a great deal of time on deck, watching the seas, lost in his own thoughts.

As it turned out, they were the only passengers and were treated like royalty. There were no problems on board the ship, and crew and officers took them at face value. They had few opportunities to speak in private, so for four days they kept to themselves and spent the time watching the ocean, reading and watching satellite television, which they found amazing out at sea, even though most of it was in one foreign language or another. They did find English-language reruns of Bonanza, and, by the end of the voyage they felt they could be on a first name basis with all of the Cartwrights. They ate far too much and were almost sad when the ship docked at Southampton, England.

36 SOUTHAMPTON, ENGLAND: THE PRESENT

Customs at Southampton were perfunctory, probably owing to their Irish passports. Their passports were glanced at, but not stamped, and they were quickly clear of Customs and Immigration.

Marisa was delighted to see how captivated Bill was with his new surroundings. Once, as they were crossing the street, she had to pull him back and point out the painted signs on the road, saying, "Look Right." She told him to be careful: cars drove on the "wrong" side of the road both in England and in Ireland and he had to look the opposite way.

They rode in the first-class compartment on the train to London. The trip passed quickly and they enjoyed seeing the green countryside but, soon their excitement caught up with them and Marisa fell asleep on Bill's shoulder. She slept until they arrived in London's Victoria Station.

37 LONDON, ENGLAND: THE PRESENT

Bill couldn't help but notice the transformation in Marisa as they arrived in London. There was a different lilt in her voice—of that he was certain—it sounded as if she had more and more of an Irish accent as the days progressed. He put it down to her surroundings—wasn't it true that people were like sponges at times, absorbing mannerisms and sounds around them? Of course, there weren't that many people they encountered who had what he'd considered to have an "Irish accent," for it wasn't as if he was any kind of expert. He'd seen enough movies, of course, including "The Commitments," but he suspected there wasn't a universal Irish accent, no more than a New York City accent was the same in the city as it was in upstate New York.

They stayed at a place called the Victory Services Club. Marisa's brother—his own alter-ego—had a membership there as a former member of the US military. It was close to Oxford Street, the main shopping or "High Street," as he'd come to learn. Even closer was Hyde Park and Marble Arch. He felt like a hick, staring up at the buildings and taking all of this foreign country in.

The American Embassy was not too far away, in Grosvenor Square, but they made a point of staying away from both it and officialdom.

Marisa, being far more adept at dealing with the "locals," handled the check-in procedure and red tape at the Victory Services Club. They were still, brother and sister and had separate rooms.

They took a taxi to the Tower of London. Bill was amazed at the black cab. It was roomy, had fold-up jump-seats and, most surprisingly, it was *clean*. He wasn't sure what it cost—he couldn't get his head around the English pound. Marisa had a supply of them and seemed to understand which odd little coins meant what. One coin, 20 pence, was particularly interesting, with it's angled edges and thinness. He imagined it was similar to an American dime, although there were coins of lesser value. He had a few of them in his pockets, if only to jingle now and then. Marisa showed him some banknotes. They all had pictures of the Queen, as did the coins.

At the Tower, Marisa soon found the massive and obviously ancient Roman wall—or what was left of it.

"This is it! I remember it!"

"You remember the wall, or pictures of the wall? How do you know it hasn't been changed, shortened or added-to in the past million years?"

"Hardly a million years. Almost two thousand, though. Did you know the Romans invented concrete? Can you imagine anything we make today lasting thousands of years?"

"I guess the Renaissance Center won't be around in 500 years, eh?" he asked.

Marisa winced at the reference to the RenCen, where her office was located—her former office. She did not reply.

They walked across the grass to the wall and both were compelled to reach out and touch it as, without a doubt, thousands of other people had over the millennia.

"And just where do you think this pirate treasure is buried?" asked Bill.

Marisa looked around furtively.

Sudden Light

She hissed, "Don't talk about it! We don't know who can hear and who's nearby!"

She'd purchased a digital camera on Oxford Street and snapped away, taking pictures of both the wall, the grass beyond and, it seemed, the presence of all the high-security, closed-circuit TV cameras that she could see. London was festooned with such CCTV cameras, a legacy of her Irish relatives, she was sure. There were some in this vicinity, but they appeared to be directed at the Tower and the more commercial areas.

Looking at a pocket guidebook, Marisa recounted the tale of the Tower, a bit about the executions here on Tower Hill, King Henry VIII and the two lost princes who were found, many years later, walled up inside the Tower. Bill found all of that interesting, but he questioned the wisdom of the two of them—wanted by the law—parading around in the daylight.

Marisa had gone to an Internet cafe and Googled Bill's name and her own. Some clever flatfoot had made the connection to her, at long last, but it appeared that the trail led to Mexico. Her feint to Mexico with the cruise seemed to have paid off. She wasn't tempted to email anyone. That would be a surefire way to send down the thunder onto them. She imagined an American Predator pilot-less drone flying over and blowing them up with a guided missile. She thought she'd watched too much television.

Acting nonchalantly, she walked a short distance from the end of the Roman wall and stopped, looking down at the ground. She appeared to accidentally drop a yellow wooden pencil, and, when she bent down, she actually rammed it into the ground so only the top inch and eraser protruded from the grass.

"Here," she whispered.

Returning to the Club, Bill joined her in her room.

"You saw me mark the spot. I was shorter than the man who paced it out those hundreds of years ago, but today, I am sure I am about his height. My pace should be about the same, or pretty close. What we need to do is go there and dig it up. Tonight."

"Tonight? Why tonight? Are you out of your gourd? Why bother? It probably isn't there, plus we've got—you've got—eight grand in cash."

"Not hardly. Something like $5,000, and it's going fast. I told you on the boat—I need to do this to prove that this isn't all some kind of opium dream. I don't mean to recover the whole cache. I remember the chalice being the last item placed in a leather bag. Of course, the leather's gone—long gone—by now, but something of the cache will still be there, unless it was destroyed in the Blitz or looted over the centuries. Perhaps something as simple as laying a drain allowed some workman to suddenly become an English lord."

"Blitz?" inquired Bill.

"The Blitz was the bombing raids on London during the Second World War. You know—the Germans? Herr Hitler?"

"I have a pretty good idea who the Germans and Mr. Hitler are, or were. I just never heard of the Blitz. No 'book larnin' you see," Bill said with an incandescent grin, all teeth and dimples. Marisa's heart jumped a bit in her chest.

"I don't mean to be condescending," she said.

"If I knew what *that* meant, I might be upset!" More teeth; another heart-flutter.

Marisa laughed. She went over to her suitcase and pulled out two sets of coveralls and two ID tags.

"They call these 'boiler suits' over here. I have no idea why. We are going to join the British Working Class. You are now an engineer with BT—British Telecom—the English telephone company. London's answer to Michigan Bell."

"They're certainly welcome to my share of Michigan Bell," answered Bill.

"I'm sure people here would be pleased to give away BT, too. Do you remember that huge, odd-shaped building with the strange top? That's the BT Tower. London's a strange mix of the ancient and the *avant*—the new."

"Where did you get these coveralls and badges?" Bill asked.

"A little online research had paid off. I found various pictures of them, as well as the badges, and had them made up. They didn't mean anything to the companies in the States that made them. Over here, you'd have to come up with some tall tale about a costume party or something. I have some stickers for hardhats, which we'll acquire locally. I spotted a shop yesterday that looks like they have the same hardhats. We will buy them, slather stickers on them, and we look like the real deal." Marisa's confidence was somewhat infectious.

"So we just slip on our suits and sashay over there and dig up the loot?" said Bill.

"Well, sort off. First of all, we're going to have tools, sawhorses, warning tape—the usual kit. Did you notice I took a number of pictures of a BT crew yesterday? Research. We don't have a van, which is going to be tough. I thought of buying an old one, but BT wouldn't have a beater. They'd have a nice, new one, smeared with BT logos and such—just like the one yesterday."

"Didn't see it," interjected Bill.

"Well, I did. Kodak moments, too. Lots of pictures. So, we'll have shovels, lights and a few of the usual things and hope for the best. Tonight's the night, in point of fact. The weather forecast is fog, which suits us to a T."

"The famous 'London fog?" asked Bill.

"Well, that fog was actually air pollution from burning sulfurous coal, mixed in with a dash of regular fog. London did away with open fires and cut way, way back on factory pollution so fog now isn't much more than in Detroit or anywhere else. People died from breathing in the fog in the not-too-distant past, not to mention getting run over by buses and taxis in the fog, falling in the Thames River and all of that."

"OK. We make it there and dig it up. What's the drill?" he said.

"The 'drill' is this: I'm the supervisor and you are the laborer. You dig the hole and I stand around and supervise."

"Unfair! This needs to be a 50/50 foxhole!"

"Not on your life, Mister. You wouldn't want to be there for two weeks while I tried to dig a 5-inch deep hole!"

They bought Army-type duffel bags at a war surplus store, along with the hardhats and work boots. Marisa added in a part of too-big leather gloves to complete the "look." Everything looked too new, though, she thought. Couldn't be helped, she concluded.

An "ironmonger" had the shovels and plastic sawhorses as well as rolls of warning tape. It didn't say "BT" on it, but maybe no one would notice.

They had a quick supper at the Colonel Sanders KFC around the corner from the Club.

"Where are the mashed potatoes and gravy? They only have fries!" was Bill's reaction.

They took a taxi to the Tower. It was already getting less-crowded. She'd looked in the newspaper at the Club to try to find the hour of sundown, couldn't find it, and finally spotted it online on one of the Club's Internet computers. It was 9:08 PM. Quite a bit later than she'd expected, but they timed it to arrive around nine.

They each went into their own public toilets to do a quick change and came out, looking very obvious. No one gave them a second glance, however. This was, after all, one of the capitals of Europe. Like any huge city, unless you grew three heads—two heads wouldn't cause any looks—no one would notice.

The fog was descending and made the darkness accelerate.

Marisa and Bill had rehearsed assembling the plastic sawhorses and they went together very quickly. Soon, they were set up on either side of the area with the yellow pencil in the ground. Marisa laid out a plastic ground cloth for the earth and Bill strung the wide, yellow plastic warning tape between the sawhorses and a light pole. Again, no one cared a whit about what they were doing. They were part of the background of London, where there was construction on an ongoing basis, 24 hours a day.

Before long, with a dramatic, heavy sigh of resignedness, Bill went under the tape and commenced to cut the sod out in a square and placed it in stacks on the ground cloth.

"Is this illegal?" Bill asked, between puffs. Marisa couldn't help but think that she loved watching this man working hard. She wanted to sniff his "manliness" but wouldn't dream of being so outrageous.

"Illegal? As opposed to being an international wanted criminal? Would they give us community service? Believe me, we're committing crimes by the second, but so what? Just dig!"

Marisa dirtied her shovel to look like she might actually had done some work, and just then, she felt someone's eyes upon her. She had been expecting this—it wouldn't be likely that they could dig up an historic lawn in the center of London's history without someone questioning this somewhat amazing event. She forced herself to look towards Bill, shoveling away industriously, as the figure approached, visible in her peripheral vision. She heard a deep, male voice clear his throat.

"And what do we have here?" said the man, in a noticeable Irish accent.

Marisa turned and flashed a luminescent smile that whisked away the fog.

"Night work in the blessed fog. Not a treat, but the unsociable hour extra pay is nice." Marisa's own Irish accent had come to full effect and it wasn't lost on the man, who Marisa could now see was a London Metropolitan Police Constable.

"Irish! As meself! Aren't the Irish the navvies who built this town?" Saying this, he leaned over and flashed his light onto her BT badge, adding, "Siobhán! Isn't that my own dear mother's name! You wouldn't be me mum, would you?" He was laying on the charm. Bill was invisible.

"A curse of a name. If I never hear, 'Siobhán your knickers, your mother's coming!' again, t'would be all right by me!"

They both laughed together.

"Where would you be from at home, my pet?" he asked.

"The North-West. And yourself?"

"A Corkman, born and bred. Walsh is my name. You know what they say about Corkmen, don't you?"

"Can't say that I do. Has to be a lie though, if you're a Corkman." she smiled coquettishly.

"My God, you are a sprightly one! Business before pleasure, however. I take it you have a permit, paperwork, that sort of thing?"

"When did BT ever do anything without papering over the entire area and wrapping it up with red tape?" she announced.

"True enough, true enough. What is it you're doing? Digging a wishing well? Going to China?" His humor was wearing thin.

"Some kind of electrical fault. Leakage of a grid shunt. I have a box here that tests for it once we get closer. If there's a leak, in come the boyos with the JCB diggers and they'll make a proper dog's breakfast of the whole area. You'll see paperwork then! We're just the surgeons who test for the leak. If you want, I can ring the super and he'll come over with some suits and they'll put you to sleep with charts and graphs."

"Oh, Christ, no. If you strike oil, I get a split!" he said, with an infectious smile. "Listen, let me give you my card. My mobile number's on it. I'm not always in the blue suit. We can have a pint or six—what do you say? Liam's the name. Cork man. Remember what they say..." he handed her a business card and she tucked it into her pocket as he risked another smile and sauntered away, trying to look both official and manly.

Marisa kept the card. If she got "inspected" again, she would drop Liam Walsh's name—the Corkman, for you know what they say about Corkmen.

Marisa didn't have a clue about what anyone might say about Corkmen, but she presumed it wasn't printable.

She was surprised herself at her accent. It seemed, on the ship, that the closer they got to Ireland and the castle, the more pronounced her Irish accent became. It was truly an amazing thing. At least she didn't sound like she came from Gross Pointe, Michigan.

She smiled with the realization that the policeman couldn't identify Bill if his life depended on it. That's just as well.

Bill was a hard worker. The pile of dirt was getting higher and higher as the darkness descended. He was easily four feet down and she began to worry that the treasure wasn't that deep—that it must have been discovered already—or, worse yet, never existed at all.

Marisa looked around her, hoping to appear nonchalant, mindful that the amorous Constable Liam may be returning to lift his leg on the pile of dirt and whisper sweet nothings in her ear. She was drolly amused that his name was "Liam," which is a form of William or Bill, and before that, Uilliam, the name the laboring man before bore so many centuries before—or so she fervently believed. They may find out the extent of her mad delusions before too long: Bill was up to his chest in the hole and was finding it difficult to wield the shovel.

Suddenly, she heard a heavy clunk, the sound jolting her out of her musings. She rushed to the side of the hole.

"Did you find it, Bill? Did you?"

"I found a rock, Marisa. It shook my very bones when I clanged into it."

"What kind of rock is it?" Marisa asked, after a moment, deep in thought.

"I don't know one rock from another. What difference does it make?"

"I mean, is it round or flat, bumpy—that sort of thing."

"Well. Let me pry a corner of it up. Just a sec."

"Is it flat?" said Marisa, in a stage whisper.

"Flat? Well, yes, it is, at that. How could you see it way down here?"

"I can't see it now, Bill, but I saw it 350 years ago. They put a flat stone over the top of the treasure!"

"Here. Hold the light while I pry it up. Wait. I can see under it."

"Gold? Do you see treasure?"

"I see—dirt," Bill replied, dejectedly, winded from the shoveling.

"Dirt. Then it isn't true." Marisa began to cry, softly.

"Hold on. I'll dig like a badger for a minute," muttered Bill.

Bill wondered to himself if he wasn't being infected by this fantasy, for his pulse quickened as he dug. It was difficult in the hole.

"Just climb out. We'll kick in the dirt. Hand me up a souvenir rock."

Bill reached down and hooked his fingers around a rock and handed the heavy stone up to her.

Marisa took the rock and held it to her, her tears falling on the soil-encrusted rock. She had thrown away her life for a heavy, filthy rock.

She turned slightly to cast some of the dim, fog-enshrouded streetlight onto the rock and gently brushed off some of the soil. No sense in carrying around most of London with her. Bill had climbed out and was rapidly shoveling the earth back into the hole. Within a short time—much more quickly, obviously, than the first time, he was placing the sod back. There was more dirt than would fit in the hole.

"What do we do with the rest of the dirt?" he asked.

"Leave it. We need to skedaddle."

"Skedaddle?" inquired Bill.

"Yup, Pilgrim. I've seen too many John Wayne movies. Wait—I take that back—you can't see *too* many John Wayne movies." She smiled.

"I like the Duke, too," Bill said.

"I knew I saw something special in you. I'd have rescued you just for the Duke!"

"I'd have rescued you right back," said Bill, with a devastating crooked smile.

"This is getting even more complicated, if that's possible," thought Marisa. "Am I falling for this guy? He's not 'The One.' Uilliam is The One! Keep your eye on the Finish Line, Marisa!"

They busied themselves, hurriedly cleaning up the site, tossing the tools into the bags, removing their hi-viz vests and hardhats. Soon they were on their way, the rock having been flung into the canvas duffel bag. The taxi drive was in two stages—one to Oxford Street and a second one to the Club. There was no point in leaving a train of breadcrumbs from the Tower to the Club, in the event anyone was looking into the excavation.

Exhausted, both from the physical exertion, Bill, obviously more than Marisa, as well as the mental and emotional strain. They both flopped on the bed, worn to the bone. Neither spoke for five minutes.

Finally, if only to fill the void of awkward silence, Bill said, "That was a treat. What say we dig up the front yard at Buckingham Palace tomorrow night?"

Marisa turned to him and let out a gale of laughter. Anyone passing by in the hallway would think there was a madwoman inside the room. Impulsively, she turned to him, held his face, raspy whiskers and all, and kissed him soundly and resolutely on the lips, shocking both of them.

Bill quickly responded, wrapping his sinewy, muscled arms around her and pulled her close to him. She mewed softly, offering no resistance.

In a throaty, low voice, he asked her, "Is that how you kiss your brother?"

"No, sir," she meekly replied, returning the kiss.

"What about everything you think you remembered? What about your lost man? We didn't find the treasure. This could all be some kind of self-hypnosis," Bill stated.

"I haven't forgotten my Lost Man. He'll always be a ghost who will haunt me until I die. You are my Found Man, Bill. I thank you for all you've done, the risks you've taken, not laughing at a silly woman's crazy talk—well, not laughing too much!"

Moving his hand up under the sweep of one of her breasts, he whispered in her ear, "I can think of a way you can show your gratitude."

She answered by unzipping his boiler suit to his naval, pressing her lips against the dark hair of his chest, drinking in the mustiness of his scent, heavy with the smell of hard, manual labor. She was intoxicated and felt herself spinning away on the winds of ecstasy. She was dimly aware of his undressing her and felt her bra unsnap and enjoyed his taking her breast into his mouth and cleverly tonguing her nipple to a point where it probably could cut glass.

Bill had somehow slipped out of his coveralls and his underwear went over his shoulder, along with hers. He played her like a violin and she loved every exquisite second of it.

Without warning, Bill had somehow brought what could only be a redwood tree into the room and thrust it deep inside her, causing her to arch her back and cry out with delighted agony.

Breathlessly, she cried out, "You have been in prison a very long time, haven't you?"

Bill chuckled at that.

Marisa asked, "Say, you wouldn't be a Corkman named 'Herman,' by any chance?"

Laughing, he set about taking her on an excursion of the planets, beginning with Venus.

38 LONDON: VICTORY SERVICES CLUB, THE PRESENT

Marisa drifted between sleep and consciousness, dreaming a half-dream that she was in Donegal, safe in the strong arms of her Uilliam, gently snoring beside her. She could even feel him—smell him! Dreamily, she half-opened her eyes and saw the curly, red hair of Bill, whom she claimed as "Her Man." She was contented, for the first time since she'd been catapulted into remembering four hundred years of torture and abject pain.

Everything was probably not going to be "all right." She was enough of a realist to recognize that. This moment of sweet happiness would come crashing down. Bill would be sent back to prison—she would be sent to prison, in disgrace. They would make TV movies about her, but she would be buried into a concrete cell deep in the catacombs of some women's prison, somewhere. She began to cry, not at what would probably befall her, but the injustice of Bill being sent back in chains, to be incarcerated in some medieval hellhole. She deserved whatever she got—she had hatched this grand escape plan. For what? A dirty rock? She'd fling that stone into the nearest garbage can at her first opportunity. What right did she have to start keeping souvenirs of her crimes? Wasn't that what always tripped up the stupid criminals, keeping panties or jewelry? What an idiot she was.

Bill slowly came to, and, seeing the state Marisa was in, was immediately concerned?

"Why the tears, my pet? Are you sorry about...you know?" he asked.

"Sorry? I'm sorry I didn't attack you five minutes after we got on that freighter! No, I'm not sorry for that. I am sorry, resoundingly, unhesitatingly, abjectly sorry that I roped you into this pipe dream. I must have been certifiable. I am certifiable!" she whispered.

"Nothing can be done about it. We're in up to our necks. I'm just glad I'm taller than you! My neck is higher out of the owl shit!"

"Owl shit! You wouldn't pull me up a little higher so I can be out of it more?" she teased.

"If you welcome me to this fine morning in a suitably womanly way, I will let you sit on my shoulders while I trudge through the lake of owl shit until we get to the shore," he jibed.

"I would do anything to escape the owl shit tide, my knight!" she laughed.

Needing no more encouragement, Bill set to work, apparently having kept the redwood tree somewhere in the room overnight. Marisa began to wonder if she would be able to survive her new lover's onslaughts. Her head spinning, she was confident she would learn how.

Marisa lay in the hollow of his arms and said, "We need to decamp."

"Decamp?" he asked.

"Yes, decamp. We need to *vamoose*. *Adios*. You know."

"Got it. Something about leaving," he said.

Marisa punched him in the arm, "Beast! Go ahead, make fun!"

"Oh, I will. Don't you worry, sister."

"Bill, I don't know how I can pretend to be your sister after flying to the moon and back."

"We will pretend. Now, the junk in the bag. Keep it? Get rid of it?"

"Just leave it in the back alley of the Club. I presume they have a back alley. We can't leave it on the street. Too many TV cameras and anything found on the street is immediately thought to be the work of the IRA or the Arabs."

"Is the IRA still around? Thought they signed a peace treaty and went away," asked Bill.

"Hardly. Someone once joked that the IRA wasn't dead, they were just sleeping and the IRA is mad because the Arabs have given terrorism a bad name," Marisa quipped.

"Well, we need to steer clear of all of those hombres, including the po-lice. Especially the po-lice."

"You have it, mister: no po-lices." Marisa laughed. It felt good to laugh again.

Bill got out of bed, treating Marisa to a magnificent view of his bare buttocks. "This can get to be habit forming," she thought.

He went into the shower and started the water. In a moment, Marisa thought, "Why not?" and joined him, thoroughly enjoying soap more than she had since she was a little girl, blowing soap bubbles in the tub.

Dressed, Bill grabbed the bag and glanced inside.

"I'll go get rid of this junk. What about the souvenir of the Great Smoky Mountains. Do we need a rock to break a window in a jewelry store heist?" asked Bill.

Amused, she answered, "No. We don't need a chunk of London. Give it a fling."

Instead, he tossed it into the sink and turned on the hot and cold water taps.

"Might as well wash it off and see if it is a ten-pound diamond or something before we give it a toss," said Bill.

Marisa busied herself packing her few belongings into her bag while looking out the window at the street below. Over her shoulder, she said, "Bill, can you fill me a glass of cold water? I need to take a little pill, if you know what I mean."

"Your 'I don't want to be a mommy yet' pill?" asked Bill.

"Yes, but don't tempt me into not taking it. My biological clock is ticking so loudly, I think it wakes me up," she said.

Bill laughed. After a moment of quiet, and running water, he asked, "No glasses. Would a cup of water do?"

"Sure. Cup, glass, saucer....I don't care."

Bill walked over to her and handed her the cup, which she accepted absently. Feeling its weight, she looked down suddenly and stared in stunned astonishment at what was in her hand—the chalice! *The* chalice with the horse! The actual chalice she thought she'd dreamed about. "Oh, Bill! My Bill! It is real. It is actually real! The stone! This was the stone?"

"Yep. One dirt-covered chalice, just for pill-taking. I guess I'm not so dumb, but I ain't so smart, either. I'm sorry for all those 'crazy lady' thoughts I've been thinking since you sprung me."

"I can't blame you. I began to doubt it myself. After we risked imprisonment to dig up the Tower of London and found nothing, I was beyond despair. But we found it!"

"Yeah. That means all the rest of the treasure is still down there. Do we go back for it?"

"Oh, hell no. It would be hotter than the center of the sun and we'd get nabbed for sure. It couldn't be sold or even given away. Someday, I'll send an anonymous letter to the British Museum and tip them off. They probably won't believe it and will just shred my letter, but I will have tried."

"It probably is a stupid question, but is that the very cup you saw in 16 hundred and something? Notice I'm saying, 'you saw,' and not, 'you think you saw.'"

"I noticed, Bill, and I thank you for that. Yes, it is the exact cup."

"So, I guess I'm this William character, then? I don't feel like him—I feel like *me.*"

"Yes, Bill. You are he, but, even more importantly, you are you. I don't love you—and I *do* love you—for who you once were, but for everything you've been. Well, maybe a little nudge from the past—I don't fall so deeply in love so quickly, so maybe you had a little help from a couple dozen ghosts!"

As they closed Marisa's suitcase, and made smalltalk, suddenly there was the sound of a catastrophic explosion in the distance and the building shook.

"What the Christ!" cried Bill.

"Gas explosion?" asked Marisa.

She grabbed the telephone and called to the desk. The line was busy and she redialed twice before getting through to the harried operator. Without asking, the operator said, "It is safe here. It isn't us. It is somewhere in the city. Turn on your telly," then hung up, without waiting for Marisa to say anything.

Marisa snapped on the television and went through the channels, finally finding Sky News. There were pictures of a mighty cloud of black smoke that drifted across what she knew to be the zoo. "How could the zoo blow up?" she asked herself.

There was no sound from the TV except the sounds of the English variety of emergency sirens. Marisa and Bill sat on the bed and stared at the television. Finally, a disembodied voice on the TV spoke:

"We have been told by witnesses that it is the American Ambassador's Residence, near the zoo. It has been blown up. No, it has been atomized. It doesn't exist. It is a monstrously huge crater, like an open-pit mine. Buildings all around the area are wrecked. It is Britain's World Trade Center."

"We have to get out of here, Bill. The Brits will put a Ring of Steel around London. We'll leave the shovels and stuff on our way out. I'll check out. You get the bags and I'll meet you downstairs at the reception desk. I'd pass on checking out, but I don't want to look suspicious."

"OK. Will do," answered Bill.

Marisa made her way to the elevator and went to the ground floor, quickly checking out. The desk clerk paid her no particular attention, half attending to her and half-watching the television nearby. All TVs were on the news.

Bill arrived shortly thereafter. Marisa asked the porter to call a taxi. "Might take a minute, Mum, what with all the furor," he said, as he hurried out to the nearby busy street, for the quiet side street would not have many taxis.

In a moment, he returned, breathlessly. "Help you with the bags, Mum?"

"Sure. Fine. Thank you," Marisa said, handing her suitcase to him.

The electric glass doors slid open and she went outside, noticing that Bill was following closely behind.

The got to the taxi and she gave the porter three round-pound coins for his trouble. He thanked her and sidled back inside the building.

"Quite a flap going on, Miss. Police everywhere. There's talk that a plane flew into the Ambassador's house," said the driver, a man in his fifties.

"How terrible! Were there many hurt and killed?"

"Ambassador, his family, staff and a couple of American senators, from what I heard. All dust now," he said.

"My God! What a tragedy!" she said, believing it.

"The world's changing, that's for sure, and it will never be the same. Not in London," said the cabbie. "Where to?" he added, back to business.

"Victoria Bus Station, please," she stated.

"Right-o. On our way."

At that, the taxi pulled away and turned towards Marble Arch and then down Park Lane. Even through the closed windows of the taxi, she could hear sirens sounding and occasionally caught sight of Army vehicles heading in the direction of what must be the Zoo. She saw several London Bobbies, traditionally unarmed, suddenly sprouting military-style helmets, flak vests and carrying sub-machine guns. Nothing would truly ever be the same, she thought. At least the heat would be off of them, she hoped, knowing it wasn't to be true.

39 ENGLAND: THE PRESENT

The taxi man left them at Victoria Bus Station and Marisa purchased two tickets on the bus to Ireland, which was to leave in a half hour.

"No airplane, no train?" inquired Bill.

"Nope. Too much scrutiny, especially after the Ambassador becoming One With the Universe today," Marisa answered.

"Got it. No self-respecting crook's going to take the bus, right? Well, except us two crooks," Bill said, with a smile.

"Careful what you say, William." She'd taken to calling him "William," perilously close to "Uilliam," his name of yore. Was Uilliam his ancestor? she thought. No, she concluded. William was Uilliam, just as she was Máire. We two are intertwined for the ages, she thought. She was self-satisfied, at least a little bit, in realizing that, even if they came to a bad end, they would be reincarnated sometime in the future. Certainly many, if not most, of those reincarnations of the past had ended horribly, but, she thought, "I'm a four-hundred year old woman. I am a born optimist!"

She said she'd be right back, and for him to keep his mouth shut, trying to sound humorous, although it wasn't. She went to a tiny shop across the street and bought a small, portable radio. She wanted to keep track of the news. Checking that it came with batteries, she quickly went back to the bus station, to find Bill staring at the passing humanity.

"Some strange hombres at this bus station," he said. "Not quite the quality of good ol' Greyhound, but they're cut from the same cloth."

Marisa smiled, looking over at the passing menagerie and agreed, taking him by the sleeve and guiding him to the parking space number assigned to their bus. The coach was already there, the driver having joined some other drivers to watch a small pocket TV. It was undoubtedly the news, the topic of all conversation she heard, in snippets.

The driver didn't seem interested in accepting their bags, so Bill tossed them under the coach, the cargo door being open. No one was accepting their tickets, so they just went on, making their way to the rear of the bus. Marisa had purchased a few drinks and snacks when she got the radio and settled into seats near the rear exit door, looking around at her fellow travelers, most of whom were young and of university age.

The driver soon returned and slammed the luggage doors shut, still apparently lost in thought and uninterested in the passengers' tickets.

The coach's brake was released and the bus was put into reverse. Just as the driver started to back out of the parking space, there was the heavy rap of a gun barrel on the glass door, seemingly heavy enough to break the glass. Not wishing to argue with a machine-gun, the driver stabbed the brakes and tossed the transmission into park, while simultaneously punching the door-opening button.

Wordlessly, two British Army soldiers, "squaddies," their faces in camouflage warpaint, came onto the bus, their machine-guns held at the ready. The chatter in the bus stopped abruptly. A few passengers who could remember the Troubles looked at each other, silently and knowingly.

Marisa clenched her fingers around Bill's arm, almost drawing blood. Neither said anything as the two soldiers, Commandos, or whatever they were, moved quickly down the aisle, staring with dead eyes at each and every passenger. Perhaps it was her imagination, but they seemed to linger over Bill and Marisa longer than the others, but she was probably just nervous. She was, in fact, terrified. What would Bill do? Would he fight them? Would they slice him in half with their machine-guns? Was this the end—once more?

The two soldiers had a short, whispered conversation and turned back towards Bill and Marisa. Marisa couldn't take his eyes off them, squeezing Bill's arm all the more. She was sure she'd cut off his circulation. Bill patted her hand and she relaxed a tiny bit, but not much.

The soldiers moved from the center of the bus back towards them and Marisa stopped breathing, knowing that they would be trundled off, beaten, shot—she didn't know. Could she wait for yet another life? What had she done to God to deserve this agony?

The soldiers reached out together and clamped their hands, vise-like, on the shoulders of a dark-skinned, Arab-looking man across from them, lifting him effortlessly out of his seat, ignoring his heavily-accented protests. The man's hand luggage, newspaper and lunch were left on the seat. If the soldiers cared what the man thought, they didn't show it. They'd bagged someone and he was off to some dungeon, or Guantanamo Bay, for all Marisa knew.

Bill broke the silence by exclaiming, "Holy Shit!" in the most American of Midwestern accents. Nervous laughter rippled through the bus, including the driver, who shut the door and backed out, over-fast, anxious to get out of the city—and England—as quickly as he could.

40 THE IRISH SEA: THE PRESENT

Marisa listened to the earphone of her portable radio in one ear, and to Bill—who wasn't saying all that much—in the other. There was endless chatter about the causes and possible perpetrators of the bombing. Besides, the BBC said, the explosion was simply too large to have been either a car bomb or a crashing aircraft, even a jetliner. References were made to a colossal explosion on the Western Front during WWI and how tunnelers, or "sappers," as one commentator described them, had dug an underground mine under the German lines, stuffed it with TNT and touched it off, sending the Hun to perdition. Marisa remembered it when it happened during the Great War.

By the time they arrived at the ferry port on the Irish sea, in Wales, the radio talkers had reported that Downing Street—meaning the British Government—concluded that whomever had sent the Ambassador to the Promised Land had done so by rafting tons of high explosive down a deep, underground river that, unknown to most people, went directly under the Ambassador's Residence. Who would have thought it? She passed this information to Bill, who nodded. He did not appear to be as interested as she was, although he did notice, as he had since they arrived in England, that she was developing more and more of an Irish accent as they got closer to their destination.

Even driving across rural England, down the quaintly-named "divided carriageway," what Americans would call an "expressway," she saw evidence of the British military buildup. There were armored cars, Jeeps and even the occasional tank—which looked especially menacing—at intersections and along the highway. Once, a long column of Army vehicles went screaming past them, escorted by several police cars, lights flashing and sirens wailing. A new world, for sure.

As the bus lumbered onto the ferry, the driver directed everyone to get off and go to the lounges on-board the large ship. He said they could come back on the bus when they arrived in Ireland. "Ireland," Marisa thought, what a sweet sound. She could hardly wait. Bill was nonplussed, but that was Bill.

When they got to the lounge, Marisa instructed Bill: "Don't say anything. You don't sound Irish; you barely look Irish, except for the red hair—which looks lovely on you, but they way. If anyone talks to you, I will tell them you are an amadán. Whenever you hear me say 'amadán,' you repeat it. Say *'amadán.'*"

"Amadán," echoed Bill. "What's an *'amadán,'* if you don't mind telling me?"

Marisa hesitated for a moment and answered, "Idiot."

"What did you just call me?" asked Bill.

"Amadán is Irish for 'idiot.' Give a goofy grin when you say it. No one can deal with an idiot."

"Oh, great. Now, I'm a brainless, Irish idiot," wailed Bill, a bit too loudly.

"Yes you are, and a big, beautiful idiot at that. Herman, my idiot 'brother!'"

They both laughed as they made their way up through the bowels of the ship.

It was a somewhat rough crossing and several people were obviously struck with *mal de mer*—seasickness. Bill looked a little green about the gills, but didn't have any other real signs. He turned down several offers of food from Marisa, however she munched merrily away on a Ploughman's sandwich, with obvious delight.

CB

In time, they arrived in Ireland. Bill, standing with her on the maindeck, said, "Looks just like where we came from."

"Not surprising. They used to be one island, a few zillion years ago," said Marisa.

"Were you just a young girl then?" Bill deadpanned.

This earned him another shot with her tiny fist into his shoulder and they made their way, wordlessly, back to the bus.

There was no sign of tanks or armored cars in Ireland and the policeman, or Garda, who came onto the bus, was armed only with a rubber stamp. He went through the bus, asking each passenger for travel documents.

When they got to Bill and Marisa, again in the back of the bus, the Garda stopped before them. Marisa handed over both passports, which he glanced at.

Turning to Bill, he began to ask him questions, to which Bill didn't reply, simply looking up at the policeman, smiling.

Slightly irked at not being answered, the policeman looked again at Bill's passport.

Marisa raised her hand, as if in class, and said to the policeman, in fluent Irish, that the man was her brother and that he was an "Amadán."

The Guard paused in mid-sentence, somewhat taken aback at the rapid Irish, which all Gardaí learned in Garda College, if they didn't know it already. He understood her, and replied in Irish. Bill, having heard his cue-word, repeated, several times, "Amadán!" Bill said it with a wide grin. The Guard, again in Irish, said he was sorry for bothering them; he had a brother just the same, and knew what she had to put up with. He patted Bill on the head like a child as he moved towards the front of the bus.

"Once is enough, Bill."

"Once-what?"

"Amadán. Just say it once if you hear me say it."

"Worked, didn't it?"

"Yes, indeed. It worked. Nice job. You'll be fluent before the day is over."

Bill smiled contentedly as the bus pulled away.

ɔ

The bus took them to the nearest Bus Éireann station, where many of the passengers—those who weren't greeted by friends and relatives—would go onward.

Bill collected their suitcases and Marisa went off to get more tickets, having exchanged many of her dollars and all of her English pounds for euro on the ferry's *Bureau de Change* money-changing booth—which, she was certain, extracted too high of a commission and exchange rate, but it couldn't be helped.

She bought two tickets for Galway, on the Atlantic Ocean. Again, they were in luck, for the bus would leave within the hour.

Soon they were off across the Irish countryside, the roads being much narrower than they'd experienced in England. Small towns whisked past and they both dozed off.

Almost before they realized it, they arrived, stiff and sore, in Galway, which was a lovely town, and they changed buses for Donegal Town, their final destination.

Galway was much more international town than many in Ireland, with the principal exception of Dublin, of course, according to Marisa's guidebook. She noticed, out of the corner of her eye, a much more evident police presence and even the occasional soldier, although they didn't have their faces painted like the English soldiers.

Different teams of two policemen and one or two soldiers—apparently for the heavy artillery back-up, moved through the crowd, looking the travelers up and down. To Marisa's horror, they seemed to immediately spot Bill and Marisa and shouldered their way over to them, stopping dead-square in front of Bill, addressing him,

"So, where are ye off to, Ginger?" the Garda said, in a deep voice, laced with malice. The policemen were not a holiday.

The policemen squared their shoulders and glanced back at the soldiers, who caught the body language and stiffened when Bill failed to answer a direct question. The policeman was directly in front of Bill and fairly spat at him from four inches away. The policeman obviously had dealt with some hard cases in the past.

Stabbing a blunt forefinger into Bill's chest for emphasis, the policeman said, 'I asked ye a feckin' question, Ginger-boy and ye will *answer!*"

Marisa wedged herself, shoulder-first, between Bill and the policeman and, with her face flushed crimson, lit into him in lightning-fast Irish.

"You feckin' Black and Tans must think you're in goddamned 1920! Who do you feckin' think you're talking to? This poor Amadán doesn't have even half a wit and you're giving him shite like you are the feckin' British Army! For shame!"

She shoved him back a millimeter, barely able to move his bulk.

It had the desired effect. The policeman's mouth was agape, unable to form a response. His partner and the soldiers snickered at his discomfort. If they couldn't understand the Irish, they could understand the tone. They were highly amused and grateful it wasn't them on the receiving end.

"I, ah, I just asked...." he answered, in textbook Irish, school-taught, not learned at his Mammy's knee.

"You thought *nothing*, you feckin' storm trooper. Leave the wee bastard alone. You want him to shite his trousers? You'll clean it up, I grant you!"

"No. Wait. There's no need. We just need to see some identification, that's all."

"I'll identify nothing, you bastard! I am a citizen of the Republic of Ireland and so is this baby boy, my wee brother, and we will show you our arses only, won't we Uilliam?"

On cue, Bill grinned and said, "Amadán."

The Garda just said, under his breath, *"Shite!"*

The policemen and soldier each laughed at the incongruity of it all and their companion's obvious agony. The second policeman tugged at his mate's sleeve and urged him to move on to net easier fish than these two.

With a wave of dismissal, the trio moved away. The policemen who received the dragon lady's fiery breath in his face said, to no one in particular, "That's the Irish Secret Weapon: a red-headed woman with the wind up her skirt. God Save Ireland!" The others laughed and moved off.

Marisa slapped Bill on the arm and said, *"Amadán!"*

Her fiery demeanor changed to laughter when Bill echoed, "Amadán!" When Bill asked her where she learned to speak such fluent Irish, she was thunderstruck. She truly didn't know...

J.A. Greenleaf

41 DONEGAL TOWN, O'DONNELL CASTLE: THE PRESENT

The white and red Bus Éireann coach with the running Irish Setter dog on the sides swayed through the corners, at what seemed to Bill to be too high a rate of speed. He was dismayed to see that there was no toilet on the bus. They'd stopped for a few minutes in Sligo, where Bill gulped down two Cokes in quick succession—something he regretted now as the bus bumped along on a particularly bad stretch of road.

Several teen-aged girls talked both rapidly and animatedly in the seats ahead of them, while supposedly listening to music on their headphones. The music was loud enough to give him a headache; he wondered what it was like between their ears.

It was early afternoon, and the sky was gray. To him, the sky seemed perpetually gray; it had rained on-and-off the entire journey. Bill had slept fitfully on the bus, but there wasn't enough legroom, even though they were in the last row. He sat behind some kind of stairwell leading to an emergency door, but a low wall ground against his knees with every lurch of the coach.

He looked over at Marisa, sitting next to him. They hadn't spoken much on the bus. She seemed fixated on watching the countryside flash by. He'd seen all he wanted to—one town looked pretty much like another. Sheep seemed everywhere, and the towns seemed to be built around the taverns. "Pubs," Marisa had called them. There was an Irish pub in Detroit, and he had been there once, with some friends. After a

282

chorus of "Oh Danny Boy," he'd had enough and left with a woman he'd met there. She'd asked him, with bright eyes, if he was Irish. He would have told her he was Hungarian if he could have had his way with her. She asked him what his Irish family's name was. He rapidly thought about what name he should give her, for he didn't want to give her his *real* name, and, for a moment couldn't recall any other Irish names, so he glanced over her shoulder and saw the draft beer pump handles, and said, "Patrick Harp Guinness Murphy—the Third." She'd laughed at that, and he knew he was not going to leave alone. "OK, Murph, you passed Immigration."

Bill noticed that they were coming into another town, just as the driver called out, "Donegal Town."

"This is it, isn't it?" he asked, looking around. Marisa didn't reply. She had her palms against the glass and was looking everywhere. She reminded him of a little girl he saw when he was a kid, peering into the Christmas window at J.L. Hudson's in downtown Detroit.

Marisa asked him, "Bill, does *any* of this seem familiar to you? Not the buildings, but the land?"

"No, can't say that it does, but, by the way, I guess the cops here don't need to carry guns. Look at those boys over there in the camouflage. Those look like they're carrying machine-guns.'

Marisa looked across to where Bill was pointing. A handful of soldiers in full battle-dress and black berets were on both sides of the street as the bus pulled to a halt in front of the Abbey Hotel. The other passengers seemed unfazed by the show of force, and stood up to leave the bus.

"I don't know what they're doing there. I didn't think there were people out and about with guns here," she said, quietly.

"Maybe it's the IRA," said Bill, half to himself.

"I doubt that. Look at their vehicles," pointing to several olive-drab four-by-four vehicles with long whip aerials. "They must be in the Irish Army," said Marisa.

"Shit, even in Detroit, Murder City, you don't see the Army waltzing around with 'cammies' on and toting sub-machine guns!" answered Bill.

As they alighted from the bus, Marisa felt something wet and cold touch the back of her hand. She recoiled in surprise, yanking her hand up and away, startling the dog that had touched a damp nose against her hand in friendly greeting.

Her fear turned to delight as she crouched down to look into the dog's dark eyes, holding the sides of its head in her hands, and started talking baby talk to it.

"What is it?" asked Bill, "A poodle?"

"Poodle! Don't say such a thing! It is Ireland's Own Dog—a wonderful Irish Kerry Blue Terrier! Let me see if it has a tag on its collar. Yes! 'Síofra' Her name is 'Síofra.' How delightful! What a pretty girl!"

"How do you know it is a she with all that fur?"

"Síofra means 'fairy.' Besides, look at her. She is so full of puppies she's about to burst!"

"She obviously loves you. I think you have a new Best Friend!"

"I had a Kerry Blue—when I was younger—Murphy—his name was Murphy," Marisa said, a little sadly.

At that moment, a dark blue armored car pulled up to the bank and a guard wearing what looked like a motorcycle helmet with a neck-protector on the back and a bullet-proof jacket stepped out of the armored car, carrying a heavy bag.

"That's it—protection for the armored car," Marisa said, confidently.

"Seems like 'overkill' to me," said Bill, as they rose to leave the bus.

ଔ

Somewhere behind them, in a plain Vauxhall sedan, one of two men began talking into the radio. Their car bore 'D' for Dublin number plates, but they were false. They actually had just driven from Northern Ireland, and had peeled off their magnetized Northern Ireland yellow rear plate and white front plate for another set of similarly magnetized white Republic of Ireland plates.

The men were members of the British MI5 Secret Intelligence Service. They were part of a team that included operatives who'd followed Bill and Marisa on foot. They had stopped at Sligo's bus stop as did the bus, and casually took photographs of the both of them. The man and woman matched the surveillance pictures from London. They didn't look like IRA, RAAD, Real IRA, Provos, or whatever it was they were, but who did?

"We should have 'popped' 'em back in Sligo. Silencer, puff, puff, end-of-story," said the man behind the wheel.

"Oh, we'll take care of them rightly enough, along with a few of their boyos later in the day! They're bound to be meeting their lads," said the radioman.

"Are the birds in the air?" asked the driver.

"Yes, indeed. Two choppers and God knows how many squaddies packed in them."

"SAS?" inquired the driver.

"I doubt it. Probably Territorial Army, would be *my* luck. No commandos for us—we don't rate! Takes the TA to violate a sovereign nation's territory!"

They both laughed at that, and the driver shook a cigarette out of a crushed pack he'd fished out of his pocket. His partner looked over disapprovingly, but said nothing.

The radioman added, "They aren't really here, of course. This is the God-blessed, piss-ant Republic of Ireland, and we aren't here either!"

They both laughed again, as the driver inhaled deeply of the cigarette smoke, making the end flare bright red.

ɔʒ

Marisa tugged at Bill, excitedly pointing at the castle, towering over the town.

"Hurry! We need to see it closer! It looks so different!" she cried. She moved towards the castle, with both Bill and Síofra trailing behind.

"What's the rush? Just another ruin. I gotta pee!"

"You can do that later. Come on! They might be closing!"

Resignedly, Bill followed behind, docilely. Maybe there was a toilet in there somewhere, he thought, hopefully.

Marisa almost ran the short distance from the Diamond in the Center of town to the castle, and stopped to pay for their admission. The girl at the counter said there would be a guided tour beginning almost immediately.

Marisa stood, breathlessly, in the courtyard, her eyes taking in every detail of the castle. She pointed at everything, with a running commentary that Bill could barely understand, except the occasional word.

"Look there! That's so different! They changed it!" said Marisa.

They fell in place behind a small group, as the guide came forward. She spoke with a strong Donegal accent, and welcomed them to the castle. She said that the castle had first been built in about 1474, and had been modified and added to by the O'Donnells since that time.

Marisa nodded and shook her head as the girl continued.

She said that the castle had passed to the Englishman, Sir Basil Brooke in the early 1600's. Brooke had added the Jacobean-style structure to one side of the original castle, and had made modifications, adding windows, blocking up the original door, building a huge, new fireplace, and making other changes.

"The Jacobean wing has not been restored by the State, but the castle itself has been completely refurbished to, we think, the way it was long ago. Let us go into the castle," announced the guide.

At that, Marisa grabbed Bill by the arm and moved towards the end of the castle. The guide seemed startled, and said, "Excuse me, Miss. The entrance is through the Jacobean addition."

"No, it is not. It is at this wall,' said Marisa, her accent thicker than the girl's, as Marisa pointed to the end of the castle.

The guide, on hearing Marisa, replied in Irish, with a little laugh, "Well, it was, four hundred years ago, but since 1630, that entrance has been blocked off!"

Marisa stopped suddenly, her face pale. She answered, "Thank you," and, her head slighted bowed, dutifully fell in behind the queue of tourists, as Bill and Síofra followed along. Apparently dogs, unlike in the United States, were more than welcome to trot along on the tour, at least as far as this particular guide was concerned.

The group went through the addition and entered the ground floor and the guide said that this was the most original part of the castle. She showed them the stone cobbles on the floor and the stone ceiling.

"Here, animals and stores would have been kept," she said, in the rapid-fire manner of someone who has told the same story countless times.

The group looked around, and flashes popped on digital cameras and phone cameras clicked.

Marisa tugged Bill's arm, and said, with obvious anticipation, "Come, Uilliam! Let us see the upper floors! Do you remember any of this? Is this something you have seen before?"

Bill shook his head, both in dismay and in answer to her question—none of this had made sense since she "kidnapped" him in Michigan.

As the party climbed the circular stone stairs set in the thick walls in the corner of the castle, Marisa moved her hands across the stone, as if in a caress.

She was truly radiant as she smiled and said, "This is so real now! The years have slipped away. We are home, Uilliam! You know it, do you not?"

To his surprise, she reached on her tiptoes and kissed him lightly on the lips, and quickly turned away, blushing fiercely at the public display of affection. Bill felt his own face redden as the other tourists snickered.

As they arrived on the next floor up, which would be the "first" floor for the Irish, but the "second" floor for them, the guide pointed out that the castle was hosting a display of Ireland's greatest artist, Jack B. Yeats, and, on exhibition were a number of Yeats' works, mostly from the Yeats collection in Sligo, as well as paintings from private collections in both Ireland and beyond, including one from as far away as Nebraska, in the US of A. She rambled on about how this and that had been done to restore the castle. She described the huge, ornate fireplace to the group, how it bore coats of arms of both Sir Basil's family and that of his wife.

Marisa was frowning at this and saying, quite loudly, *"English* fireplace!" A few of the tourists were obviously English, and they looked at each other wordlessly.

Marisa looked at the paintings with obvious interest, for there was something familiar about them that she could not quite place—until she rooted herself firmly in front of a large seascape. The bronze plaque affixed to the frame read, *"Donegal Coast,'* painted in 1927 by Jack B. Yeats (1871-1957)"

She cried out, "Jack! It is the same 'Jack'—*Jack B. Yeats!* This is *my* painting! Jack gave it to me in 1927!"

Bill saw everyone looking at her as the most crazy of crazy ladies. Bill put his arm through Marisa's and said, quietly, "Come on, Marisa. Let's look over here."

She looked at him hotly and said, in precise tones, *"Máire.* I am *Máire.* You are *Uilliam,* and this is your clan's castle. I am your wife and we are *home.* This painting is *my* painting!'

Bill removed his arm from hers at this, and stepped back, quite speechless.

Marisa said something harsh in Irish, and, with a toss of her head, boldly stepped across the floor to hear the guide, standing at the foot of a large, wooden staircase, say that the old fireplace, during restoration, was found to be backed by a secret staircase set inside the heavy stone walls.

"Where does it lead?" asked Marisa, obviously excited at this news. "I did not know of a secret passageway in this wall!"

"Well, there would be no way you would, Miss, unless you took this tour before!" joked the guide. The other tourists laughed at Marisa's expense, but she was oblivious to them.

"It leads to where?" Marisa insisted.

"It descends from the top floor and passes behind this fireplace and probably goes to the ground floor, or even lower. The restorers found it. It has been blocked up too, like the original entrance. I imagine this was done by the Brookes. Secret passages have a way of letting people in as well as out," she said, smilingly. "Besides, it wouldn't have been much of a secret—everyone in the castle at the time of the O'Donnells would have known about it!"

Marisa shook her head, and whispered in Bill's ear, "I did not know about it. Did you? Oh, *Uilliam.* We could have *escaped from the fire!*"

He shook his head, for he truly did not know about it. How could he? He had never been on this island before, much less this rocky little corner of it.

Marisa fairly flew up the stairs, leaving the rest behind. Bill, not knowing what to do, followed her.

She looked up and down the huge room, and moved quickly to a small alcove, pierced by a window.

She didn't look back when the guide appeared, saying, to both her and the others who had arrived, "Stones filled the secret staircase. We have no idea when, or why, it was blocked off, as the existing records do not mention it. But, if you look up the chimney of the fireplace downstairs, you can see light coming through a chink in the rocks.'

Marisa looked back at Bill with a stricken look, as if she might faint.

She said once more, "Uilliam. We could have escaped. We could have gone down those stairs! There was furniture here—always. A large chest with brass handles. Remember it? It never moved. Oh, *Uilliam!*'

She began to cry, and the group self-consciously moved away to listen to the rest of the presentation.

Bill didn't know what to do, but her sorrow seemed genuine. He had no idea what she was talking about, and it was clear to him that she was mentally unbalanced. Her tears moved him, though, and he put his arms around her and held her closely. She formed herself to his body, and pressed her head against his chest as she sobbed.

Beyond sight of them, two British Army helicopters zigzagged across the fields at low level. They avoided any buildings and towns. If seen, they would be thought to be the Irish Air Corps, as they were unmarked. If they were recognized, that was too bad, thought the young Captain commanding the small force. His name was Seán O'Keeffe. He took a great deal of ribbing from the other officers, who called him "Mick." or "Paddy." He bore absolutely no allegiance to the Ireland that his great-grandfather left many years ago. He spoke English with a thick Home Counties accent and was a Londoner, through-and-through. He even hated his name as being 'too Irish,' and had considered changing it, but realized that the Army knew him by that, and that is what he would remain.

He looked at the hard faces of the young soldiers in the jump seat. They clutched their automatic rifles with tight fists, their eyes staring straight ahead from their war-painted faces. One held a light machine-gun, and his mate, boxes of ammunition for it, along with his own automatic rifle. They were ready for war, but this was, of course, merely an "incursion," and error of navigation. To hell with the European Union, thought the captain. This was enemy territory. Good Friday/Bad Friday; it made no difference to him.

He heard static in his headphones, and the pilot's voice sounded in his ears. "Coming up on Donegal Town, Cap. We will lay back in the countryside, away from civilization."

"'Civilization!' There's no civilization here. Trained monkeys, driving cars, breeding...should be stamped out!" said O'Keeffe, vehemently.

The tone of voice and anger in Captain O'Keeffe surprised the pilot, who knew of O'Keeffe's ancestry. It must be true, he thought, that there is nothing worse than someone who has turned on his own. He kept quiet, and concentrated on the ground whipping past below.

"What do you say to a high-speed run over the town? You know, let them know we're here, and raise some dust?" asked O'Keeffe.

The pilot was incredulous. He quickly responded, "That's precisely against standing orders. We are not here, you understand. We never left British territory."

O'Keeffe didn't say anything, as he looked intently out the front windscreen of the helicopter with his massive field glasses.

Suddenly he spoke out, in an excited voice. He was pointing at something the two pilots could not see. "Armed men! Armed men! Dressed in camouflage! There must be a half-dozen that I can see. They have weapons displayed!"

His sergeant, listening to the radio on his own earphones, made hand signals to the troops, who grew agitated and began to tighten straps and pat their uniforms, as if confirming they had their equipment and ammunition. One drew a long, wicked knife with a black blade—obviously not Army issue—from his boot and examined it intently.

"Make the pass. We'll just give them some rotor wash," O'Keeffe ordered over the intercom. The pilot looked over at his co-pilot, shrugged his shoulders, and nodded, speaking rapidly by radio to his wing-man.

Both helicopters, as one, banked to the left and dove towards the Center of the town.

The Irish Army soldiers guarding the armored car looked skyward as they heard the familiar thump, thump, thump of fast-approaching helicopters. One, who had been smoking a cigarette, spit it out onto the street and raised his weapon towards the helicopters to get a better view through his optical gun sight. Simultaneously, the door gunner in the lead helicopter, catching the movement, swung his machine-gun in the direction of the Irish soldier. In a microsecond, his training overrode his orders not to fire, and, recognizing what he took to be imminent enemy fire, he squeezed off a burst of machine-gun fire.

Two of the heavy bullets struck the soldier solidly in the chest, penetrating his body armor. His arms splayed out reactively and he fell back against a car, dead before his body thudded against the pavement.

The armored car guard stood stock-still at the action before him, then suddenly threw the moneybags into the trap at the rear of the truck and ran to the side door.

The door gunner, seeing movement again, swung his machine-gun toward the armored car and let go a burst, catching the guard in mid-stride. As he fell, the bullets showed a stitching pattern along the sides of the truck, except where the man had been a second before. Two bullets had struck the bulletproof glass on the right side, starring the glass crazily. The driver, stunned by the sound and impact, punched the radio alarm button instinctively, and stomped on the accelerator. The heavy truck struck a small car ahead of it, and then another on the street.

Horns were blowing on crushed cars, as the soldiers took cover. They began firing in disciplined, rapid-fire bursts of automatic fire at the two helicopters as the choppers wheeled to the right to move away from the Diamond.

The tour group in the castle rushed to the west windows to see smoke from one of the cars hit by the armored car as the struck car burst into flames. They pointed excitedly at the two dun-colored helicopters as they flitted overhead, smoke and gunfire now coming from the doors of both helicopters.

The second helicopter seemed to stagger in the air as bullets from the Irish soldiers impacted against the thin aluminum sides. To the tourists' shock and horror, a camouflaged soldier, holding a rifle, tumbled from the helicopter, in the disjointed manner of the recently dead, and plummeted to the castle grounds.

The stricken helicopter began to pirouette after its tail-rotor noisily flew off.

The tourists could see the goggled, helmeted pilots rapidly try to gain control, but the helicopter auto-rotated and crash-landed at the foot of the bridge over the River Eske, to the south of the castle. They moved to the south windows to see a few of the soldiers from the wrecked helicopter stumble out, still holding their weapons. Some were obviously badly injured.

To the surprise of others in the tour group, some of the tourists began to video the crash, as if this were, somehow, part of the day's entertainment. Only when one of the injured soldiers, seeing something pointed at him from the castle windows, raised his rifle and fired a burst did the tourists recognize that this was not for their viewing pleasure. The bullets ricocheted harmlessly off the stone above the window they had been looking out of, but it was enough for them. They quickly ran to the wooden staircase at the far end of the castle, getting as much distance as possible between them and these soldiers, whomever they were.

Bill protectively moved in front of Marisa, and told her to stay where she was; she was safest in the alcove, he thought.

The Irish soldiers, seeing the helicopter go down, ran down the lane toward the castle, fanning out to move along each side of the street. As they spotted the soldier firing at the castle, two of the Irish soldiers took up firing positions across parked cars and fired their Steyrs at the British troopers, hitting the one who had been firing a moment before.

The British soldier with the light machine-gun took up a position at the end of the castle wall, and, hidden by a car, lay on the pavement and began the staccato beat of his machine gun.

Tracers flew like rampant supersonic wasps and windshields and building windows shattered. His mates recovered from their momentary daze, and those who were able-bodied took up defensive positions, and the wounded fed them ammunition and acted as spotters.

The Irishmen, recognizing they were outgunned, and still facing the remaining airborne helicopter, now swinging around to attack them, signaled to one another to move into the castle grounds, the most defensible location in the town. One of the Irish soldiers was shot in the leg as he dashed across the street, but another grabbed him under the arms and pulled him through the doorway of the reception room.

The receptionist was cowering on the floor behind the counter, blubbering. She was relieved to see the Irish tricolor flag and the word, 'Ireland' on a patch on the soldiers' uniform.

'Thank Jaysus, ye are ours!' she stammered.

"Get out, girl. Don't go in the street. Go into the castle. You'll be safe enough there."

She looked at him gratefully and, sniffing, ran quickly across the grassy courtyard to the castle entrance.

"We need to take high ground, Corp," said one of the Irishmen to his corporal.

Wordlessly, the remaining soldiers ran, zigzag, to the castle entrance, and slammed the heavy door behind them. To their chagrin, there was no deadbolt on the inside.

"Not a proper castle!" scowled one of the soldiers, and the others laughed, to their surprise, considering the circumstances.

They rolled a heavy barrel from inside up against the door, standing it on end.

"Hope that will keep out the—whatever they are," said one.

"Who the fuck are they, Corp?"

"My best guess is, yon squaddies are Soldiers of the Queen, young sir. Why or how, I don't know. For all the fuck I know, we are at war with England. Wouldn't be the first goddamn time!"

They positioned the wounded soldier behind some other barrels and a cart, with orders to cover the door. He nodded, knowing it was the end of him if the British came through the door.

The others ran up the circular stairs, and the corporal told one to guard the door at the far end, while they went up to the top floor.

As the last two got to the top floor, they quickly took in the situation, with the crying and wailing bunch at the far end, and the couple in the center alcove.

Bill walked forward, his hands in the air, as Marisa called to him to stay where he was.

"What can I do to help?" he asked.

"You a sojer?" asked the corporal.

"No. But I can help. Let me help," said Bill.

The corporal paused for a moment and said, "All right. Spot for me. Those feckers are down on the street, and they'll be coming in here. We have damn little ammunition, and virtually no kit. We were guarding an armored car, for Christ-sake, not fighting a war!"

The three of them moved to the windows on the south end of the castle, and immediately fired on the surprised British soldiers in the street below.

The British troops scattered, and, after a moment's pause, began firing on the castle. One of them was talking into a radio, with apparent result, for the circling helicopter, its talons out, swung toward the castle.

One of the Irish soldiers fired on the helicopter at too great a range, holding down the trigger until the bolt stayed back over an empty magazine. He pressed the catch and the empty magazine clattered to the floor. He reached into his magazine pouch to find nothing—he had expended his last magazine.

The corporal, seeing this, handed him his own last magazine.

"Make them count, Private," he added, needlessly.

The corporal turned to Bill and said, 'I have a man on the floor below, and one on the ground floor. Their names are Séan and Michael. Call out their names. Micheal's on the ground floor. Tell them the "corp" sent you, before you show yourself, or you'll get your ass blown off. Get all of their mags but one each. Damn, I wish I had my canteen!'

Bill still had a bottle of Coke left in his pack, and gave it to the corporal, who took a deep swallow and handed it to his mate.

"Thanks, friend," he said, unnecessarily.

To Marisa's dismay, Bill descended the circular stairwell. She had no idea what he was doing, or where he was going. She only knew he was leaving her alone—again! She clutched the dog around the neck.

In a short time, he reappeared, carrying something that he gave to the soldiers. She was concerned that he was staying with them, but she knew, in the center of his soul, that he was a warrior, and that, at the most basic of levels, he knew he was defending both her and his castle!

The helicopter hovered low above the street. The soldiers leapt out, forming a skirmish line at the entrance to the castle. One ran forward with a satchel charge and placed it at the foot of the locked iron gate, ran back, and moments later, the explosives detonated, flinging shards of broken iron in all directions.

This provided them with a wide opening to enter the courtyard without having to filter through the reception room and its "choke-point."

They drew fire from the Irishmen in the castle as they ran into the courtyard, and, the helicopter, seeing this, raked the castle windows with machine-gun fire.

As it swung to the south, it fired rockets at the castle. One hit the wall with a tremendous explosion, and the other whistled through the window where the soldiers and Bill were, like a fiery lance. It roared past Marisa in her alcove and passed through one of the English tourists, exploding tumultuously against the wall, emulsifying several of the tourists and killed the others with madly whirling shrapnel.

The shrapnel whined harmlessly past Marisa and the Kerry Blue, protected in her alcove.

The soldiers and Bill stared, transfixed, at the carnage at the far end of the castle, and then, realizing that nothing could be done, turned back towards the attack below.

"Cover that window there, mate," as the corporal gestured with his rifle toward the south window.

The soldier ran there, and immediately began firing. After the first burst, he shouted over his shoulder, "They're in the courtyard! 10-12 of 'em!"

The corporal looked out his window and, seeing none of the enemy, joined the other at the south window, as Bill followed.

At that moment, the soldier who had been stationed on the first floor, came up the wooden stairway, and promptly slipped on the gore covering the floor. He recovered, and, pale-faced, came over to the corporal's position.

"I ordered you to hold the floor below! What the feck you doing up here?" growled the corporal, after glancing over to see who was coming toward him.

"No floor below, Corp. Whole place is on fire. Grenades or rockets, I don't know. I had to 'book or cook'."

The corporal thought for a moment and lowered his voice and said, softly, "OK, mate. We're fucked anyway. We might as well go out together."

One of the British soldiers fired a long burst at them and, by worst luck, one bullet hit the Irish soldier at the window squarely in the forehead, disintegrating his head and sending his beret flying across the room, almost in slow motion. The others were covered with brain matter and bone chips, and looked as if they had been in a train wreck.

The corporal picked up his comrade's weapon and moved the firing selector to single shot and handed it to Bill with the simple command, "Kill them. Kill them all. Look through there and pull the trigger."

Bill leaned against the window frame and began to methodically fire at the advancing enemy until the gun snapped empty. He looked at the corporal, who said, "No more. Go see to your lady. We don't have long. This place is going up in smoke. Thanks. Thanks a lot. Nice knowing you."

Bill clutched the man's shoulder for a moment and moved across the scarred floor to where Marisa was.

"Uilliam! Can we get out?" she cried.

Bill had seen that great gouts of smoke were coming from both the wooden staircase and the circular stone stairwell. Smoke was also filtering through the cracks between the planks of the wooden floor beneath them.

He shook his head in answer, and she clutched him tightly.

"Oh, Uilliam! I had such hopes that this would bring you back to me. After four hundred years, that we should die again in the same place, knowing now that we could have escaped in the very beginning, had we known of that accursed secret passage! Damn those who knew yet did not tell us!"

"In the here-and-now, we are done for, Marisa. We are not going to make it. There's no way out."

"Uilliam, I am so bone-grindingly sorry to have put you through this. Come to me. A kiss before dying."

The smoke was filling the chamber, and they crouched closer to the floor to be able to breathe. Marisa could feel her lungs being choked of air and felt the burn of lack of oxygen. This was not déjà vú; this was history truly repeating itself. How could God be so cruel? she thought, as she began to cough and choke.

She could no longer see the soldiers across the room, and their gunfire had stopped. She looked at Uilliam and saw that his lips were turning blue and he was very still.

She knew they would, somehow meet again in the future, someday, somehow, but she felt a terrible sadness. Of course, he did not know her—he never did—but to die here, again, by fire, in this castle. This was the ultimate cruelty.

She intertwined her fingers in Uilliam's still hand, and prayed for a speedy death and a new life, hoping and praying that the future Uilliam would smile his old smile and say, in Irish, "It is you, Máire!"

She smiled to herself at this pleasant dream, and felt herself drifting away, to a certain peace in the tumult all around her.

As the room darkened and the gentle goodnight of death came to her, she felt a sudden searing pain in her chest, and heaved a great cough, which seemed to cause her to recover slightly.

Her eyes burned from the smoke, but, somehow, things seemed different. She felt different, and even the floor felt different. Rather than the smooth, evenness of sawmill timber, this was the rough-hewn floor of her youth, covered with woven rushes, of so many centuries before. She squinted at her arms, and saw that she was wearing a long-sleeved dress. The dress she wore back then! Was this the last dream of death?

She rolled over, and moved up against Uilliam. Through squinting, irritated eyes, she saw that it was her Uilliam! Uilliam! He was barely conscious. Directly behind him, she could see the massive cabinet that blocked what she knew now to be the secret passage.

She simultaneously remembered what was—or will—happen in the future, but surely she must somehow be in the past!

She crawled through the smoke and began to tug at the massive cabinet. It would not budge. She braced her legs against the stonewall and pulled with every fiber of her being, and, to her amazement, it moved a little. Heartened by a draft of fresh air that rushed upward, she pulled mightily once more, knowing that she only had this last bit of strength.

The cabinet came forward and, catching on an uneven board on the floor, crashed down, barely missing Uilliam who lay on the floor.

She dragged Uilliam toward the more clear air by the passage entrance, and could see him reviving in the better air.

She watched him lovingly as he began to stir.

"Quickly, my love. This place is burning down. We must escape!"

With only a half-understanding of what he was doing, and not knowing why, Uilliam brought himself to his knees and crawled with Marisa—to the alcove and its passageway.

She helped Uilliam into the alcove and was about to follow when she heard a whimpering across the room. It was Síofra, the Kerry Blue Terrier.

Síofra crawled across the floor and found Marisa, making sounds that indicated she was both miserable and scared. Síofra lay on the floor, and next to her was the Yeats painting Jack had given Mary in 1927.

Marisa pulled the painting toward her and called to Síofra, "Come, girl! Come with me!" Síofra followed obediently.

The stone stairs were small, and the passageway was dark and damp, but the air was somewhat clear, and the lower they went, the more they revived.

Feeling their way along the narrow stairs, the roof above was so low they had to crouch. Some types of animals scurried in the darkness as they descended.

Soon they found themselves on a somewhat level section, and were no longer on the stairs.

"River. We are going under the river," muttered Uilliam.

"Yes. It is true," answered Marisa, with wonderment.

Water in the passageway was amazingly cold, and came to their knees, but they continued on.

The tunnel began to rise upward, and the water level decreased to ankle level. Uilliam led the way until they came to a large, flat stone blocking their way. Síofra stayed close to Marisa.

He put his shoulder against the stone and heaved. To his surprise, the stone moved slightly, and a blaze of daylight lit their passage. Through the narrow opening, they could see a radiant rainbow, welcoming them. Marisa's heart fluttered when she saw fingers missing on Uilliam's right hand. Uilliam let the stone back down and said, "We must wait until darkness and we can make it through the forest beyond. The English could be atop us, for all we know, Máire."

"*Máire?*' Did you call me *Máire?*" she said, gleefully.

"Hush, little one. They might hear. Is that not your name? Have I not called, cried, whispered, and shouted your name for all time?"

"Not quite for 'all time,' Uilliam, but *this* time will do quite nicely!' she whispered, as she held him close.

–The Beginning–

ॐ

SUDDEN LIGHT

I have been here before,
But when or how I cannot tell:
I know the grass beyond the door,
The sweet keen smell,
The sighing sound, the lights around the shore.

You have been mine before,—
How long ago I may not know;
But just when at that swallow's soar
Your neck turned so,
Some veil did fall,—I knew it all of yore.

Has this been thus before?
And shall not thus time's eddying flight
Still with our lives our love restore
In death's despite,
And day and night yield one delight once more?

Dante Rossetti, 1863

EPILOGUE

W hether or not people live on, long after death, is a question that everyone must answer for him or herself. There are many explanations for the phenomenon of déjà vu, but it is never explained to my satisfaction.

The physicists tell us that matter can neither be created nor destroyed, and that DNA continues, with its mystical double-helix of information about us, carried through the ages.

Who is to say that these long-lost remnants, these snatches of memories, scents of balsam in the air and tastes of honey do not survive our mortal bodies?

As the Indians say, no man ever dies who is remembered by his friends.

Parapsychologists call remembrance of past-life skills, talents, and knowledge "information leakage."

The locales in Detroit, including the Renaissance Center and the look of Detroit are real. All of the characters are imaginary.

Donegal Castle exists. It did burn in 1589. It was the stronghold of the O'Donnells, my clan. My son, Joseph, and I were walking up a path in Donegal Town many years ago, and an old man stopped us, as he walked his dogs.

We said hello to both him and the dogs and he asked, "So what is your family name in Ireland?"

"O'Donnell," I said.

"Ah," he answered, "so that will be your castle there," pointing to the ruins of the castle, dismissing, in an instant, 400 years of history, a capture by the English, occupation by a Jacobite friend of the Crown, ruins, possession by the Irish Government, which, with the help of the European Union (those generous souls) is restoring the castle for the tourists.

He would think it quite natural if I were to lay claim to "my" castle.

The walls and layout are as described, as is the staircase in the walls. The secret passageway? When I first wrote this chapter, I included a secret passageway. I've always liked secret rooms and passageways, but I recognized that such things are more romantic than practical. Castles were often flung up in haste, and were practical, utilitarian structures. After the restoration of the castle was completed, my wife and I toured the castle. To my great surprise the guide pointed out—the secret passage! Amazingly enough, it is in the same place as in my fictional writing. It has not been explored. The guide said it ended at ground level, but this doesn't make sense. If the castle is besieged, even if there was a door to the outside, who could—or would—use it? Wouldn't this same door be an easy entry point to the enemy? I think an in-depth survey of the castle would find that there really is a tunnel under the river. Even on the Aran Islands there are ring-forts that have underground tunnels.

The Great Fire of London did take place in 1666, at the King's Baker's bakehouse on Pudding Lane. His name and the names of many others are historical facts. Samuel Pepys was a friend of Sir William, an historical figure, and Pepys, at least, did bury his wine in his garden.

The Roman Wall still exists, in sight of the Tower of London, which stands, on-guard, on the banks of the River Thames, downriver from the site of the old London Bridge, which, at the time of the fire, had many houses and shops built on it.

St. Paul's Cathedral, as we presently know it, was designed by Sir Christopher Wren, whose genius is apparent throughout London. The "Old" St. Paul's, built of stone, was destroyed in the fire, and eyewitnesses told of rivers of lead flowing in the street and granite stones exploding in the fire, sending shrapnel in all directions.

Cannibals in Borneo called their human victims, 'long pigs.' The incident where the chief tears the ear from the victim actually happened. The ears, penis and vagina of human victims were delicacies for cannibals.

Máire cried out, in Irish, "William! Till I burn myself with a hundred sorrows!"

There was a famine in 1740 and 1741 in Ireland, caused by, it is believed, a volcanic eruption in the Far East, which caused a darkening of the skies around the world, and the temperature to plummet. In Ireland, fuel and wood set aside to last through the winter did not last. The crops of the following Spring and Summer failed, and by the Winter of 1741, the situation in Ireland was desperate. Ireland had Arctic conditions. The incident depicting the dead mother on the street with her child, still alive, nursing at her breast, actually happened.

The historical events and characters in Paris are accurate. The story characters are fictitious. One of Henry VIII's wives was beheaded in the Tower of London by a Frenchman wielding a French executioner's sword, while she knelt. I'm confident that such swords were used during the Reign of Terror.

William Burke, a native of Ireland, was accurately described, as was his partner in crime, the McDougal woman. Not content to supply the ever-burgeoning need of fresh bodies to physicians, Burke, Hare and McDougal began killing people. At least two of their victims were named "Mary," Mary Paterson or Mitchell, whom they killed in April 1828, and the Mary portrayed here, Mary McGonegal, whom they murdered on the 31st of October 1828. The account of the murder is taken from court records at the time.

Their crimes were notorious, and the expression "Burking," for strangulation, came into common usage.

Burke was convicted and sentenced to be hanged on the 28th of January 1829. McDougal was acquitted. As the hangman was about to adjust the rope around Burke's neck, the crowd cried out, "Burke him! Burke him! Give him no rope!"

Donald McKay, the greatest builder of clipper ships, was an historical figure, as was Daniel O'Connell. O'Connell did conduct his "monster meeting" at the Hill of Tara, but our man was not there. He and all the other characters are imaginary. The Rainbow was the first true clipper ship, but it had no such captain. The captain of another square-rigged sailing ship did, in fact, jump over the side of the ship holding a rope to successfully rescue a crewmember who'd fallen overboard. It was an incredibly brave thing to do.

The Bird Cage Theater, the O.K. Corral, Boot Hill and the Silver Dollar Saloon still exist in Tombstone, Arizona, as do other sites. There was, amazingly enough, a "Russian Bill," visiting Tombstone. He was said to be a brother or cousin of the Tsar or Czar Nicholas of Russia. "Russian Bill" did rent the first "bird cage" of the Bird Cage, paying $25-40 a night—a tremendous sum in those days.

If you go there today, you can see not only the box, but the bullet hole in the stage, fired by a customer during a magician's show.

While the "soiled doves" did take gentlemen under the stage, there is no record that Russian Bill ever saw a dancer and "dove" named Marianna—an Apache with no nose.

Russian Bill did want to experience the old west, and wanted to see what it was like to steal a horse. The last "experience" Bill had in Tombstone, Arizona Territory, was at the end of a rope. It is said that they sent his body back to Russia with an accompanying letter saying, "We're sorry, but your brother died of a high fall."

The "Patricia's" did fight—and die—in Ypres, France, on that day, gassed by the enemy.

The abortion and murder of the perfectly-formed little blonde boy by the doctor, did actually take place in the 1940's, as depicted, although the doctor then was a man. The husband was not on the *Arizona*, however. The couple never did have any other children.

There is, in fact, an underground river that runs under the American Ambassador's residence near the London Zoo. Over the centuries, the Londoners buried most of the rivers and streams that used to flow through the city to the Thames River. Don't tell anyone...

Sudden Light

ABOUT THE AUTHOR

J.A. Greenleaf has been a sailor, Polar explorer, policeman, military officer, lawyer and an author. He is a Michigan Master Lawyer.

He lives at the northernmost tip of Ireland in County Donegal with his wife, Karlene and assorted cats and dogs, including two Kerry Blue Terriers, Murphy and Síofra and the moody black Lab, Molly. They also have a home in the Omaha, Nebraska, area.

You can email him at JAGreenleaf@Swordpoint.com or write him in either in care of the Publisher or at J.A. Greenleaf, Malin Head, Co Donegal, Ireland. Please enclose an International Postal Reply Coupon, available from your post office anywhere in the world, if you'd like a reply.